Anna's
HEALING

Books by Vannetta Chapman

PLAIN AND SIMPLE MIRACLES

Brian's Choice
(ebook-only novella prequel)

Anna's Healing

THE PEBBLE CREEK AMISH

A Promise for Miriam

A Home for Lydia

A Wedding for Julia

"Home to Pebble Creek"
(free short story e-romance)

"Christmas at Pebble Creek"
(free short story e-romance)

Anna's HEALING

VANNETTA CHAPMAN

HARVEST HOUSE PUBLISHERS
EUGENE, OREGON

Scripture verses are taken from

The Holy Bible, New International Version®, NIV®. Copyright © 1973, 1978, 1984, 2011 by Biblica, Inc.® Used by permission. All rights reserved worldwide.

The King James Version of the Bible.

Cover by Koechel Peterson & Associates, Minneapolis, Minnesota

Cover photos © Nancy Brammer, Willard, Givaga, Jim_Pintar / Thinkstock

ANNA'S HEALING
Copyright © 2015 Vannetta Chapman
Published by Harvest House Publishers
Eugene, Oregon 97402
www.harvesthousepublishers.com

Library of Congress Cataloging-in-Publication Data
    Chapman, Vannetta.
    Anna's healing / Vannetta Chapman.
    pages ; cm.—(The plain and simple miracles series ; book 1)
    ISBN 978-0-7369-5603-1 (pbk.)
    ISBN 978-0-7369-5604-8 (eBook)
    I. Title.
    PS3603.H3744A82 2015
    813'.6—dc23

                                                                    2014044241

Printed in the United States of America

            15 16 17 18 19 20 21 22 23 / LB-JH / 10 9 8 7 6 5 4 3 2 1

For my friend,
Kim Moore

Acknowledgments

This book is dedicated to Kim Moore. God smiled on me the evening I found myself sitting next to Kim at the ACFW gala. We didn't know each other at the time, but what has proceeded from that moment is a lovely friendship and a superb professional relationship. She is an encouragement and a blessing to me, and we enjoy swapping photos of our pets. What more could one want in an editor?

I'd also like to thank the many believers who shared with me the miraculous works of God in their lives.

Thanks to my prereaders: Dorsey, Donna, and Kristy. They have been with me through each release, and they always do a wonderful job finding my mistakes and pointing them out. I appreciate my family and friends who encourage me to continue down this path of sharing God's grace through fiction. I'm grateful for the help of my agent, Steve Laube, as well as the wonderful staff at Harvest House for publishing this story.

Lastly, I would like to express my gratitude to the Amish communities in Oklahoma. The folks there are friendly and gracious, and I appreciate their help with this manuscript.

If you find yourself near Tulsa, drive east on US-412 for forty minutes until you reach the town of Chouteau. You'll be blessed by your journey.

And finally...always giving thanks to God the Father for everything, in the name of our Lord Jesus Christ (Ephesians 5:20).

He performs wonders that cannot be fathomed,
miracles that cannot be counted.

~Job 5:9

There are only two ways to live your life.
One is as though nothing is a miracle.
The other is as though everything is a miracle.

~Albert Einstein

PROLOGUE

Oklahoma
Late October

"Was Anna healed?"

That's the question I'm most frequently asked. I might be at a high school football game interviewing players and coaches, or at a council meeting covering the newest city ordinance. Sometimes I'm not even on the clock, but Cody's Creek is a small town, and people know I write for the paper.

Always the question is the same and often it comes out of nowhere. I could be eating a club sandwich at the local diner when someone comes up behind me and, without even an introduction, asks, "Is it true, Chloe? Was Anna healed?"

I suppose they know my name from the newspaper column I write. It's a biweekly paper, called the *Mayes County Chronicle*. My name is on half of the bylines. Maybe they recognize me from the accompanying postage-stamp picture.

Why do they ask me about Anna?

After all of the national coverage—the television spots, newspaper columns, magazine features, and an unauthorized book that is coming out with alarming speed—why do they ask me, Chloe Roberts, small-town reporter?

Perhaps because I was there, from the beginning. Or maybe because, as a reporter, I have the reputation for being objective. Honestly, I don't

9

know how anyone could be impartial in a situation like this, though I'll try. In my heart I suspect that you either believe what you see or you reject it. Whichever side you land on, you then go in search of facts to support that position.

I first met Anna in the fall three years ago. She had moved to Cody's Creek the summer of that same year. We had no idea, in those first days, how our lives would become intertwined. We couldn't have envisioned what was ahead—the heartache and joy and confusion. Everyone involved found their lives and their beliefs irrevocably changed. To say we'll never be the same would be equal to staring down into the majesty of the Grand Canyon and calling it *nice*. Even when we're old and these days lie far in the past, I believe the memories of the events surrounding Anna will remain crystal clear.

No, I'm not afraid I'll forget. That's not why I'm once again sitting in front of my tablet, with Anna's name front and center on the blank page.

The reason is actually quite simple. I want to share the details of her story in black-and-white and allow you to choose. I want to cut through all of the fear and controversy. I want to do what I was trained to do—answer who, what, where, and when. As to the why, I'm not sure any of us can answer that question. The *why* is something you'll have to wrestle against within your own heart.

You may wonder how I could remember whole conversations, exact times, and precise reactions. I do remember, is the easy answer. But in case you're skeptical, I also conducted hundreds of hours of interviews and filed dozens of stories. As a reporter, I assure you I've done my homework.

I'll lay out the facts as best I can, and I'll resist the temptation to sugarcoat any parts. There are moments I'd rather forget, but this story isn't about us and what we did or didn't do.

It's about Anna.

To understand exactly what happened, we'll need to go back to the beginning, to that day in September when I visited Cody's Creek and first spoke with Anna Schwartz.

CHAPTER 1

Oklahoma
Tuesday morning, three years earlier

Anna didn't mind working in the produce stand situated next to the two-lane road. At least the August heat had given way to a slight September breeze, though it didn't bring much relief. There were times when she wondered if leaving Indiana had been the right thing to do. Oklahoma's weather was more extreme than she had imagined. The summer had been hotter than anything she'd ever experienced. The heat had brought wave after wave of storms. Warnings of golf-ball-sized hail and tornadoes and strong winds became commonplace.

From the produce stand Anna could see miles of green fields, a few rolling hills in the distance, and an occasional grove of trees. Three white-tailed deer foraged along the edge of the pasture. The sky was a vibrant blue, punctuated by white fluffy clouds. There was no sign of extreme weather that she could see, but then there was the ever popular saying among locals—*If you don't like the weather, wait a minute. It will change.*

In the beginning she had been terrified each time she heard the weather alerts from someone who stopped by the stand. The ominous clouds building in the west set her teeth on edge and stole her sleep at night. Now she met such dire warnings with a shrug, same as most of the other residents in Cody's Creek, Oklahoma, which went to show that a person could become accustomed to anything.

From what she'd heard, the winters were every bit as cold as those in Indiana, with the wind howling across the hills and the snow piling high. After the summer they'd had, Anna almost looked forward to a freezing walk to the phone shack or a buggy ride through snow drifts.

Except buggy rides were few and far between. The black mare was only hitched to the buggy on Sundays and special occasions— weddings and funerals. Anna felt sorry for the old gal and would often walk out to where she was pastured to offer her a piece of apple or carrot. Duchess should be living on a farm up north, where she would be used more often than the tractors which had become a part of everyday life in Cody's Creek.

Yes, some days she missed home. Other days she still savored the adventure of living in a new place.

Her eyes had opened that morning when she felt the slight northern breeze tickling the sheet she lay beneath. Perhaps she could withstand another Oklahoma summer. Maybe she'd been right to move in with her *aenti*. Two hours later, she was in the shed they had converted into a produce stand—selling fresh corn, green beans, tomatoes, and squash to anyone who passed by.

Though she'd been in Oklahoma for three months, she still hadn't found her "place," or so it seemed to her. At breakfast her *aenti* had again brought up the Sunday singing as well as which boys would be willing to accompany her on the youth outing. Anna had tried to remain polite but had finally blurted out, "If I'm a burden, please tell me and I'll go."

Onkel Samuel had scowled as he shoved another spoonful of oatmeal into his mouth. *Aenti* Erin had tsk-tsked, but it was *Mammi* who had gently reminded her, "Children are never a burden, Anna."

She wasn't a child, but she didn't point that out to *Mammi*. Her grandmother was a bright spot in Anna's move to central Oklahoma. Samuel and Erin were stern and strict. Perhaps the difficulties of farming the red clay soil had soured their disposition, but Anna imagined they had been that way since birth.

Mammi, on the other hand, was sunshine personified.

A car pulled into the drive, and Anna set aside her mending. She wasn't very good at it anyway. She'd never cared much for sewing and it showed, but her *onkel* insisted she stay busy while minding the booth.

The woman who walked toward her was pure *Englisch*. Black curls bounced inches above her shoulders, and dark sunglasses accented her high cheekbones. She wore tight blue jeans, a light fluffy shirt trimmed in lace, and leather boots. Anna had never considered leaving the Amish, but there were times she'd trade in all four dresses hanging in her bedroom for one Western outfit.

"Good morning."

Definitely from Oklahoma, her accent was strong and Southern. As she removed her glasses, Anna realized the visitor was also a tad older than she had first thought. She revised her estimate of the woman's age to somewhere between twenty-five and thirty.

"*Gudemariye*. Can I interest you in some vegetables?"

"Yes." The woman smiled and then confessed, "Actually, I don't cook much, but I imagine my mother would love some of the green beans. You could throw in a few tomatoes and four ears of corn too."

As Anna filled the order, the woman fiddled with her sunglasses, finally tucking them into her purse. Pulling out a ten-dollar bill, she placed it on the counter with a smile. "My name is Chloe Roberts, and I'm a reporter for the *Mayes County Chronicle*."

"My name is Anna. Anna Schwartz. Your job must be very challenging. There's not much to report on around these parts."

"My main office is in Tulsa, but my area is Cody's Creek. It's true we don't have the excitement of a large city, but folks like to read stories about their neighbors."

Anna only nodded as she made the change for Chloe's order and pushed it across the counter to her.

"Especially their Amish neighbors." Now there was a definite twinkle in Chloe's eyes.

"Oh, *ya*? Curious, are they?"

"Indeed. I get questions every week."

"Like what?"

"Mostly about your way of life. For example, the tractor thing has people stumped. Lots of folks don't understand why so many Amish now drive them into town. How did that happen? Why not drive a car if you're going to abandon the horse and buggy?"

Anna waved away the questions. "It's difficult to explain to an *Englischer*." In truth, she barely understood it herself, but why bring that up?

"Today I'm working on a different subject entirely. I'm reporting on the growth of the cottage industries among Amish families." She paused, and then she added, "By cottage I don't mean small homes—"

"*Ya*, I know what cottage industry means. I work in one."

Chloe pocketed the change. "Do people do that to you often?"

"Do what?"

"Assume you don't understand something."

"Often enough."

"I apologize. Let me begin again. My boss wants me to report on the Amish in Mayes County, and in particular the rise of home businesses. Could I ask you a few questions? I promise not to sneak any pictures with my phone."

Anna couldn't help laughing at that. It had been a slow morning, as most weekdays were, and it was nice to have someone to talk to. "If you promise, then I would be happy to help."

"Have you lived here all your life?"

"*Nein*. I moved here..." She stared at the top of the shed as if it would crystallize the events since she'd left home. "A few months ago. It was early July."

Chloe had pulled out a small pad of paper and a pen and was taking notes. "Where did you live before?"

"Indiana. Goshen, Indiana."

"Also a small town."

"It is. Have you been there?"

"We used to visit Chicago once a year to see my cousins. My mom would always insist that we take the toll road east and shop in the Amish communities."

"And now you have your own Amish community." Anna was actually enjoying this conversation. The woman was easy to talk to, especially for a newspaper reporter. Though come to think of it, her *onkel* probably wouldn't approve.

"You take all of this interest well. I know many Amish are irritated by it."

"No use being irritated by what you can't change, or so my *mammi* says."

Chloe nodded. "She sounds a lot like my mother."

Anna considered that a minute. She didn't believe her grandmother and this woman's mother would have much in common, but perhaps she was wrong. "What can I tell you about operating a vegetable booth?"

They spoke for another ten minutes about farming, the tourist traffic, and the response from the local grocery stores. The answer to the last topic was mixed. While they were willing to buy farm-fresh produce from the Amish and mark up the prices to sell in their stores, they were less enthusiastic about all of the independent produce stands popping up.

"Certainly, what we're doing is not unique to the Amish." Anna twirled her *kapp* string around one finger. "After all, folks have been selling their extra produce in stands like this for ages—much longer than the hundred years the Amish have lived in Cody's Creek."

Chloe's pen hovered over the sheet of paper. "I read that your community has existed for that long, but it's hard to believe. I grew up here and don't remember much about the Amish."

"From what I've heard, the community was quite small at first. I believe the population began growing when land prices increased in the northeast."

Chloe clicked her pen once, and then she placed it back inside her bag, which was a tooled brown leather. "You've been a big help, Anna. I appreciate it. Do you mind if I use your name in the article?"

"I suppose that would be okay." It made no difference to her what Chloe put in her *Englisch* paper. She rarely ever saw a copy.

Anna watched the reporter walk back to her car, and something inside her—probably the same thing that had whispered *move to Oklahoma*—caused her to call out, "We'll have the corn maze open in another week. You should come back. You can even take pictures—of the corn, that is."

Chloe hitched her purse strap up on her shoulder. "I'd love that." She opened the door to her little car, a small blue thing that looked as if it wouldn't go much faster than a buggy, and started the engine.

As she pulled away, it occurred to Anna that their conversation was the most exciting thing to happen to her in a week. Perhaps her *aenti* was right. Maybe she should go to the singing.

CHAPTER 2

*C*hloe had barely driven her small car out onto the blacktop when Anna's *onkel* pulled the tractor up to the house.

Tractors!

When Anna had first heard that the Amish communities in Oklahoma had allowed them, she'd envisioned all sorts of things—differences in their dress, a broader role for women, maybe even a chance to do something she'd never done before. But when she'd arrived she had found that everything—except for the tractors—was the same as back home in Goshen.

She understood the allowance. She'd spent part of July and August helping with the family vegetable garden. The dirt was like the Play-Doh her little sister, Bethany, had once brought home from school—malleable at first but quickly turning to something that resembled concrete. Plowing with the big workhorses was difficult, and in some spots, impossible.

It was a mystery to her why her uncle insisted on keeping Snickers and Doodle, two workhorses he'd bought for a good price five years earlier. She'd asked her *aenti* about that.

"It seems the other Amish families here don't have any workhorses at all."

"You're right." Erin had continued hanging laundry as she spoke. "They use the tractors for everything, as is allowed."

"But not *Onkel* Samuel."

"*Nein.*"

Anna waited for more, but as usual her *aenti* was not very forthcoming.

"Is there a reason? That he keeps the horses, I mean. Is it better for the crops?"

"I couldn't say." Erin pushed hair back into her *kapp*. The summer sun was hot, though it was early in the morning. "Your *onkel*, he's stubborn. That's the best explanation I can give you."

Thinking back on those words, Anna realized her *aenti* wasn't criticizing her *onkel*, but rather stating a fact.

Regardless, Anna thought Snickers and Doodle were fine geldings. Both were chestnut-colored Percherons. Snickers had a dark-brown patch that stretched from between his ears to his nose. Doodle had white patches covering her head and neck. Both were strong horses, and she understood why her *onkel* was unwilling to part with them. What she didn't understand was why he'd bought them in the first place. Tractors had been allowed for many years before her family had moved into the area. What had he seen in the two Percherons to cause him to spend so much money on them? That money could have been used as a down payment on a new tractor.

Whatever the reason, Anna was glad he had. She enjoyed visiting the horses, especially when she was homesick for Indiana. Life in Oklahoma had certainly not turned out the way she'd imagined it would. Yes, farming was different and they drove tractors to town—something she still wasn't comfortable with, but that was the full extent of their *liberal* lifestyle.

Her *aenti* appeared on the porch, holding a plate filled with lunch. In Anna's opinion, *Aenti* Erin was thin to the point of unhealthiness. The woman looked as if she stood in danger of being whisked away by the Oklahoma wind. She insisted on wearing drab colors of black, dark blue, and gray—though their *Ordnung* allowed for much more diversity. Her skin was pale and creased, more wrinkled than someone her age should be, as if life's trials and tribulations had etched themselves on her skin.

Erin's hair was a different matter. Thick, chestnut brown, and wavy, she attempted to keep it tightly pulled under her *kapp*. Always, though, tendrils snuck out. Anna loved her *aenti*'s hair because it looked like that of a much younger woman. It proved that *Aenti* wasn't as old as she perhaps behaved.

Anna popped out of the booth and met her halfway.

"*Danki.*"

"It's no problem, child. How was your morning?"

"*Gut.* A little slow."

"The woman in the car stayed a long time."

Anna almost told *Aenti* Erin about Chloe Roberts and her news stories. Realizing any such information would be met with a lecture on remaining separate, she focused on her lunch instead. The plate held fresh bread covered with homemade peanut butter accompanied by an apple and two oatmeal cookies. She still had half the water in her thermos, the one she'd carried out with her earlier that morning.

"This looks *wunderbaar*." Throwing a smile over her shoulder, Anna made her way back to the produce booth. If she had thought she would lose weight in Oklahoma, she was wrong. Her *aenti* and *onkel* might be stricter than even her own parents, but the meals were the same— chock-full of calories and fat. That didn't stop her from closing her eyes in a prayer of appreciation before she bit into the fresh bread.

Some might wonder how *Aenti* remained so thin, but Anna had watched her eat. The woman pecked at her food like a small wren.

The rest of the afternoon passed quickly, probably because instead of darning she spent a good portion of the time reading the book she'd brought home from the library. A prairie romance, it boasted a sticker on the side proclaiming it to be *Christian fiction*. Soon she was lost in another life, one similar to hers in many respects; however, it was set in a different place with unusual problems and interesting strangers. That alone was enough to bring a smile to Anna's face.

CHAPTER 3

*T*hree days later, Anna found herself driving the tractor into town. This was a first! *Onkel* Samuel had never trusted her to drive alone anywhere before, but to be fair that may have been because there was rarely a need to go into town, and someone had to watch over the vegetable stand.

She would rather have driven the buggy, but Samuel had merely scratched his head and walked off when she'd mentioned it. He'd showed her three times how to operate the tractor. She was to put it in first gear to plow, but that wasn't something she needed to know. Neither was second or third, which were used for pulling heavy loads and mowing. She only needed to know neutral and fourth.

She stopped at a red light and checked her purse again. Yes, she still had the list.

The light changed and she attempted to pull through, but she popped the clutch and the tractor stalled. She ran Samuel's instructions through her mind—break, clutch in, start the engine, clutch out. The engine started, but she again let the clutch out too quickly. The tractor jerked forward a few feet, so that it now rested in the middle of the intersection, and then the engine again died. A car behind her honked, and several folks walking down the street turned to stare.

Anna ignored them. She'd driven a pony cart when she was in fourth grade, a buggy since she was in eighth, and even the large workhorses her father used when harvesting. She could certainly handle an old blue tractor with a faded blue canopy, pulling the truck bed of a white Ford pickup.

This time when she started the tractor, it jerked and sputtered but didn't die. Breathing a prayer of relief, she continued on through the intersection and then turned right into Bylers' Dry Goods. Her mind slipped back to a simpler time, when she'd driven her parents' mare to town in Goshen.

But she'd wanted change, or she'd thought that was what she wanted. It seemed that Duchess had looked at her accusingly when she had left her *onkel*'s farm. She'd take the mare an extra apple when she returned home.

Dropping the tractor keys into her purse, Anna scrambled out of the contraption and turned toward the store. She fairly bounced up the old wooden steps.

"*Gudemariye*, Anna." Rebecca Byler smiled at her as she walked inside.

It was nearly noon, so the good morning greeting caught her by surprise, but Anna responded in kind.

"It's not often we see you out. I suppose Erin is home caring for your *Mammi* Ruth."

"*Ya*. Doc says she needs to stay in bed a few more days, at least until she's able to eat all three meals again."

"Summer colds can be terrible, especially for older ones."

Anna nodded as she picked up a shopping basket. She spent the next twenty minutes filling it with items from her *aenti*'s list. She also paused in the book aisle and perused the latest offerings. Rebecca didn't carry much, and what she did carry didn't actually appeal to Anna—books on farming, herbal remedies, and a small section titled "Plain and Simple Reading." No doubt those books were for the tourists who stopped in, as no one Anna knew needed a book on *A Plain Life Without Electricity* or *Attending Amish Schools*.

Still, she enjoyed glancing over the entire selection. The book covers were crisp, shiny, and unbent. Opening one, she took a deep sniff.

"I'm going to have to charge you for smelling that book." Joseph Byler leaned against his broom, trying to hide his smile by pulling down on his beard.

"Charge me? Will it be fifty cents or a dollar?"

Now Joseph laughed. "You'd probably pay it. I've never seen a gal who loves the book section quite like you do."

Anna sighed and replaced the book on the shelf. "*Onkel* doesn't approve. He says my time is better spent on something useful."

Instead of arguing with that, Joseph patted her shoulder with a large clumsy hand. As he walked away, he said, "Rebecca has something put back for you behind the counter."

Rebecca and Joseph were probably the same age as Anna's *aenti* and *onkel*. She guessed they were in their early fifties. The difference was that while *Aenti* Erin and *Onkel* Samuel approached each day as if it was a huge burden, Rebecca and Joseph seemed to find joy in the smallest things.

Had their lives been so different? Or were people merely different in their hearts? In the way they went about their rest and worship and chores? Joseph couldn't be thrilled about sweeping the shop floor again, yet she'd never seen him when he wasn't smiling about one thing or laughing about another. Rebecca always had a pleasant word for everyone.

Anna had only been in the community a few months, and already these two were her favorite people. Their shop was often filled with tourists and Amish and *grandkinner* all at the same time. At the moment, one of Rebecca's youngest grandsons, a toddler named Simon, was seated on a stool playing with a small toy hammer and pegs.

Rebecca rang up her purchases, chatting about the weather and remarking on a baby that had been born to one of the couples in their district.

"I remember Katie because she was at the last church service looking ready to have that *boppli* any minute."

"*Ya*, she's the one. Blond hair with a tint of red in it, what my *mamm* used to call a strawberry blond. Her husband's name is Brian. He's the teacher at the school nearest to you."

"Isn't he an *Englischer*?"

"Was. He's Amish now."

"We had a few try to convert to Amish while I was growing up in Goshen," Anna admitted. "It never stuck."

"Brian is a special man, though no doubt the changes are difficult. We should keep them both in our prayers." Rebecca handed her the receipt and change, and then she reached under the counter and pulled out a copy of the *Mayes County Chronicle*.

"I was hoping you'd come in today. I saved you a copy of the paper." Rebecca opened it up across the counter and pointed to an article on the top of the second page. "The writer mentions your *onkel*'s farm."

The article was titled "Plain Produce."

Anna couldn't help rolling her eyes at the heading, but then she caught site of the byline—Chloe Roberts.

"Take it home with you." Rebecca tapped the paper. "No charge. I thought you'd like to read it."

"*Danki*, I will. Though it may be best to do my reading in the tractor. *Onkel* can't abide *Englisch* papers, only the *Budget*. He doesn't outright forbid such things. In fact, he caught me reading a library book last week and simply walked away mumbling about young girls and wasted time."

"I don't mean to suggest you go against Samuel's wishes, but I think he may be interested in this article. It's bound to bring more tourists out to your place. *Gut* news, *ya*?"

"It is." Anna carefully refolded the paper and placed it in the sack with her purchases. She glanced left and right. Assured that they had the store to themselves for the moment, she plunged ahead with something that had been circling her mind.

"I'd like to ask you a personal question, Rebecca."

"I'll answer if I can."

"Why is *Onkel* Samuel so harsh? I've been here for more than two months now, and I rarely see him smile."

Rebecca didn't answer immediately. Instead, she pulled out a roll of "New Product" stickers and began placing them on a stack of cookbooks. "I wouldn't be judging your *onkel*, Anna."

"*Nein*, of course not. It's only that I've been wondering...is it me? Is it because I've come to stay with them? When we wrote to ask about my coming, it seemed as if they wanted me, but—"

"There's no doubt they do want you." Rebecca set down the roll of stickers and met Anna's gaze directly. "It's as you say. Samuel and Erin have always had a serious disposition. Perhaps they were born that way."

"But *Mammi* is so joyful."

"*Ya*. It's true. Though her husband, your *Grossdaddi* Menno, could be a very somber man at times. I believe Ruth had a positive effect on him. But though she taught him to smile and to appreciate the blessings of our life, his natural temperament was more serious."

"So that's why Samuel and Erin are so sour?"

Instead of being offended, Rebecca laughed. "I don't know if 'sour' is the right word, but I understand why you would use it. Some of that answer lies in the past, and it's not my place to share it."

"My *dat* and Samuel are *bruders*. I always thought *Dat* was a bit strict and even a little somber at times, but next to *Onkel* Samuel, *Dat* looks like a blushing schoolboy."

"Speaking of blushing boys..." Rebecca nodded toward the door, where three of the boys from their district were stomping dirt off their boots before stepping inside.

Each boy had asked Anna to the singings, and she had turned down all three. The reason that she'd given her *aenti* was they were too young, and it was true they were one to two years younger than she. But the real reason was she wasn't ready to settle down. She hadn't even lived yet. How could she be expected to begin dating—which would no doubt lead to marrying—one of the local boys? She didn't even know if she wanted to stay in Oklahoma.

So she said goodbye to Rebecca, tucked her package under her arm, and only offered a brief nod to Neal, Adam, and Thomas, who were indeed blushing.

Anna walked to her tractor without looking back, though she suspected they were watching her. Was she that odd of an occurrence? An out of town Amish girl? She couldn't get used to being a minor celebrity among the boys. In Goshen, most of them didn't give her a second glance.

Or perhaps she was remembering that wrong. She'd had no more interest in dating back home than she did here. The difference was that when she was still on her parents' farm, she'd thought a change of scenery would calm the restlessness in her heart.

It hadn't.

She climbed up into the tractor, but instead of putting in the key and fighting the clutch, she opened the paper across her lap and found the article she was looking for.

Plain Produce
By Chloe Roberts
Mayes County Chronicle

CODY'S CREEK—If it's wholesome food and fair prices you're looking for, you need look no farther than a few local Amish farms.

Corn, green beans, tomatoes, okra, bell peppers, radishes, and squash—plump, fresh, and picture-perfect—can be had when you pull over to one of the small produce booths that dot the countryside. Amish farmers do not use insecticides or chemically produced fertilizer on their crops. What you buy will be organic in the truest sense of the word.

The Amish population in Mayes County has doubled over the last ten years, bringing with it a resurgence of small farms. Unlike conglomerates with vast acreage and the latest technology, farms owned by the Amish insist on using the old ways and only farming what each family needs to earn a living and feed their own. Though they remain faithful to the Amish faith, their day-to-day practices differ somewhat from larger Amish communities in Indiana, Ohio, and Pennsylvania.

You have probably seen the canopied tractors pulling the bed of a pickup truck. Amish in the area use tractors for farming and for local travel. However, a horse and buggy can still be found on most homesteads. Their life here in Oklahoma is one of necessary compromises due to the difficulty of the area's claylike soil.

If you've visited the area on Sunday, you've no doubt had to slow down behind the iconic horse-drawn buggies and Plain-clothed families making their way to church or visiting neighbors. What you may not have realized is that this community east of Tulsa is now home to four Amish church districts and more than six hundred Amish people.

City manager Lex Carlson considers that a plus. "They make good neighbors. Not too much crime among the Amish, and what many folks don't realize is that they pay the same local taxes as everyone else."

Judy Scotts with the Cody's Creek Chamber of Commerce also believes the Amish community is a real asset. She explained that Amish families have been a plus to the local economy. "It only takes one stop by the Amish Cheese House, Dutch Pantry, or Ropp Farm and Bakery to win folks over."

Located near the intersection of Highways 69 and 412, Cody's Creek has become a stopping point for travelers in the market for handmade furniture, fresh produce, or a piece of homemade pie. But not everyone is happy about the Amish move into local tourist, restaurant, and produce businesses. Local farmer Leo Stuebner III admitted, "You cannot underprice these people. Family members work for extremely low wages or nothing at all."

The Amish of Cody's Creek have indeed made a name for their community in the produce business, and their businesses are usually family owned and operated. Anna Schwartz recently moved to the area from Goshen, Indiana. Anna is twenty-four and lives on her *onkel's* farm. She has chestnut hair covered with the traditional *kapp*, and a pretty round face. Standing a few inches over five feet, she could be the cover girl for Amish women. When asked about the rise of cottage industries among Plain folks, Anna said, "What we're doing is not unique to the Amish. Folks have been selling their extra produce in stands like this for ages."

See the enclosed map for locations of various produce stands, including the Schwartzes'. In addition to fresh vegetables, you can find homemade sweets and the occasional quilt or birdhouse. Mr. Schwartz will also be offering tourists a walk through their corn maze beginning next weekend for a nominal fee.

Anna wanted to reread the article, but she realized her *aenti* would be worried about her if she didn't hurry home. So she folded the paper, set it back inside her shopping bag, and started the tractor, pulling out onto the blacktop and turning it toward the farm.

She didn't know if her *onkel* would be pleased about the article, but she imagined it would increase the number of folks who stopped by the produce stand. In Anna's mind, publicity could be a good thing. She was in favor of anything that would keep her busy enough that she didn't have to mend socks or sew patches on work pants.

CHAPTER 4

Samuel hadn't, in fact, been particularly pleased about the article. As usual, his expression drooped into a frown, which looked rather comical to Anna. It caused his beard to fall even lower, and often it seemed in danger of reaching his plate. In contrast, the top of his head was as bare as that of most newborns.

At six feet, he was a large man and still fit and able to do the work in the fields. Anna wondered who would help once he was too old. He and Erin had no sons, no children at all.

"Best not to have long conversations with the *Englisch*," he had muttered at dinner that evening.

Her *aenti* almost smiled at Samuel's conservative response to the article in the *Mayes County Chronicle*.

Mammi, though, was thrilled.

Anna's grandmother sat across from her at the dinner table. Her blue eyes sparkled behind large glasses, reminding Anna of an owl she'd seen the day before. As usual, *Mammi*'s face crinkled in a smile. To Anna, she looked like a child in adult clothes. Though she claimed to have once been five feet two inches, the top of her head barely reached Anna's shoulders. As further proof that she was getting smaller, her dresses nearly reached the tops of her shoes. With skin wrinkled like the pages of an old book, *Mammi* looked every inch of her eighty-nine years.

In Goshen, Anna had had the support and guidance of her parents, her four siblings, and the other six *onkels*. All of *Mammi's* sons were married with large families of their own. Only Samuel and Erin were childless, and only Samuel and Erin had moved to Oklahoma. Anna knew that *Mammi* missed her other children and grandchildren. Once a year she traveled to Indiana to visit, and each day she wrote a letter to a different family member, always inviting them to visit Oklahoma.

Why had Anna taken *Mammi* up on the offer? Why had she left so many relatives to live with this small family of three in the middle of northeastern Oklahoma?

She supposed there were several reasons for her decision to move south—and she'd explained all of them to her family several times. Although large families could be a blessing, Anna often felt smothered by hers. Everywhere she went there were family members, and always they asked the same thing—"When are you marrying, Anna?" This would be followed by a smile and a hug. No one meant any harm by the inquiry. Still, each time she would clench her teeth and dream of living in another place.

Also, she wanted to see more of the world than Goshen, Indiana. Was that such a sin? She didn't know, but even with Samuel and Erin's gloomy dispositions she was glad she had come. Though she often found herself bored on the farm, she was determined to remain in Oklahoma the twelve months she had committed to staying.

But the single biggest reason that Anna was glad to have taken *Mammi* up on her offer was sitting across from her, smiling behind her oversized glasses as she looked up from the chicken leg she was holding.

"*Gotte* can use that article in the paper. Perhaps more of the *Englisch* will bring their children to the maze, Samuel. That would be *gut*. Children need a chance to run through the fields." She took a bite and then chewed thoughtfully before adding, "Even though we live in a rural area, it seems that many of the *Englisch* children know nothing about farming. They should learn how food is grown and harvested."

Samuel grunted, *Mammi* chewed, and Erin pushed the platter filled with chicken she had battered and fried toward Anna.

Anna had passed on the chicken the first time her *aenti* had put the plate in her hands. It seemed to her that no matter how carefully she watched what she ate, the waistline of her dresses grew tighter. She'd settled for one spoonful of potatoes, some of the baked carrots, and a slice of Erin's homemade bread.

She nearly passed a second time on the chicken, but decided a single piece couldn't hurt. Her *aenti*'s cooking was nearly as good as her mother's, and the smell of the chicken frying had reached out to the front porch when Anna had returned to the house. She'd been envisioning it for hours. Taking the first bite, she closed her eyes and savored the rich, crisp taste of the batter.

Mammi laughed and shook her finger at Anna. "You look as if you've met your new best friend. Erin is a *gut* cook, *ya*?"

Anna nodded.

"There was no use trying to teach my boys to cook. Eight boys and not a single one of them could break an egg correctly. So when my *kinner* married, I thanked the Lord I would finally have a chance to pass on the skills of the kitchen."

Mammi grinned and pushed back at the white hair that had escaped from her *kapp*. Samuel continued eating without comment, and Erin, as usual, remained silent.

"I can teach you too, Anna. You will want to be able to feed a young man one day."

"Are you going to Sunday's singing, Anna?" Erin finally appeared interested in the conversation.

Anna wanted to say no. What she'd like to do Sunday was enjoy their time of family worship, rest, relish her time out of the produce booth, and maybe take a long walk. On the Sundays they didn't meet for church, most Amish families visited friends or kinfolk. But since she'd been in Oklahoma, that hadn't happened with her *onkel* and *aenti*. They had no family to visit, though they were welcome at any of their neighbors' homes.

The look of hope on Erin's face caused Anna to reconsider her answer. There was little she seemed to do that actually pleased her *aenti*. Would it be such a burden for her to agree to go to the singing?

"I was thinking I might."

"With Neal or Adam?" As an afterthought Erin added, "Or Thomas?"

"Actually, I thought I would go alone." Anna peeked up from her food, steeling herself against her *aenti*'s disappointment. She needn't have worried.

"It's *gut* you're going. And maybe you are right. I can think of at least two other boys who are older and still searching for a *fraa*. If you go alone, perhaps they will understand they may have a chance."

Samuel had finished his meal. He pushed away his plate, leaned back, and sipped his coffee. "All fine boys. We're not rushing you, Anna, but understand that when a woman hesitates to make such a commitment, eventually the time for choosing will pass. Think of your future and realize there are only a limited number of chances."

"You're worried about my future?" Anna aimed for a light tone, but the question came out accusatory nonetheless, at least to her ears.

"You mock me, but it's true. Your *dat* wrote me before you came about how you had turned down the boys back in Goshen."

"But I'm only twenty-four—"

"Twenty-four is maybe not old in the *Englisch* culture, but for us it is..." Erin swiped at a crumb on the table. "It is unusual for a girl to wait so long."

"*Gotte* has a plan for Anna." *Mammi* continued to peck at her chicken and potatoes. "You two do not need to worry over her future. You need to pray and be kind to one another."

Samuel didn't respond to that. He only stood and walked out the back door to complete his evening chores.

CHAPTER 5

hile Anna was washing the dishes with her *aenti*, she thought back over the conversation she'd had with Rebecca at the dry goods store. With Samuel out of the house, Erin was sometimes in a more talkative mood. Her temperament seemed better this evening, perhaps because Anna had agreed to go to the singing. Maybe it was a good time to ask her some questions.

"I don't remember meeting *Daddi* Menno."

"You did when you were a small *boppli*. It's no surprise you don't remember."

"This was before you moved from Goshen?"

"*Ya.*"

"Why did *Mammi* and *Daddi* move with you? Didn't they like Goshen?"

Erin shrugged. "Everyone needs the support of family. Perhaps they thought that because we had no children, we needed them all the more."

Anna hesitated for less time than it took to wash one plate. "Did you ever learn why you couldn't have children?"

"The why is less important than the fact." Erin vigorously dried a plate and set it in the cabinet with a clatter. If the memory upset her, Anna couldn't tell by the expression on her face, which remained neutral.

"I'm sorry. That must have been very difficult."

"*Gottes wille.*"

"But—"

"There is no use struggling against what is, Anna. A kite rises only against the wind."

Anna splashed soapy water at a fly. "I've grown up hearing proverbs all my life, but I have no idea what that even means."

"It means what it says. On a windless day a kite will only fall, but if there is a good breeze, if a storm is coming, then the kite will fly high."

"I'm the kite?"

"We all are, to some degree."

"So wind and storms are *gut*?" Anna teased, but Erin only shook her head and remained serious.

"The proverb is saying that adversity is *gut* when it brings us closer to *Gotte*."

"Do you believe that?"

"I suppose I do." Erin draped the damp dish towel over a hook on the cabinet. "I'd best get to the darning before the light fades."

Erin and Samuel rarely used the gas lanterns that sat in each room. Why would they? Each evening they were in bed by the time it was dark, though perhaps it was different in the winter. Summer days in Oklahoma seemed to stretch forever, and even Anna was usually worn out by the time darkness cloaked the fields.

She finished cleaning up the kitchen, grabbed her shawl, and stepped out onto the front porch. *Mammi* sat on the top step, playing with one of the cats that had wandered over from the barn. The image made her smile, and for a moment Anna wished she could paint—with pencils or brushes or even words. She wished she could put this memory of her grandmother down on paper.

"Come sit with me, Anna."

The setting sun splashed a dazzling array of color across the Oklahoma sky—orange melted into red, purple, and blue.

"If I could quilt something that looked like the evening sky, I might be interested in quilting."

Instead of admonishing her, *Mammi* laughed. "You struggle against the rules, Anna. You are not the first."

"Some rules make no sense to me."

"*Ya.* I can tell."

"Why do we not quilt with red?"

Mammi continued to tease the cat with a piece of yarn.

"Why do we insist on only using the old patterns?"

The cat pounced on the yarn, causing them both to laugh.

"Why are girls supposed to choose whom to marry when we barely know who we are?"

"No one is rushing you, Anna." *Mammi* gave her a side glance, and then she turned her attention back to the cat. "Like this barn cat, you have a playful spirit."

"If you mean I am easily bored, yes. You're right."

"You have not learned to find contentment in simple day-to-day pleasures."

"I'm pretty content watching you play with that cat."

Mammi reached over and patted her knee. "I am glad you came to stay with us. This house needed your youth and energy. *Gotte* has blessed us with you, Anna."

And with that announcement, *Mammi* stood and moved into the house, leaving Anna with the cat.

"I'm a blessing," Anna assured the cat. Somehow when *Mammi* said it, Anna could believe her.

Perhaps good would come from her time in Oklahoma.

Maybe she would find the answers to how she was supposed to live her life, and where, and with whom.

Possibly, as *Mammi* had suggested, her impatient spirit wasn't such a terrible thing after all.

As she watched the cat pounce and roll and then pause to clean its face, she realized that she and the cat had a lot in common. They both were young, both enjoyed amusement more than work, and both had short attention spans. And God had created them, and what He created was good. The Bible promised her as much. It was with those optimistic thoughts that she watched the sunset give way to darkness.

CHAPTER 6

A familiar restlessness claimed Jacob Graber the second week of September. He'd spent fourteen days harvesting sorghum in South Dakota. He'd become quite good at scouring the *Budget* and figuring out which communities could use an extra hand. Not that they advertised outright for "Help Wanted." No, you had to read between the lines. When someone posted about a "better than expected crop" and in the same paragraph mentioned a "short harvesting window," it usually meant there weren't enough men in the family. Though neighbors would help, each farmer had his own crops to bring in, which could result in a stressful time for all involved.

Jacob had picked up a copy of the *Budget* in Montana. While riding the bus south, he'd deduced that there was work at an Amish community an hour southwest of Sioux Falls.

His reasoning had been solid, and he'd easily found a job harvesting the last of the summer crops. Jacob knew his build helped in that hiring—folks looked at him and saw a big, strong farmer. He was five feet eleven and two hundred and five pounds. He was also a hard worker, evidenced by the callouses on his hands.

Matthew Hochstettler was a good boss. He was more than fair, he paid well, and he provided a place to sleep as well as meals.

"I could use you around this place. My boys help as they can, but I've been thinking of taking someone on permanently."

Jacob stared out the buggy window. The Dakota hills tumbled into the distance, one after another, until they seemed to him like the waves he had seen in Sarasota.

The day before he'd woken to a brisk north wind and the smell of fall. He didn't need any other excuse to pack his bag and head toward town. Matthew was quick to offer him a ride.

"The job is yours if you'll have it. You're a *gut* worker, Jacob. We'd be happy to have you."

What went unsaid was that Matthew had three daughters at home—all of marrying age. All easy to look at and with sweet personalities. Too sweet? Jacob didn't know. He only knew it was time to go.

"*Danki.*"

"Which means no."

"I suppose it does."

The silence stretched and rose to fill the buggy as it should, as it always had. Amish men weren't famous for their ability to make conversation. Jacob had affirmed that truth in the nine states he'd visited. The horse's hooves against the road soothed something in him—the thing that made his foot tap and his eyes seek the horizon.

Soon they reached the outskirts of town. Matthew pulled his horses to a stop beside an asphalt parking area. The community in Dakota was growing but still on the small side. Only two other people waited for the bus in the shade of the dry goods store. Matthew set the brake on the buggy. They both stepped out onto the asphalt, savoring the warmth of the day.

Jacob retrieved his one piece of luggage. The battered black leather looked more like a sports bag than a suitcase. More importantly, it held the things Jacob needed. Inside were two changes of clothes, his shaving kit and a toothbrush, and his reading material—a Bible and the paperback he'd traded for at the town library's swap section.

Turning to Matthew, he clasped the older man's hand. "*Danki* for your kindness, Matthew. I enjoyed the work and your family treated me as if I belonged."

"*Ya,* it seemed to me you fit right in." The older man rubbed at his right eyebrow and stared off into the distance. Finally he returned his gaze to Jacob. "Once you begin traveling, it can be hard to stop."

Jacob didn't bother answering.

"But if you must, we will keep you in our prayers. We'll pray for your safety and ask *Gotte* to lead you where you belong." Matthew reached into his pocket and pulled out a small piece of paper folded in half. He pushed it into Jacob's hands. "I know you have family back home. You've told me as much, but if you find you need help from someone closer, give me a call. That's the number to my *bruder's* harness shop here in town. He can get hold of me."

With one last slap on the back, he climbed back into his buggy and turned toward home. Jacob picked up his bag and walked up the steps of the dry goods store. The clerk greeted him by name, which wasn't much of a surprise given the lack of business.

"Where would you like a ticket to?"

Now that was a very good question.

He hadn't given it too much thought. He'd even pretended he might stay. But as soon as that thought entered his head the restlessness growled in his stomach. "Whatcha got?"

The old man ducked his head and looked at him over his reading glasses. "Can you give me a direction?"

There was no use going back north. The harvesting season was done there and there would be little or no work. He pointed to a spot on the map.

"South, it is." The clerk printed out a ticket and told him the amount. After depositing the money in his cash drawer, he passed the ticket over the counter.

It was a transaction Jacob had made dozens of times, and it never failed to produce a smile. He reached down, unzipped his bag, and extracted the paperback he was only halfway through. He placed the ticket as a marker in the book.

Thanking the clerk, he made his way outside.

Twenty minutes until the bus arrived. Enough time to lose himself in the history of the Dakotas. And why would he be reading a book about a place he was leaving? That irony wasn't lost on him, but he'd always been a reader. Another trait not prevalent among Amish men, but then as his mother had pointed out, "*Gotte* made you to be the person you are, Jacob. Sure, sin should be fought against, and I trust you will. But your personality and interests? *Gotte* gave you those, son. Never be ashamed of who or what you are."

The words eased some of the questions in his heart.

While most of the people he met—and certainly those he worked for—didn't understand his need to move on, he had the blessing of those who mattered most. His family back in Clymer, New York, had always accepted that he was a bit different. Though his six brothers teased him about it, they also were supportive, suggesting he "get it out of his system" while he could. Whatever that meant. His dad was less understanding but not one to argue. Instead, he assured Jacob that a place would be waiting for him when he returned.

By the time the bus arrived, he was deep into the history of the Dakota Territory, the geography of its black hills, and the Sioux Indians who had lived there long before any white men, let alone Amish, set foot in the area.

As he boarded the bus, he quietly took inventory of the other passengers. He'd been traveling for three years now, ever since his twenty-third birthday. It had always amused him the type of people who still used the bus system. Perhaps it was different in a large urban area, but for cross-country? He'd counted five groups.

There were the poor who couldn't afford private transportation, let alone airfare. Second, he could always count on a few older folks—sometimes couples, sometimes alone. Several had shared with him that they couldn't abide flying, and others had admitted they had grown up riding the bus system and preferred it. The third group was the most troublesome for Jacob—the homeless. Not well washed, they always wore a hungry look, and their eyes darted about constantly. What would cause a person to take to the roads when they had nowhere else to live? Wouldn't it be better to live within a community? To have the support and help of a shared group of family and friends?

He supposed the same questions could be asked of him. The difference was that he had a place if he ever chose to settle there.

The fourth group he saw on most trips, though certainly not all. He'd first sat beside a military person on the bus from Pennsylvania to

New York. He knew they were military not because they were in uniform—usually they weren't—but because of the short haircuts and the closed down expressions. Polite, they remained distant and offered little in the way of details or conversation.

Then there were the Amish. One bus he'd taken out of Sugar Creek had been nearly all Amish. He supposed the driver was used to it as he'd greeted them with a robust "*Gudemariye.*" These folks were usually on their way to a well-earned vacation or family visit in another part of the country. Occasionally, he'd met someone like himself, someone who traveled for the joy of it.

Jacob claimed a seat halfway back and set his bag on the empty spot next to him. Matthew's wife had packed him a lunch, and he was tempted to open it up even though it was only nine in the morning. Best to wait. He had a long ride ahead of him.

CHAPTER 7

Anna was astonished at how the look and feel of her *onkel's* farm changed over the next week. She'd walked the corn maze on the north side of the house many times in the last few months, taking her time as she investigated the paths and explored the borders, and she'd even walked down the two-lane road to see what it looked like from that side. When she'd arrived in the middle of the summer, the corn was no more than waist high, but now it towered far above her, golden husks waving in the September breeze. The maze looked like a different place entirely, a hidden path to an unknown destination.

Actually, it only went round and round with various twists and turns, ending on the far side of the field—the side closest to the Millers' property.

Friday morning Anna walked to her booth in a bit of a daze. The booth had been moved closer to the house, and the yard was filled with people. She hadn't realized that so many from the community joined in with the weekend's festivities, but then she'd never spent a fall in Oklahoma before.

The Millers, who had three children under four years old, brought bales of hay and set them up in a kiddie maze on the south side of the house. Other families from their church brought items to be sold in Anna's booth, and soon it was filled with fruit pies, loaves of bread, and cookies baked fresh by the women in their district.

"How will I ever keep it all straight?" she asked *Mammi*.

"No worries. Each woman takes turns working in the booth, and we keep a tablet with everyone's name on it." *Mammi* reached under the counter and found the tablet and pen. How had Anna not noticed that before? But then she hadn't needed it. The produce she'd sold had been from *Onkel* Samuel's field. There'd been no need to keep track of money or items.

"Write down the amount of each sale and who brought the item." *Mammi* held up a jar of preserved okra. "See? A name is written on the labels."

Anna glanced up when she sensed even more activity across from where they sat. Neal and Adam waved at her as they finished setting up the refreshment booth, which was directly across the large front yard. According to the sign they put in front of it, there would be hot cider, coffee, hot chocolate, and fresh-squeezed lemonade.

Even Levi Troyer, their bishop, participated. When Anna had first arrived in the district, she'd been surprised to see that the bishop was handicapped, but she quickly learned his limp didn't slow Levi down much. He needed a cane to walk, and the injury he'd suffered still seemed to cause him some pain, but she'd never heard him complain about it.

He'd shown up the previous afternoon with two goats, a small donkey, three sheep, and a chicken. Levi was also their neighbor. His place was to the east. Though his children were grown and scattered throughout the district, the oldest son had remained home and raised his family there. Anna had been over to their place several times, and always there were children and grandchildren about.

He'd walked the animals over with the help of some of his grandchildren. The goats, donkey, and sheep each had a lead rope tied around them, but one of his granddaughters carried the chicken. They looked like a traveling farm.

"For the petting zoo," he explained with a wink. And indeed, two more men from their church soon arrived with a makeshift pen and a pony.

"I'm overwhelmed," Anna admitted to *Mammi*. But she was also excited. Who wouldn't be? This was the most activity she had seen in months.

"You thought we were only having a walk through the corn?" *Mammi* sat on one of the chairs inside the produce stand. Though the morning was warm, she wore a long-sleeved dress. Her grandmother was obviously enjoying herself. It occurred to Anna that this was a precious memory she would look back on for years to come.

"Why does he do it, *Mammi*?"

"He?"

"*Onkel* Samuel."

"He does it because I ask him to." *Mammi* patted her arm, and added, "This was something your *grossdaddi* started years ago."

Her *grossdaddi*? Hadn't Rebecca said that Menno Schwartz was as serious as his sons? She could hardly picture him planning a fall festival on his land, and this was definitely turning into quite the celebration.

"He also did it because I asked. You see, Anna, I grew up on a farm back in Goshen. Back in the day when land was plentiful and roads were few. My parents would have two weekends in September where they invited anyone who would come out to their farm to celebrate *Gotte*'s goodness. Each year something else was added. What started as a simple maze for children to meander through became much more. Members from our church district began to participate until finally it was much like what you see here."

"This was in Goshen?"

"*Ya*. It was a time we used to thank the Lord together. We celebrated the harvest. Even when there was drought or floods or war, we held the festival. Even when the harvest was less than we hoped, we thanked the Lord. It became a tradition that was dear to me." *Mammi* seemed lost in thought for a moment, lost in memories of long ago. "Not long after I married Menno, my parents were killed in a buggy accident."

Mammi reached under her glasses and rubbed at her eyes. Anna thought she was crying, but *Mammi* repositioned the glasses and smiled at her—clear blue eyes and wrinkles fanning out in every direction. "My heart was broken. I did not understand then that *Gotte* has His reasons. For months I went through the motions, feeling nothing, saying little. Three weeks before the harvest, Menno asked me what he could do, how he could comfort me."

Anna turned her back to the activity in the yard and focused completely on her grandmother. "What did you say?"

"I asked him to hold the harvest celebration as a way to remember my *mamm* and *dat*. Menno, he was a solemn thing, much like my sons. But he loved me. *Ya*, he would have done anything to ease the pain in my heart."

"And the festival did that?"

"*Nein*. Not the first year or even the second. But eventually the memories of my parents and the smiles of the children eased my pain. Each fall I found myself looking forward to those weekends when it seemed I could hear their laughter again."

"The harvest celebration healed you."

"The Lord did that, Anna. He brought the harvest. I was able to be thankful again, and gratitude will bring healing every time."

"I don't remember having any harvest celebration in Goshen."

"You were a babe the last time. When we moved here, we brought the tradition with us. Samuel continues it to honor his father's memory and because he knows it is important to me."

"And now Amish and *Englischers* come."

"*Ya*. It seems that at various points our lives do intersect, even though we strive to be separate. It's a *gut* thing to see these families bring their *kinner*, to see them run through the maze as my children once did."

Mammi changed subjects when she saw Neal Eberly walking in their direction. "Looks as if you're about to have company, Anna."

Before she could think of a way to avoid him, Neal was standing at her booth. Anna had made the mistake of riding home with him on Sunday evening after the singing. Perhaps calling it a "mistake" was a bit strong, but she didn't want to give him the wrong impression.

"Hello, Anna. Ruth."

Anna was a little surprised that he knew her *Mammi*'s name, but then he'd grown up in the district. Probably she was like family to him. That thought caused Anna to smile, which didn't go unnoticed by young Neal.

"We were preparing the booth for the start of the festival," Anna said. "It looks *gut, ya*?"

"It does." Neal seemed about to say more, but then he clamped his mouth shut and stuffed his hands into his pockets.

"Was there something you needed, Neal?" *Mammi* asked gently.

"*Ya*, I was wondering if you'd like some of the cold lemonade I brought for the refreshment booth."

"Lemonade sounds *gut*, Anna. Please fetch me a glass." *Mammi*'s smile widened. "*Danki*, Neal. That's very nice of you."

Anna didn't have much choice, so she tossed *Mammi* a we'll-talk-about-this-later look and walked beside Neal to the refreshment stand. The yard was as full as Anna had ever seen it with children of all sizes, parents, grandparents, and, from the looks of cars pulling off the road, *Englischers*.

Neal fetched a glass of lemonade for *Mammi*. "Wait here," he said, and then he carried the drink back over to her. When he returned, he poured them each some and motioned toward the porch. "Want to sit for a minute? I noticed you've been working all morning."

"I stopped for a sandwich."

"Which you ate standing up in the booth."

Anna squirmed uncomfortably. Had Neal been watching her that closely? She needed to nip any romantic ideas he had in the bud because a relationship was not blossoming between them."

"I enjoyed driving you home Sunday night."

"And I appreciate your doing so."

"I was wondering if perhaps you'd like me to pick you up this Sunday evening. Our church service will be at the Bylers', and they'll hold the singing in their barn. Of course you could stay, but that sometimes makes for a long day. If you went home after the luncheon I could—"

Anna reached out and touched his arm. "I appreciate the offer, Neal, and I suppose I will see you at the singing..."

"But..."

"But I don't think we should go as a couple. I'm not ready for that kind of commitment yet."

"It's only a singing." Neal stared into his glass, as if the answers he sought might be floating among slices of lemon.

"It *is* only a singing," Anna agreed. "And I noticed several nice young girls watching you at the last one. I wouldn't want them to think you're already taken."

"I wouldn't mind being taken, though."

Anna sighed and pressed her glass of lemonade against her forehead. "Is it because I'm fat?"

"You are not fat. You're the same size I am."

Neal smiled for the first time since they sat down. "Well, no one could ever call us skinny."

"True, but fat is...well, you know. It's people who sit around and eat whoopie pies all day."

"We're too busy for that."

"Of course we are. You can't eat while you're building furniture, and I can't eat while I'm selling produce or doing whatever *Aenti* Erin has planned for me next. Say, why do you make furniture? Do you actually enjoy it?"

Neal launched into a long description of the different types of woods and what made for the best table or chair.

Finally, Anna held up her hand to stop him. "You love what you do. I can tell. You're a very fortunate person, Neal Eberly."

"And what do you love to do?"

"I don't know." Anna stood and handed Neal her empty glass. "I honestly do not know."

Then she turned and headed back toward the booth, hoping and praying he was no longer watching her every move.

Mammi was still sipping her lemonade and apparently enjoying the activity surrounding her. "You turned him down, didn't you? I could tell the moment it happened. His shoulders fell as if he'd been crushed by a gigantic weight."

"*Danki.* That makes me feel better."

Mammi smiled and smacked her lips after another sip of the tart lemonade. "Why did you do it, then? Is there something wrong with him?"

"*Nein*. Maybe there's something wrong with me, *Mammi*. Did you ever think of that?"

"You are as *Gotte* made you, Anna."

"So why am I not interested in courting Neal Eberly? He's a perfectly nice boy with a *gut* job. He doesn't smell bad. His hair is cut nicely, and he has *wunderbaar* manners."

"It takes more than the good manners and a nice haircut."

"How did you know?"

Mammi waited.

"How did you know you were in *lieb* with *Grossdaddi*?"

The next words surprised Anna as much as anything that had happened that day.

"I don't know that I was…at first. In my day girls didn't marry for love so much as for someone to be a *gut* partner through life. But by the time I had my first *boppli*? Oh, yes. I loved your *grossdaddi* by then, and though he died eleven years ago, I still do."

Anna thought about that as families continued to fill their yard and a line developed at her booth. Loving someone for your whole life. For years and years. For decades.

She supposed her parents loved each other like that, though it had always seemed to her that they were friends more than anything else.

And her *aenti* and *onkel*?

Maybe.

It was possible that love looked entirely different from what she had imagined.

CHAPTER 8

$\mathcal{T}$hat first weekend they opened the corn maze passed in a blur.
Anna forgot about all the questions in her life and enjoyed
being where she was. She didn't mind working in the booth, but her
favorite thing was leading the children through the maze of corn. The
small ones giggled and shrieked and ran as the corn swayed around
them.

Occasionally she'd have a young girl or boy who didn't believe it
was actually corn towering so high above their heads. Then she'd pick
them up and pull down one of the cornstalks. Peeling back the husk,
she'd point at the yellow and white kernels. "See? Corn, the same as
you eat at home."

Each time the child's eyes would brighten, and when they had completed the maze they would run to their parents proclaiming, "I saw
the corn. Anna showed me."

"Perhaps your calling is to be a teacher," Erin suggested as they were
about to begin the second weekend of the maze.

They both knew the flipside of what her *aenti* was saying—perhaps
she wasn't meant to marry.

Anna didn't know about marrying, but she did know that teaching wasn't for her. "Homework and parent meetings and lesson plans?
No thank you."

Erin shook her head as they cleaned up the breakfast dishes. It was
Friday morning, and the crowds would be arriving by noon.

"Did you always want to be married? To be a housewife?"

"*Ya.* Why wouldn't I?"

"I don't know. I just wondered."

Erin was always reticent, never answering more than she had been asked. But on this one occasion she looked directly at Anna and said, "I love your *onkel*, you know."

There was something in her gaze—a deep hurt and a fierce honesty that brought tears to Anna's eyes.

Why had she asked?

Why did she pry?

She mumbled, "Of course you do," and hurried outside.

The cars and buggies began arriving after lunch. There was less set-up to do than there had been the week before, and things moved along smoothly. The day flew by, and soon Anna was busy once again leading groups of children through the maze. On the return of one such trip, she was surprised to see a familiar face waiting for her at the booth.

Chloe smiled and waved. When she did, the silver bracelets she wore jangled and reflected the bright fall sunshine. As before, she wore a pair of Western jeans and boots, and this time a short-sleeved, snap button Western shirt made of a brown, paisley material. Her black curls bounced as she wove her way over to where Anna stood.

"Hi. I was hoping to see you today."

"Well, you certainly looked in the right place. Are you here to write another article?"

Chloe hitched her purse over her shoulder. "Maybe. Or I might be here simply to enjoy the afternoon."

"There's plenty of food and a booth with drinks too."

"Can you take off for a moment? I'd love to buy you a coffee or..."

"Apple cider would be *gut*."

The bishop's wife, Mary Beth, was manning the produce stand. "Go on, Anna," she said. "You've barely taken a break since the day started."

Chloe purchased two cups of cider at the refreshment booth and then they settled under the large cottonwood tree near the front porch. Someone had set up benches there which were about half filled with parents waiting for their children. It was interesting to see so many *Englischers* on her *onkel*'s property. Everyone looked as if they were enjoying the day.

"I read your article."

"Did you? I thought you only read the *Budget*."

"Personally, I read anything I can get my hands on. In this case Rebecca Byler—"

"She runs the dry goods store, right?"

"*Ya*. She saved me a copy of your paper, thinking I'd like to see the article."

"And it met with your approval?" Chloe grinned impishly.

"Oh, it did. You write very well, and I liked how you presented the different opinions."

"Well, it's true that not everyone is happy with the increase in Amish businesses, but I have a feeling the big farmers—the Leo Stuebners of the world—will do fine in spite of a few Amish roadside booths."

"I wouldn't think our small produce stand is a threat to any business."

They sipped their cider and sat watching the coming and going of families. Anna was surprised at how comfortable she felt with Chloe. She'd never had an *Englisch* friend before, not that they were friends exactly. Maybe it was because they were both women, both older than twenty-two, and both unmarried. She supposed Chloe was not married but snuck a glance at her left hand to be sure.

Nope. No ring.

"Say, Anna. I'd like to do a piece on the women in your community who make quilts for sale. Do you know anyone like that?"

"Sure. Many of our women quilt for extra money. It helps supplement their family income—one of those cottage industries you spoke about."

"Would you be interested in going with me to see them? I have a feeling they might be more willing to talk with me if you were there."

Anna thought about it. She hadn't been off the farm for anything other than services at church, a few singings, and the occasional visit to the dry goods store. Her *aenti* had reminded her the night before that if she wanted time off she could have it. Anna was quite sure that Erin was hoping the time off would be for a romantic date, but some girlfriend time sounded better to her.

"I'll need to check with my *onkel* first, but I think I'd like that."

So they set a day and hour for the next week, and Anna promised to call her from the phone shack if she couldn't make it.

Anna returned to her booth to work. Occasionally she'd glance up and see Chloe speaking with a family or examining some of the items for sale. She noticed, for the first time, that the reporter had not brought her camera with her. No doubt pictures would be good for her newspaper articles, but the fact that she knew it would make people uncomfortable and chose not to bring it said a lot about the woman.

The rest of the day passed quickly. By the time she closed the booth for the evening, Anna had decided she would go with Chloe on her quest to find Amish quilts. Surely her *onkel* wouldn't forbid her to do so. Tuesdays were usually quiet days—Mondays being taken up with laundry and Wednesdays with baking. She'd go Tuesday, ride in the little blue car, and enjoy a day traveling around their district.

The thought brought a smile to her face, and soon she was humming as she made her way once again into her *onkel*'s house.

CHAPTER 9

*J*acob had found work right after he had exited the bus in Yoder, Kansas. He'd stopped by the men's room to splash his face with water. Then, stepping out onto the main street, a buggy pulled past him, stopped, and waited. When he walked up beside it, a middle-aged Amish man slid open the side window. The man had a gray beard, bright blue eyes, and looked to be between forty and fifty.

"New in town?"

"*Ya*. Just off the bus."

The man took a moment to size him up. Finally he said, "Name's Saul Yoder."

At the look of surprise on Jacob's face, he grinned. "*Ya*. I know. The town is Yoder and my name is Yoder. There are a lot of Yoders in these parts, and most of us are kin to the original founder."

Jacob laughed. "Nice to meet you, Saul. I step off the bus and am greeted by a town celebrity. What are the odds?"

"Hardly a celebrity, and the meeting isn't happenchance. One of my workers had a family emergency and needed to go back to Indiana. I dropped him off where the bus picks up, the store you just came from. Too much coming and going if you ask me, but I never was one for travel." He shrugged and added, "I'm bringing in my sorghum crop and could use some help."

It happened more often than most people would believe. There weren't many Amish itinerant workers, and Jacob had never had trouble finding work unless he landed in an area when there was little work to do. Which is why he followed the seasons and headed south when the winter months approached.

The work at Saul Yoder's farm was like the work on any other farm—though his spread was somewhat bigger and the crops therefore more numerous. The small community also allowed tractors in the field, but Jacob learned that was mostly for the planting. The bulk of the harvesting was still done by hand.

Jacob had read about Amish communities in Oklahoma allowing tractors, but he'd never seen them himself. The two tractors on Yoder's farm had been converted for off-road use, meaning they had steel rim tires. No teen on their *rumspringa* would be taking their dad's tractor to town.

Surprisingly, there was still as much work as he'd seen on places without the vehicles. Perhaps the farmers were able to plant a little more or more easily pull in a second harvest.

Either way, the yield had been good. The sorghum cane had grown to ten feet, and the cluster of seeds at the top were a nice size. The harvest involved using a thin-bladed stick to strip the leaves from each side of the stalk, after which you could remove the head of seeds. Once that was done, another worker followed behind and cut the stalk off close to the ground. It was then taken into the barn, where Saul had a processing machine that crushed the cane and harvested the juice, which was collected into large containers and cooked.

The sorghum would be used in the silage to feed the farmer's animals. And some was also traditionally put back for cooking—a sweet syrup that Jacob liked even better than molasses.

The size of the harvest explained why Saul had several hired workers, including a few *Englisch* ones. Together they worked long hours to bring in the crop, hurrying to do it before predicted storms arrived the following week.

He'd been there for a little over a week and everything had gone well. Saul paid on Fridays, even when the men were expected to work on Saturday. He said if he couldn't trust them to stay around for the last day of the week, he supposed he hadn't made a wise decision in hiring them.

Giving them their wages on Friday allowed them to knock off an hour early and go into town to buy any supplies they needed.

The trouble began on the second Friday evening, after they had received their wages.

Jacob had been in the fields all day—they all had, even Saul's wife and daughters. The harvest had gone well. One more day, and they should be finished. He could tell that Saul was relieved. No Amish farmer would be caught working on a Sunday, and heavy storms were still predicted for the next Monday, including high winds and hail that would likely ruin whatever was left standing in the fields.

Jacob accepted his pay, thanked Saul for the work, and walked slowly to the old barn to wash up. He and the other three hired hands were bunking in a converted workroom that had been cleaned up and furnished with cots. Jacob had recently been reading *Grapes of Wrath*. Though he rarely read fiction, Steinbeck's book had been on a SWAP shelf at a bus station in Nebraska, halfway through his trip. He'd finished the Dakotas history and readily selected the new title and replaced it with his.

John Steinbeck's book was on his mind as he walked toward the barn. It seemed to him that very little had changed in the way of farming since the 1930s, at least not for the Amish. However, the economic and political aspects of the novel challenged him. Mulling those ideas over in his mind and dead tired from a day in the fields, he pushed open the barn door. A separate part of his mind was thinking of washing up, filling his belly, and settling down to finish the story of migrant workers during the Great Depression.

He stepped into the cool darkness of the barn, and that was when he first heard the muffled sound, something that didn't belong. Perhaps a hurt animal or...

There it was again.

As he walked to the back of the barn, something in his stomach twisted and turned.

The sound was clearer now. He recognized it as a low, quiet, desperate sob, and it wasn't from an animal.

When he reached the back stall, there was barely enough light to discern what was happening, but then it didn't take a spotlight or an explanation. One look was all Jacob needed.

"Leave him alone."

Cory Shoals, one of the *Englisch* hired hands, momentarily froze. Cory was only medium sized, but he had calloused hands, and he was strong in the way of most harvest workers. He was also a bully. Jacob had caught him taking Miguel's lunch and harassing him in the bunk room. Each time, Jacob had ignored it, opting instead to help Miguel. But this time was different. This time, blood had been shed.

Cory had Miguel Garza backed up to the wall and was holding the kid's wallet. Blood dripped from Miguel's nose and his right eye was beginning to swell. Miguel was what Amish folk called *special*. He was a hard worker but somewhat slow in understanding things. It wasn't a problem when harvesting. Miguel was a grown man, but in many ways he had the attitude of a child. The first day Jacob had arrived, Miguel had found a dead bird among the crops. It had been a strange sight to see the six foot, muscular man sitting on the ground, crying, and holding the small animal.

"I said leave him alone."

Miguel's eyes were wide with fear, and tears streamed down his cheeks. He glanced at Jacob and then down at the ground, as if he could make himself invisible.

"I heard you, Amish boy. We all know that Miguel here is your friend, but this is none of your business."

Cory turned his attention back to Miguel, who was literally cowering away from the man. Miguel was bigger and stronger than Cory, but he didn't know that. He only knew that he was afraid and that someone had hurt him.

"Looks like you've been saving up your money for a couple of weeks, Miguel. This just happens to be the amount I need." Cory snatched the bills and dropped the wallet on the ground.

Red spots floated in front of Jacob's vision. Convinced he could control his anger, and with his eyesight having grown accustomed to the darkness, he strode into the stall and pulled Cory away from Miguel.

"This is none of your business, Jacob." Cory's tone landed somewhere between a sneer and a laugh. "So stay out of it."

"I said leave him alone and give him back that money."

"Or what? Are you going to run and tell the boss?" Cory turned back to Miguel and pushed him once more, causing Miguel to trip over a pail and land on the ground. "Go ahead and tell. By the time you get back, I'll be packed and long gone."

Miguel struggled to his feet at the same moment Jacob snapped.

He certainly couldn't say later that he thoughtfully considered his options.

Instead, his instinct to protect simply flooded every other part of his brain. His pulse and blood pressure accelerated. His muscles tensed as his brain sent signals that the danger was still present and very real. Adrenaline pumped through his veins.

He grabbed Cory's shoulder and attempted to drag him away from Miguel. When the man resisted, Jacob pulled back his arm, clenched his hand into a fist, and knocked him out in a single punch.

Miguel barely hesitated. His eyes still cast down, he picked up his wallet off the ground, not bothering to gather his money, and fled.

Cory didn't move. He lay there on the barn floor, a small amount of spittle drying at the corner of the mouth, his face turned toward the roof of the barn, his eyes closed.

Had he killed the man with a single punch? Unlikely, but Cory was definitely out.

Jacob found an empty feed crate, turned it over, and sat down on it. He'd keep an eye on Cory in case he came to and attempted to run.

He doubted he would be alone for very long.

CHAPTER 10

The next day Jacob sat down for his second meeting with the local bishop.

Saul Yoder was also in attendance.

As before, the meeting took place in Saul's kitchen. The air was rich with the smell of bread recently baked, and a blackberry pie cooled on the counter. A full pot of coffee sat on the stove. It was an indicator of the seriousness of the meeting that no refreshments were offered.

Bishop Schrock was the first to speak. "Jacob, I want you to know we called the phone number you gave us yesterday. The one for..." He stopped and ran a finger down a sheet of paper where he'd written a few notes during their first meeting.

"Matthew. Matthew Hochstettler. He was able to verify that you did indeed work for him." Schrock took off his glasses and swiped at the dust on them. "He gave you a *wunderbaar* character reference. Said he'd had no trouble from you at all."

Instead of asking what the man had expected to hear, Jacob simply nodded once.

"Which makes this situation all the more puzzling."

Jacob remained silent. He'd given his version of what had happened the day before. As far as he knew, Cory was still in the *Englischer*'s jail, and that was what mattered. Miguel was safe, and his money had been returned to him. Jacob wouldn't apologize for what he'd done. Given the chance, he was certain he would do the same thing again.

"I've also spoken to your bishop in Clymer. He had *gut* things to say about you, though he's puzzled by your desire to travel instead of settle down. He told me he's spoken with you about this several times, and he even warned you that it could only result in trouble."

Jacob remembered that conversation well enough, but he chose not to elaborate on it.

"I appreciate what you did for Miguel, Jacob. He lives in the next town and works for us every harvest." Saul rubbed at his eyes. No doubt he'd had little sleep the night before. "However, you know it's not our way to respond in a violent manner to any situation."

Bishop Schrock picked up where Saul left off. "Jacob, you are young, so your transgression can be forgiven. However—"

"Transgression?" In spite of his vow to remain calm, Jacob's temper flared. "Saving Miguel was no transgression."

"But the use of violence was. In the fifth chapter of the Gospel of Matthew we are instructed not to 'resist an evil person.' If anyone slaps you on the right cheek, you are commanded to turn the other also. "

"I'm familiar with Christ's words, and if I had been slapped I am certain I would have been able to turn the other cheek."

"The commandment is the same regardless—"

"It is not!" Jacob closed his eyes and pulled in a calming breath. "I beg your pardon, Bishop Schrock. I do not mean to argue with you."

"And yet you are."

"But the Scripture does not forbid us from protecting women and children. Miguel...he is like a child."

"The Scripture is plain, Jacob. I understand that at your age this is difficult to understand. When we respond with violence, we preempt God's intervention."

"You're saying an angel might have appeared to save him."

"I'm saying we are to trust in Him."

"And if Cory had hurt Miguel badly?"

Saul's eyes locked with his, but the man said nothing. No doubt he had been wrestling with the same thought throughout the night.

Schrock tapped his Bible. "We choose a nonviolent approach because of our commitment to Christ as our Lord. It is not a transaction where God promises to save us from every danger."

Jacob clenched his teeth together until his jaw began to ache.

Schrock was on a roll now, waving his arms for emphasis and occasionally picking up his Bible as if that would lend credence to his words. Ten minutes later he wound down and got to the real point of the meeting. "We are not asking you to leave our community, Jacob. Your bishop shared with me the fact of your baptism and subsequent commitment to the teachings of Christ. But when you joined the church, you also vowed to uphold the rules of the *Ordnung*. Though some Amish communities may differ in manners of technology or dress, there is no difference in regard to violence. It is not allowed, and it will not be tolerated here."

He cleared his throat. "If you stay within our community, you have two options. You may offer a confession at church a week from Sunday, or you will be shunned until such time as you make such confession. Of course, should you decide to move on this matter will stay here. You have no history of violence, and we feel no need to share it with other communities unless they should inquire about you. In that case, we would be honest in our answer."

Jacob wasn't surprised or even disappointed. He'd been in enough different communities to understand that a bishop's job was a difficult one. Were Bishop Schrock to allow violence to go uncorrected within his flock, his problems would increase exponentially. The last thing Jacob wanted to be was a divisive factor within a community. Yes, he understood the bishop's position, but in this situation he couldn't say he agreed with his assessment.

He stood and pushed his hands into his pockets. "*Danki* for meeting with me and explaining your position." Turning to Saul, he added, "And *danki* for the opportunity to work on your harvest."

Then he turned and walked out into the afternoon.

CHAPTER 11

*C*hloe shuffled the papers in front of her into a neat stack, clicked the "Sleep" button on her computer, and then she pushed her chair back from her desk. The desk was old and scarred, and one leg was shorter than the other three. Long ago she'd stuck a telephone directory under it and forgot about it. Because she was in the office at all sorts of odd hours, she rarely ever turned off the computer. Her schedule was one thing she loved about being a newspaper reporter. She also realized she was probably the last generation to be able to claim that title. Already they were outnumbered by bloggers, and the trend was expected to continue.

Jobs for traditional newspapers were predicted to decline thirteen percent over the next ten years—she knew that exact number because one of the other reporters had pinned an article to their bulletin board the week before. In addition to the reduction in jobs, many newspapers had closed or gone to online-only editions. The distinction between bloggers and news reporters had blurred over the years, and recently the U.S. Ninth Circuit had ruled that bloggers had the same First Amendment protection as news reporters.

Chloe was glad about that. She had friends who were bloggers. She didn't think anyone should be prosecuted for what they wrote, but she wasn't ready to trade in her shoddy desk for the dining room table in her little apartment, where she could research, virtually file her reports, and immerse herself in social media. She liked going in to work in an actual office. She liked having a line of separation, even though she often did work on stories from home.

But she always submitted them in the office. She received new assignments in the office. And she learned the ropes from the older reporters in the office.

The newspaper room itself was a large, busy, chaotic, and vibrant place. It practically hummed with activity, reminding her of a bee-hive. She liked interacting with people and the feeling of being part of a group—part of something bigger than herself. Sometimes, she even liked her boss.

Other times, not so much.

Eric Knowles leaned over the partition that divided Chloe's space from the sports writer. *Leaned over* wasn't an exaggeration. The partition was short and her boss was nearly seven feet tall. He never missed an opportunity to remind folks that he once played college basketball at Oklahoma University. The man could work that tidbit into any conversation.

"Headed out to cover the quilting piece?" At the moment Eric was studying her with a dopey smile, so apparently his day was going well. As usual, he wore tan-colored pants and a button-down shirt. Where did he find clothes to fit his tall frame? Did he have to special order them? Is that why he wore the identical, or nearly identical, thing every day?

Her well-developed radar told her things were going well around the office but Eric was slightly bored. She didn't mind the bored Eric too much. It was the insanely upset Eric that she avoided. When there were problems—missed deadlines, bad photos, absence of a juicy story—he resembled a tall, thin, angry bear.

"I'm headed out to Cody's Creek now."

"Cool." He sipped the coffee he'd probably reheated four times. Eric carried around a mug with him everywhere, as if he might need a shot of caffeine and didn't want to be unprepared. He didn't seem to actually consume much, though. Maybe he thought the caffeine would leap into his system by osmosis.

Chloe stuck her cell phone in her purse and looped the purse strap over her shoulder. "Cool, but…"

"No but."

"Yes, there was. I heard it in your voice. You think this is a lame story."

"I approved it, didn't I?"

"You did."

"Quilts." He shook his head as if the topic offended him.

"Sorry I don't have anything more catastrophic."

"It's okay. We had a lot of good response on your produce piece. Readers are interested in this Amish thing."

Chloe didn't bother calling him on the *Amish thing*, which seemed rather offensive to her. What if she talked about the *sports thing* or the *stock thing* or, heaven forbid, the *proliferation of red cars thing*. Eric treated his Porsche like the child he'd never had. He even hung a framed picture of it in his office. The man could probably use some therapy. She couldn't imagine how he afforded the sports car on an editor's salary. For all she knew, he was a trust fund baby and played at being an editor for the sheer fun of it.

Which was not her problem. She was supposed to meet Anna in forty minutes and she didn't want to be late.

Unfortunately, Eric wasn't finished.

"It's just…we're in tight competition with Cherokee County for the small-town newspaper awards this year."

"They haven't even named the semifinalists yet. It's only September. There are still a lot of news reports to file." When Eric looked as if he were going to argue, she pushed on. "Also, we have a lot of fine papers as our competition. The *Claremore Daily Progress* and *Delaware News* both had good coverage of the flooding in their area last spring and—"

Eric waved her objections away as if he were batting at a pesky fly. His voice took on a nostalgic tone. "Last year we had that piece on the four dead bodies down by Saline Creek."

"Only the one body was at the creek."

"Your reporting literally catapulted us over the competition. You showed the real stuff then, Chloe. The way you attacked that story, you showed the makings of a seasoned reporter."

"I didn't attack anything. My car broke down. I happened to hear the call come in on the tow truck's CB radio, and because it was close to where we were—"

"And the pictures!" Eric smiled fondly at the memory. "Wow."

"I need to go."

"Sure. Yeah. The quilt thing."

Chloe didn't look back as she hurried from the room. She was not going to let Eric ruin her day.

She relaxed as she exited the office and climbed into her little blue Chevy Cavalier. It was nearly ten years old and had a horrendous amount of mileage on it, but the car was hanging together. She glanced down at the gas gauge. Early in her career, Martin Star would pull her aside and give her advice, always by relating some mishap of his own career.

The conversation she remembered best was how he missed the biggest story of his life—one featuring a nationally known movie star who had parachuted near a local lake. The guy was a superb actor and his movies were always well attended and well reviewed, but he was terrible with GPS equipment. The pilot had apparently tried to warn him, but Mr. Movie Star had been sure he was landing on a flat area to the east of the lake. Instead, he'd landed in the water and had been rescued by a couple of local fishing buddies. Martin had been called by one of the guys with a "You won't believe who is in our boat" message. He'd hurried out with the camera tech, but missed the entire event because he'd run out of gas.

"They can teach you a lot of things at those fancy schools." Martin had nodded at the college diploma she'd hung on her cubicle wall. "But if you don't keep gas in the tank, it won't matter one bit. Learn from me, kid. Keep it topped off."

Martin was part-time now—a victim of budget cuts, which he said was fine. His wife wanted him to clean out the garage anyway. He had a weekly column on agriculture and hunting, and he occasionally covered local conferences or legislation on the same.

Chloe liked Martin, and she missed seeing his old, wrinkled face around the office. Pulling into the gas station at the corner, she topped off her tank even though it was two-thirds full.

"Learn from me, kid."

That was exactly what she'd done. She didn't plan on missing any career-making stories. Though today, she was ridiculously psyched about going to look at a bunch of quilts.

CHAPTER 12

They had been to three houses, and Anna had several more on her list.

"I've never paid much attention to quilts before."

"When you grow up Amish, it's like a rite of passage."

"So you quilt?"

"Some." Anna studied the scene passing outside their window.

"Does that mean you don't want to talk about it? Or you have nothing to say?"

Anna laughed. "You ask more questions than I do, which I didn't know was possible."

"I'm a reporter. I'm supposed to ask questions. It helps when you're trying to get information from folks for an article. Of course, some people I interview actually want to be in the paper. It's hard to get them to stop talking."

"Not so much with the Amish."

"Not so much..." The afternoon had turned out better than Chloe could have imagined. She never would have found Amish women who sold quilts for additional income on her own unless she'd passed their roadside sign by sheer luck.

"Explain to me why there isn't a quilt shop located somewhere central that these women could sell their quilts from. Somewhere *Englischers* could find."

Anna shrugged. "If *Gotte* wants them to sell..."

"He'll bring folks down their lane? Come on now."

Anna only smiled.

Chloe was learning that her new Amish friend wasn't easily offended. She was surprised at how comfortable she felt with Anna. There had been no awkward silences or dead-end topics, though at times—like now—Anna didn't exactly offer volumes of information.

"If there was a central shop—"

"But there's not."

"If there were, it would bring more tourists and more quilts would sell. Mrs. Troyer..."

"Our bishop's wife."

"She had more than a dozen beautiful quilts completed. I'm sure plenty of woman would love to have those in their home. They would sell quickly if anyone knew about them."

"Who would work at this shop?" Anna cornered herself in the car seat so she could face Chloe.

She certainly seemed comfortable riding in the car. Chloe had no idea why she had worried that this might be her first time, that she might not know how to work the seat belt. She realized suddenly that many of her thoughts about the Amish were stereotypes. As a reporter, she should have known better.

"That would depend on how many women you had contributing quilts. If you had at least twelve, I suppose each woman could spend half a day —"

"Amish women don't work outside the home."

"Never?"

"They don't if they're married. For one thing, there's too much for them to do at home. There's the cooking and cleaning and raising of the younger *kinner.*"

"*Kinner?*"

"Children."

"What about when they're older? When the *kinner* are gone?"

"Still there is much to do—helping with the *grandkinner.* Plus all of the work on a farm remains the same. Look at my *aenti*. She has no children, and still the work is almost too much for her. At least in big families the children grow older and can help."

"Is that why you came? To help her?"

Anna shook her head and popped her finger joints one by one. A nervous gesture? Maybe. Chloe turned the subject back to the prospective quilt shop.

"What about younger women, like you?"

"Most women my age are married already and expecting their first *boppli*."

"Really?"

"Yes. Why would you be surprised at that?"

"Well, you're not so old. Probably younger than I am."

"Twenty-four." Anna again popped the index finger on her left hand.

If Chloe didn't stay away from sensitive subjects, the girl was going to have an early case of arthritis. "I'm thirty-two."

"And not married?" As soon as she said that, Anna covered her mouth as if she wanted to snatch the words back.

"It's okay. My mom says the same thing, often in the same tone of voice." She immediately regretted the words. There was no use in being angry at her mother, and she had vowed she would bury the hatchet. Some days it seemed to her that they had been fighting for years, though they never raised their voices. But tension always simmered beneath the surface.

She slowed down as they entered a school zone adjacent to the local elementary school. "But before Amish women marry..."

"Sometimes young girls will work at a shop in town or in one of our local schools, but a woman's place is most often on the farm. We believe it is *Gotte's wille*."

"I don't understand. I know there are plenty of shops in places like Pennsylvania and Indiana and even Ohio. Why not here?"

"Those areas have a bigger Mennonite population, which can help with establishing businesses. For example, Lolly's Fabrics in Shipshe—"

"Shipshe?"

"Shipshewana. It's near my town of Goshen, in northeast Indiana."

"Okay."

"Lolly's is run by a Mennonite woman. That helps, because women working outside of the home is more accepted in the Mennonite culture. She hires Amish girls, but she and her husband run the business."

Chloe shook her head. She was going to have to resist her urge to fix things, and really, was the Amish way broken? The families they had visited seemed to be doing fine. No one was going hungry because a quilt hadn't sold.

They were driving through Cody's Creek on the way to the next quilter on her list.

Chloe nodded toward the dry goods store. "The owner there is Amish, right? I've been in a few times."

"*Ya*, Rebecca and Joseph Byler own the store." Anna glanced out the window as the signal light changed and they passed by. "I hadn't given much thought to the fact that Rebecca works in the store. Maybe, because they live behind the store instead of on a farm, it's natural for her to help her husband."

"She could carry a few locally made quilts in her store."

"Perhaps."

Chloe's stomach rumbled the moment she saw the Dairy Queen sign up ahead. She turned on her right blinker and changed lanes. "Hungry?"

"A little."

"Let's get some ice cream, then. I'll buy yours since you are giving up your afternoon to show me around."

"And I'll buy yours since you gave me an excuse to get off the farm for a few hours."

CHAPTER 13

The last home Chloe and Anna visited was in the northern part of the district.

"Naomi Hershberger is one of the best quilters in our area, or so my *aenti* says. I've never seen her work."

"You moved here just a few months ago. How do you know where everyone lives?"

"I don't. I'm only taking you to the homes I've visited during our church meetings."

"I read about that. The Amish have church in their homes. How does that work?"

"Each family hosts the meeting twice a year."

"Oh. I guess that makes sense."

"*Ya.* It's the same in nearly every Amish community, though some New Order districts have church buildings like the *Englisch* and like the Mennonites."

"It must be crowded when you meet in a home."

"It is, but it also assures your house receives a thorough cleaning twice a year."

Chloe pulled into the drive of a large two-story home. Like the others they had visited, this one had a massive garden to the side and a huge barn to the back. A trampoline adorned the front yard, but no children were on it.

"The older ones are in school today," Anna explained.

It turned out plenty of younger children were not in school. A woman in her early fifties opened the front door.

"Anna, it's *gut* to see you."

"And you, Naomi. This is Chloe Roberts. She works for the newspaper and is doing a piece on quilting."

"Please come inside." Naomi stepped aside and introduced her daughter-in-law, Sally, who was nursing an infant.

Sally sat quietly. She didn't smile, and she avoided looking directly at them.

Chloe guessed that the younger woman was about her age, probably in her early to mid-thirties. Around her, scattered throughout the sitting room floor, were four youngsters in addition to the one she was holding. The oldest boy proudly proclaimed himself four years old by holding up the corresponding number of fingers. The twins were in the middle at age two and a half, and there was another toddler that looked to be a year, if that.

Five children under five years of age. Chloe couldn't imagine.

Naomi had gray in her hair and a few extra pounds around her middle. She was the quintessential grandmother, and Chloe's fingers itched to pull out her camera and snap a few photos. She didn't, of course. She understood the rules. Naomi had a slow, genuine smile that lit up her face.

But there was a profound sadness about Sally. Her expression was grave, and she only interacted with them if asked a direct question. Her face was drawn tight, perhaps owing to her thinness. Dark circles under her eyes indicated she wasn't receiving nearly enough sleep.

Naomi corralled the twins toward the kitchen table, where she placed crayons and sheets of paper. Bending down, she asked the oldest, the four-year-old, to watch over his baby brothers.

"Don't let them eat the crayons," she reminded the boy as she turned back toward her guests.

"I apologize if this is a bad time." Chloe couldn't imagine a good time. Maybe in six years when they were all in school?

"One time is as *gut* as any other," Naomi assured her, walking her guests to a back porch that had been converted into another sitting area. Two chairs were positioned by the windows with a small table between them. On the table was a checkerboard. The room was full of sunshine and warmth. Chloe found herself wishing Sally would come out with them, but she'd said she needed to finish nursing the baby.

Naomi was bustling about, opening the back door to let in the breeze and raising one of the shades to allow even more sunshine into the room. "Sally has other *kinner* who are older and in school now. It's a bit busier when they're home, though they are *gut* helpers. When they're gone for the day, the house seems somewhat quiet and empty. Sally and I are ready to see them by the time they return in the afternoon."

Chloe glanced at Anna, who waved four fingers at her.

They had four more at school? That made for nine.

"You look surprised." Naomi smiled and patted Chloe's arm. "Nine *kinner* is not unusual for an Amish family."

"So I'm learning."

In a corner of the room was a full-sized bed, and Naomi motioned toward it. "Here's where we keep the quilts. We don't have closets in our homes, and this is an easy way to show the quilts to *Englischers* who stop by."

On the top of the bed was a sheet, which Naomi removed and folded. Under it was a quilt that looked plain until Chloe stepped closer to examine it.

"This is a polished cream double wedding ring quilt," Naomi explained.

"It's stunning. And this was all done by hand?"

"*Ya*. None of the women in our district use treadle machines, though some Amish do." Naomi folded back the top quilt, revealing another off-white quilt, but this one was designed with black squares set off diagonally. "This is a black-and-cream nine patch."

Chloe glanced at Anna, who smiled and turned to Naomi. "Chloe would like to take a picture of the quilt with her phone if that's okay with you."

Naomi's brow furrowed in concern. "I'm afraid that would be quite prideful of me. Though I enjoy the work Sally and I do, and I'm grateful we are able to do it, I wouldn't want to be bragging about it."

"We've visited several homes today, and all of the quilts have been lovely. I'd like to list your address in a sidebar, and perhaps that will bring more people out to see what you have for sale."

"Listing our address would be all right, I suppose."

"How about if I include a few photographs but don't put your name beside the photos?"

Sally had finished feeding her youngest and was now standing in the doorway of the little back room. "I saw photos of Rebecca Byler's shop in the paper once. It was a few years ago."

"I suppose it's okay with our bishop then." Naomi reached forward and pulled back the next quilt, revealing another of the same pattern, but this one was pastel blue and cream. "All right. As long as you don't mention my name—only the family name to the side, where you list our address. That would be allowed, I'm sure. Rather like an ad."

"*Ya*, except this advertisement will be free," Anna said brightly.

In all, Naomi and Sally had twenty-two quilts for sale, a staggering number in Chloe's opinion.

She'd taken pictures of three of them and hoped that Eric would agree to run the photos with her piece and the sidebar with driving directions.

Naomi invited them to stay for tea, but it seemed to Chloe the woman had her hands full. Sally had returned to her rocker, still holding her baby and staring off into the distance.

They said their goodbyes, with both Chloe and Anna thanking them.

Though the home had been clean and orderly, Chloe took in a deep breath when they walked outside. There was an oppressive atmosphere in Naomi's home, something Chloe couldn't quite put her finger on. She waited until they were once again on the main road, and then she began to pepper Anna with questions.

CHAPTER 14

Anna wasn't surprised Chloe had a lot of questions.

"So many children. Is that normal? If so, when do they find the time to quilt?" They were once again traveling through Cody's Creek, headed back to Anna's. "As you said, there's plenty of work to do on a farm, and with all of those babies…"

"*Ya*, but quilting is one of the ways we relax." She pulled one of the strings from her prayer *kapp* forward and fiddled with it. "What do you do when you go home in the evening?"

"Microwave a dinner, watch some television, and maybe work a little."

"We can't bring the field work into the house at night, we don't watch television, and we never microwave dinners."

"Cooking for all of those people and then doing the dishes by hand?" Chloe gave a fake shudder. "That must take forever."

"Hardly. Remember, we have lots of little helpers."

"Huh."

"But my point is that our evenings are very different from yours. There's not much to do after dinner other than sit on the porch or play a game of checkers. Maybe read a little, though most Amish only read the *Budget*."

"You read other things. I saw the book you had tucked under the receipt pad at your produce stand."

Anna's face warmed, but she laughed along with Chloe. "I do like to read the occasional story, and no one mentions it because I'm relatively young and unmarried. But *Englisch* newspapers? Few Amish read those."

"I'm offended."

"*Ya*, I thought you might be."

"Surely you can sell subscriptions of my paper to your neighbors."

It seemed funny to Anna that she didn't have to wonder if Chloe was kidding. She knew her that well after only a few times together.

"So quilting is a nice way to rest."

"It doesn't sound restful."

"Many Amish women also work on a quilt at odd moments during the day. Remember when we went by Mary Beth's?"

"She's the bishop's wife?"

"*Ya*. She keeps a quilt on a stand in the corner of her sitting room. That way, if she has a free half hour, it's easy enough to take a break and quilt a bit."

"You're suggesting that if I gave up television, I could learn to quilt?"

"Probably anyone can learn, but not everyone is as talented as Mary Beth or Naomi."

"And you?"

"My *mamm* taught me well enough, but my mind often wanders. It's not unusual for me to find I've sewn the wrong two pieces together."

"Great!"

Anna looked at her in surprise. "Great?"

"Yes. There are at least two of us in Mayes County who aren't quilters."

She pulled into the lane and followed the gravel road to the side of the house. Before Anna could hop out, Chloe reached over and stayed her with a touch to the arm.

"What was wrong with Sally? Why was she so...sad?"

Anna removed her hand from the door handle and placed it in her lap. "It happened before I arrived, in June. Sally had the twins—"

"Twins?"

"Her second set. *Ya*, but one, a little girl, didn't make it."

"She died?"

"The doctors assured Sally that it wasn't the midwife's fault. They said whether Sally had been at a hospital or at home, the baby would not have been born breathing. Apparently, it had not developed correctly."

Chloe thought about that a minute. "All the children I saw were boys."

"They were, and the older ones are as well. The one who died was her first girl."

"That's so sad, Anna."

Instead of reminding her that it was *Gotte's wille*, Anna opened the door of the car and climbed out.

She gave Chloe a little wave goodbye and started toward the porch, but she turned when she heard the window of the car slide down. Chloe called out to her, so she walked back.

"I don't visit my mother nearly enough." Chloe was leaning across the seat, so she could see her better. "My mom's a quilter too."

"Is she now?"

"It's a different kind of quilting, but you might find the things she makes interesting. We could go and see her next Tuesday if you want. Same time?"

Anna pretended to hesitate, crossing her arms and tapping her right index finger against her lips. "It seems that...I might be free next Tuesday afternoon. *Ya*, I suppose I am."

Chloe laughed. "Thanks for checking your schedule. I'll see you then."

She made a three-point turn, and then she started back down the driveway. As Anna stood and watched her, Chloe stuck a hand out the window and waved.

She had an *Englisch* friend.

She hadn't ever considered such a thing, but she supposed it was—as her *aenti* was apt to say—*Gotte's wille*.

Which might be the best thing that had happened to her since moving to Oklahoma.

CHAPTER 15

*J*acob never intended to show up in Mayes County, Oklahoma. His plan had been to keep moving south, slowly curving toward Florida. If he'd written out a travel route, it would have been something like Kansas to Missouri, then Arkansas to Tennessee. From there he could work his way through Georgia and on to Florida. He'd never envisioned Oklahoma in his future.

But the situation at Saul Yoder's had thrown a hitch in his buggy, figuratively speaking. He didn't actually own a buggy, but his mind and emotions were still reeling from what had happened. He had walked out of the meeting with the bishop, picked up his single bag, which he'd left on the front porch, and headed to town. To give Saul credit, the man had stopped him before he reached the end of the lane.

"I stand by any decisions made by my bishop."

"Of course you do."

"He's a fair man."

Jacob didn't answer that. Was the bishop a fair man? Maybe, but it seemed that he'd landed on the wrong side of the situation with Miguel Garza. Jacob wouldn't attempt to argue that, though. There was no point, and he could see it in the set of Saul's jaw. He'd expected as much. What he hadn't anticipated was the look of misery and compassion in the older man's eyes.

"You saved a young man from harm." Saul looked incredibly older to Jacob, older than the day he'd picked him up near the bus station.

He had aged in the last few days, a fact evident in the extra lines around his eyes and the slope of his shoulders, as if the world had suddenly become a weightier place. He set a weathered hand on Jacob's arm. "I can't be approving of what you did, but I love you for it."

With those words, he turned and began walking back to his house.

Jacob called out before he was three yards away. "*Gotte's* blessing on your family, Saul."

"And you as well, Jacob."

The walk into town had been an easier trek because of those words of grace and forgiveness shared between the two. But when Jacob reached the bus ticket booth, he had no idea where he was going.

"Pick a direction," the middle-aged *Englisch* woman had said, a look of amusement on her face.

"South," he'd muttered.

Without any other question, the woman had printed out a ticket to Oklahoma.

Fair enough. What other Amish settlement was south of Kansas? None that he knew of. He'd temporarily forgotten that his ultimate destination for the winter was Florida.

Feeling suddenly exhausted, he had boarded the bus and scrunched down on a seat that had no one near it. He'd pulled down the brim of his hat to cover his eyes, pushed away any thoughts of the last several days, and slept most of the trip.

When he'd awakened he was rested but completely disoriented. Where had the woman with the short gray hair sent him? Oklahoma?

A sign across the street proclaimed "Tulsa Pawn and Loan Shop."

Tulsa, Oklahoma. What would he do in a city the size of Tulsa? Situated on the Arkansas River, the area boasted more than a million people. Jacob had spent some time in large urban areas before. He couldn't claim to like it very much, and he certainly didn't want to be there during harvest. He needed to be working out in the fields.

He spent three nights at a local mission that provided housing for those in need. One of the counselors informed him that there were only two Amish communities in Oklahoma—one in Cody's Creek, an hour to the east. The other was in Clarita, more than two hours to the south.

"It's quite small."

They were sitting at one of the long tables where volunteers had served dinner an hour earlier. Jacob had insisted on working to pay for his room and board, but he realized this was not a place he wanted to stay, so he'd sought out the counselor.

"Exactly how small is Clarita?"

"It's a one-church district." The older man rubbed a hand over the top of his bald head. "Your best bet is to head east to Cody's Creek. It's bigger with four church districts, and I'm sure you can find some work there. They're only now pulling in their harvest, or so I'm told."

The man had then offered him bus money, which Jacob refused. He had more than enough left from his work in Yoder for the bus fare. It was a short ride to Cody's Creek, and the cost reflected that. So he once again boarded the bus on a Tuesday evening. There were times, like this leg of his trip, when he wondered why he didn't go home, settle down on the family farm, and become an active member of the church. But each time that thought passed through his mind, he would experience a feeling of being trapped, much like a hog he had seen in one of the fields in Yoder. Wild hogs were a problem, and Jacob understood why the farmers felt the need to trap them. However, he wasn't ready to be that settled. Best to head east as the man at the mission had suggested.

By the time the bus pulled into Mayes County, Jacob was no longer certain he had made the right decision. The place looked deserted, but then it was nine thirty in the evening.

He remembered reading something about the area, but he couldn't recall any of the details. Stretching, he grabbed his bag off the empty seat next to him and walked out into a dark evening. There weren't a lot of businesses in Cody's Creek—though the town's name was proclaimed boldly over an *Englisch* bank. The few businesses that existed were closed.

Shouldering his bag, he followed the signs to a local park, made himself a passable bed on a wooden bench, and set in for a long night.

The hours on the bus from Yoder followed by the days in Tulsa had left him restless. The last thing he wanted to do was waste time on a park bench, and he wasn't sure he wanted to be in Cody's Creek. Perhaps in the morning he would board the bus again and continue heading east.

He pulled out his wallet and counted the money he had left from his work at Saul's farm. It wasn't a lot, but it was enough to last him a couple of weeks if he was careful.

Then again, his last phone call home had revealed that his parents were struggling financially. It wasn't something his mom had said, but rather what she didn't say. No references to a good harvest. No mention of fall clothes for his brothers. There must have been some problem, though when he asked after their health she'd assured him everyone was fine. Perhaps the crop hadn't produced as well as they had hoped. There were dozens of things that could go wrong with a crop. Jacob felt he'd seen every one of them in the last few years. Suddenly he was tired and dreaming of home. He drifted off for an hour or so. When he woke, the moon was high and the stars shone like so many fireflies.

He sat up, fetched his water bottle from his bag, and drank deeply from it.

He realized as he studied that darkness that he couldn't say why he went where he went, or how he made his decisions. He knew Sarasota was a good winter community. At this point he was drifting through his life. He realized that truth, though he didn't know exactly what to do about it.

Did God have a plan for him? He couldn't say, but Jacob did know right from wrong.

As he stowed the water bottle, he was sure of one thing. He wouldn't be boarding the bus in the morning. He'd go to the bank and wire the bulk of his money home. Then he'd find work. If God was guiding his path, there would be something he could do here in Cody's Creek.

CHAPTER 16

*T*he next morning Jacob had no luck finding what he was looking for.

He asked about work at the small grocer and the restaurant. He hung out at the feed store, hoping an Amish farmer would drive up, but the place was dead.

Finally he gave up and walked down to the dry goods store.

Owned by an Amish couple, the woman listened to his situation, nodded in understanding, and called her husband from the back room.

"Joseph, this is Jacob Graber."

"*Ya*? Pleased to meet you."

Joseph and Rebecca seemed pleasant enough, but he could tell from the lack of traffic that they did not need help at the moment.

"Where is everyone?" Jacob asked. "If it weren't for the occasional sign for buggy parking and the two of you, I wouldn't know there was an Amish community here."

"Oh, *ya*. We're here all right." Rebecca shared an amused smile with her husband.

"Where are you from?" Joseph bent to pick up one of the *grandkinner* who had begun to fuss.

Jacob had noticed several young ones scattered behind the counter. One little boy walked around, tugged on his pants leg, and offered him a small toy horse.

"My folks live in upstate New York."

"We've been there before. Haven't we, Becca?"

"Sure, when the boys were young."

Jacob was worried these two were going to trot down memory lane, but to his relief Joseph tapped on the counter and redirected the conversation. "In Oklahoma the communities are a bit more spread out than in the northeast."

"I heard there was more than one church district in this area."

"For sure and for certain." Joseph didn't elaborate.

Jacob removed his hat, wiped at the sweat on his brow, and set the hat back on his head. "I am looking for work. I'm *gut* in the fields, and I have references."

"No need for that. The reason you're not seeing any families is because everyone is in the fields, which are located outside of town a little ways."

"*Ya*, this is the slowest week we have all year long." Rebecca resumed restocking the display near the register. "No one has time to go to town if they can help it."

"So there's probably work…" Jacob felt the first stirrings of optimism since he had entered the store.

"Could be." Joseph scratched at his beard, a mixture of white, gray, and brown. "I couldn't say for sure."

"But surely if everyone is in the fields at once…"

"Storm's predicted for the weekend." Rebecca finished adding candy to the display. She stood, walked to a peg on the wall, and removed Joseph's hat. "Our bishop, Levi, will know who needs an extra hand."

"*Gut* idea." Joseph accepted the hat from his wife and motioned for Jacob to follow him.

For his part, Jacob was in no hurry to see another bishop, but then again he needed work. Besides, there was no avoiding church leadership in an Amish community, not that he intended to do any such thing. He'd done nothing wrong in Yoder, or at least in his opinion he hadn't.

Soon they were at a house virtually overflowing with children. The bishop was on the front porch. He had the full attention of the entire brood as he showed several young ones between the ages of two and six how to blow bubbles with a wad of gum. The youngsters were trying, without much luck but with a lot of laughter.

One reached forward and tried to pop his grandpa's rather large bubble, but the old man was too quick for him. He looked up and waved as Joseph and Jacob walked toward the house.

Jacob initially wondered why he wasn't helping with the crops. Even when an Amish man didn't have crops of his own, he always lent a hand to his neighbors. Then the bishop reached for a cane with his left hand and stood, leaning heavily on it, and Jacob understood. Though he was younger than Jacob initially thought, probably in his early fifties, he moved with an obviously painful limp. No wonder he was left tending to the children.

If Levi Troyer was a bit handicapped as far as his walking ability, he lacked nothing in arm strength. One of the children had begun to cry, and he easily swung the tike up onto his shoulder.

Joseph explained why Jacob was there. While he was talking, Mrs. Troyer walked out onto the porch. She listened for a moment and stepped forward when her husband said, "I'm sure we can find something for you to do."

"I'm Mary Beth, and you can stay here with us. There's always room for one more."

Jacob rather doubted that by the passel of children on the porch, but he simply thanked her.

"Have you had any lunch, Jacob?"

"No, ma'am, but I'm happy to wait on that if you know of any work I could get to this afternoon."

Levi's eyes sparkled as he glanced at his wife, "A young and energetic one, *Mamm*. Maybe we should keep him around here for ourselves."

"Indeed, but I am thinking the Stutzmans are in a greater need for help, what with one son laid up with a broken leg. You won't be able to work well on an empty stomach, though. Come inside."

Mary Beth insisted on feeding Jacob a hearty lunch of ham sandwiches and potato salad. By the time he'd devoured the food, Joseph was gone and Levi had hitched up the buggy. "Let's go see Daniel

Stutzman. I believe he'll be happy to have you lend a hand, though he may be close to finished."

"I heard a storm is predicted for the weekend."

"It is, and though I'm skeptical of many *Englisch* things, their weather-predicting ability has improved over the years. We'll do our best to have all of our crops in before the front hits the western border of Mayes County. That you can be sure of."

It was obvious that Daniel was indeed finishing his harvest as they walked down the rows of freshly cut corn.

"Samuel could use a hand," Daniel said. "He's the final man in our rotation this year, so we won't get there until Friday afternoon. The more he can have finished before we arrive, the better."

Levi thanked him and turned to hobble back toward his buggy. "Sounds as if the Lord has sent you exactly when Samuel Schwartz needs you, Jacob."

"*Ya*, maybe so."

"Samuel has no sons, no kin of any type here in Cody's Creek. He's a *gut* man and a real asset to our community. For better or worse, the man plants as if he's feeding a household of twelve, so there will be plenty to do." Levi popped his gum and then added, "I should have thought of him first."

On the ride to Levi's, Joseph had said the storm was due in Saturday morning, or Sunday at the latest. It was supposed to bring large-sized hail, heavy rain, and the possibility of tornadoes, which gave them three days to harvest Samuel's crops—four if the front slowed. Jacob quickly did the math in his head. Three days of work times the going wage was easy enough to calculate. It wouldn't be a lot of money, but the wages would be enough to put a little in his pocket and buy a bus ticket.

This time he'd head east and south as he'd originally intended.

CHAPTER 17

*A*nna woke Friday morning and put on her oldest dress, a *kapp* that had seen better days, and her work boots. The air outside was thick with humidity. There was little doubt that the forecasted storm was indeed headed their way. It was something everyone spoke of the last few days, and she wasn't sure she understood the concern. They'd had alerts all summer—constant storms that traveled west to east and brought hail, strong winds, and heavy rains. She no longer paid much mind to the talk. She couldn't do anything about the weather.

This week the folks in their community had seemed more than a little worried. Erin had told her the previous evening that in recent years Oklahoma had been hit hard. She described the tornado that had hit Oklahoma City and the suburb of Moore. "It wasn't only the destruction, Anna. It was also the width and length of the path of the tornado. There was much loss of life, and the *Englischers* estimated the cost of that storm at more than two billion dollars."

"Two *billion*?"

"*Ya.*"

"But Oklahoma City isn't near us."

"The storms appear all over the state. It is important to be vigilant and to head for the cellar at the first sign of trouble."

The cellar was next to the back porch. It was a large room built into the ground, where Erin kept her canned vegetables. The door on the room was sturdy and could be bolted from the inside.

Anna supposed she understood the urgency to harvest the crop before the storm arrived. Crops not only fed their families but also fed their livestock. If it was a good year, any extra harvest could be sold to local grocers or families. The extra income helped to cover unexpected expenses.

Leaving her room, she walked down the hall hoping she wasn't late for breakfast, but she needn't have worried. She stumbled to a stop as she peeked into the kitchen. *Mammi* tottered in from the back porch. Already sitting at the table was her *onkel*, her *aenti*, and the man they had hired to help with the harvest.

Jacob had shown up at the farm two days before with Bishop Levi. He was polite enough but terribly quiet. Though they had been working in the same field the day before, they hadn't exchanged more than a dozen words.

Taking her place at the table, Anna nodded to Jacob, said good morning to her *aenti* and *onkel*, grinned at *Mammi*, and bowed her head for prayer. When she finished and reached for the large pot of oatmeal, she noticed Jacob studying her. She smiled at him, but he quickly ducked his head.

Polite and quiet and shy.

"You did well with the horses yesterday, Anna." Her *onkel* reached for his coffee cup. "If you like, Jacob can take the team today."

"*Nein*. I enjoy driving Snickers and Doodle. They are *gut* horses."

Jacob again glanced up from his breakfast, but he didn't say anything.

How did he arrive so early? Did he walk? Or did someone drive him? She'd heard through her *aenti* that he was staying with the bishop. It wasn't a far piece, but he would have had to rise at least an hour early in order to dress and walk to her *onkel's* farm for breakfast. No wonder he ate as if he hadn't seen a full plate in years, though he certainly didn't look as if he were starving.

Anna snuck glances as she ate her breakfast.

Jacob was tall—nearly six feet if she were to guess.

He obviously wasn't married. His face was clean shaven.

But he was older, probably older than she was. So why wasn't he married?

Anna shook her head. She hated it when people asked her that question, and here she was wondering the same thing about him.

His blond hair needed a cut, and his blue eyes had such a calm, serious look that she wondered what he had seen in his traveling. The only thing she knew for certain about him was that his parents lived in New York and he didn't have any family in the area. So why was he here? Simply for the work? But they would be done by the end of the day. As far as Anna knew, Cody's Creek wasn't on the way to anywhere. How had he picked their little community?

Samuel was obviously happy with his help.

By the looks of him, he was strong enough to do anything her *onkel* needed. But he didn't argue with her wanting to drive the team. They only used two geldings and had a small harvester. The tractor, on the other hand, was a complicated piece of machinery—much bigger than the tractor she had driven to town. While part of her would like to learn to work it, another part shied away. She'd heard about accidents with the contraptions, and she would rather learn when they weren't rushed to complete a job.

It seemed ironic, even to her, that though women were discouraged from working outside the home, working in the fields during harvesttime was accepted by nearly all communities. Then again, Amish didn't usually hire outside the family. When the entire family pitched in, a field could be cleared and put in the barn fairly easily. The problem with her *aenti* and *onkel* was they had no sons to help.

"The work crew will be here this afternoon, but I'd like to have the northern field cleared by then. Jacob and I will do that with the tractor if you and Erin can take care of the maze with the horses."

"*Ya*, sure."

"That will leave only the southern and eastern fields for the afternoon. Though they are larger, with help we should be able to finish today." Samuel ran his hand over the back of his neck.

"I will be fine, *Onkel*."

"You worked with the horses back in Indiana..."

"I worked with the horses here, yesterday."

"Yes, but only for a little while. Today will be all morning."

"I often helped out back home, and we had more than two horses. I pestered *Dat* so much he finally taught me how to drive them and turn. They're no different than a buggy horse."

"They are when you've six of them harnessed." It was the first opinion Jacob had offered.

"*Ya*, I can see that would be harder. But Snickers and Doodle? They're gentle as lambs. Besides, I have no idea how to run the tractor in the fields."

"You did all right driving to town," Erin pointed out.

Anna remembered stalling the tractor in the middle of the intersection and smiled. "Maybe before next year's harvest you can teach me how to use the tractor in the fields."

This brought a smile to her *aenti's* face. Anna had never mentioned staying beyond the year they had agreed to. It was something they didn't discuss.

But it had been a good week. The crowds had been sizable the previous weekend for the corn maze, her day trip with Chloe had gone well, and now she was actually helping in the fields rather than sitting in a booth.

"The storm will be here today." *Mammi* seemed completely focused on the biscuit she had broken in two. Steam drifted out of the warm bread. She reached for the fresh butter, carefully covering each side. When she glanced up, Anna was surprised to see such concern in her eyes. *Mammi* was always the cheerful optimist of their little group. Today she pushed up her glasses and added, "It's apt to be bad, but *Gotte* will always care for His children."

"A *gut* reminder, *Mamm*." Samuel pushed back from the table. "Now Jacob and I had best get to work."

Jacob again glanced at Anna before thanking Erin for the food and following Samuel outside.

"He's a *gut* worker, *ya*?" Erin carried the pot of oatmeal to the sink and began to scrape it clean.

"Seems like it." Anna helped to clear the table.

As the sky lightened, she saw two mourning doves sitting on the fence of the nearest pasture. Splashes of pink and dark violet spread across the sky. Behind that, building ominously far on the horizon, was layer upon layer of tall, dark clouds.

"Don't worry. Bishop Levi checked with the storm center in Tulsa before Jacob came over this morning. The heaviest rains are still predicted to arrive late today." Erin hung the dish towel on a peg beside the sink. "Remember to watch the sky, and if you see anything that concerns you, head for the house."

Earlier that morning Anna had been thinking of the storms they'd had in Goshen. They had even endured the occasional tornado. Now, as she stood looking out the kitchen window, she admitted that the Oklahoma sky was different in some way. She would often catch herself standing and staring heavenward. There was something about the vastness of it, the way the landscape stretched as far as the eye could see, unhindered and unbroken. Her arms pebbled with goose bumps, and she inwardly chided herself. There was no danger in a little rain, but she understood that the crops could mold if left in the field.

They quickly put away the dishes as *Mammi* settled into her rocker, which sat by the windows. She would put out ham sandwiches for everyone at lunch, but most of the work for that was already done. She'd only need to pull the meat out of the refrigerator, slice the bread, and serve up the beans cooking on the stove.

Opening her Bible, she began to rock gently. When Anna walked by, *Mammi* reached out and touched her hand. "You're a blessing to us, Anna. For sure and for certain." Anna bent and kissed her grandmother on the cheek, and then she followed Erin out the back door.

Either Samuel or Jacob had already hitched up the horses to the wagon. Behind the wagon was the harvester. It was a slow way to harvest the corn, but every row done was a help to her *onkel*. Anna enjoyed leading the team, and they had responded well the day before. Her *aenti* sat in the wagon, her back to Anna. She watched the harvester and alerted her if there was any problem.

Samuel had insisted that neither of them work the team alone. That seemed a tad cautious to Anna. She knew her father and brothers often did so, but then this was her *onkel's* place and his decision. She was simply glad to have a different type of chore for a few days.

The sky grew increasingly dark as the morning wore on. The clouds slowly overtook the sky, though there was little wind and no rain. The darkness, though, was a bit unnerving. Because Anna was so focused on the horses and the rows of corn, she had trouble telling how much time had passed. She'd been leading children through the maze she was now harvesting only a few days before. She thought of the little *Englisch* boy and his look of surprise when she'd shown him the kernels of corn. When her *aenti* tapped her on the shoulder, she nearly jumped out of her *kapp*.

Erin gestured with her hands and hollered, "Let me off at the end of the row. I'll help *Mammi* fix our lunch."

Anna nodded. As she pulled to a stop, she swiped at the sweat running down her face.

"Seems to be getting hotter."

"*Ya*, no wind at all." Erin studied the sky, concern shadowing her features. "Maybe you should come inside."

"I'll go down once more and back, and then I'll pull the team to rest under the oak tree."

"*Gut* idea."

Snickers and Doodle tossed their heads as she turned east, away from the house. With some effort and a stern voice, she finally convinced them to move in the right direction. Anna's heart thumped against her chest, and she wondered that her pulse was racing so. Perhaps she was more tired than she had thought.

She reached the end of the row and turned the team toward the west, and that was when she saw the funnel cloud dip out of the sky. A scream tore from her throat as she attempted to steady the team and lead them toward the shelter of the barn. Would they be safe there? Or would it be better to leave them in the field?

A terrible sound filled the air—like the roar of a train set on a collision course, only they had no train tracks anywhere near her *onkel's* farm. The horses were now galloping, cutting across uncut rows and pulling Anna and the harvester at breakneck speed as they shook their heads. Anna stood to better pull on the reins, and that was when they reared.

She was thrown into the air, flying through it as if she were no more consequential than a leaf dropped from a nearby tree. She felt herself falling, falling, unable to grab the stalks near her because suddenly they were gone. Her mind tried to comprehend that and couldn't.

Three thoughts flashed through her mind in the space of a single breath.

The first was that the tornado had indeed come early.

This thought was quickly followed with *Mammi*'s assurance that "*Gotte* will always care for His children."

And last, it occurred to her that she wanted to see her parents one more time.

CHAPTER 18

$\mathcal{J}$ acob and Samuel had shut down the tractor and were walking toward the house from the field they had been harvesting. Suddenly Samuel stopped, turned toward the west, and his mouth fell open. Jacob's heart rate kicked up a notch at the expression on the older man's face, but he still didn't understand the danger. He still hadn't looked toward the sky.

"Get to the cellar!" Samuel grabbed Jacob by the shoulders and pushed his face close, but still his words were barely discernible. "Behind the house. Go!"

Samuel turned without another word of explanation and ran toward the front porch. He left Jacob to gape at the black, churning funnel cloud barreling toward them. Even as Jacob watched, it dipped down from the sky and devoured everything in its path.

He started after Samuel, but a cry over the noise of the storm stopped him. The sound was not from the girl, but from the horses. Was Anna still outside? Was she trying to steer the team? He ran toward the maze, or what had been the maze when he'd arrived a few hours earlier. As the tornado bore down on him, Jacob stumbled to his knees and slapped his hands over his ears. He had to silence the howl of the twister or surely his eardrums would burst. As he crouched in the dirt, the team appeared out of the darkness—running wildly, eyes flashing, heads tossing. He barely had time to roll out of the way as the workhorses tore past him. The rigging between the wagon and the harvester was damaged and the harvester jostled left, then right, and finally broke free. It occurred to Jacob that the severed hitch probably saved the horses. If the connection between the harvester and wagon had held, they would have been pulled over with the harvester, which now lay on its side.

But where was Anna?

He ran in the direction the horses had come from, down a strip of field that was now without any crop. He prayed as he ran, his mind repeating over and over, "Please, *Gotte*. Please." The fear in his heart could find no other words, and his mind was as chaotic as the scene around him.

Part of the maze had been harvested. Another part had been ripped away, leaving a cleared field. The terrible howl had stopped and now a gentle rain fell. No lightning. No thunder. Only a path of destruction and silence. Suddenly he saw her up ahead and to the right. She was lying on the ground—lifeless and still.

He ran, stumbled, struggled to his feet, and ran some more. It seemed to take an eternity to reach her side. Jacob's hands trembled as he knelt beside her.

From the angle of her body, he could tell that something was terribly wrong. He placed his hand on her neck to check her pulse, a procedure he had read about in a first aid book he'd picked up in Ohio.

She was unconscious but still breathing.

"Please save her, *Gotte*. Don't let her die. Not today. Not here, like this."

The prayer sprang from his heart with the same intensity as the stalks of corn had been ripped from the field. The words flowed from him as he unpinned the collar of her dress and again put his fingers to the side of her neck.

Still breathing, but if anything she looked worse to him.

Her skin was unnaturally pale, and she hadn't moved.

Should he stay or go for help?

Suddenly a horrendous popping sound assaulted his ears, and a second tornado barreled down on them, dipped, and sucked up what remained of Samuel's corn.

Jacob threw his body over Anna to protect her from the violence of the funnel cloud. As suddenly as it dipped down upon them, it vanished, leaving a completely cleared field without a single stalk of corn in it.

He didn't know how much time passed as he knelt beside her, praying and watching the sky for signs of any additional twisters. Suddenly he was aware of Samuel and Erin calling, frantically searching for them.

He released Anna's hand, which he had been clutching. Standing in the muddy, barren field, he waved and jumped and screamed for their help.

Erin saw him first and began running in his direction.

Samuel wasn't far behind, and in the distance Jacob could see Anna's grandmother hobbling down off the porch.

"Anna!" The agony of Erin's voice would follow Jacob the rest of his life.

Erin threw herself on the ground at Anna's side, sobbing and crying out in German. Jacob caught the words "mercy" and "*Gotte*" and "please, please, Lord" as he turned to Samuel.

The man's face was a ghastly white. "Is she—"

"*Nein*. But we can't move her. Do you have a phone? In your barn?"

Samuel shook his head. "Next door. There's a phone shack next to the road."

"Which direction?"

Samuel pointed in the opposite direction from Bishop Levi's place. "I'll go," he said, but Jacob reached out to stop him.

If Anna died, she should do so surrounded by her family, not with a stranger at her side.

"*Nein*. Stay with your wife and Anna. Don't move her. She's breathing, but something's...something's wrong. If she wakes, keep her still." Then he was gone, running faster than he ever had before, praying help would arrive in time. As he ran, he petitioned God for this family he barely knew, aware that his prayers were echoing Erin's as she knelt in the mud beside her niece.

CHAPTER 19

*J*acob stood next to Anna's grandmother, and together they watched the medical personnel work on the young woman. The run to the phone shack and back had taken less than twenty minutes. In that time, Anna still hadn't moved. She hadn't awakened at all. The neighbors began showing up, Bishop Levi and others whom Jacob didn't know.

An ambulance had dashed down the lane, lights flashing and siren wailing, coming to a stop next to where the small group was assembled. A middle-aged woman with red hair stepped out, followed by a younger man who looked to be about Jacob's age. She took one look, muttered, "Don't move her," and ducked back into the vehicle. When she stepped back out, she walked straight to Anna and knelt beside her, slipping a large plastic collar around her neck.

"Has she spoken?"

Samuel merely shook his head, which the woman couldn't see, so she barked the question again.

"*Nein.*" Jacob stepped forward. "She hasn't moved at all."

"Who found her?"

"I did."

"How long ago?"

Jacob had no idea, so he didn't answer.

This time the woman turned her head and met his gaze with a look of understanding and compassion. "My name is Brenda, and I want to help your—"

"Friend." Jacob began to shake. He crossed his arms in an attempt to still the tremors. "Anna is my friend."

"I need to know whatever you know. How long ago did it happen?"

"Maybe thirty minutes."

"And she hasn't spoken or moved at all?"

"Not a word, and I was afraid to move her."

"You did well. In fact, you may have saved her life." Brenda pulled a radio off her belt and pushed the button. "Unit seventeen."

"Go ahead." The dispatcher was male and sounded as if he were standing in the field with them.

"We have a twenty-five-year-old female..."

"Twenty-four." Erin's words shook and trembled. Samuel had pulled her away when the medical personnel arrived. Otherwise, she'd still be clinging to Anna. "She's only twenty-four."

"She's waking up." The young man was on the right side of Anna and the woman on the left.

Jacob couldn't see Anna's expression. Erin had thrown herself down at the girl's head and was once more praying.

"Ma'am, I need you to give us some room."

Samuel again pulled Erin away. She turned to him and collapsed in his arms, sobbing and praying and hiding her face.

"Anna, try not to move. We're here to help you."

"My neck...it hurts." Anna's voice was weak, and Jacob had to lean closer to hear. A little color had returned to her face, and her eyes were darting left and then right but focusing on nothing. "Why can't I move my head?"

"We have a collar on you to keep your neck in one position. I want you to hold very still for me." Brenda didn't look at the other paramedic but began barking orders as she continued to examine Anna for other injuries. "In-line spinal stabilization. I want it started now, and bring me a splint for her leg."

She'd finished her preliminary exam and took a moment to listen to Anna's breathing with her stethoscope. Replacing the instrument around her neck, she asked, "Can you squeeze my hand, Anna?"

"*Ya.* I think so."

Jacob realized now what his mind had blocked out earlier. Her legs were splayed out awkwardly, unnaturally.

"We need to move your legs, Anna. It may hurt. I want you to keep your eyes on Charlie and let him know if the pain is too much."

Anna nodded as tears began to stream down her face. "What's wrong with me? Why does my head hurt so?"

"We're going to give you something for that, but I need to be sure there are no fractures first." Brenda was already moving and straightening her legs.

Anna never complained at all. Jacob was watching her closely, and she didn't so much as flinch as the paramedics went about their work.

Brenda again pulled her radio. "This is unit seventeen."

"Go ahead, seventeen."

"We have a twenty-four-year-old female with a possible SCI and multiple contusions. The patient is alert and responding to questions. I'm requesting a med-vac stat."

"I have your location, seventeen. Hold please while I contact Tulsa." The voice came back in less than a minute. "Med-vac is on its way. ETA twenty minutes."

Brenda looked around until she spotted Jacob. Standing, she walked over to him. "I need you to come and talk to her until her mother—"

"*Aenti.*"

"All right, until her *aenti* calms down. We want to keep her alert and responsive. Can you help me with that?"

Jacob nodded and tried to swallow, but his throat felt as if he'd drank a glass of sand. The rain was still falling, and he had the strange thought to tilt his head back and let the drops moisten his mouth. Instead, he swiped a hand across his face and moved to kneel beside a girl he had known for less than forty-eight hours.

"Hi, Anna."

"Jacob. What happened?"

He looked to Brenda for permission to share about the tornado, but she shook her head. She helped Charlie to start an IV in Anna's arm and was again checking her breathing.

"Had an accident, is all. You're going to be okay." He prayed those words were true as soon as they had slipped off his tongue.

"*Aenti* and *Onkel*?"

"They're here." He glanced over toward the couple. Erin seemed to be pulling herself together, and Samuel's color was some better. They both hovered close, but Anna couldn't see them with the brace on her neck. She could only see what was directly in front of her, which at the moment was Jacob.

"I remember harvesting the corn, the storm, and then...then the horses running. I couldn't hold them."

"You did well. The horses are fine."

"*Ya?*"

"Sure. The harvester is broken, but it was old anyway."

Erin pulled away from Samuel and sank down in the mud next to Jacob.

"Anna, are you okay? Are you hurting?"

"Only my head. Did I bump it?"

Instead of answering, Jacob said, "The paramedics are taking *gut* care of you."

"Will you hold my hand? I'm scared."

He reached for her hand, which seemed impossibly small and fragile. Now her grandmother knelt with them so that they made a sort of circle around the top of Anna's head.

"*Mammi*—"

"Don't worry, child. *Gotte* is going to take *gut* care of you." She reached out a hand covered in wrinkles and spots. Her fingers caressed Anna's face. "He is your rock and your fortress. He is your deliverer, child—your *Gotte* and your strength. You can trust in Him."

As she'd spoken the verse from the book of Psalms, Anna had closed her eyes, and it seemed she must have drifted off to sleep. Jacob was glad for that because the fear in her eyes had torn at his heart. He'd been afraid he might break down and weep. He didn't mind crying in front of others, but he didn't want to frighten Anna more.

Then he remembered he was supposed to be keeping her alert and responsive. "Anna. Look at me, Anna."

She opened her eyes and glanced left and then right without moving her head. "You won't leave me, will you?"

"*Nein*. I'll stay right here, but you need to keep awake."

Mammi continued to quote the Psalms, softly and tenderly. Behind them, Bishop Levi was leading those who were standing around in prayer. Jacob thought he heard weeping, but he couldn't be sure from whom. Brenda and Charlie continued to monitor her condition.

When they heard the *thump, thump, thump* of a helicopter, Brenda nodded toward the ambulance and told Charlie to "get the backboard."

The family was moved out of the way as Anna was surrounded by medical personnel. Four paramedics transferred her to the backboard and placed the board on a gurney that they wheeled to the waiting helicopter.

"I want to go with her," Erin said.

"You may ride in the helicopter with her." Brenda stepped closer to Erin. "But you have to leave now. There's no time to go to your house for clothes or your purse. It might be better to—"

But Erin was already running toward the chopper. One of the paramedics reached down to help her up. For a moment, it looked as if her feet would tangle in her long, dark dress, but she jerked the fabric tighter around her legs and scrambled aboard.

A few moments later the helicopter rose into the sky, and then it was gone.

Jacob wondered what they should do next. How many other farms had been hit? Were there other injuries?

Samuel had moved to the side, halfway between the ambulance and where the helicopter had been. He stood alone, his shoulders bowed as if from the enormous burden that had been placed there.

While Jacob wondered if perhaps they should have one of the emergency workers look at him, Samuel squared his shoulders and turned toward them. His face was grim, but his color was better than it had been.

"I'll need your help, Jacob."

"Of course."

"First we find the horses. Then we find a way to the hospital."

"I'll take care of a driver, Samuel." Bishop Levi stepped forward. "The horses will respond better to you, and it looks as if your home and outbuildings weren't damaged. Put them in the barn."

"I can check on them morning and night, Samuel." This from an older Amish man Jacob hadn't met yet.

The bishop nodded in approval. "By the time you're done, we'll have a car here to drive you to Tulsa."

"I'll go inside and pack Erin and Anna a bag." *Mammi* waved away the bishop's offer of help. "Go and find that ride, Levi. I'm fine."

Jacob stared out over the destruction. He'd seen pictures of tornadoes and their path of devastation before—once or twice he'd read articles about such an event in the newspaper, and one of the books he had borrowed described tornadoes in the Midwest. Always they spoke of collapsed buildings and piles of debris. That wasn't what he was looking at.

Samuel's fields were clear as far as the eye could see. It was as if the tornado had whisked everything up but set nothing back down. "The horses were headed to the east last I saw them."

They were walking toward the barn when Samuel stopped, turned, and went back to Brenda and Charlie, who were packing up their equipment.

"*Danki* for your help. For arriving so fast and helping with my niece."

Brenda reached out and touched his arm. "You don't have to thank us, Mr. Schwartz. It's our job."

"But you did it with kindness and compassion." Samuel stared at the ground when he added, "If you would give the bishop directions as to where we should go, I would appreciate it. I...I want to be there with my family."

"Of course." Brenda pulled out a pad of paper and wrote down the name and address of the hospital.

Samuel nodded once to Jacob, and they left the little crowd behind. Would the neighbors go in search of Samuel's crops? But they could have been carried miles away. Perhaps they would check the surrounding farms to be sure no one else was hurt. Jacob had never been through anything remotely similar to this before. As they hurried in the direction of the barn, moving across the barren fields, it occurred to him that soon he would be leaving. There was no harvesting left to do. The work crew wouldn't be needed and neither would he.

CHAPTER 20

*C*hloe was working on a story about the increased use of fracking to extract natural gas in the area when Eric appeared in the doorway to her cubicle. The expression on his face told her something was up. Eric had a police scanner in his office as well as a CB radio. He kept them both on all the time. Often he had reporters at crime scenes or accidents before emergency personnel managed to arrive. For Eric, it was all about the thrill of the hunt—always the never-ending search—for more and faster and better news. Turning to study him, Chloe realized that today his expression was an odd mixture of excitement and compassion.

Compassion? From Eric?

"What's up?"

"Accident reported. I want you to cover it."

"All right." Chloe picked up her purse and began shutting down her computer. "Any details? Where am I going?"

"Farming accident." Eric cleared his throat as he stared down into his coffee cup. "Amish girl. It's the girl you have been using in your last couple of pieces."

"Anna?"

"Yeah. Anna Schwartz."

Chloe sank back down onto her chair. "What happened?"

"From what I heard on the scanner, there were several sightings of a tornado touching down. Anna was helping with the harvest when it happened. According to the chatter, it must have spooked the horses of the team she was driving."

"And she was thrown?"

"Apparently." The somber look returned. "I know you're close to the girl, Chloe. Can you be objective about this? We need to get the details, and if you're fast enough we can include it in the next edition of the—"

"I'll send in something before the five o'clock deadline."

"She's in Tulsa at Oklahoma Surgical Hospital."

Why OSH? Why not Saint Francis or OSU Medical Center? Accident victims were often taken to St. John's as well. Chloe jumped up and then barreled out of her cubicle, but she realized she had left her phone on her desk and turned back. When she brushed past Eric to retrieve it, he put a hand on her shoulder.

"Get the story. Get the facts. Get out."

Chloe wanted to bat his hand away. She wanted to stop and argue with him. More than anything she wanted to ask him what had happened to him along the way. Where had he lost his compassion? When had he forgotten that the people they wrote about were people they lived by, ate with, and shopped with? People they went to school and church with.

She flew out the door. Her hands trembled when she tried to put her key in the ignition of her car.

Anna. She was so young. How did this happen? Why did it happen?

Chloe didn't spend much time arguing with God. She'd seen and written about enough of the dark side of human nature to understand that some people simply turned bad somewhere along the way, like an apple left in the bottom of a basket too long. If that was a cold perspective, so be it. She'd seen the destruction that such people left in their wake, and it wasn't a pretty sight.

No, she didn't argue with God about those people or the people they hurt. It might be unfair, but the world was a harsh place. Her years on the newspaper staff had taught her that.

But a farming accident caused by a tornado? Why did things like that happen? And if they had to happen, why not take the bad people instead of the good? People walked around as if life would always proceed as it had the day before, but often it didn't.

Because they were a county newspaper, their offices were located on the east side of Tulsa, a fair distance from the downtown area. Making a right out of their parking lot, Chloe accelerated onto 412 West, which would take her downtown. Glancing out the side window, she saw a busload of schoolchildren, laughing and talking. That was when she realized her thoughts were assuming the worst. There were many reasons a med flight may have been called in for Anna. Perhaps it wasn't as bad as she feared.

She turned on her radio in time to here an announcer give an emergency update.

> Approximately one hour ago at least two tornadoes touched down in the small community of Cody's Creek. Multiple sightings report the funnels hopscotched through at least a dozen fields before going back up into the sky and heading east.
>
> There have been several reports of injuries. Many Amish as well as non-Amish farmers were working outside in their fields at the time of the tornado's appearance. According to Dereck Hess with Cody's Creek Emergency Services, all but one of those injuries have been minor.
>
> Because the storm has moved off to the east, the Shelter-in-Place warning has been lifted. At this point we'll resume our regular programming, but we will break in the moment we have additional details.

Chloe pushed her little blue car up to the speed limit. Usually she treated the engine gently. The car was old and needed to last her at least another couple of years, but worrying about the life of her vehicle today seemed trivial. Her friend was injured. Anna was on her way to Tulsa, maybe flying over her right at this moment. She glanced down at her gas gauge—it was on full.

Eighteen miles. She'd be at the hospital within the half hour.

CHAPTER 21

*C*hloe had met Anna's aunt twice—the night she'd attended the corn maze festival and the morning she'd picked Anna up so they could go and look at quilts. The woman had seemed pleasant enough, if a bit subdued.

Today everything had changed.

As Chloe walked into the surgical waiting room, she understood immediately how serious the situation was.

Erin sat ramrod straight on the edge of her seat and barely glanced at Chloe when she rushed into the room. From the looks of her, she was still in shock as to what had happened. And where was the rest of Anna's family? An older *Englisch* woman was sitting beside Erin, dressed in black slacks and a light-blue blouse, her gray hair cut in a short bob. She was as round as she was tall, and she wore a name tag that said, "Dora Smith, Chaplain."

Chloe nodded but didn't offer her own name. Her attention was completely focused on Anna's Aunt Erin. "Mrs. Schwartz, I don't know if you remember me..."

Erin raised her eyes but didn't seem to process what Chloe had said.

"I write for the *Mayes County Chronicle*, and I've been to your farm a couple of times. Anna and I went to—"

"You went to look at the quilts. *Ya.* I remember." The words were spoken softly, as if she were afraid of disturbing someone, but they were the only people in the waiting room.

"I heard about the tornado. Is...is Anna okay?"

Instead of answering, Erin covered her face with her hands and began to weep.

Chloe sat beside her and placed a hand on her back. Glancing over at the chaplain, she asked, "Do you know? How is Anna?"

"I'm afraid I can't share any family information, and if you're asking as a reporter—"

"No, I'm not. I'm asking as Anna's friend." She pulled in her bottom lip and fought against the tears that stung her eyes. "That is to say, my boss sent me here to report on what happened, but I would have come anyway. I'm concerned about her."

Erin gained control of her emotions long enough to glance at the chaplain and say, "Tell her. It makes no difference to me. How could it matter? Anna, dear Anna..." and then she dissolved once again into tears.

"Most of Anna's injuries were minor..." The chaplain hesitated, ran her hand over the Bible she was holding, and then slowly continued. "She sustained some lacerations and bruises. There's a possibility she's suffering from a concussion as well."

"What else? I can tell there's more. Please, I need to know."

"The doctors fear she also suffered a spinal fracture. They have ordered X-rays, a CT scan, and an MRI. Anna is having those tests now."

A spinal fracture sounded terrible. "They can fix that though, right? They brought her here because it's a surgical hospital."

"I don't know any more than that." The woman's gaze was sympathetic. No doubt she had sat beside many grieving families before. She wasn't going to offer false hope.

So they waited.

Once Dora asked if Erin would like her to pray. When she nodded yes, the chaplain commenced to petition God on Anna's behalf. It had been years since Chloe had heard an audible prayer. Somewhere along the way she'd simply stopped attending her parents' church. But she bowed her head and listened respectfully. Perhaps it would calm

Erin. Maybe, just maybe, God was listening. She didn't know what she believed, and suddenly she felt her lack of faith more than ever before.

Silence again fell across the room, the only sound the ticking of the clock and the occasional echo of someone in padded shoes going down a hall.

Then the double doors across from them opened. A tall, athletic, middle-aged man with brown hair mostly tucked under a surgical cap walked into the room. Actually, he looked younger than that, possibly mid-thirties if Chloe were to guess. She noticed he wore no wedding ring, and then she was embarrassed that she had looked. She told herself to chalk it up to possessing a reporter's inquisitive nature.

"I'm Dr. Hartman. Are you Anna's family?"

Erin nodded her head. Then she unexpectedly reached over and clasped Chloe's hand. Chloe had been wondering if she should leave, but the look of panic on Erin's face convinced her to stay.

"I'm Erin Schwartz, Anna's *aenti*, and this is Chloe, her friend. How is she? How is Anna?"

"She's stable." Dr. Hartman nodded toward a chair opposite Erin. "Do you mind if I sit?"

"*Nein.* So she's out of danger? She'll live?"

"Anna is stable, and yes she will live." He clasped his hands in front of himself, his elbows resting on his knees, and Chloe knew that his next words would change their lives forever.

"Mrs. Schwartz, I'm sorry to inform you that your niece suffered an SCI—a spinal cord injury."

Erin clasped her hands to her heart. "What does that mean?"

"It means the damage is irreparable."

CHAPTER 22

*C*hloe filed her report by the deadline. She respected the Schwartzes' desire for privacy and kept her column brief and to the point. Though Eric may have preferred a more sensational piece, she was determined to keep her emotions at bay. She could do that when she was writing, but the rest of the time she struggled.

What had happened was terrible, and it seemed to haunt her hour after hour. Like a stone in the pit of her stomach, she carried her worry and grief with her everywhere. It colored the morning sunrise, turned her food bitter, and stole her sleep. How could such a thing happen to an innocent young woman in the prime of her life? How could it happen to anyone? What kind of God allowed tragedy and heartache to randomly destroy innocent people? Her faith, which she'd largely ignored since her father's death, wavered. Did she believe what she'd always been taught? Was their God a loving God? Why did terrible, awful things happen to good Christian people?

Chloe found none of those answers as she tossed and turned each night, but she would rise the next day and continue with her work. It was the one thing she knew she was good at, and the rhythm of investigating, researching, and reporting calmed her turbulent soul.

She constantly reminded herself to focus on the who, what, when, and where of the story. As to the why, she wouldn't attempt to address that question.

Tornadoes Rip Path Through Cody's Creek
By Chloe Roberts
Mayes County Chronicle

CODY'S CREEK—Two tornadoes briefly touched down in Cody's Creek yesterday, damaging crops and livestock. Multiple injuries were reported across the area but were minor in nature. Only Anna Schwartz sustained massive injuries. She was care-flighted to Oklahoma Surgical Hospital in Tulsa, where it was determined that she had suffered an irreversible spinal cord injury. The family had no comment.

The National Weather Service confirmed both tornadoes hopscotched across the area beginning at 11:54 a.m. and lasting approximately 12 minutes. The storm was confirmed to be an F-3 with winds reaching 170 miles per hour. The area sustained some damage to structures. Both funnel clouds repeatedly dipped into fields, decimating crops but leaving houses and barns largely in tact.

Dr. Greg Gardner with the National Weather Service issued the following reminder. "The Emergency Alert System now issues emergency warnings over wireless systems. You can sign up to receive text alerts through your carrier. Details can also be found at www.ctia.org/wea. Many local agencies also issue texts regarding critical weather events. Be alert, be aware, be alive."

Approximately 1000 tornadoes occur each year in the U.S., and Oklahoma records on average 52 per year. The weather service reports that annually 60 people are killed by tornadoes, most from flying or falling debris.

CHAPTER 23

*A*nna dreamed.

In one dream she tried repeatedly to sew a quilt, only she continually pieced it together incorrectly. She was holding the fabric wrong, and her needle always had a small length of thread in it, causing her to bend over the work and take increasingly tiny stitches. Each time she turned the fabric over and began to sew, she looked down and found herself staring at a large needle and a too-short length of thread. Slowly she would begin to sew again and the entire scene would repeat, looping endlessly until she thought she would scream.

Another time she was walking through her *aenti*'s fields. Wildflowers stretched in front of them as far as her eye could see. That made Anna laugh, as she'd never imagined a land that had been so tough to farm could be so beautiful. A bird chirped in the background. She could never see it but felt as if the bird was following them as she walked through the sea of wildflowers. Anna ran through the flowers, only to find that she was suddenly stuck in a field thick with corn about to be harvested. When she looked up, a rainbow adorned the sky.

It was the last dream that bothered her the most. In it, a handsome, strong young man hovered over her, concern etched across his face. He looked as if he was about to cry, and she wanted to reach up and smooth the worry from his face. She didn't know who the man was or why he would be so worried. She didn't know what she could say to relieve his fears. Occasionally he would speak, whispering, "You're going to be okay." She wanted to believe him, but there was such fear in his eyes—a deep, lasting misery. For some reason she couldn't fathom, she asked him to hold her hand and he did. The tenderness in his touch was more than she could have imagined, but the grief never left his eyes.

The dreams repeated themselves, always the same, always ending in confusion and fear. She longed to open her eyes but found it too difficult. She was too tired. So she would give in to the need for rest and allow herself to drift off, only to be pulled again into a cycle of nightmares.

When the man began to cry, the man who was holding her hand, Anna knew then that she could stand it no longer. She made up her mind to scream out, to cry for help, but someone was again standing over her, murmuring.

"It's all right, Anna. It's only a dream. Relax. Try to relax."

She opened her eyes with a heroic effort. Bending over her, gray hair peeking out from her *kapp*, brown eyes assuring her that all was fine, all was okay, was her mother.

"*Mamm?*"

"Shh. Don't try to sit up yet. You've been resting a long time. Take a moment."

Anna allowed her eyes to travel around the unfamiliar room. It was too bright, owing to electric lights in the ceiling. Machines were lined up on the left-hand side of her bed. One showed a display with a line going up and down, and it beeped occasionally. The other held a bag of fluid that was connected to the needle in her arm. Directly across from her bed and mounted on the wall was a television, which was turned off. There was also a long row of windows with their blinds partially open.

"*Mamm?*"

How was it that her mother was here? Her mother was supposed to be in Indiana. It was harvesting time. She would be needed to help her father.

Those thoughts were immediately followed by a question. "How sick am I?" The machine began to beep and a red light flashed over the zigzag line.

"Look at me, *dochder*. Deep breaths. I am here with you. Don't be afraid." Her mother's voice remained calm. "You're all right, Anna."

While her eyes held compassion and a mysterious kind of sadness, Anna knew she was telling the truth. She must be. As far as Anna knew, her mother had never lied. She might occasionally avoid an answer, but lie? No. She seemed incapable of such a thing.

Anna wanted to speak, to ask her mother about the grief in her eyes and more, but when she tried, her voice came out a croak.

The door opened and a nurse walked in—a woman with short, spiky gray hair. "Our patient is awake and no doubt quite thirsty. Let's see if these ice chips will ease that dryness in your throat."

The nurse handed the cup to Anna's mom, and then she walked over to the machine and touched a button that turned off the flashing red light.

"It's good to see you awake, Anna. I'm Nancy, and I'll be your nurse this afternoon."

Anna accepted the ice chips. Her lips felt dry and cracked when she ran her tongue over them. The cold water instantly eased the pain in her throat.

"Where...where am I?"

"More ice, Anna." Her mom popped in another spoonful before she could argue.

"You're at Oklahoma Surgical Hospital in Tulsa, and you've had quite a lot of visitors these past few days." The nurse noted something on a tablet she held in her hands, glancing again at the machines occasionally.

Something squeezed her arm, and she attempted to pull herself free from it.

"That's only a blood pressure cuff. It's reading your vital signs, and then they appear here on this screen." The nurse tapped on one of the monitors. "Both your heart rate and blood pressure. If either number becomes too high or low, the monitor you heard goes off. We're very high-tech here."

This seemed to be some sort of joke between the nurse and her mother, who exchanged a smile.

The beeping sounded like the bird in her dream. Why had there been birds in her dreams and how long had she been in the hospital?

Nancy stepped closer, her attention now completely focused on her patient. "How does your head feel, Anna?"

"Fine. I guess." She wanted to raise her hand, to check if her *kapp* was on, but she was connected to so many machines she couldn't actually move her arm.

"No headaches or blurry vision?"

"*Nein.* What happened?" Anna cleared her throat and tried again. "I remember driving the team and then...nothing."

Aenti Erin pushed through the door and into the room at that moment. The panic that Anna had felt on waking returned full force when her *aenti* rushed across the room and grabbed her hand.

"Anna. Oh, praise *Gotte.* It's so *gut* to see your eyes open."

Anna glanced at her mother, who shrugged and smiled at the same time. "Your *aenti* is a worrier, but you probably know that by now."

"Why are you here, *Mamm*?"

Her mother pulled a chair closer and sat on it. Beside the chair was her knitting bag, balls of blue, pink, and white yarn poking out of the top. Someone in their family must be expecting another baby.

The nurse made an adjustment to the bag of fluid. "Dr. Hartman will stop by soon. He is on his rounds if you would like him to explain to Anna—"

"*Nein.* We have waited and prayed for this moment."

"All right. I'll give you some privacy. If you need me for anything, push the call button."

Her mother waited until the door had closed behind the nurse, and then she signaled to Erin to pull the other chair closer. They sat next to one another, their knees touching Anna's bed, her mother's left hand still holding tightly to Anna's right.

"You say you remember helping with the harvest. Do you remember anything else?"

"*Nein.*" Anna's heart beat faster as she searched her memory. "Only, maybe the horses. I...I was driving them after I dropped *aenti* off near the house to help prepare lunch."

"I should have never done that, Anna. I should have stayed with you."

"Hush, Erin." Her mother reached over with her right hand and squeezed her sister-in-law's fingers. "We spoke of this, and it is not your fault. What happened, happened. It was *Gottes wille* whether we understand it or not."

"You're scaring me, *Mamm*. What happened?"

"Do you remember the storm?"

"Maybe. A little."

"It was three days ago." Her mother met her gaze, willing her to remember that which Anna would rather forget.

"The tornado came from the west." Erin's voice had calmed. She stared out the window now, as if she expected to see what she was describing.

Anna glanced that way, relieved to see blue skies and an occasional white, fluffy cloud.

"We weren't there. Samuel ran into the house, urging *Mammi* and me to go to the cellar. We looked up and saw the funnel cloud and ran outside to find you, but Jacob reached you first."

"Jacob—" Anna remembered the dream, remembered the man's worried look and asking him to hold her hand.

"He's a fine young man, Anna. *Gotte* sent him, for sure and for certain." Her *mamm* wiped at her eyes, at the tears that threatened to spill.

"The horses, they passed him first, dragging the harvester, which broke before they thundered away." Erin plucked at the blanket covering Anna. "He saw you, ran to you, and waited there until we came. He protected you when the second tornado dropped from the sky. Jacob knew what to do, and then...then he ran to the phone to call for help."

Her mother squeezed her hand. "The horses must have seen the tornado, or sensed it, before you did. They threw you, Anna."

"Threw me?"

"*Ya.*"

"Snickers and Doodle, are they okay?"

"They are. Jacob and your *onkel* found them. They were frightened but unharmed."

Anna felt sweet relief flood her system. The horses were dear to her *onkel*, and she'd become quite attached to them herself.

"The doctor says it's a miracle you weren't trampled, that you lived at all."

Anna thought of all her mother and *aenti* had revealed. It all made sense. It jived with her memories, which were fuzzy, and her dreams, which still seemed quite clear.

But there was an important detail they were leaving out. She could tell it by the way they glanced at each other.

"There's something you're not telling me, *Mamm*. What is it?" Though she wanted to scream, her voice had in fact become a whisper. One part of her longed to hear the answer to her question, and yet another part of her, the young girl she had been, wanted desperately to clap her hands over her ears and block out her mother's next words.

"Your spine was fractured—in the lower part, which is a blessing. Higher up and you wouldn't be able to use your arms."

Anna glanced down at her right hand and rubbed her thumbnail against her index finger.

"The break couldn't be repaired. It's why you can't feel your legs. They say..." Her mother hesitated but didn't look away. "They say you will not walk again."

CHAPTER 24

Anna heard her mother's words, but they didn't make sense. Wouldn't she know if her legs no longer worked? She certainly wouldn't need someone to tell her. Then again, she had been asleep in the hospital for three days.

There had been some misunderstanding.

Her *aenti* stood and walked toward the window, sniffling and swiping at her cheeks.

Her mother patted her hand. "It's a heavy burden, Anna, but you will learn to bear it. And we will help you, all of your family. We will do whatever needs to be done."

Anna felt the corners of her mouth turn up in a smile. Her mother was so sincere. She didn't realize this was all a mistake. Perhaps when the doctor came in, he could straighten them out.

Her mother asked if she had any questions, but she only shook her head. What she needed was to rest. When she woke this nightmare would be over. Perhaps it was another dream—like the quilting and the flowers and the man. She would wake to find herself in her room at her *aenti's* house beneath her center diamond quilt.

But when she woke it wasn't to her old room. The door opened, and a tall *Englisch* man walked inside with her mother.

"Hi, Anna. I'm Dr. Hartman."

This was her doctor? She'd expected someone older—someone with gray hair and spectacles.

"How are you feeling?" He didn't check her pulse or use the

stethoscope that was draped around his neck. Instead, he pulled up a chair and sat near her bed.

"*Gut*, I guess. Tired."

"That's to be expected. We've been giving you a sedative the last few days. With injuries like yours, it's very important that the patient remain still for forty-eight to seventy-two hours. This decreases the amount of swelling around your spinal cord and the chances of further damage."

Anna nodded her head as if she understood.

"Your mother told me she explained about your injury."

"*Ya*, but..."

Her mother moved to the other side of the bed and placed a hand on Anna's shoulder. "It's all right, dear. You can ask any question. Dr. Hartman is here to help you."

"Well, it's only that I believe there's been a mistake." Once she started speaking, the words tumbled out of her like so much water washing over the fields. "*Mamm* says I won't be able to walk, but I don't think there's anything wrong with my legs. I would know, right? I feel the same."

A look of compassion passed over Dr. Hartman's features, and Anna felt embarrassed. But this was too important. They were wrong, and she needed to show them.

"Perhaps if someone could help me swing my legs over the side of the bed, I could show you that I can still walk."

"It's common for SCI patients to be in denial—"

"I am not in denial." Her voice was louder now—stronger and more confident. She needed to show them, and if she was sure she could walk, then they would listen to what she had to say. "Could you help me move my legs to the side of the bed?"

"Did you need help before?"

Dr. Hartman's words landed on Anna's heart like a slap to the face. "*Nein*, but—"

"Can you move your legs?" He stood now and moved to the end of her bed.

Anna closed her eyes and focused, but nothing happened. Nothing at all!

"Close your eyes again." Dr. Hartman's voice was quiet but firm.

Anna closed her eyes and heard him moving the covers on her bed.

"I'm using the end of my pen to touch pressure points on your foot. Can you tell me which foot I'm touching?"

Anna shook her head.

"Now?"

Again she shook her head.

"What about now?"

"*Nein.*" She opened her eyes and watched as he re-covered her feet.

"The tests were quite clear, Anna. When the horses tossed you into the air, you hit the ground hard. The spinal cord is eighteen inches long and goes from the base of your neck to near your waist. Are you following me?"

She focused on his words and ignored the teardrops sliding down her cheeks.

"Your break occurred in the lumbar vertebrae, the lower back. If it had been higher you might have lost the use of your arms as well. Because the injury was in the lower portion, you have lost use of the lower part of your body."

Her tears were falling in earnest now, and she was powerless to stop them. Though Dr. Hartman appeared sympathetic, he continued with his explanation.

"You had a complete SCI, meaning a complete break. There is no surgery to repair this type of injury. However, with time and therapy, you may one day be able to learn to control your bowel and bladder function."

The information was too much. Anna still didn't believe it was true. She didn't believe that she would be bedridden and wearing a diaper for the rest of her life. It wasn't possible.

"Anna, I know this is a lot for you to digest, but I believe in being completely honest with my patients."

"When can I go home?" An ache burned in Anna's heart. Suddenly, more than anything, she wanted to be away from this hospital.

"Your blood pressure is stable and your breathing is fine. I'd like to do a more extensive test to document the strength and responsiveness of your muscles." He quickly added, "It's only small pinpricks and light touches—what I did with your feet a few minutes ago."

"After this test may I go home?"

Dr. Hartman and her mother exchanged a knowing glance. "We have all agreed that it would be best for you to move to a rehab center for a few weeks."

"But—"

"The rehab facility connected with our hospital is very good. There are others you may choose from here in Tulsa if you'd rather."

Her mother waved away that idea. "You've taken *gut* care of Anna. I've spoken with her father, and we would rather she stay with your rehab."

"But I want to go home!" Anna didn't think she could endure one more thing. She wanted to stamp her foot so badly that tears coursed down her cheeks. No one was listening to her or asking her what *she* wanted. They'd simply made decisions without her knowing, and she was powerless to do anything about it.

"I think this is something you two should discuss in private. I have a few more patients to check on and then I'll stop back by."

When he'd left the room, her mother sat in the chair and resumed her knitting. Instead of exasperating Anna more, watching her mother perform the everyday task calmed her nerves. After a few moments, her emotions settled and she was able to ask "Why, *Mamm*? Why can't I go home with you? Or back to *Aenti*'s?"

Her mother didn't answer immediately. Instead, she finished the row she was knitting and pushed the needles into the ball of yarn. Focusing her complete attention on Anna, she said, "I've spoken with your *dat* about this. We want you home, Anna, but moving you now does not seem practical. Also Dr. Hartman has taken very good care of you. Perhaps after some time has passed and you've grown accustomed—"

"To being handicapped, a burden on everyone around me?" The words felt like a shout as they burst from Anna's throat, but in fact they were barely a whisper.

"*Nein.* Your legs may not work, *dochder*, but you do not have to be a burden. You will choose how you follow the path set before you." Her *mamm* hesitated and then glanced at her *aenti* before she continued. "We have all cried many tears, Anna. My heart—all of our hearts— breaks for you and what has happened. But we believe *Gotte* has not turned His back, and that there is a purpose and a plan for what you are enduring."

Anna stared at the blanket covering her. She heard what her mother was saying. She'd heard such sentiments all of her life, but it was difficult to believe them now.

"We want you to come home with us, Anna." Erin moved closer to the bed. "I feel it is my fault for leaving you alone that day—"

"*Nein*." Anna didn't know whose fault it was, but it wasn't her *aenti*'s. The woman had done nothing wrong. If she'd stayed with Anna, she might be in a hospital bed beside her.

"Your *bruders* and *schweschder* are all praying. They have offered to come and help if you need them, but moving you now would be unwise."

"We want you to come home," Erin repeated. "Samuel has already spoken with the bishop, and a work crew is coming to the house to widen the doors for your wheelchair and install a ramp."

Anna looked out the window, unwilling to envision herself in a wheelchair.

"Also the bathroom needs to be modified."

"It's a lot of expense to go to if I'll be going home eventually."

"You are worth any expense."

"It is the best way, Anna. I will stay as long as you need me, and the hospital here is *gut*. I'm sure the rehab center will be exactly what you need. By the time you're finished there, Erin and Samuel's house will be ready for you to return to it."

"And when will I go home? To Goshen?"

"I want you to give it six months at least. Dr. Hartman has assured us that the first six months are the most critical. If you still want to come home then, we'll get permission from our bishop to fly you back to Indiana."

The knowledge that she would eventually be home—really home— eased some of the panic clawing inside of Anna. She suddenly had an overwhelming need to close her eyes and sleep. Even the dreams would be an improvement over her new reality.

CHAPTER 25

*J*acob plopped chicken salad onto fresh bread and added a spoonful of beans to his plate. Thanking the girl who was standing behind the spread of food, he accepted a glass of water and turned toward the makeshift picnic tables.

All of the workers bowed their heads in prayer at the same moment, and a familiar silence permeated the worksite. On Levi's "Amen," the noise and clatter of thirty men eating filled the area.

"*Gut* weather for rebuilding a barn," Adam King said.

It was actually the third barn they had rebuilt in the last week, and it was indeed good weather. Adam had worked on most of them, as had Jacob. The two weren't exactly friends yet, but they were acquainted.

Jacob grunted and bit into his sandwich.

Adam managed to talk around the rather large bite he had taken. "I heard the work has gone well on Samuel's house. Sorry I couldn't be there to help."

"Quite a few showed up," Jacob said. "The ramp is done and the bathroom made ready. Widening the doorframes is going to be a bit harder."

"*Ya.* I would imagine so."

"Fortunately, Samuel's house has a rather open floor plan, so only three doors need to be widened."

"Front door."

"Sure, as well as the bathroom and Anna's room."

"When does she come home?"

Jacob had been asked the question more times than he could count, and each time he wished he had a better answer. "When she's ready."

He finished the rest of his meal in silence. He'd been in the community for nearly four weeks. The names and faces were beginning to come together in his mind. The Amish in Cody's Creek made up a small community, especially compared to his parents' home in New York. Unlike some communities he'd visited, they were also close-knit. Perhaps the harshness of Oklahoma had drawn them together.

He'd heard the rumors. Originally, many families had moved away when the leaders made the decision to allow tractors. That was more than ten years ago. Since that time, the ones who were left had to depend on one another to survive, and now they had become a tight group of families. Surprisingly, they still accepted Jacob, though he suspected that had to do with the number of unwed daughters.

Jacob didn't consider himself a prime catch, but he understood how Amish communities worked in regard to marrying. There were four church districts in Cody's Creek totaling more than 600 folks. That equaled a lot of courting, marrying, and babies born—which continued the cycle. With seven to ten children per family, all Amish districts grew quickly.

There wasn't exactly a shortage of people Jacob's age, but someone from out of state was much preferred to someone local simply because so many family lines crossed. And still it was up to the bishop to confirm that those marrying were not first cousins, or in some communities second cousins. The task was made difficult because they came from a fairly restrictive gene pool, as one bishop had explained to Jacob. He'd had a twinkle in his eyes when he had explained, "With so many children in each family, counting your first cousins can easily result in a number over a hundred. Do the math, son. Some days I need my *fraa* to help me with the family lines when counseling a couple. Lots of Millers and Yoders, you know."

Jacob didn't consider himself ready to marry, but he'd caught enough glances to understand he was the right age to do so. They would figure out soon enough that he didn't plan to stay in the area. He finished his sandwich, gathered up his plate and cup, and carried them to the washbasin.

"If you see Anna, tell her we're praying for her."

"Sure will," Jacob said, and then he made his way back toward the barn.

Though a few families had made the trip to Tulsa to visit Anna, Jacob knew that the boys who had been courting her had not. He'd heard that bit of information from Erin one night. He couldn't blame Neal, Adam, and Thomas for losing interest in Anna. An Amish wife confined to a wheelchair? That would require a very special husband indeed.

He spent the next three hours carrying roof slats up ladders, working in the afternoon sun, and hoping the labor would stop the questions whirling through his mind.

How long should he stay in Oklahoma? Could he leave without seeing Anna again? Could he leave when Erin and Samuel so obviously needed his help?

Or should he stay and continue to earn money to send back home? His mother had finally admitted that his younger brother's health had worsened. It was nothing serious, she had assured him, but it had required a short hospital stay. The cost was prohibitive, and his father had stepped in and used the family savings.

Perhaps he should stay in Cody's Creek.

He wasn't sure how long Samuel could pay him, but there were larger farms that might hire him. The work they were doing to help others rebuild from the storm's damage was free—of course it was. An Amish community would never charge a family to help them out in their time of need. But Jacob was also helping Samuel in the mornings and Levi in the afternoons when they weren't rebuilding barns or outbuildings. Levi provided food and a place to stay in exchange for a few hours of work. Samuel paid him as he was able, though with the near total loss of his harvest it didn't seem that could last much longer. Regardless, the money was adding up. He'd need to go into town the next week so that he could wire more money home.

Which had nothing to do with the real reason he had a strong desire to stay. No, the truth was that he'd felt something for Anna Schwartz that he'd never experienced—even before the storm.

Before he'd seen her lying on the ground.

Certainly before she'd stared up at him with fear flooding her brown eyes and asked that he hold her hand.

An Amish wife confined to a wheelchair?

Jacob wasn't naive. He understood how difficult that would be, and he wasn't saying he was considering marrying Anna. He barely knew her. All he knew for certain was that he needed to see her again before he decided to move on.

One of his questions was answered as he was leaving the job site. Bishop Levi limped his way—something that had looked odd to Jacob when he first arrived but now looked natural. Levi didn't allow his infirmity to slow him down. The older man fell into step beside Jacob, asked about his health, discussed the weather, and finally got to the point.

"Samuel tells me you've been a real help around his place."

"Doing my best."

"We appreciate it. The entire community does." Levi stopped and turned to study the barn that was now nearly complete. "*Gotte* blessed us in spite of the storm. There were few injuries and no real damage to homes. Still the barns must be rebuilt and the winter crops planted."

"Samuel hopes to have his winter wheat in the ground next week."

"*Ya*. He told me as much. You know, Jacob, things turn out best for the people who make the best of the way things turn out."

Jacob couldn't help smiling at the impish look in the bishop's eyes. "*Ya*, my *grossdaddi* used to say that."

"The proverbs are *gut*. They guide us in much the same way as the *Ordnung*."

"But you didn't stop me to share Amish proverbs."

"Indeed. There have been many donations made for Anna."

"Donations—"

"From Amish and *Englisch*. It seems the news reports written by the woman with the Mayes County paper have drawn quite a bit of attention."

"Chloe."

"You know her?"

"No, but Anna spoke of her."

Levi nodded. "Samuel and Erin have asked me to oversee the

contributions. They are somewhat embarrassed by the attention. However, we did speak about using some of the money to pay you."

"Me?"

"Samuel has no sons."

"That's not a new situation."

"He needs the winter crop planted, and he'll need more help than ever around the farm. Anna's situation will require his attention to be diverted from his normal work. There will be constant doctor appointments, not to mention she will need help to get out of bed in the morning. He won't be able to work in the fields for hours without interruption. His new responsibilities will cut into his time, and that's where you come in. If you can stay, we'll be happy to pay you."

The amount the bishop named was more than fair. "I'll continue to provide your room and food in exchange for ten hours of work each week around my place. The rest of your time will be spent at Samuel's."

"But I don't want to take money that's earmarked for Anna."

Levi pulled out a small pocketknife and proceeded to clean the dirt from under his nails. After he'd finished with one hand, he glanced at Jacob and said, "Folks donating these funds want them used for the entire family."

"But if Anna needs—"

"Anna needs time and prayers, as well as a wheelchair and an updated bathroom. Help Anna's famly, and you will be helping her." Levi allowed his words to sink in as he cleaned the nails on his other hand, closed the knife, and slipped it into his pocket. "Are we in agreement?"

Jacob nodded. Levi slapped him on the back, and then the two men walked in separate directions.

It seemed God had provided a way for him to stay. He would be able to see Anna again. After she came home, he could decide whether he should move on or not. In the meantime, the money he was making would certainly help his family.

Now, if he could figure out what to do with the feelings that were bouncing and colliding in the pit of his stomach.

CHAPTER 26

*C*hloe filed continual updates on the tragedy at Cody's Creek over the next several months. It was her assigned area to report on, but it also seemed she had become an Amish expert of sorts, perhaps because of her connection to Anna.

There was certainly other news to report, and she did. The opening of a new store. Changes in city council members. School happenings. She attended all of those things, interviewed individuals involved, and took along a cameraman when the piece could be complemented by photos. And though her heart wasn't in those things, her readership grew. Eric received numerous emails praising her column. She knew that because the letters were always copied to her as well; however, he never mentioned them to her. He was still looking for the next *big story*.

Cody's Creek was not that story. Though tragedy had struck and people were hurt, life moved on.

But not for Chloe. Her heart was stuck trying to make some sort of sense out of what had happened. She watched the families in Cody's Creek rebuild from the destruction they had suffered. She participated in charity drives and blood donations and work teams. She became close to a community that six weeks before she'd known little about. Yes, she'd reported on the area for some time, but she hadn't known the people. She hadn't worked and sweated and ate and cried with them—until now.

She tried to keep her reports factual, to wring out the emotion before she sat down to write the latest piece. She tried to be professional.

October 10

Barn Building
By Chloe Roberts
Mayes County Chronicle

CODY'S CREEK—A barn raising will take place in Cody's Creek this weekend. Preliminary work has already begun on the Millers' barn, which was destroyed during the recent tornado. The barn will be rebuilt in the traditional Amish way with families from the area helping in order to complete the work in a single day.

Across the county, several structures were rendered unusable due to the late September storm. The majority of those buildings have already been repaired. According to Cody's Creek city manager, Lex Carlson, "Not only did the Amish repair their own damaged buildings, they also helped other folks. We had a few families who had received insurance compensation but were unable to procure the services of builders in the area." The surge of new construction in Tulsa combined with damage from the tornadoes resulted in long waiting lists for local builders.

Skip Newsome found himself in that exact situation. "The insurance money does me no good if I can't use it to have my barn repaired. I needed that work done before winter sets in. Levi Troyer found out the trouble we were having and had a work crew out the second week." The Newsomes went on to donate the insurance money they had received to a local fund set up for Anna Schwartz. "We felt like it was the least we could do. They helped us in our need, and we wanted to return the favor."

Anna Schwartz suffered a spinal cord injury and paralysis in the September 26 storm. She remains in a rehabilitation center in Tulsa. Donations can be directed to Cody Creek Bank, c/o the Anna Schwartz Fund.

October 21

Benefit Auction
By Chloe Roberts
Mayes County Chronicle

CODY'S CREEK—A benefit auction will be held in Cody's Creek this Friday and Saturday. Proceeds will benefit those Amish families affected by September's tornadoes. Levi Troyer, bishop for one of the local Amish communities, explained that half a dozen families suffered partial or total crop loss from the storm system.

Structural damage was limited to barns and outhouses. Those have all been repaired or rebuilt. Moneys received from the auction will compensate farmers for the loss of their crops. A portion will also go to Anna Schwartz, who was severely injured in the tornado (Cody Creek Bank, c/o the Anna Schwartz Fund).

This weekend's benefit will take place at the Kings' farm next to the old fire station in Cody's Creek on the north side of town. Items available will include Amish-made furniture and quilts, as well as fresh baked goods and canned items. Animals and farming equipment will also be auctioned.

November 4

Anna's Homecoming
By Chloe Roberts
Mayes County Chronicle

CODY'S CREEK—Anna Schwartz returned to Cody's Creek this week. Anna is a young Amish woman who was thrown from a wagon during the September 26 tornadoes. Now a paraplegic, Anna spent the last five weeks in a rehab center in Tulsa.

Bishop Troyer declined to be interviewed at length, but he said, "Anna is a strong girl. We appreciate your prayers as she continues on the difficult road before her."

Amish and *Englisch* families in the Cody's Creek and Tulsa area have raised nearly $150,000 to offset medical bills from the accident. Expenses for the Schwartzes include a remodel that was necessary to accommodate a wheelchair at her uncle's house.

Mr. Schwartz said, "The community pitched in and helped us to widen doors and install a ramp as well as a handicap-accessible bathroom. We're very grateful to those who came out to the work frolic and pitched in a hand. Also the folks who attended the auction and purchased items, that helped tremendously." The benefit auction was a huge success with folks parking up to a mile away in order to attend.

Anna's rehabilitation will continue as an outpatient. Although Mr. Schwartz was unwilling to discuss their financial situation, neighbors shared—off the record—that Anna's medical bills had surpassed $425,000. In addition, Mr. Schwartz's corn crop was a total loss. Donations for the family can be made to the Cody Creek bank, c/o the Anna Schwartz fund.

March 6

Spring Sale
By Chloe Roberts
Mayes County Chronicle

CODY'S CREEK—The town of Cody's Creek is holding a spring sale on the town square this Saturday from 8:00 a.m. until 5:00 p.m. Proceeds will benefit the Anna Schwartz fund. Anna was injured during the September storm and is now a paraplegic. She's twice suffered bouts of pneumonia and the family's medical bills have continued to mount. "Anna's strong. We're grateful to everyone for the cards, contributions, and prayers," said Erin Schwartz, Anna's aunt. Anna is originally from Indiana. She had moved to Oklahoma in order to spend a year with her aunt and uncle when the tornadoes hit.

Nearly six months have passed since the fateful September day when an F-3 tornado swept down and destroyed local crops and buildings, injuring several local residents, though none as seriously as Anna Schwartz, who suffered a spinal cord injury. Driving through Cody's Creek, there is little sign of the destruction wrought that Friday afternoon, but locals say it's a day they will never forget.

"I saw that black funnel cloud barreling out of the west, and I thought my time on this earth was over." Janice Tripp has lived in Cody's Creek her entire life. "Eighty-nine years," she informed me with a smile and a chuckle. "I suppose the Lord wasn't ready to take me in that storm. I might be old, but I'm still pretty tough."

Mrs. Tripp was one of several residents featured in the *Tulsa Daily* after the storm. Instead of heading for her cellar after spotting the tornado, she ran to her barn and released the prize horses her husband raises.

"Scott was in town at the feed store. I knew those horses were better off out of the barn than in it. Horses have a strong instinct for survival, and they headed to the south pasture as soon as I opened their stalls." Mrs. Tripp barely escaped before the storm barreled through their barn, leveling it. "A bruise on my forehead. That's all I got."

Local Amish farmers helped the Tripps rebuild the barn. Saturday's spring sale will include bedding plants, birdhouses, outdoor benches and swings, quilts, and fresh baked goods. Local businesses—both Amish and *Englisch*—will also be donating items for purchase in a silent auction. All proceeds will be deposited in the Cody Creek bank, c/o the Anna Schwartz fund.

CHAPTER 27

Early June

Anna awoke to a summer breeze floating through the window and the sound of her *mammi*'s murmured prayers. Her grandmother literally washed her in the Psalms before each day began, though often she would change the pronouns to make the reading more personal.

We trust in Your unfailing love; our hearts rejoice in Your salvation.
Keep Anna safe, my God, for in You we take refuge.
Show us Your ways, Lord, teach us Your paths.

The words of Scripture, spoken in her grandmother's German accent, calmed and soothed her. They provided a foundation Anna sorely needed as she adjusted to her new life.

Sleeping wasn't too difficult. By the end of the day she was often more tired then a newborn babe.

Waking, now that was a different matter.

Some mornings she would wake slowly, the prayers of her grandmother pulling her from her sleep. Other mornings, she woke with her heart racing, her pulse loud and rapid in her ears, echoing like the sound of thunder. Occasionally she woke rested and ready to bound from the bed, temporarily forgetting that she could no longer bound anywhere.

Her eyes would open, she'd take in the view outside her window and glance around her room, and then her eyes would fall on the wheelchair and the real nightmare she was enduring would come crashing back around her. She almost preferred waking from the terrifying dreams. Forgetting her disability, while sweet, was too painful. She understood that she needed to accept her situation, needed to move on with her life—whatever that meant. But something in her mind, or heart, was holding her back. She'd stare down at her toes under the old quilt and she would try to move them. Nothing. She couldn't even feel the weight of the covers on her legs. It was as if everything simply stopped below her waist.

Though the doctors had explained it to her, she couldn't understand, couldn't quite accept what had happened. Her legs appeared normal when covered by the quilt. They looked as if they would support her.

Once she threw the covers back, the ugly truth was revealed. In spite of the therapy and exercises, her legs had lost much of their muscle tone. They looked almost like *Mammi*'s minus the wrinkles. Though, of course, her grandmother could still move around just fine.

On the difficult mornings, Anna would lie in her bed, unwilling to move. Better to pretend to be asleep and try to understand what had happened, why it had happened, and what purpose God could have. Why her? Why anyone? Even after her meetings with Bishop Levi, the answers eluded her. Sinking into despair, she would close her eyes and hope to fall back asleep.

But *Mammi* always knew, and she was not one to tolerate self-pity. "*Gotte* has blessed us with another day, Anna."

She loved her grandmother dearly. She did. But often her optimism exhausted Anna before she rose in the morning.

Mammi shuffled over, pulling the chair closer beside Anna's bed. "Samuel will be inside soon to help you to the bathroom."

Anna nodded but didn't say anything. Some days she didn't trust herself to speak. The terrible questions she had might begin tumbling out, and once released, she wasn't sure she'd ever be able to stop them.

"I've been praying for you, Anna." *Mammi* clasped her hand. "*Gotte* has a plan for you. I am sure."

Instead of answering, Anna looked away.

"Mornings are difficult. *Ya*. I imagine they are." *Mammi*'s voice softened as she picked up the jar of lotion from the night stand. Anna's mother had sent it from Indiana. Someone in their community made it, claiming it would prevent bedsores and help restore muscle tone. Anna doubted an ointment could do all of that, but it seemed to please her grandmother to smooth the lemon-scented balm over her arms and legs.

"*Gotte* is mighty, Anna. Never doubt that. Oh, no. Our Lord, He does great things—things we cannot understand." *Mammi* pushed up on her glasses.

When Anna looked at her grandmother, she saw such complete faith and trust that she had to turn away. Her grandmother's life had not been easy. Though she hadn't suffered an injury like Anna's, she had endured the death of one child and her husband. Her own legs hurt her, and she walked slightly stooped due to osteoporosis. None of that dimmed her outlook.

"Today will be special. You'll see, child. Better even than yesterday."

Yesterday had consisted of shelling spring peas on the front porch. Anna had been happy to have something to do besides mending, but she failed to see how a plain old Wednesday in June could be special.

Then she remembered, and a sense of dread and anticipation flooded through her. "Maybe I shouldn't go."

"Nonsense. Chloe has called the phone shack three times in the last week. She even ordered the handicap van."

Great. That made for a special day. She'd get to ride in a white van with a strange driver who would glance at her with pity before pointedly looking away.

"I feel a little rattle in my chest. Maybe I should stay in and—"

"You were snoring like an old Amish man when I came into your room. I think your chest is good. Those herbs I gave you worked."

Hmm. Best not to fake an illness with *Mammi*. The woman's herbal remedies might work, but swallowing the bitter teas was often more painful than the ailment. Not to mention that faking was a form of lying. She had enough sins without adding another to the count before her day had even officially begun.

Samuel's boots clomping down the hall pulled Anna from her morose thoughts.

"Morning, Anna."

Anna had noticed a marked change in her *onkel*'s attitude toward her over the last several months. Was it because he felt a sense of guilt for what had happened? That was a ridiculous thought. He had nothing to feel guilty about. More likely it was because he'd joined their community of believers again—in spirit as well as body. Whatever had caused him to hold himself apart for so many years had dissolved over the last six months. It was difficult to remain distant when folks brought meals for your table, feed for your animals, and seed for your field. Not to mention the monetary donations from the benefits, auctions, and even strangers.

"Ready?" he asked.

She nodded, placing her arms around his neck. Instead of putting her in the wheelchair, Samuel insisted on carrying her to the bathroom each day. Then *Mammi* would come in and help her take care of her toiletries and dress. The weeks in therapy had done little good, in Anna's opinion. She had not regained any use of her legs. She had learned to maneuver the wheelchair, become convinced of the importance of eating right and doing her exercises, and regained her ability to use the toilet. There wasn't a day that passed when she didn't thank the Lord for that.

At first she had been astonished that her *onkel* was not too embarrassed to carry her into the bathroom. He'd been such a quiet, reserved man the first few months she'd lived with them. He was still quiet, but their relationship was different. Perhaps when you walked through the valley of death together, you grew closer. Not that Anna had been so very near death, except for the bouts with pneumonia that had frightened everyone.

Today her lungs felt strong, and though she did not understand the turn her life had taken, she was able to be objective enough to recognize the changes that had been good. Each time she placed her arms around her *onkel*'s neck and rested against him, Samuel would smile—a slow genuine smile. Was it for her? Was it a reflection of his heart? She didn't know. There was so much she didn't understand.

Mammi helped her with her toiletries. Her clothes had been hung in the bathroom the night before, and Anna was able to pull the dress over her head. She could now fix her own hair and even pin on her *kapp*. However putting on her socks and shoes was impossible. She would have tumbled right out of her chair if she tried, and then—if no one was there—she'd have to lie there on the floor until someone came. The thought frightened her. She let *Mammi* take care of those things. It wasn't easy for the old gal. She couldn't bend to the ground either. They were like two peas in a pod in many ways. She had to raise Anna's foot and place it on the side of the tub. Then she would fetch Anna's shoes and socks and put them on.

She was grateful for her aunt and uncle and grandmother. She appreciated the many letters from her siblings and parents, all of who continually offered to come and visit. But none of those things changed what she had become. She was a paraplegic, and that wasn't something she would ever get used to. Thoughts of going back to Indiana had faded away. Why? What did it matter whether she sat in a wheelchair here or there? Her life had become meaningless, and it seemed to her that it would always remain that way.

CHAPTER 28

*J*acob wasn't in the kitchen when Anna rolled her chair into the room. Some days he joined them for breakfast if the work allowed. More often, he would eat a large breakfast at the bishop's and work in the barn or on the fences or with the animals until lunch. Those were long mornings for Anna. Her time with Jacob was special, though she didn't want to focus on that either. She wasn't ready to examine her feelings, which she realized were as futile as wishing she could fly.

"Chloe should be here by ten, and she scheduled the van for half past the hour." Her *aenti* set a hot mug of coffee in front of her. Anna never drank the stuff before...it seemed her life was divided into before and after the accident. She'd always thought of coffee as an old married person's drink. But now she found the warm beverage helped to jumpstart her brain and even improved her attitude a little.

"I don't like the van," Anna confessed.

"*Ya.* The old ways were better. Though I agree with the necessity of using the tractors." Samuel paused before adding, "If you had been driving a tractor instead of the horses, maybe you'd still be able to walk."

"I don't think so. If the tractor had turned over on top of me, it could have killed me. The horses ran away, and maybe that saved my life."

They had spoken of the accident many times, but it seemed as if Samuel hadn't been able to let go of his sense of guilt. He heaped a large pile of scrambled eggs on his plate, and then he passed the bowl to her.

Anna took one spoonful and passed it to her *mammi*. No matter how little she ate, her clothes grew tighter. She'd struggled with her weight before the accident, but in the last eight months she had lost that battle. Her entire body had changed, had rebelled against her and what had happened. It had embarrassed her when she'd needed newer, bigger dresses, though her *aenti* seemed happy to sew them for her.

"I'm glad we still take the buggy to church," Anna said.

"And to weddings and funerals." *Mammi* pushed up on her glasses.

"The buggy is what I like best." Anna stirred the food on her plate. "Even when we have to strap my chair on the back, it's soothing to ride behind a horse."

"I'm surprised you aren't a little bit afraid of them." Erin set a tray of hot biscuits on the table, sat down, and began to fill her own plate.

Once she'd done so, her *onkel* said, "Let's bow."

Anna wasn't sure what others prayed about during this silent time. She prayed that *Gotte* would help her through one more day. That seemed monumental enough of a request. And she tried to remember to be thankful for the food.

"Amen," Samuel said.

He smiled at his wife as she passed him the bowl of grits. Erin had also changed since the accident. Hadn't they all? Where before she was painfully thin, she'd put on a few pounds and they looked good on her. There was now color in her cheeks and she moved with more energy. It had occurred to Anna that being needed had changed her *aenti* into a different person.

"Anna loves the horses." Samuel picked up the conversation where they had dropped it. "You should have seen her last week when Jacob took her to the barn."

Anna blushed at the thought of Jacob pushing her wheelchair across the yard. He'd done so four times now, and each of those trips was burned into her memory. On the first they'd been watching the sunset when a bobcat loped across the yard in front of them. Anna had heard about them but never seen one. The cat moved gracefully, the sun bouncing off its brown coat. She'd been able to make out black-tipped ears and whiskers before it darted out of sight.

On the second time they had gone to the edge of the field so she could see the progress of the crops. The ache in her heart had been terrible then. She'd wanted so badly to stand up and walk down the rows. She'd insisted they go back inside, and though Jacob was obviously confused by her mood change, he'd quietly agreed.

The third time was what her uncle was referring to, when they'd gone to the barn. She did still love the horses. When Jacob took her to the horse stalls, and she was able to feed Snickers and Doodle a treat, it was as if a small part of her had healed.

It was the last trip with Jacob that stood out in her mind the strongest. He'd pushed her out to the mailbox, which sat near the two-lane road. She'd been so happy to be away from the house, to be somewhere different, that she'd felt a curious lightness. She'd felt free. On the way back, a red-tailed hawk dove down in front of them, caught something up from the grass, and soared away. Its majesty and beauty had stunned them both, and they had remained there for a few minutes hoping it might return.

Jacob seemed to enjoy those walks as much as she did, though she couldn't imagine why. Surely he had more important things to do than push a wheelchair around the yard. He had even suggested she allow him to put her on the tractor so they could head off toward the tank on the back side of the property to fish. Jacob often put preposterous ideas in her mind.

"She fed Snickers by hand," Samuel continued. "That horse is becoming spoiled."

"I'm not afraid of Duchess or the workhorses, and I do prefer them to the van or any *Englisch* vehicle. The horses, they did me a favor." It was Anna's opinion that if the horses hadn't thrown her, she would have continued driving straight into the storm. She would have died after being sucked up into the tornado. The horses' instincts had saved her, though at a terrible cost.

"We could have helped you into Chloe's car, but she wasn't sure she could get you back out. The van is a good compromise." Samuel continued to shovel food into his mouth, pausing once in a while to swipe at his beard.

"We're fortunate Mayes County offers such a service," *Mammi* said. She sipped her coffee slowly as the steam rose up from her cup.

Conversation died as each person focused on their plate.

The door to the mudroom banged open, followed by the sound of Jacob stomping his feet on the rug.

"Sorry I'm late."

"No problem, Jacob. Sit here. I'll fetch you a plate."

He sat across from Anna, saying good morning to *Mammi* and assuring Samuel that the animals had all been cared for. "The cow was in a mood this morning. She tried to kick me once."

"Sounds like Bella. She's been cranky the last few weeks."

"But she still gives *gut* milk," *Mammi* added.

"Speaking of which, I thought we might make a buttermilk pie this afternoon, *Mammi*."

Anna nearly winced. She loved her *aenti*'s cooking, but she had to find a way to eat less or burn up more calories.

"Going to town today, huh?" Jacob winked at her as he heaped food high on his plate.

"*Ya*, in the van." Anna squirreled her nose, feeling like a moody child and not caring how silly she looked.

Why did it matter? She was convinced that he thought of her as a little sister. He no doubt felt he needed to protect her, but he didn't care for her, not the way she cared for him. Her mood continued to drop as she considered a day away from the farm. She wouldn't see him at lunch, and he'd likely be gone by the time she returned.

Jacob was still working for Bishop Levi a few hours in the afternoon when Samuel could spare him. The weather had been good and the crops were coming in well. There was work on any farm, but Samuel and Levi seemed to have more than their share. All but one of Levi's sons had farms of their own, and Samuel had no sons. They had both adopted Jacob, who appeared content to split his time between the two places.

Soon the men were gone, Jacob pausing to whisper, "Enjoy your day in town and stay out of trouble."

What trouble could she get into from a wheelchair?

She tried to control the blush creeping up her neck, but if he noticed he didn't mention it. Instead, he thanked Erin for the breakfast, wished *Mammi* a good day, and hurried out after Samuel.

As the calories settled into her stomach and the dreams of the night before fell away, Anna's mood improved. By the time there was a knock at the door, she was actually looking forward to the trip she had dreaded on rising.

CHAPTER 29

*C*hloe waited by the door after knocking briskly. She worried that her friend might have changed her mind. Anna suffered from depression and boredom. Chloe had done a lot of research on spinal cord injuries and paraplegics. Both said this was normal and might or might not pass as the injured person grew accustomed to their new life.

Chloe had visited once a week since the accident. At first Anna had been happy to see her, but then she'd decided that Chloe was visiting her out of pity. One day Anna had said as much. "I don't need or want your sympathy. You don't have to keep coming to see me."

Those had been a rough few months through the darkest part of winter. Perhaps that was why Chloe had begun calling her mother again, several times a week. She needed someone to talk to, someone who understood about loss and pain and suffering. They didn't talk about Chloe's dad during those conversations—about his illness or his death. But her mother counseled her to have patience, to pray, and to keep visiting her friend.

When spring arrived Anna's mood had improved, and she seemed to look forward to Chloe's visits as long as they stayed at her uncle's farm. She'd always found an excuse when Chloe discussed them going to town together. One night Chloe remembered her promise in the fall, after they had gone to see the Amish quilts. They had set a date to see the quilts Chloe's mom made, but that plan had fallen away with so many others after Anna's injury.

Now it seemed to Chloe that it would be good for Anna to enjoy an afternoon away from the farm. She'd spoken with Erin about it twice, and Anna's aunt had agreed that it would be a good idea. But each time Chloe had tried to plan it, Anna had dodged and hedged and generally become difficult.

When Erin opened the door, Chloe blew out a sigh of relief. They were still going. She could tell by the smile on Erin's face.

"It's *gut* to see you, Chloe."

"You too, Mrs. Schwartz. How is Anna today?"

"I'm fine, and I can hear you."

Erin cocked an eyebrow and said, "She's ready."

Chloe walked into the sitting room and tried not to wince. The sight of Anna in a wheelchair still came as a shock, even after so many months. She'd been so vibrant and full of life when Chloe had first met her. Now she seemed like a mere shadow of her former self. Everyone said to give her time and Anna would find her way back to them, back to the person they knew and loved. But Chloe was beginning to worry that might never happen.

"Tell me you are not in a complaining mood today, Anna Schwartz. I've been looking forward to this trip for a week."

Anna stared at her and attempted to frown, but when Chloe stuck out her tongue, she laughed. "You look like a child when you do that."

"And you sound like one, which is why we make perfect friends."

It was true. They'd become fast friends over the last eight, no nearly nine, months. Chloe realized with a start that in many ways Anna was the little sister she'd never had.

"I'm so glad you're finally going to meet my mom."

"I thought I met her in the hospital."

"She met you. You were rather out of it."

"*Ya*, so you tell me."

"The van will be here any minute," Erin said. "You girls had best hurry outside."

Chloe moved behind the chair and released the brake. "Do you have everything you need?"

"What do I need?"

"I don't know. Your purse? Maybe a pillow or..."

"I wasn't planning on sleeping."

"For your back! Weren't you complaining about your back last week when we were on the porch looking through magazines?"

"Maybe, but I'm not going to look through magazines today."

Chloe rolled her eyes, and Anna said, "I saw that. Well, I didn't see it, but I know you either rolled your eyes or made a face."

"She's feisty today." Chloe stopped in front of *Mammi*'s chair. "Can you explain that to me?"

Chloe had been teasing, but *Mammi* answered seriously. "Anna had a difficult morning because of the dreams, but I know she is looking forward to spending time with you." *Mammi* patted Anna's hand and squeezed Chloe's arm. "You two have a *gut* day."

Erin returned with Anna's purse. "Here you go. Be careful, girls."

By the time Chloe pushed Anna outside and down the wheelchair ramp, they could see the van turning into the lane.

"What nightmares? You didn't tell me about those."

"Nothing to tell. I'm moody. Didn't you hear?" Anna plucked at the fabric of her dark blue sleeve as she added, "I suppose I thought you might cancel."

Chloe moved in front of the chair and squatted down in front of her so that they were eye to eye. "I'm not going to cancel. I've looked forward to this as much as you have."

"Why? Why would you want to spend the day with someone like me who can't...can't do much of anything?"

Anna looked so vulnerable that Chloe longed to enfold her in a hug. Instead, she pulled a *kapp* string to the front that had caught behind her shoulder.

"I don't know. Maybe I'm the crazy one, but I actually like spending a day with my friend instead of working."

"We don't have to work?" The teasing note was back in Anna's voice.

"I thought about having you fold newspapers for me."

"Next you'll have me deliver them from my wheelchair."

"Not a bad idea if you were in town where there are sidewalks."

The van pulled to a stop and a black man jumped out. "Hello, ladies."

"*Gudemariye.*"

Chloe was relieved to see it was Clarence driving. She understood full well how much Anna disliked riding in the van, though it was sometimes necessary in order to make one of her doctor appointments in Cody's Creek. Many of the appointments were in Tulsa. For those trips, Erin and Samuel paid a neighbor with a vehicle that was equipped for wheelchairs.

Anna had complained about the van on more than one occasion after a doctor's appointment or trip to the therapist. Chloe thought the problem was that Anna felt vulnerable in the van, especially when the driver was a stranger, but she had mentioned Clarence before. There was a smile on her face as she held a palm up and high-fived him.

"Morning, Anna." Clarence's voice was soft and Southern, reminding Chloe of molasses.

He lowered the lift with a button inside the door. Chloe pushed the chair onto the lift and Clarence locked the chair into place with clamps on the floor. "Don't want you flying about," he said and offered a toothy grin.

When Chloe climbed into the van beside her, Anna turned to her in surprise. "I thought you'd take your own car."

"Nope. When we come back, I'm staying for dinner. Your *aenti* already asked and I agreed. I hear that *Mammi* is making a buttermilk pie."

"*Ya.* Very fattening."

"Are you saying I'm fat?"

"I'm saying we'll need to go light on your mother's lunch if we're planning on *Mammi*'s pie."

"No worries. Mom always makes salads for lunch."

After watching Chloe buckle up, Clarence slammed the van door shut. He jumped into the driver's seat, put on his own seat belt, and started the engine.

Butterflies fluttered in Chloe's stomach. What was that about?

Ever since she was a small girl, she'd had quirky, butterfly-like feelings when something good was about to happen. Maybe it was excitement about an unusual day, or maybe some part of her could actually tell when life was about to take a big turn.

CHAPTER 30

*C*hloe's mom lived on the eastern edge of Tulsa, not far from the farm. When she opened the door to her home, Anna almost giggled. Looking at Chloe's mom was like seeing a mirror image of Chloe.

They both had bouncy black curls, slim figures, and a no-nonsense attitude. Chloe's mom introduced herself as Teri, wore small reader glasses, and had soft lines around her eyes. Anna guessed she was probably in her mid-fifties.

Anna noticed that when Chloe and her mom hugged, something passed between them. What? It was almost as if they were tentative around each other, unsure how to act or what to say. Now that she thought about it, Chloe had not talked much about her mom other than to reveal that she was a quilter.

"It's about time I met you, Anna." She bent down and enfolded Anna in a hug. "I've been praying for you, child."

"*Danki.*"

"And I would have visited, but Chloe tells me you're still adjusting to all the therapy sessions and doctor appointments."

"*Ya*, it is a lot of coming and going." She motioned toward her legs, and then she remembered her manners, which did not include keeping the conversation on herself. "It's nice to have a day away from the house."

"Understandable. I was on bed rest when I was pregnant with Chloe. At the time I thought I might lose my mind being confined to one spot for so long. Once she was born and consuming all my time, I wished for a day in bed."

"Are you saying I was a lot of trouble?"

"I would never say that, darling." Teri smiled and motioned toward the living room. "I've set out some iced tea. It's sweetened with fresh raspberries and oranges. Of course, if you'd like something different..."

"The tea sounds *gut*." Anna's eyes widened as Chloe pushed her chair into the sitting room. Unlike Amish homes, Teri's was decorated with a soft mocha color on the walls. Large bay windows sported sheer curtains to soften the morning sun, and dark green curtains across the top and sides complemented the earth tones nicely.

Anna had only been in a few *Englisch* houses. Many of them were overdecorated, in her opinion. Not Teri's. The room was open, airy, and held enough color to brighten but not overwhelm.

The tea was fresh, and the fruit added a lovely flavor. Anna's shoulders relaxed, and she temporarily forgot to worry about the many problems in her life.

They talked about the wet summer they'd had and changes in Cody's Creek, which included a remodel of the public library and the building of a new strip mall.

"Mom's particularly interested in the shopping center because it's going to include a quilt shop."

"*Ya*? I hadn't heard—"

"I only know because my daughter interviewed the man who manages and leases the shops." Teri smiled at Chloe. "I get inside information."

"Everyone will know Friday when the paper comes out," Chloe reminded her. Turning her attention to Anna, she added, "The other businesses will include a yogurt shop, an optometrist, and a nail salon."

"Can't say I'll use the nail salon," Teri studied her nails, which she kept neat and filed but unadorned by polish. "The quilt shop will be a huge blessing."

"Wouldn't you rather go to a store in Tulsa?" Anna asked.

Teri tilted her head as if considering. "There are several fabric stores in the city, but I'd prefer to drive to Cody's Creek. It's the same distance and a much pleasanter trip."

Anna said, "We buy our fabric at Bylers' Dry Goods."

"I've been there a few times, but never to purchase fabric."

"Rebecca carries mostly solid colors because that's what we use in our clothing and our quilts."

"Do you quilt, Anna?"

Chloe and Anna shared a smile.

"I quilt a little." Anna hesitated, sipped her tea, and finally continued. "My *mamm* taught me. All Amish girls learn to quilt, but I was never very good at it. I quickly grow bored using the same colors and patterns. When I came here, I was happy to help with the produce booth rather than spend my time with fabric."

Teri nodded as if she understood, and maybe she did. Anna thought she was an intriguing woman.

Chloe had mentioned during one of their porch talks that her father had died a few years before after a long struggle with multiple sclerosis. When Anna had asked questions, Chloe changed the subject. She'd noticed that Chloe did that when asked any questions about her family—she clammed up or responded with a question about something else.

Teri seemed to have recovered completely from the shock of becoming a rather young widow. There wasn't even a hint of bitterness in her demeanor. Was it because of her faith? The cross and a framed Bible verse on the wall behind them indicated she was a Christian. Had that helped her? Or did her personality allow her to accept trouble more easily than others, more easily than Anna?

"I'm pleased you wanted to come see my little operation. I don't consider myself a master quilter, but I'm proud of what we've been able to do."

Anna glanced at Chloe, uncertain how to respond. They had an operation? Who was the *we* she referred to?

"Mom, I think you're baffling Anna. Why don't we show her what you're talking about?"

"Absolutely, and then we'll have lunch. I've made a cranberry walnut salad."

Chloe once again pushed Anna's chair. The house was on a single level with a somewhat open floor plan. Anna could see the dining room and the kitchen from where she sat, but Chloe turned her in the opposite direction.

"This was originally a den when Chloe's father was alive. I've been quilting in a casual way for about ten years. When I first started, I used a small bedroom at the back of the house. After I opted for early retirement from teaching, quilting became more than a hobby. Then Gus died two years ago, and I decided to convert the den into a quilting room."

It had only been two years since Chloe's father passed? Anna turned to look at her friend, but she was quietly studying her nails.

"The light is good in this room." Teri added, "Gus always teased that I had my eye on his space."

Chloe walked back behind Anna's chair and pushed her through a wide double doorway into a room that literally took Anna's breath away. Stunned, she put her hand on the top of the wheel to stop the chair.

"I've got it now, Chloe."

The room was beautiful—wide windows on one side and double doors that led out to a veranda on the other. There was certainly a lot of light. A sewing machine sat on an L-shaped table in one corner of the room. A third wall was covered with felt, and that seemed to be where Teri placed her quilts as she sewed them. A countertop had been built along the fourth wall. This was where she cut her fabric. Under the countertop were dozens of clear plastic bins filled with supplies.

All of those details passed through Anna's mind quickly. The quilts, on the other hand, amazed her. She slowly rolled her chair from one to another, drinking in the sight of them.

A teddy bear flannel print, cut into large half squares, placed in a *V* shape, alternated with bright green fabric and was trimmed in yellow rickrack.

A nine patch made from bright calico prints.

A cat print, alternated with polka dots and used in an hourglass pattern.

"What is this one?" She'd stopped in front of a quilt that reminded her of a large garden. The colors were haphazardly placed, and the effect was delicious.

"That's a string quilt. It's how I use all of my leftover pieces. They're very easy to make."

Some of the quilts were hung from a long wooden strip fastened across the top of one wall. Others had been folded and stacked on top of a cabinet. More were draped over two chairs. They filled the room with their color and energy.

Anna rolled to the wall that held a covered board from floor to ceiling.

"This is my design wall."

Anna reached out and touched the cloth that covered the design wall. "This fabric—"

"It's felt, which allows me to place smaller pieces on there without pins in the early stages of a quilt. Once I've begun sewing the blocks, I usually do pin them. This way I can see the quilt and decide if I like the color placement before I actually start sewing."

Anna nodded and rolled her chair in front of a white board that held a chart of sorts. On the left-hand side was a list of names, to the right were the words—"requested," "designed," "pieced," "quilted," and "mailed."

"Mom likes to have several projects going at once." Chloe seemed more relaxed now that they were in the quilt room. In fact, it was obvious that she was proud of her mother. "The board helps to keep her organized."

"Yes, charting my projects was Chloe's stroke of genius. I was always forgetting that I had started something until I came across it in another pile."

Taped to the top of the white board was a picture of a child, fingers in one mouth and clutching a blanket with his other hand. The words "Project Linus" were written across the top of the board next to the picture.

"They're all for children." Anna scanned the names again—Ben, Candace, Stefanie, Mandi, Baby Joe. She turned her chair in a circle so that she was facing Teri. "Your board is full of children's names, and the quilts. They're all done in patterns and colors that will please young ones."

"Yes. That's what Project Linus does. We provide blankets or quilts to seriously ill or traumatized children."

"We?"

"I'm a blanketeer—officially. Project Linus actually began in 1998, well before I became involved. Today there are chapters in all fifty states. I can give you some brochures on it if you're interested."

Anna nodded but didn't say anything else. Instead, she turned to look at the quilts again. Then her gaze drifted toward the list of names.

Since her accident she had forgotten that other people were hurting. Her focus had been completely on herself—her problems, her pains, and the unfairness of her life. She'd struggled and cried and confessed and prayed, but always the focus had been on her. For the first time in many months, her mind and heart were flooded with sympathy for others.

"Mom runs the Tulsa County chapter—"

"I have plenty of help. I don't make all of the blankets myself."

"Helpers come here?" Anna glanced around the room. It was large, but she didn't think it would hold a lot of quilters.

"No. Mostly we communicate via phone, email, and texts. But I stop in and visit the area groups when I'm in Tulsa or Oklahoma City."

"Mom stays very busy."

"It's difficult to fill all the requests we receive, but we come closer to that goal every year."

"You're a very *gut* quilter."

"Thank you. The patterns aren't intricate. After all, a child doesn't care how expert we are at cutting triangles or quilting elaborate designs. They merely want something that will make them smile on a gloomy day." She stopped and allowed her gaze to drift around the room. "Working with the Project Linus is something I enjoy doing. The focus isn't on the quality of the quilt, but rather on the love and prayers that go into each one."

Anna nodded again as if it all made sense, but she had a lot of questions. Of course, her community made quilts for benefit auctions. There had been quite a few sold at the auction to help with her medical bills. But this was different. This was strangers helping one another on a regular basis.

"You girls must be starved. Anna, would you like to wash up before we eat?"

"*Ya*. That would be good." She was surprised to see that the bathroom was outfitted for a handicapped person with support bars next to the toilet, a step-in shower with a seat, and a low sink that she could roll up to and wash at. Chloe had told her once that her father was wheelchair bound for several years. This house must have been adapted to accommodate his handicap.

She washed up quickly, comforted by the fact that if she did need to use the toilet it wouldn't be too cumbersome to do so.

The meal was filling and delicious. Anna forgot to wonder about calories and happily devoured cheese, crackers, and a second helping of salad.

They talked about Chloe's latest assignments and Teri's recent scare over an irregular mammogram.

"They decided it was nothing but a calcium deposit."

"I'm sure you were relieved."

"I was, but it gave me a lot of empathy for women going through breast cancer—for men and women going through any types of cancer. Gus's illness was...well, it was different."

Chloe stood to remove dishes as her mother spoke. It was clear she wasn't comfortable with the direction the conversation was taking.

"The important thing was that we had time together," Teri continued. "We didn't worry about the end until the last few months. Gus was able to spend the days he had left with our family, those we loved, and with me."

By the time Chloe returned from the kitchen, their conversation had circled back around to Project Linus.

"It's very interesting," Anna admitted. "I like the idea of making something for hurting children, of being able to help someone else."

Chloe beamed as Teri leaned forward, crossing her arms on the table. "I'd love to have your help, Anna. Do you think you'd like to make a quilt for us?"

"Oh. I don't know. That is, I'd love to..." Anna stared down at the table. "It's only that I'm not making any money, and I hate to ask for anything else from my *aenti* and *onkel*."

Glancing back up, she continued, "I wouldn't be able to buy the supplies, though the Lord knows I have plenty of time on my hands."

Teri stood and pushed in her chair. "Supplies? That's not a problem."

CHAPTER 31

*J*acob noticed a dramatic change in Anna over the next few days as she began to make quilts for children. She was engaged and excited for the first time since the accident. Gone were the times when she stared off into space, her hands motionless in her lap and her face blank of expression. It was as if she'd rejoined them, as if she'd picked up the pieces of her life and was eager to start living again.

Mornings were still occasionally difficult. Twice he'd heard *Mammi* mention the nightmares that were plaguing her, but he hadn't had a chance to discuss them with Anna. They had very little time together—nowhere near what he would have liked.

He vowed he would speak with her alone after Sunday's worship service.

He'd glanced at her occasionally throughout the singing and during the sermons. Once he looked across the room to see her wiping tears from her cheeks. Another time she had been staring down at the open Bible in her lap. He considered all of this an improvement. At previous services she'd stared straight ahead and said little, never participating in the singing. Today, he thought he could pick her voice out from the others—not especially loud, but with a certain ring to it. He might have been imagining that—how could he possibly tell one voice from another? Still, in matters of Anna, it seemed he could.

Now she sat at the end of one of the luncheon tables. There was a plate of food in front of her, but her attention was momentarily occupied by a small passel of young children

Jacob stopped a few feet behind her chair and listened.

"Why don't your legs work?" One of the boys asked.

"Your mind sends a message down your back." She touched her head and a point on her back just below her neck. "Since I was thrown to the ground, the messages don't carry so well."

One little girl's eyes widened, and she exclaimed, "I never want that to happen to me!"

The girl's blunt statement didn't seem to upset Anna. Instead, she nodded slightly and said, "I would never want it to happen to you, either."

"How fast can you make that chair go?" Another boy asked.

Anna didn't answer immediately, so Jacob used the moment to interrupt.

"I think that's enough questions for now. If Anna doesn't eat, she won't have the energy to roll her chair anywhere."

Somber faces nodded in understanding. One of them was called away by his mother. The rest soon followed.

"Mind if I join you?"

Anna waved to the area the children had vacated. "Sure. Have a seat."

"You handled that well."

"The *kinner* are only curious. They mean no harm by their questions."

"Indeed."

Anna bit into a piece of fried chicken, studying him thoughtfully while she chewed.

"What? Am I wearing my food?" He swiped at his chin with a napkin.

"*Nein*. You haven't started eating yet. How could you be?"

"What is it then? You're looking at me strangely."

"Am I?"

"You are and you know it." Jacob sunk his fork into a mound of potato salad and popped it into his mouth.

Anna took a sip of water before leaning forward. "I was wondering why you're sitting with me. I suspect it's because you don't want to see the girl in the wheelchair sitting all alone."

"But you weren't alone when I sat down."

Instead of refuting his point, she said, "Isn't there someone else you'd rather sit with? I've noticed several girls giving you long looks."

Anna tilted her head toward a trio of girls standing near the dessert table. When Jacob looked their way, each girl blushed and began to giggle.

"Are you trying to get rid of me?"

"Not at all."

"Did it ever occur to you that I might prefer sitting with you?"

"Oh, it occurred to me, but I decided there was probably another explanation."

He picked up his knife and cut through the large slice of ham on his plate. Spearing a piece of it on his fork, he pointed it at Anna and said, "The only explanation is that I enjoy your company—"

"Which you have nearly every day."

"And I hardly ever have a moment alone with you."

She only cocked an eyebrow and continued chewing on the chicken. He was glad to see she wasn't picking at her food. He'd heard her mention her weight to Erin on several occasions. In Jacob's opinion that was a silly concern. Her body needed calories, healthy food, and vitamins. If she'd gained a little weight since the accident, maybe that was a good thing too. She should trust her body.

While they finished their food they discussed inconsequential things—the storm of the week before, new neighbors who had moved in down the street, and a recent letter from her mother.

When their plates were empty, Jacob asked, "Dessert?"

"Not yet. I'm too full from the extra roll you gave me off your plate."

"I gave it to you because you love bread."

"I do." Anna's hands slipped to cover her stomach. "But now I wish I hadn't eaten it."

"Ridiculous. A little exercise and you'll be ready for pie."

"What did you have in mind? Should I join the game of baseball?"

"You probably could wheel around the bases faster than Jonas King can run them. That boy is slower than my *dat*'s old mule." Jacob stood and cleaned off their end of the table, taking their plates to the tub set up for dishes and dumping the water left in their cups onto a flowering bush. He paused for a moment to speak with Erin, stopped by the vegetable table to put a few raw carrots in his pocket, and then he made his way back to where Anna was waiting.

The service had been held at the Millers'. It was close enough that Jacob had walked. He'd passed the barn on the way in, and now he had an idea. He moved behind Anna's wheelchair and asked her to release the brake.

"Where are we going?"

"It's a surprise."

"What kind of surprise?"

"Wouldn't be much of one if I told you."

He backed the wheelchair away from the table and started pushing her across the lawn.

"Maybe I should tell my *aenti*—"

"I already took care of that." He slowed the chair, leaned down, and whispered, "Trust me."

More loudly he said, "And hold on."

He pushed the chair much faster than usual. The lawn was smooth and Anna didn't seem in danger of falling out. In fact, he was sure he heard a laugh escape her pretty lips.

By the time he reached the far side of the barn, they were both breathless.

"This is it? You wanted me to see the back of the Millers' barn?"

Jacob put two fingers to his lips and whistled. When he did, a beautiful roan mare stepped out from the barn. Directly behind her was the foal that he had spied when walking to the service. Somewhat unsure on its feet, the foal followed closely behind its mother, trying to nurse when the mare stopped next to the fence.

Jacob reached into his pocket and handed the carrots to Anna. "She looks hungry to me."

"The foal is beautiful." Anna held a carrot piece out to the mare, who accepted it between her large front teeth. After crunching it, she stayed close to the fence, poking her head through the fence rail, obviously hoping for another treat. Anna leaned forward in her chair and stroked the white splash of fur between the horse's ears, feeding her all of the carrots one by one until they were gone.

"I think she likes you."

"I think she likes carrots."

They both laughed when the horse attempted to stick her head all the way through the fence.

"That's all I have, girl. Go on now."

Nodding her head, the mare turned and walked away, her foal toddling behind.

"Tell me about your family," Anna said.

"What's there to tell? Typical Amish family."

"*Bruders* and *schweschdern*?"

"Only boys—seven of us."

"So your *mamm* is a patient woman."

"She is."

Anna rolled her chair forward and back. For a moment her eyes were on the foal, who had settled in the shade on the far side of the pasture. When she turned her attention back toward him, Jacob knew that the next question was very important to her.

"Why did you leave them?"

"Some days I can't remember why." He stuck his hands in his pockets and allowed his memory to comb back over the years. "I was a middle child, and I guess I thought no one would notice."

"Did they?"

"Of course. *Dat* wanted me to stay. He said he needed my help, but he didn't. There were too many boys for the small amount of acreage we had."

"There must have been plenty of other jobs."

"Yes, but I've always enjoyed working outside. I couldn't see myself as a cabinetmaker."

Anna nodded as if that made sense. "How long have you been away?"

"Four years now. I've been back to visit twice."

"And you didn't want to stay?"

"Part of me did, but another part had become used to the road—as my bishop predicted."

Anna ran the fingers of her right hand over the wheel of her chair. "I'm glad you stayed here—that you seem content here."

"This is where I'm supposed to be, Anna. I can't imagine moving away now. I wouldn't want to." Jacob glanced again at her as he said the last four words. The mixture of emotions on her face and the tears in her eyes caused him to squat in front of her chair, reach out, and touch her cheek.

As he did, the last of bit of reserve he'd carefully placed around his heart began to crumble.

CHAPTER 32

*A*nna's emotions soared high and plummeted to the bottom of her stomach in a matter of seconds. When Jacob squatted in front of her, his kind eyes probing hers, and reached out to touch her face, she didn't know whether to laugh or cry.

Instead of doing either, she decided to be honest.

"Thank you, Jacob." Her voice was soft and sincere. "There are many things I've missed since the accident, but I suppose what I miss most is being able to enjoy the little surprises of each day."

She ran her hand over the top of the right wheel. "Most of my days are very much the same, with little to break up the tedium."

"Except your sewing."

"*Ya.* The sewing has helped."

"But you're still sad at times. I can tell, and I want...I want to help. That's why I brought you out here, hoping it might lift your spirits."

Anna nodded, but she didn't smile. How could she when her heart was being squeezed so tightly she had trouble pulling in a full breath. "Maybe you could push me over toward that bench?"

Jacob moved behind her chair and pushed her the few feet to the bench that sat along the back wall of the barn. When he'd positioned her chair next to the end, he took a seat.

"I appreciate you're attentiveness, Jacob. I do. It means more to me than you could know."

"I hear a *but* coming."

"*Ya*, I suppose so. I like you Jacob, more than I want to admit, and sometimes I think you feel the same."

Instead of answering that question, he said, "The first day I saw you, the first afternoon I arrived to work for your *onkel*, I knew you were special."

"I'm not that person anymore. I'm...broken now."

"You *are* the same person, Anna. How can you say that? You have the same heart, the same smile, you care about others, and I think I've loved you since that first day because—"

He'd turned toward her, and though it hurt her to do so, Anna reached out and put a finger on his lips. "Let's not speak of love."

"Why would you say that?"

The fist around her stomach tightened, but she pushed on. "Because I would not make a good wife, and we both know that. I don't know if I could have children, and I would be very little good around the house."

"Those things don't matter—"

"I would be a burden." Tears slipped down her cheeks, but she didn't let them slow the words she needed to share. She wiped the tears away and pushed on. "You deserve someone better, someone who is whole."

"Anna, that is not true. I've cared about you—no, don't try to stop me again. I've cared about you since that first day. When I covered you with my body as the tornado passed by, our lives were sealed together. And when I held your hand as we waited for help, we both knew that we were meant for one another. I dare you to tell me I'm wrong, to tell me you did not feel what I felt."

"Feelings are not always a good basis—"

"I've waited, Anna. It's been nearly nine months, and I've tried to be patient, waiting for you to heal. Waiting for the right moment because I knew you needed time. Now the time for waiting has passed. I don't want to be patient anymore."

"But you don't know me!" She closed her eyes until the hammering in her heart calmed. When she realized how ridiculous that must look, she opened them, but instead of looking at Jacob, she sought out the mare and colt. The sight calmed her and allowed her to confess the things on her heart. "I'm angry a lot of the time. More angry than you can imagine, Jacob. Why did this happen to me? What did I do wrong? Does *Gotte* hate me?"

He started to speak, but she reached out her hand and stopped him. "Other times I know those questions are wrong. My mood calms, and I wonder what purpose *Gotte* could have...how He could possibly use me now, in this chair. *Mammi* is always talking of *Gotte*'s plan for me, but I can't begin to imagine what that might be."

"We can't always know."

"So Bishop Levi says."

"The bishop is right. You should listen to him."

Anna couldn't help smiling at the scolding in Jacob's voice. One minute he was confessing his love, and the next he was speaking to her like a schoolgirl.

"What I'm saying is that not only is my body broken, but so is my heart."

"Anna—"

"I do need to heal, Jacob, on the inside. And that could take months or it could take years."

Now he stood, stuffed his hands in his pockets, and faced her. "Then I'll wait."

"You will?" Anna gave him her best skeptical look. "When you were speaking to my *onkel* at breakfast last week, you weren't sure if you'd be here for the fall harvest."

"Because I wasn't sure you wanted me to be here. I wasn't sure I could bear to stay if you didn't feel the same way that I do."

Jacob waited, but Anna didn't utter the words he wanted to hear. It would only encourage him, and she refused to do that.

"You may not be ready to say you care for me, Anna Schwartz, but you're too honest to deny it." Now a smile tugged at the corners of his mouth. "I'm glad we've had this talk. I'll tell your *onkel* I can stay as long as he needs me."

Anna shook her head, wanting to warn him that waiting on her was the wrong thing to do. But he was no longer listening. He moved behind her chair and began to push it back toward the group of folks now talking and resting and playing underneath the shade of the Millers' pecan trees.

After a moment of silence, he said rather gruffly, "And since you won't speak of your feelings, tell me about this sewing that you've begun."

So she did. She described in detail her visit to Teri's, the program that provided blankets for children, and how she was able to receive free supplies because fabric was often donated by stores and individuals. Thinking of the quilting lifted her spirits. It was the one thing she could do that benefited someone else.

By the time they had reached the picnic tables, Jacob was teasing her about using *Englisch* patterns and fabrics. He wheeled her into an open spot between Erin and the bishop's wife. "I'm sure my *mamm* has never seen puppy print fabric, and she's quilted since I was small."

"Oh, *ya*. Anna likes the animal prints—dogs and cats, as well as rainbows and flowers." Erin smiled fondly at her niece. "She's quite the wild one when it comes to fabric."

The teasing soothed her raw emotions. Jacob whispered, "Visit with the women. I'll go and supervise that ball game."

With a smile and a touch of his hand on her shoulder, he was gone.

Anna mostly listened to the talk of recipes and children as her mind went back over what had happened in the last half hour. Jacob had declared his love for her! Part of her heart wanted to tell her *aenti*, whisper the news to *Mammi*, and hurry home to write a letter to her mother. Another part was filled with dread, convinced that once he realized how damaged she was, he would change his mind.

CHAPTER 33

The next few days should have been easier, but instead they were more difficult than any Anna had endured since waking to find herself paralyzed and in an *Englisch* hospital.

The quilting was going well, but perhaps she worked on it too much. Her eyes would begin to burn from staring at the tiny stitches and her shoulders ached from sitting in one position for so long. Twice she stitched blocks together wrong, and the second time she threw the fabric on the kitchen table and declared, "Take it away from me. All I do is mess up everything I touch!"

Instead of reprimanding her, *Mammi* toddled over, folded up the quilt piece, and set it in Anna's sewing basket. "Let's go to the porch. Sometimes watching *Gotte's* rain helps my moods."

But the rain didn't help. The sight of it falling and saturating Samuel's fields only made Anna more irritable. Even the smell of the rain, which she had once found so delightful, scratched against her nerves. After a few moments, she insisted on going inside and being transferred to her bed, but there she only stared at the wall, unable to sleep.

Erin came in to help her with her exercises, and Anna snapped. "Why even bother doing them? What is the point?"

"Dr. Hartman says your exercises are very important, Anna."

"I'll never walk again. We both know that. The exercises make no difference at all. It would be better for everyone if I had died in the storm."

Erin may have been shocked the first time her niece said this, but no longer. Everyone, including Anna, was well past being surprised by her tantrums. Even as the words left her mouth, she wondered how they could possibly endure her presence. She heard herself. She was aware of how bitter and angry she sounded, and she realized that the person she had become was someone she didn't like very much.

None of which stopped Erin. She simply reached for the lotion and began rubbing it methodically into Anna's hands and arms and legs and feet.

"Did you read through the magazine the doctor sent? Exercise promotes neural recovery—"

"It's hopeless, *Aenti*."

"And it reduces the risk of secondary complications."

Anna stopped arguing. No one listened. No one understood what it was like to be her, to be trapped in her chair and to have no hope for a normal future.

Erin finished with the lotion and moved on to the physical therapy. She began to move Anna's right leg through the range-of-motion exercises. Anna watched but didn't speak, didn't actually participate in any way. It was like watching someone else's legs being pushed and pulled. By the time Erin had finished with both legs, Samuel appeared and moved her to the floor.

Anna didn't put her arms around his neck as she usually did. Instead, she sat on the rag rug *Mammi* had crocheted and stared at the wall on the other side of the room. She didn't want to meet her uncle's gaze. She didn't want to see the compassion on his face. It would be her undoing. Once her tears started, she would drown in them.

"Having a hard afternoon?"

Erin answered when Anna wouldn't. "*Ya*, but the exercises always help, and Jacob said that tomorrow is supposed to be sunny. This rain can pull anyone's emotions down."

"But it's *gut* for the crops." Samuel touched Erin's arm, and then he walked out of the room, whistling one of the hymns from Sunday's service.

Had it been just Sunday that Anna had shared those special

moments with Jacob? Though he appeared at breakfast every morning, they hadn't spent any other time together. On Tuesday he'd suggested they go to look at the corn maze that had been replanted, but she'd refused. Already her mood had been plummeting.

At times like this, she would have an outburst, followed by moments of silence. She couldn't help the fact that she clammed up. It was as if she had no words left, no more cries of despair.

She went through her routine with the stretchy band and small weights. She performed the shoulder shrugs and deep breathing exercises, though she was convinced they weren't helping at all.

When she'd completed all of the tasks and Erin had placed a check mark beside each one listed on her chart, Samuel again appeared. How did he know when they would be done? She couldn't begin to guess and after her outburst she refused to look him in the eye and ask.

"Wheelchair?" he asked softly.

"*Nein.*"

"Bed, then. Perhaps you need some rest."

But she didn't rest. She lay in her bed pretending to sleep until she was alone. When he left the room, she stared at the wall and wept for all that might have been.

CHAPTER 34

*A*nna woke the following morning as she usually did, to the sound of her *mammi*'s voice.

"We call on You, our God, for You will answer us; turn Your ear to us and hear our prayer. Show us the wonders of Your great love." *Mammi* loved the Psalms. It had been that way since the day Anna first arrived in Oklahoma. She'd barely known her grandmother then. Now she couldn't imagine her life without the dear woman.

She did have things to be grateful for. There had been no nightmares last night. Perhaps she'd been too tired after the emotional low of the day before. The memory of it embarrassed her, and she wondered if she might be able to hide under the quilt all day.

Mammi had other ideas. "*Gudemariye*, Anna."

"*Gudemariye, Mammi.*" She doubted it would be a good day, but she didn't see how it could be much worse than the day before.

"Some days are difficult, *ya?*" *Mammi* reached for the lotion and began to work it into Anna's right arm. This time the scent of the lemon balm made her think of sun tea and picnics. She relaxed, closed her eyes, and enjoyed the ministrations of her grandmother.

"Other days are better. I think today will be a *gut* day."

Anna grunted, but she didn't open her eyes. Few days were good days. Some days were less bad than others. It was the most she hoped for.

"Do you believe in miracles, child?"

Anna's eyes popped open, and she stared at her grandmother. What was she asking? What did it have to do with her situation?

"Our *Gotte* is a *Gotte* of miracles."

Anna shook her head. Miracles? Seriously? She was a paraplegic now, forever confined to her wheelchair. All of her hopes and dreams had been ripped from her. She would probably never marry, probably never have children, probably remain dependent on her family the rest of her life.

Did she believe in miracles? What difference did it make? She hadn't received one.

"I've been reading. The miracles in the Bible occur to a variety of people in very different places."

Anna wanted to slap her hands over her ears. Why was *Mammi* bringing this up today? Hadn't yesterday been bad enough? She couldn't sit around and hope for a miracle.

No.

Mammi proceeded to recount the miracles Christ performed as recorded in the book of Matthew, the eighth chapter. The man with leprosy was healed. The centurion's servant was healed. Peter's mother-in-law was healed.

Anna heard her grandmother, but her mind zoomed off in another direction. She could wait on a miracle and pin her hopes on the improbable or the impossible. If she worked at it, she might be able to convince herself that the right lotion or the right herb or the right prayer would make her into the person she had been.

She could, but how many miracles had she seen or heard of in her lifetime?

None.

The wiser course seemed to be to learn to accept the facts of her life. She was unmarried and would remain that way. Jacob's confession of love was touching, but it would be wrong for her to encourage him. Deep down in the pit of her stomach, she knew it was time to accept her life. That was the right course.

Samuel came into the room. "Morning, Anna."

She wrapped her arms around his neck and smiled. He was a good man and hadn't asked for the troubles he'd received. The least she could do was show her gratitude, and she was thankful for her family and their help.

He carried her to the bathroom and left her alone.

As she went about the business of preparing for another day, her thoughts returned to what *Mammi* had said.

Was God still in the business of miracles?

She honestly didn't know, though it might be an interesting question to ask the bishop. No doubt he would give her a look of pure sympathy. Anna didn't need more incidents of people feeling sorry for her. No, she wouldn't be asking that question of Bishop Levi.

She was twenty-four years old and she was paralyzed. She could sew blankets for needy children. She could bless others in her small way. She could cheerfully do her exercises and be less of a burden on her family. She could make the best of the life that she had.

Anna still didn't know if she would remain in Oklahoma after the harvest or return to Indiana. Her mother and father had promised to visit at that time, and together they would come to a decision. What difference did it make? Life in a wheelchair was her future no matter where she lived.

Mammi joined her in the bathroom and helped with her socks and shoes. She'd left talk of miracles in the bedroom, and for that Anna was grateful.

She struggled to make it through each day and such lofty thoughts— such theological debates—seemed pointless.

If only she could make her family see her as she actually was. Her *aenti* insisted on talking about her future. Jacob visited each day and looked at her as if she held the secret to his dreams.

And her grandmother? She continued to pray and to believe in Anna's healing.

CHAPTER 35

*J*acob understood that the last few days had been particularly hard for Anna. He blamed himself. He shouldn't have pushed. He shouldn't have told her about his feelings, but then again, how could he not? In spite of his worries he whistled as he finished the project he was working on for her. The fields had been too muddy to work in the rain, so there had been plenty of extra time the last few days.

He'd actually thought of the project the week before. While he'd worked outside the barn brushing down the buggy horse, he'd watched Anna. She had sat idly on the porch, staring out toward the garden. Erin and *Mammi* had been weeding around the vegetables, and he'd realized that Anna looked trapped up there in her chair. He'd begun the work that evening.

On Sunday Anna had told him that her days were "very much the same, with little to break up the tedium," and he'd known that completing the project was the right thing to do. He'd also come up with another idea—one that wasn't yet completed but soon would be.

The day had dawned clear. With Samuel helping, they finished the first job and much of the second by the middle of the afternoon.

"Let's go tell her." He looked at Samuel, whose boots were caked with mud. "I believe she's sitting on the porch, which is a good thing since Erin would never let you inside with those boots."

"Your boots don't look any cleaner." A smile broke across the man's face. "This was a *gut* idea, Jacob. The last few days have been particularly hard on Anna. Maybe the worst I've seen since she's come home."

Jacob wondered if that had anything to do with their conversation on Sunday. Maybe, but he still didn't regret it. She couldn't dwell on her injuries forever. She had to begin looking toward the future, and he was determined that her future would be spent by his side.

"This will help."

"*Ya*, I think so."

They trudged to the front porch and up the steps. The porch was a wraparound, stretching across the entire west side of the house, which fronted toward the lane, turning at the corner, and continuing across most of the south side of the house. Anna usually came out to the front and sat there watching the yard and looking out toward the lane, which was probably why she hadn't heard what they were doing. If she had, the sound of hammering would have piqued her curiosity, and she would have learned of the surprise before Jacob was ready.

The handicap ramp started at the front of the house, before making a turn and coming to an end on the south side. The ramp itself hadn't been used much, not nearly enough in Jacob's opinion. Anna rarely had a reason to go down it, other than the occasional trip for a doctor's visit. He hoped that was about to change.

"You don't look very busy," Jacob said.

Anna apparently hadn't noticed their approach. She pulled her gaze from the road toward them. Her hands were idle in her lap.

"Run out of fabric?" Samuel asked.

"*Nein. Aenti* and I decided perhaps I should sew in the morning and rest in the afternoon. Perhaps I was pushing too hard and that was the reason for my...moods." She blushed prettily at the confession.

"Can't sit on the porch and do nothing every afternoon." Jacob walked up behind her and released the brake on the chair. As he did, Erin and *Mammi* walked out onto the porch.

"About to show Anna her surprise?" Erin crossed her arms and smiled.

"We are," Samuel grunted. "Might as well make it a family outing."

"Let me grab my cane." *Mammi* rarely bothered with the maple walking stick that the doctor had insisted she use, but the weather had worsened her limp the last few days.

"What surprise?" Anna asked. "Where are we going?"

"Wouldn't be a surprise if we told you." Jacob brushed her *kapp* strings behind her shoulders. When *Mammi* returned from the sitting room, he pushed her chair down the ramp. They made quite a group with Jacob in front pushing Anna in her wheelchair, followed by Samuel, *Mammi*, and Erin.

At the end of the ramp was a wooden boardwalk.

"When…when did you build this?"

"Last few days," Samuel said. "We had some leftover lumber in the barn."

Jacob chuckled. It wasn't exactly a lie, but it was an exaggeration. The leftover timber in the barn had given him the idea. After discussing it with Samuel, he had gone from farm to farm asking for donations of what other folks had left. Because nearly everyone had needed to rebuild something on their property after last year's big storm, most people had a few boards or boxes of nails they were willing to donate.

"We'll need to weatherproof them." Samuel stuck his thumbs under his suspenders, glancing toward the garden and then back at Anna.

"How did you manage with all the rain we've had the last few weeks? When did you find the time?"

"Jacob was able to build these in sections in the barn. We moved them out this morning."

Jacob stepped away from the back of her wheelchair. "See if you can do it, Anna."

She gave the wheels a tentative push and her chair trundled a few feet.

"Nice and even boardwalk," Samuel said. "*Gut* work, Jacob."

"But why? And where does it end?" Anna's voice held a note of awe, and Jacob was relieved to see that she was smiling again—something she hadn't done in several days.

"Well, that's the best part." He resumed pushing her chair. The boardwalk stretched from the wheelchair ramp on the porch to the first row of Erin's garden.

"You raised the plants." Anna put her hand on top of the wheels and gave them another good strong push. She trundled past miniature rose bushes, moved slowly along a row of herbs, and stopped when she reached radishes, scallions, and cherry tomato plants. "You raised up the plants. You made garden window boxes."

Anna made a three-point turn, something Jacob had never seen her do before, and turned to stare at them.

"We thought you might enjoy working in the garden again." Jacob ignored the tears pricking his eyes. He didn't want to stain Anna's day with his own emotions, but the look of wonder on her face satisfied a spot deep in his heart.

"*Mammi* made you a tool pouch you can keep in your lap. There's even a strap to wrap it around your waist so it doesn't topple off." Erin pulled the cloth bag from behind one of the plants, where she'd hidden it earlier that day. Peeking out of the top was a small hand-sized shovel, rake, trimmers, and a new pair of garden gloves.

"I hope you don't mind that I used your leftover scraps for the bag." *Mammi* pointed toward the colorful prints. "Seemed to me that those cats and dogs wanted out for some sunshine."

"I...I don't know how to thank you all. This is...it's *wunderbaar*." Anna raised her face to the sun. "It's absolutely *wunderbaar*."

"Guess you'd better show her the rest, Jacob," Samuel muttered. Though his voice was a bit gruff, a smile tugged at the corners of his mouth. "I'd best get back to the barn."

"Aren't you all coming?" Jacob asked.

"Oh, I need to check on dinner," Erin said.

"*Ya*, and I'll help her." A mischievous look sparkled in *Mammi's* eyes.

Jacob had the distinct feeling they were purposely scattering in different directions so he could have time alone with Anna, and he didn't mind one bit.

"There's more?" Anna asked.

"*Ya*. It's not finished, but—" Jacob again stepped behind her chair and pushed it toward the ramp on the south side of the front porch. This time, instead of returning back to the house, he turned left toward the produce stand, which had been vacant all of spring and now the first few weeks of summer. Erin didn't have time to work there, and no one wanted to leave *Mammi* out in it alone.

"It'll probably take a few more weeks to complete the boardwalk to the produce stand. It's good that the rains have stopped, which makes it much easier to lay the wood for the walk. I'm not sure it will be ready before we have to start working in the fields again, but I promise you I will finish it. Until then, you'll have to let one of us know when you want to come out here."

"Why would I—" Anna's voice stopped as he paused at the back of the produce stand. They had widened the door for her wheelchair, and remodeled the inside.

"You lowered the shelves."

"And the window, so you can easily help customers."

"I can't imagine how much time this took."

"Not so much, Anna, and you're worth it."

"You expect me to work out here again?" Her voice rose in hope.

"Only if you want to. We were thinking that we'd begin with Friday and Saturday mornings if that's all right with you." When she didn't answer, he hurried on. "Chloe already made a sign for the road. She left it here last time she visited. She didn't want to spoil the surprise until we were ready. I think folks will start coming again once we put it out—if you want us to do that."

"Of course I do!" She rolled around the produce stand. She could hardly go three feet before she had to turn and go another direction, but she didn't seem to mind. "I feel funny admitting this, but I've actually missed this place."

"Erin thought you might be ready to get back to work."

"Work, yes. But it will also be nice to see people." She laughed, probably at the look of surprise on his face. "Don't get me wrong. I adore you and Samuel and Erin and *Mammi*, but it's also nice to see different people, which I hardly ever do other than during Sunday services."

Jacob turned around and leaned against the tabletop she would use for laying out customer's goods and accepting money.

"Are you saying you're tired of us?" He pretended to look hurt. "And here I thought we were such good company."

"You are." Anna rolled forward and back, forward and back. "It's just...um...the last week has been pretty hard."

"I heard."

"I don't know why. Sometimes it all seems too much."

"That's understandable." ·

"But this...and the garden. They give me things to look forward to."

Jacob waited a moment, weighed the wisdom of what he longed to say, and then he knelt in front of her chair. "Don't you see, Anna? This is how it would be if we married. There is still so much you can do. It's only a matter of thinking it through and understanding what accommodations you need to be able to do it."

"Jacob Graber. Are you saying you would build a house to fit me?"

"I could."

"I know you could." Her voice softened and she stared down at her lap.

"And I would." He reached out and claimed her hand. "But we don't have to decide that now. All we have to do is find ways to help you through the rough spots. One day at a time, Anna."

"Indeed." She squeezed his hand, and then she ducked her head, pushing the chair through the back door of the produce stand, where she promptly became stuck.

"I believe you're going to need help there—"

"Until my carpenter finishes my boardwalk."

"You need to get him right on that."

"Yes, I do."

Her laughter was light and too brief, but it was a drastic improvement from the girl sitting somberly on the front porch. One day at a time. Jacob thought those were wise words. What he hadn't told Anna was that he'd been meeting with Bishop Levi and they'd been praying together about Anna, about what they could do to help, and that God's will would be done in her life.

Perhaps they'd taken a step in the right direction. Working in a produce stand? That was a little thing, something children often did. But giving her back a sense of independence was a huge step.

The question was what they should do next.

CHAPTER 36

*C*hloe walked toward the produce stand, her purse over her right shoulder, the bag from her mother over her left. The smile on her face grew the closer she came to Anna's window. It did her heart such good to see her friend again sitting in the same place she'd occupied the first day they had met. More importantly, Anna looked as if she was enjoying herself immensely.

"Do you have peaches? I heard you have peaches."

"Check the sign, *Englischer*."

"Yeah? I'm sure I saw the word *peaches*."

"There are no peaches on the sign! Do we look like a peach grove?" Anna had been aiming for exasperated, but she couldn't hold on to it. Soon she was laughing right along with Chloe.

"You joke, but sometimes it happens. I had a woman stop by last weekend who wanted fresh mangoes. No kidding."

"Who doesn't love a fresh mango?"

"I've never had one," Anna confessed.

"Now I know what to buy you for your birthday." Chloe was kidding, but Anna's expression became suddenly serious.

"I turn twenty-five in a few weeks—the first of July. Last year, I was still at home with my family. Think about it, Chloe. If I hadn't moved here..." A wave of her hand encompassed her legs and wheelchair. "None of this would have happened."

Chloe sat in the lawn chair they kept near the booth window for customers who were older, turning it first so she was facing Anna.

"I know that look." Anna rolled her chair back and forth. "You're trying to put a positive spin on my handicap."

"No. No, I'm not."

"Then what?"

"Selfish thoughts—mostly. If you hadn't moved here, we would never have met."

"True."

"I'm not sure I've told you how much you've helped me."

"In what way?" Anna cocked her head to the side, waiting and watching.

"When we first met, my mom and I weren't particularly close."

"Because…"

Chloe tapped the handles of the lawn chair. "I'd like to say because of my dad's death, but honestly I think the problem was due to my immaturity."

"You blamed your mom?"

"Not exactly, but I had to lash out at someone, and I lashed out at the person left standing." Chloe sat up straighter and stared out across the farmland. "I was so angry…"

"For sure and for certain I know what you're talking about."

"You do." Chloe turned back to Anna and smiled. "That's the miracle of this—that you do understand, that anyone can understand. After a while I wasn't angry anymore, but I didn't know how to bridge the distance I'd created. When you were injured, I began calling my mom more. We'd have long talks over the phone about faith and family and how to live through hard times."

"Your mother seems like a wise woman."

"She is. And now with your quilting, I've fallen in the habit of visiting her again. You've given me back my relationship with my mom, Anna. That's a very big thing."

"Well, I suppose if you wanted to thank me you could at least buy some fresh vegetables."

They both laughed, but then Chloe turned the conversation to where it had begun. "If you hadn't moved here, it might have taken me years to reconcile with my mom."

"That was *Gotte's* doing, not mine."

"I suppose. There's more though. If you'd stayed in Indiana, you wouldn't have met Jacob."

Anna had shared Jacob's confession of love the week before when Chloe had visited. The information hadn't come as a surprise to her. The man was positively smitten, and it had been obvious to everyone but Anna for quite some time.

"*Ya.* I have thought of that. Also..." She hesitated as she looked back toward the house. "My *aenti* and *onkel,* they are very special people. They've changed too. They have become less closed up to me and to others. Something good did come of the accident, not to mention the time I've spent with *Mammi.* I can't imagine my life without her."

"I'm glad you're seeing the bright side."

Anna shrugged. "Not always, but it's a *gut* day today because I'm out of the house."

"And you get to see my pretty face."

"Uh-huh."

"And..." She dramatically held the word for an extra beat. "I brought fabric!"

She set the bag from her mother on Anna's counter. "Mom loved what you sent her. She says your quilting has improved more in a month than hers did in a year."

"I always knew how to quilt. I just never enjoyed it before. When you're quilting for someone else, when you're envisioning and praying for the child you're sewing for..." She let out a gasp as she pulled the fabric from the bed. "Frogs? She sent me *frogs?*"

"Happy frogs. Don't they look happy to you? We both thought you'd like the bright colors."

"I love it, though to be honest I've never been a fan of frogs. They jump too quickly, and you never can tell what direction they're bound to hop."

"I can take it back—"

"No, you don't. I will love quilting with them, but don't bring me any real specimens."

They spent the next half hour catching up on the events of the last week. Twice they were interrupted by customers. Chloe moved to the side and pretended to study the corn maze behind them. It was coming along quite well. She had a hard time grasping that it had been nearly a year since she first met Anna.

Chloe's life had changed in many ways since that time—small things, but they made a big difference. She once again was attending church with her mother, and she'd said yes to a handful of dates over the last six months. None of them had turned into anything lasting, but at least she was allowing for the idea that she might fall in love. Anna's accident had reminded her that life was precious and should be lived to the very fullest. Figuring out how to do that was a bit harder.

When they were once again alone, she repositioned her chair and rested her elbows on the counter that extended to the outside of the stand. "I came to visit and bring the fabric, but also because I wanted to see how you were getting on in the stand. You look as if you're doing very well. I'm impressed!"

"If you think I'm impressive here, you should see me in the garden."

"I'd love that. There is one more reason I came, though. My boss wants me to run another piece on you."

Anna groaned.

"We always receive a great response from articles about you—"

"People are bound to get tired of the poor handicapped girl story."

"Actually, you inspire them. Go figure."

"You're joking."

"I'm not. Perhaps it's because they don't have to hear your sarcasm."

Anna cocked her head and tapped a finger against her lips. "I had the perfect response to that, but it was sarcastic. I'll keep it to myself."

"Will you do the article?"

"I suppose. If it helps you. No pictures, though."

"I know the drill."

"And we need to run it by *Onkel* Samuel and get his approval."

"I already did. He was coming out of the house as I drove up."

Anna reached forward and flipped the homemade sign to indicate the stand was closed. "You'd better take me in to lunch if I'm going to have the energy to answer your questions."

Chloe hurried to the back of the stand to help her friend through the door, but she didn't need her help. The boardwalk was finished now, and she was able to maneuver quite well. The only thing she couldn't do on her own was push the chair up the ramp. Her arms weren't quite that strong yet, though at the rate she was improving, Chloe expected Anna would be able to do that soon.

CHAPTER 37

*A*nna was happy to help her friend. In truth she didn't mind the interviews much. The Schwartzes didn't receive the *Mayes County Chronicle*, so she never actually saw the pieces. Chloe had offered to bring by a copy, but Anna had joked, "It's hard enough for me to get through doorways in this wheelchair. Add a giant head from seeing my name in print, and I might get stuck."

No, she didn't see the articles, and she didn't mind answering the questions, but such days always exhausted her in ways that ran deep and touched an old ache. She was grateful when the sun brushed the western horizon and she could go to bed without anyone wondering if something was wrong.

"Remembering is exhausting, *ya?*" *Mammi* sat by her bed, knitting a brightly colored lap blanket.

Anna had a sneaking suspicion the blanket was for her, but she didn't say anything that might spoil the surprise.

"I suppose. Just when I think I'm beginning to accept the way things are, a part of my heart rises up to rebel."

"Any change is difficult, Anna. Yours more than most."

They sat in silence for several moments. Anna stared at the wall. *Mammi* continued to knit.

"Usually you ask me to turn out the light when you're tired. Something tells me that tonight you're tired but hesitant to sleep."

Anna glanced sharply at her grandmother. There was very little that the old dear didn't notice.

"Is it because of the dreams?"

"You know about them?"

"I'm here after you fall asleep and before you wake in the morning. It's one of the great blessings of my life that I can minister to you." She pulled more yarn from the ball of bright yellow cotton blend with a flick of her wrist. "Of course I know."

"They don't come every night, but when I'm especially tired, like now, they tend to plague me. It seems as if they play repeatedly in my mind as I lay here, but that's probably my imagination. I read somewhere that you only dream the last few minutes of your sleep."

"I can't tell you how long or when a dream occurs, but I can tell you that *Gotte* often speaks to us during our dreams."

"Do you believe that?"

"*Ya*. Says so in the Bible. Abraham, Jacob, Joseph—they all had dreams sent by *Gotte*."

"Yes, but—"

"Samuel, Daniel, Peter, and Paul too."

"Those are all men."

"Pontius Pilate's wife had a dream."

"I don't think *Gotte* does that anymore." Anna remembered her grandmother's talk of miracles, but she shied away from that topic. She didn't need one more thing on her mind.

"You think *Gotte* has changed?"

"Well, I don't know if He's changed, but—"

"*Gotte* loves you, Anna. He loves all of His children." *Mammi* knit another row before turning her eyes toward her granddaughter. "He'll use whatever He wants in order to tell you so."

"These three dreams aren't about love, though. They're...disturbing."

"Tell me about them."

Anna ran her hand over the quilt on her bed. She remembered the dreams, remembered every detail, but where should she start?

"Begin with the one that bothers you the least."

"That would be the dream about Jacob."

"*Ya*? It's not unusual for a young woman to dream about a young man, especially when he's as sweet on her as Jacob is on you."

"I've had the dreams since my time in the hospital, when they gave me medications to keep me asleep. The dream about Jacob...it bothered me more than any other at first because I couldn't remember who he was. When I woke, and *Aenti* mentioned Jacob often, the memories of that day started coming back to me."

"Go on."

"I'm lying somewhere, but I don't know where. He is hovering over me, and the look on his face...what I want most is to reach up and assure him that everything will be all right, but I can't move my hands."

"Often in dreams we move about but are unable to do what we want to do. When I was a young woman, I had a recurring dream that a cake was burning in the oven. I could look in the little window and see it, but I couldn't reach forward, open the oven, and remove it. That dream bothered me something fierce." *Mammi* raised an eyebrow as she glanced again at Anna. "I hadn't thought of it in years."

"In this dream, I can hear Jacob whispering that I'll be okay. I want to believe him, but I don't because he is so worried, so concerned. There's fear flooding his eyes, and I know that there is something he's not telling me. Then I ask him to hold my hand and he does. His touch is tender and calming, but the grief never leaves his eyes."

"I was there when Jacob reached forward to hold your hand. This was a traumatic moment in your life, Anna. Maybe the most traumatic you will ever experience. It's understandable that you would dream of it."

Anna took a sip from the glass of water on her nightstand. "The second dream is almost silly, but when I'm dreaming it I feel very anxious."

Mammi pushed up on the bridge of her glasses and waited.

"I'm sewing a quilt, but I put it together wrong every time. In fact, I'm doing everything wrong. Holding the fabric at an odd angle, using a ridiculously large sewing needle and a tiny amount of thread—I have to bend over to see what I'm doing, and my stitches get smaller and smaller until I can't see them at all."

"Sounds like some of my early attempts to quilt."

"Sometimes in the dream—not every time, but sometimes—I'm convinced that it's terribly important for me to finish the quilt, but I can't. I don't have the skills. I can't even stitch a straight line. The strange thing? I know I can't sew even as I pick up the needle and begin. It's unbelievably frustrating."

Mammi sighed. "I don't have the gift of interpreting dreams—"

"It's not that kind of dream, *Mammi*."

"But it seems to me that there might be a deeper meaning to this one than the Jacob dream. The Jacob dream is a remembering, a way to mourn what has happened even as you sleep. This dream of the quilt, it seems as if it might mean something else. Perhaps you should share it with the bishop."

Anna shrugged. Though she didn't mind sharing such private thoughts with her family, she wasn't sure she wanted to share them with Levi. The man had been a tremendous support to her, but she felt vulnerable when she spoke of such things.

"You said there were three dreams."

"*Ya*. The last one makes no sense at all. I'm walking through *Aenti*'s fields—for some reason I always think of them that way, in the dream, as being *Aenti*'s."

Mammi had stopped knitting and was now staring at her curiously.

"In front of us, the wildflowers stretch as far as we can see. It's beautiful, and it always fills my heart with...with song, and I know how silly that sounds. I begin to laugh. I'm surprised that the land which *Onkel* works so hard to cultivate is suddenly brimming with color."

"Are they like the wildflowers we have growing alongside the road?"

"Some are, I suppose. Maybe." Anna paused, before telling the rest. "But, *Mammi*, they are thick like wheat and the smell is heavenly. A bird chirps nearby, but I can never see it. Even as I'm looking I know that I won't see it and still I search. The bird seems to be following me as I walk through the sea of wildflowers."

"And then what happens?"

"I look up and see a rainbow. Its colors are amazing. In the dream, I'm surprised to see it, as I don't remember any rain. My heart begins to beat quickly and my palms sweat. Maybe I'm afraid of being lost in the rows of flowers. But then I look up and see the rainbow. I want to reach out and touch it, but I can't...it's at that point I always wake up."

Mammi's voice shook as she turned her gaze to the world outside Anna's window. "The rainbow—it is God's promise to us. *Ya?*"

"I suppose."

Mammi clasped her hands in her lap. "Is that the end of it?"

"*Ya.* They sound so simple. I wish I could describe how I felt. Everything is so vivid and real. Sometimes...sometimes those dreams seem more real than the life I'm living."

Mammi bowed her head for several moments, not speaking.

Anna flipped over onto her side, which she'd learned to do, though it was an awkward movement and her legs flopped after the rest of her body had turned. She lay there, studying her grandmother.

When *Mammi* opened her eyes, she smiled, reached out, and patted Anna's hand. "Perhaps it will help, now that you have shared your dreams."

"Maybe. It felt good to talk about them." She yawned and admitted, "I suppose I'm ready for you to turn out the light, unless you'd like to continue knitting."

Mammi reached toward the battery-powered lantern—everyone had agreed that Anna shouldn't have gas lanterns in her room. The batteries had to be recharged, but Chloe happily took two sets home and recharged them each time she visited.

Anna closed her eyes, allowing sleep to claim her as she listened to the sound of her grandmother rocking in the dark.

CHAPTER 38

*I*t started as a summer cold the last week of June. A small cough. The occasional low-grade fever, which always broke in the morning. An ache seeping deep into her body.

By the first full week of July, Dr. Hartman was wanting to admit Anna to the hospital, and she was resisting with her last ounce of strength. She couldn't bear to leave her family again. She wouldn't. What difference would it make if she was miserable in the hospital or miserable in her own bed? She cried, pleaded, and eventually won.

Instead, they tried stronger antibiotics. A specially trained nurse arrived with the doctor the next day.

Her name was Mary Jo.

"Hi, Anna. I'm here to help you with your PICC line."

She was round and pleasant and smiling. More importantly, she was adept at what she was doing.

"First I'll give you a little local anesthetic to numb the skin and tissue." She donned a pair of plastic gloves from the box kept near Anna's bed. Then she tore open a sterile pad and dabbed at the large vein in her patient's arm above where the elbow was bent.

Anna coughed, caught her breath, and asked, "I won't need the shots anymore?"

"You won't. Everything will go through here, and it will be easier to maintain IV fluids you need." Mary Joe worked as she talked, and the doctor assisted her.

Anna thought that was funny, but she couldn't find the energy to share the joke. The doctor was assisting the nurse. The world was upside down.

Mary Jo inserted the PICC line, which she explained was a "peripherally inserted central catheter."

Anna was nearly asleep by the time they finished stitching around the catheter. Mary Jo sat beside her and squeezed her hand. Once she had Anna's attention she said, "Your regular visiting nurse will stop by each day. If this starts bothering you at all, have your aunt or uncle call us. I'll come back out right away and check on you."

Anna nodded, but she was already drifting off. For the rest of the day, she was aware of very little going on around her. She occasionally caught looks of concern passed over her head and heard whispered conferences that took place in the hall.

Her birthday came and went with a promise to celebrate once she was better, and behind those words she heard the unspoken concern— if she was better.

All work on the quilts and the produce stand and the garden stopped, but those same things filled her dreams. Fabrics sporting ponies, cows, and birds. Sunlight bouncing off buckets of fresh vegetables. Her fingers dipping into the dirt around the garden plants. Her parents and brothers and sister. Erin and Samuel and Jacob and *Mammi*.

Always her grandmother provided a bridge between sleeping and waking. At one point Anna thought to ask her if she ever left her room. Was she getting enough sleep? Was she eating? Perhaps it was time *Mammi* allowed someone else to sit beside her bed. When she managed to voice those concerns, *Mammi* would smile, pat her hand, and continue doing whatever piece of quilting or knitting that occupied her.

Time passed, hours and days when her condition stayed the same, until one afternoon for no apparent reason she suddenly worsened.

There was talk again of moving her, but there was little more that the doctors could do at the hospital. As Amish, the family did not believe in extreme measures. She was receiving excellent twenty-four-hour care from her loved ones and the nurses. Occasionally, a second bag of fluids was piggybacked on the IV because she became dehydrated. She simply couldn't stay awake long enough to eat or drink.

The visiting nurse easily managed these things, and the word *hospice* whispered through Anna's mind.

Was she dying? Would they tell her?

When her condition continued to deteriorate, it was decided—again—that she would fight this latest battle at home.

Each time Anna opened her eyes, it was *Mammi* that she saw, sitting beside her bed, knitting, reading the Bible—her voice a low steady melody that washed over Anna and cooled her brow.

"Why am I still here?" she asked one morning as a summer sun blazed outside the window.

"No one wants you back in the hospital."

"Doc Hartman—"

"Even he says you're receiving the same medicines here you would have there." *Mammi* nodded toward the side of Anna's bed.

She turned her head and saw a small metal stand holding a stack of medical supplies and the tall metal pole holding the IV bag.

"The nurses, they take *gut* care of you, Anna. Don't worry about having to return to the hospital. We all agree you'll get better faster in your home."

Anna blinked back tears and accepted the chips of ice *Mammi* spooned into her mouth.

"My *mamm*?"

"She will come next week if you haven't improved." *Mammi* returned to her chair, which she had scooted even closer to the bed. Reaching out, she claimed Anna's hand. "You have many visitors, Anna. Erin and Samuel, Jacob, and Bishop Levi. Some of the girls from church came by yesterday, and Rebecca Byler came the day before. She brought you some magazines from the store. All of these people are praying for you. Stay strong, child. Focus on letting the medicine work."

Anna's mind went back to her original question. She hadn't meant why was she still here—at her home. She'd meant why was she still here—on this earth. What was the point? She was such a burden to others. If she could not get well, could not return to the small things she enjoyed, what was the reason to tarry in this life? But she didn't say any of those things. Instead, she allowed herself to sink back into a restless, dream-filled sleep.

CHAPTER 39

The next time Anna woke, *Mammi* was not in the chair by her bed. Outside the window was a deep darkness. She could make out a smattering of stars and a quarter moon. The lantern beside the chair in the corner of the room was turned down low. She blinked again, wanting to clear the sleep from her eyes. Her mind felt fuzzy and full of cobwebs, but she made a valiant effort to focus on what was happening around her. That was when she recognized the sound—a soft sobbing. Glancing to her right, toward the door, she saw Erin and *Mammi*. Erin was swiping at her cheeks and *Mammi* was rubbing her back.

Why was she crying? What had happened?

Her heart raced as she imagined another tornado or someone hurt by the tractor. Then she heard Erin whisper her name and break into tears again. "Should we take her to the hospital?"

"Doc says it won't make any difference."

"But—"

"She'll either get better or she won't."

"I can't bear it. I can't lose another child. I know Anna is not mine, but it feels as if she is. I simply cannot go through that again."

"*Gotte* never gives us too much," *Mammi* reminded her. "Let's pray together, both of us, that He will spare our Anna."

She woke several times the next day, when Dr. Hartman was examining her, as the nurse administered still more meds through her catheter, and when they changed her sheets. None of those things bothered her. She was overwhelmed by the desperate need to fall back asleep. Her struggle to wake fully never lasted more than a couple of minutes. Eventually, she closed her eyes and stopped fighting the weariness. She allowed it to claim her.

That evening she dreamed again. These weren't the nightmares that had become familiar. These were new dreams, and they frightened her with their brightness and hope.

Her and Jacob, walking through a field and holding the hand of a small boy.

Erin preparing a large meal.

The bark of a dog, and Samuel working on the tractor, a smile on his face as the crops grew tall and thick around him.

Her mother and father, bending to kiss her.

Mammi, smiling as she touched the Bible in her lap.

Mammi, whispering the promises of God.

Mammi, believing.

Anna woke suddenly. Though the small battery-powered lamp dimly lit the room, there was enough light for Anna to see her grandmother. *Mammi* was there, sleeping in the living room chair, which had been brought into the corner of Anna's room. Her glasses were on the table beside her, resting on top of the Bible. Her face looked older without them, an assortment of lines and wrinkles—the map of a life rich and full and blessed by God.

Suddenly, Anna wanted to live.

More than she had ever wanted anything before, she longed to see another sunrise and to breathe with healthy lungs. She wanted to roll her chair out among the harvest. She wanted to marry Jacob. Tears flowed down her cheeks as she realized she'd been looking at her life all wrong. She'd been so focused on what she had lost since her accident that she hadn't stopped to consider what she'd gained.

She was no longer a stranger in her *aenti*'s home.

Her *onkel* cared for her deeply.

Jacob—always her heart returned to Jacob and his kind eyes, gentle touch, soft words.

They lived in a caring community that looked after one another.

Bishop Levi was a *gut* man. He would guide them through any troubles they faced. Hadn't he sat by her bed and prayed for her, for all of them?

The quilting allowed her to help others. She wanted to feel the pull of thread through fabric again, to piece together blankets of love for the children.

Anna saw it all clearly as she lay in the dimly lit room in the middle of the night and wept.

She saw her life, as it truly was, and she longed to grasp it and hold it to her breast.

"Please, *Gotte*. Give me another chance. Forgive me—*ya*, forgive me for all my sins. For not believing. For not appreciating." Sobs shook her body, and she squirmed down underneath the summer quilt on her bed. She didn't want to wake *Mammi*. She didn't want to alarm anyone, but suddenly the desire to cry out to God was overwhelming. She could no longer deny the need to bare her heart to Him and to share her hopes, her fears, and her dreams.

She wept and she prayed and she cast all of her cares on her heavenly Father. Once she had done so, she fell into a deep and restful sleep.

As she slept, her dreams were filled with light, warmth, and a peace unlike any she had ever experienced. Again she walked through a field of wildflowers that winked and nodded in the late afternoon sun. She held a folded quilt in her arms. When she glanced down she saw that rainbows danced across bright blue fabric. Hugging the quilt to her, she walked through the field of flowers and into crops which were ripe and ready for harvest. In the middle of what should have been Samuel's field, picnic tables had been arranged like those they set up after Sunday services. Sitting around the table was everyone Anna had ever loved—her parents, brothers and sister, and the members of her new community. Chloe and Jacob sat together, smiling at her.

"How can I see everyone...everyone in one place?" she murmured.

The answer seemed to come from all around her. Did she hear it? Or was it merely a truth beating in her heart? "They all love you, Anna. Everyone wanted to be here for this."

"I don't understand."

"It's not important for you to."

Anna realized the answers were correct. These people loved her. They always would. And she didn't need to understand what she was seeing. She only needed to experience this moment of complete peace and surrender to it. So she stepped forward, into the group, and she was surrounded by the unconditional, unlimited love of her family.

The sun was suddenly brighter, and she had the urge to cover her eyes.

Excitement rippled through the crowd, and fear quickened her pulse, but one look at Jacob assured her she had nothing to be afraid of. He motioned for her to look up. When she did she saw a clear blue sky, the sun setting and stars beginning to appear. Above and below, over and through the sunset and stars were rainbows—not one but hundreds of rainbows. The sight was more beautiful than anything she had ever seen.

Suddenly she remembered the bishop's words as he sat and prayed by her side.

And God said, "This is the sign of the covenant I am making between me and you and every living creature with you, a covenant for all generations to come."

She closed her eyes and allowed herself to bathe in the beautiful promise and healing warmth of God's Son.

CHAPTER 40

*A*nna woke early the next morning as the dawn began to streak across the eastern sky. The blind covering her window was raised, as it had been since she'd been bedridden, allowing her to study the colors of pink and lavender against the blue of a summer sky. It was beautiful—absolutely beautiful.

Mammi was once again in the straight-back chair beside her bed. She was quietly reading—from the Psalms—words of blessing and hope. "The whole earth is filled with awe at your wonders; where morning dawns, where evening fades, you call forth songs of joy." Anna was distracted by a distant memory, a dream of light and life-sustaining warmth. Gooseflesh pebbled her arms and her heart—her heart felt light.

She stretched. The breeze through the window tickled her skin. It was early, based on the softness of the light outside the window, but no doubt Samuel was already in the barn. Did she smell biscuits cooking? Her stomach growled, and she realized she was hungry. Ravenous, in fact.

"You're awake." *Mammi* placed her hand on top of her open Bible.

"*Ya*. Something smells *gut*."

"That would be Erin's biscuits. We also have fresh eggs that Mary Beth brought over."

"Sounds *wunderbaar*."

191

Mammi studied her, pushing her glasses up on her nose as if she needed to see better. "You look *gut*."

"*Ya?*" Anna smiled, realizing she felt good.

Mammi reached for the bottle of lotion and began rubbing it into Anna's arms.

"You never left me."

"Where would I go?"

"*Nein.* I mean that you stayed here—since I've been sick."

"I couldn't leave you, child, and don't look as if you're going to scold me, though you must be quite a bit better if you're feeling well enough to do that." *Mammi*'s smile was pure joy, and Anna thought of the picnic tables, and her family, and the rainbows.

"Have you ever seen a double rainbow?" She reached out and covered *Mammi*'s hand with her own.

"*Ya.* I have. It's a beautiful sight indeed." *Mammi* peered more closely at her. "Did you have the dreams again?"

Anna shrugged. A memory danced beyond her reach.

"Erin will be so happy to see you..." *Mammi* reached out and ran her fingertips across Anna's forehead. "To see that you're better. You gave us quite a scare."

"But you aren't afraid any longer."

"*Nein.*"

Anna felt an itch and rubbed her toe against the mattress to stop it.

Mammi turned quickly and stared at the bottom of the bed, where the quilt was tented over Anna's feet.

"What is it?" Anna asked, yawning again and shaking the last of sleep's cobwebs from her mind. She ran her hand through her hair, which felt as if it needed to be washed. "What are you staring at?"

"You—"

Anna met her grandmother's gaze, and she realized what *Mammi* was speaking of. She understood what had just happened. A slow smile spread across both of their faces. A smile which said this can't be, but maybe...maybe it was. Or was she dreaming again? But she had never dreamed this, never considered it could be possible.

"Anna, can you..." *Mammi* put a finger to her lips, closed her eyes for a moment, and popped them open again. "Can you move your feet?"

She pointed her feet to the left, to the right, and then she wiggled them back and forth.

Mammi reached under the blanket and pinched her right calf.

"Ouch!"

"You can feel that?"

"*Ya*, and it hurt!"

Mammi let out a whoop of pure joy. "Erin! Come here, Erin! Hurry!"

Erin ran into the room, a spatula in one hand, an egg in the other. "What is it? Is she—"

"Anna's well."

Erin closed her eyes, "*Danki. Danki*, Lord." She rushed to Anna's side. "Your color is better." She too placed a hand on Anna's forehead. "No fever. None at all."

"No, Erin. I'm not talking about the fever. Anna is *well*." *Mammi* motioned toward the end of the bed and gave Anna a pointed look. "Do it again."

Anna was suddenly filled with fear. What if they'd imagined it? What if she'd dreamed it? But *Mammi*'s pinch. That was real. She started with a small wriggle, scooting her feet left and right, left and right.

And she knew it was real.

She knew she was healed when Erin's eyes widened in surprise and all color left her face. She backed away from the bed and then fainted, dropping the spatula and the egg. The spatula bounced once, and the egg splattered on the wood floor. Anna stared at the brown eggshell and yellow yoke and remembered the girl with the quilt—ducks and a yellow border. She suddenly remembered, in complete detail, the dream of the night before. She remembered her family, the picnic tables, the bright sun, and the many rainbows.

Mammi rushed to Erin's side and knelt beside her. Anna tossed off her covers and swung her legs over the side of the bed, but then she was pulled back by the tug of the IV line. She swung her feet to the other side, stood, and pulled the IV pole with her as she walked over to Erin's side. *Mammi* looked up at her, her eyes widened in complete surprise, and her hand shaking as she reached for Anna's arm.

"What is it? What's wrong with *Aenti*?"

"Erin is fine. She only fainted. But Anna...Anna, you walked."

CHAPTER 41

*J*acob was working in the barn with Samuel. They'd both had their head stuck into the engine of the old tractor for the last hour.

"Try it now," Samuel said.

Jacob walked around and started the engine. The clatter was still there, but it no longer threatened to die. Maybe if they changed—

His thoughts were interrupted when he heard something that didn't belong. Something that caused his heart to skitter and his palms to sweat. It was *Mammi,* hollering at the top of her lungs. He reached back toward the steering column and turned off the tractor.

Samuel popped his head out from under the hood of the tractor. "Why did you—"

Then he heard it too. He dropped the rag and wrench, and together they ran toward the house.

What could have possibly happened? Why hadn't she used the emergency bell? Why was she running toward the barn?

"What is it? What's wrong?" Samuel grasped her by the shoulders. "Is it Anna?"

"*Ya. Ya.* It is." *Mammi's* hands were out, waving wildly toward the house. "Go to the house. Run! You too, Jacob. Run and see. Anna's well. Anna's healed."

Shock followed by doubt filled his heart and played across Samuel's face, but Jacob didn't stay to hear the rest of their conversation. He turned and ran to the house.

Not bothering to knock the mud off his shoes, he sprinted through the kitchen and down the hall to Anna's room. His mind was a white blur of confusion and anxiousness and hope.

Erin was in a sitting position but paler than the sheets on Anna's bed. Beside her, a spatula lay in a puddle of splattered egg.

Then he saw her.

Anna was kneeling on the floor beside Erin. Her IV pole had hung up on a bedside rug, and the line to her arm was drawn tight.

Why was she kneeling? How could she sit that way? And why was she consoling Erin?

His arms began to tremble, and he wondered if his legs would support him.

At that moment Anna looked up. Her eyes met his, and a smile crept across her face.

She got to her feet, reached for the IV pole, and walked toward him, rolling the pole beside her. She walked straight into his arms.

He didn't realize he was crying until she reached up to wipe away his tears.

"It's *gut, ya?*"

"But...how..."

Samuel crowded into the room, followed by *Mammi* and the nurse who had arrived for the morning shift.

"Anna?" Samuel's voice trembled. "Anna—"

She turned toward her uncle as he covered the few steps between them.

"Is it true? Are you...are you healed?"

Anna stared down at her legs—they all did. She was still wearing her nightgown, which reached nearly to her ankles. She wiggled her toes against the floor. "The wood is warm. It feels *gut.*"

Samuel let out a holler, swept her up in his arms, and twirled left and then right—going as far as the IV would allow. He laughed and kissed the top of her head. *Mammi* was shouting, "Our Lord is merciful! He has blessed us! He has heard our prayers!"

Sandy, the nurse who came daily to care for Anna, had arrived early this morning, and she went to Erin's side to help her to her feet. Erin walked to Anna and put both hands on her face, rubbing her thumbs back and forth as if she needed to touch her to believe her eyes. "Anna. How can this be? How can you walk?"

Instead of answering, Anna placed her arms around Erin, who was now openly weeping.

Sandy had been staring at Anna, her eyes wide and her mouth partially open. When Erin began crying, she seemed to snap out of her reverie. "I'll call Dr. Hartman." She hurried out of the room and to the front porch, clutching the phone she'd pulled from her pocket.

Suddenly Jacob's brain caught up with his heart. The enormity of what they were seeing smacked him, causing him to collapse onto Anna's bed.

A miracle.

Anna had experienced a miracle. She was healed. She was walking. His mind kept repeating those things, as if doing so would make the believing easier. He didn't need to believe, though. He only needed to look at the beautiful girl standing a few feet from him.

Everyone was talking at once. Erin was crying and *Mammi* was practically dancing a jig. Samuel had one arm around his wife and the other around his niece.

Jacob wanted to fall on his knees. Tears coursed down his face, and he reached up to wipe them away. He couldn't be dreaming. He tasted the salt of his tears and heard the weeping of Erin. He glanced at the floor and saw the track of mud he had left. Glanced across the room and saw the egg shell in a puddle of yolk.

This was real.

And Anna? She stood in the middle of it all, as a shaft of light broke through the window and bathed her in its rays.

His Anna was standing, watching him.

He didn't understand it, couldn't explain it, and would never have predicted it. But somehow, Anna was healed.

CHAPTER 42

Anna had trouble processing all of the emotions surging through her heart.

She might think she was dreaming but for the looks of wonder on Erin's, Samuel's, and Jacob's faces. The nurse seemed almost afraid, and she had quickly fled the room. *Mammi*, she accepted the mystery of what had happened better than anyone—as if what she'd longed for, hoped for, and prayed for had finally come true.

No one wanted to believe that she could dress herself without assistance. She asked them to send the nurse into the room to disconnect the PICC line.

The nurse came in a bit breathless. She'd always been kind, orderly, and efficient. Anna guessed she was in her mid-forties, possibly fifty. Neither large nor small, she always wore plain-colored scrubs. She was not an overly sentimental woman, but she now looked completely shaken.

"I called Dr. Hartman. He thinks you're having involuntary muscle spasms. He thinks—"

Anna reached out and touched the woman's arm. "I experienced the spasms in rehab. I know what they are like, Sandy, and they are not like this. I can walk."

The nurse gulped and sank into the chair beside Anna's bed.

"He's coming. He's coming to see. I told him—" Her hands waved toward the window. "And he's coming."

"I appreciate your taking care of me all these weeks." Anna smiled and kept her voice calm and low, trying to settle the woman's nerves. "The reason I asked for you is that I'd like you to remove my IV."

The nurse shook her head, as if she didn't understand the request.

"My fever is gone. I'd like to be able to move—to walk about—freely."

"But those weren't Dr. Hartman's orders. He said..." She met Anna's eyes and nodded slowly. "All right. If you insist."

"I do."

The process took a few minutes. Sandy cut and removed the sutures that held the line in place. She slowly pulled the catheter out, and then she covered the incision site with sterile gauze.

"Can you put light pressure on it for me?"

"*Ya*. Of course."

Sandy covered the entire area with a dressing. She nodded when Anna asked if she was finished.

"Do you need help?"

"*Nein*. I'm fine now. Would you tell my family I'll be out in a few moments?"

Sandy looked as if she might argue. Anna didn't wait to hear. She stood and walked to the bathroom, where she quietly but firmly shut the door. In all honesty, she needed a few moments alone.

To look at her feet. To feel the wondrous miracle of being able to stand. To fall to her knees and thank God for what He had done.

When she stood and began to dress, she reveled in the feeling of being able to put on her own shoes and stockings. She was just pinning her *kapp* when a tap on the door reminded her that her family was waiting to see her.

"Are you okay?" Erin opened the door and peeked inside.

Anna was standing in front of the sink, running water over her hands. She looked over at Erin before she reached forward and turned off the water. "I can't tell you how good it feels to be able to stand in front of a sink and wash my face. To feel the floor again. To move about. It's...it's truly amazing."

Erin nodded but remained silent.

Anna walked toward her, stopping a few feet shy. "*Aenti*, I can't thank you enough for taking such *wunderbaar* care of me."

Tears cascaded down Erin's cheeks. She nodded, clasped Anna's hand, and together they walked to the kitchen. When they entered the room, Anna saw that everyone was sitting around the table, except for the nurse, who stood in the doorway—watching her with unbelieving eyes.

"I'm starved," Anna said.

Suddenly everyone was talking at once. Jacob jumped up and dragged her chair to the table. For nearly a year that chair had sat in a corner of the room. She'd been in her wheelchair instead. But she wouldn't need that anymore. She would never have to sit in it again.

Samuel said, "Let's pray." The silence which surrounded her reminded Anna of the dream, of her family joined together there in the field of corn. Suddenly she could feel the presence of each of those persons. She knew, without a doubt, how much her family cared for her and how much she loved them.

The moment was broken by the cry of a bird outside the window. Jacob smiled at her, his eyes glued to her face. She glanced down at her plate in embarrassment. Had she walked into his arms? She had! And he had held her as if he would never let go.

Erin began to pass around the food, though no one started eating until Anna broke open a biscuit and sniffed it appreciatively.

"Butter?" *Mammi* asked.

"*Ya* and jam, please. I really am hungry."

They each began asking her questions, but it was Sandy who asked what was on everyone's mind.

She'd finally taken a seat at the far end of the table and was clasping a cup of coffee between her hands. Her face was still pale. "How did it happen, Anna?"

Anna dropped the biscuit on her plate and placed her hands in her lap, covering one with the other.

"I know this is real. It must be." The nurse glanced around at each of them. "I've been coming to your home for nearly a month. I've seen the X-rays in Anna's chart."

Now she looked directly at Anna. "You had a complete spinal cord break—a severe, irreparable, spinal cord injury. How is it that you can…" She swallowed and with great effort pushed on. "How can you walk?"

"I'm not sure." Anna hesitated, but only for a few seconds. She told them about waking in the middle of the night, about weeping and praying and calling out to God, about her desire to live. She began to tell them about the dream. Before she'd finished describing it, she was overcome by a sense of fullness and joy. She shook her head and said, "*Mammi* asked me once if I believed in miracles."

She glanced at her grandmother, who was nodding.

"You were filled with despair that day," *Mammi* said.

"I feared—I was certain that *Gotte* doesn't bless us with miracles anymore." Anna tapped her shoes against the floor. "But I was wrong."

"So it is a miracle?" Sandy asked.

"What else can it be?" Erin reached for the bowl of scrambled eggs and passed it to Samuel. "She couldn't walk and now she can. She was ill, on the edge of death's door, and now she is well."

Samuel had begun to eat, but he suddenly dropped his fork. It clattered against his plate. "We should tell the bishop." Without another word he pushed back from the table and hurried from the room.

Erin stood and ran after him. Anna could hear her on the porch. "Call Anna's mother and tell her, Samuel. Tell Martha about the miracle."

Through the kitchen window, Anna could see him hurrying across the yard. He didn't bother to get the tractor or hitch the horse to the buggy. He didn't look back.

Erin returned to the table.

Sandy was frowning into her coffee now. "But miracles don't happen. I've been a nurse for more than twenty years, and I've seen things that are hard to explain, sure. But a miracle? No."

Jacob nudged Anna's foot with his under the table. When she glanced up at him, he asked, "Do you think…can you tell if it's permanent?"

She shrugged. "I was afraid I might be imagining things, but this isn't a dream." She put her hand against the table and ran her fingers over the smooth grain of the wood. "This is real."

They managed to eat breakfast, stopping often to recount their first thoughts, their surprise, their gratitude to God.

Sandy tried to convince Anna to rest. She didn't want her patient to push herself too hard. "Perhaps you should take it easy until the doctor gets here. Until we can be sure—"

"*Nein.* I've been in that bed long enough. What I'd like…"

Jacob had barely taken his eyes off her throughout the meal. Now he leaned forward. "What is it? Tell me."

"I'd like to walk out in the garden and in the fields."

So they did.

Mammi said she was too tired to join them. Sandy wanted to wait in the house for Dr. Hartman. Erin stayed at the sink, claiming she needed to wash the dishes. But when Anna glanced back, she saw her staring out of the window at them. Anna waved, and then she turned back to Jacob.

"You're okay?" he asked. "You don't feel tired or—"

"I feel fine. I am. I would tell you if I was tired."

They walked to the garden. Anna allowed her fingers to trail up and down the plants that had been placed in containers and elevated so she could work on them. "Someone has been looking after my garden."

"*Ya.* We didn't want it to wither while you were sleeping your days away."

The fact that he could joke helped Anna to relax.

"Those days seemed to drag on forever." She raised her face to the sun, sat on a bench, and took off her shoes and socks.

"Is something wrong?"

She pushed her toes into the warm Oklahoma dirt. "*Nein.* I wanted to feel—"

He covered her hand with his. "I understand."

"You do?" She cocked her head to the side and smiled.

"Yes. I've been waiting, Anna. Not for you to be healed. I never thought…" He ran his hand through his hair. "I never thought that was possible. My faith, it should have been stronger."

"I didn't believe it could happen either!"

"I should have though. I should have believed." He turned to her now, his face colored by his emotions. "But it never mattered. Your injury wasn't important. All that was important was what I felt for you, and how sure I was that *Gotte* had connected our lives for a reason."

She reached out and squeezed his arm. Her emotions mirrored his exactly, but suddenly she felt too shy to admit it. He knew anyway. She could tell from the way he looked at her that he understood how she felt about him.

"Let's go and see the corn," she said, picking up her socks and shoes and carrying them to the porch. She placed them side by side on the bottom step, wiggled her toes again into the dirt, and smiled up at Jacob.

They continued into the fields as the morning sun rose in the sky. The cornstalks were shoulder high. Anna held Jacob's right hand with her left and let the fingers of her right hand graze the plants. The earth felt delicious between her toes. The sun was a caress to her face. They didn't talk but rather enjoyed the moments of peace. She couldn't have said why, but something told her it wasn't going to last for long.

CHAPTER 43

*C*hloe was on her way to cover the noon dedication of a new skateboard park in Pryor Creek when she received a call from her boss.

"I need you to get to Cody's Creek right now!" Eric's words came out fast and jumbled, as if he had been running.

"Cody's Creek? What about the skateboard park?"

"Forget that story. I'll send someone else. Where are you?"

"North side of town."

"How long will it take you to get there?"

"Maybe an hour?"

"Do it. I'll have a cameraman meet you outside of Anna's."

Chloe had been talking on her phone while driving, something she was loathe to do. Too many people didn't pay attention while on the road. A call from Eric wasn't one she could ignore, so she'd answered it. At the mention of Anna's name, she took the upcoming exit and pulled over in a gas station parking lot.

"What are you talking about, Eric? Why do you sound so strange? And what's wrong with Anna?"

"So you haven't heard?"

"Heard what?"

"They're saying she's healed."

"*What?*" The word came out louder than she intended. Her friend had been through enough in the last year, and her recent illness had left her on the steps of death's door. She didn't need rumors like this and the media attention it would bring.

"Our weatherman lives out that way. He stopped in at the Dutch Pantry for breakfast and heard about it. He says there's a big group of people already at her place."

"She's paralyzed, Eric. I was there when the doctor explained that the injury to her spinal cord was irreversible."

"Great point. You'll also want to interview the doctor as soon as you can corner him. But first get to Cody's Creek. I want this story. We'll run video on our website, and I want pictures for our next edition." Eric hung up the phone before Chloe could remind him that the Amish did not allow themselves to be recorded on camera. She started up her car, but before putting it into drive she called her mother. The call went to voicemail.

"Mom, something has happened with Anna. I'm headed out there now, but please say a prayer for her. I think this could be bad. It's not that she's worse. Nothing like that. I'll call back with more details when I have a chance."

She envisioned a dozen different scenarios as she drove toward Samuel's farm, but nothing prepared her for the sight that confronted her when she turned down the road which led to their lane.

Cars had parked haphazardly down both sides of the road. She noticed Manuel, their photographer, standing beside his old pickup and waving at her. He'd somehow managed to save an area big enough for her to park in. By the time she got out of her car, he'd retrieved his camera equipment.

She opened the back door of her car, grabbed her purse and, as an afterthought, a ball cap. They might be standing in the sun for hours. The last thing she needed was a sunburn on her scalp.

"What's going on?"

"No idea." Manuel adjusted the ball cap he always wore. "Some are saying she's healed. Others are saying it's a hoax. The police department arrived thirty minutes ago to keep folks off the property."

"Good grief. What is wrong with people?"

"Aren't you curious? It's not every day you get to see a miracle." Manuel grinned at her as they hiked toward the entrance to Samuel's farm.

"Is that supposed to be funny?"

Manuel hitched his camera bag up higher on his shoulder. "Don't know. The whole thing is kind of freaky."

Chloe had to remind herself that Manuel was barely out of college. He couldn't possibly understand how disturbing this type of public attention could be to an Amish family. Instead of trying to explain, she said, "Catch B roll of the crowd and police officers. Remember, no photos of the Amish."

"But Eric said—"

"No photos, Manuel. We're going to do our job, but we're also going to respect their wishes."

They both stopped abruptly when they came around the corner of the lane.

There was a large group of people, more than a hundred if Chloe were to guess, standing on their side of a police barricade. The crowd seemed to be half Amish and half *Englisch*. Everyone's attention was focused on the house, which could barely be seen from where they stood.

Manuel glanced at Chloe, and she gave him the okay sign. They would only be catching the size of the crowd and the back of folks. She knew from experience that Amish didn't mind having their pictures taken as long as they weren't identifiable in the photo.

Chloe noticed reporters from several of the big newspapers and even a few television crews. All were on her side of the barricade. Two sheriff's deputies stood at the barricade to make sure no one crossed the line.

Chloe pushed her way through to the front of the crowd.

"Ma'am, I'm going to have to ask you to step back." The man looked to be in his forties, had a crew cut, and wore a name tag that said "Starnes."

"Officer Starnes, I'm a friend of the family—"

"Uh-huh." He stared pointedly at her press pass.

Chloe yanked it off. "Yes, I'm with the paper, but I'm also Anna's friend. I need to be in there."

"Sorry, miss. The boss's orders were *no one* passes these barricades, especially press."

"Please, call. Call your boss and ask him. Tell him to ask Anna. She will want to see me."

Starnes looked toward the other officer, who had been listening to their conversation. He shrugged, and Starnes pulled the radio off his belt.

Two minutes later, Chloe was walking up the lane.

There had been quite the ruckus when the officers let her through. One lady had thrown herself at Chloe. "I need to go with you. I have cancer—brain cancer. Please, let me go—"

The officers had stepped in to pull the woman away. The entire episode had unnerved Chloe, though she noticed that Manuel snapped several pictures of the event.

Now that she was walking toward the house, with the crowd behind her, she allowed her mind to go over what had happened so far.

Someone had reported that Anna was healed. Word had leaked out, as word is bound to do in a small town. And now there was a crowd of folks—some gawkers, some people in search of a miracle—desperate to see her friend.

To think that when she got out of bed that morning, she had feared it would be a slow news day.

There appeared to be no one working in the barn and no one on the front porch. Three cars were parked in the gravel area between the barn and house. One was obviously the sheriff's patrol car. Chloe thought she recognized the white sedan. She'd seen it there before, so it must belong to one of the visiting nurses. The third car—a black Mercedes with tinted windows—she'd never seen.

She walked to the front door and tapped lightly.

All of the shades were pulled down, which struck her as odd. Usually the shades were up and the windows raised.

Then she saw that the windows were open, allowing a small amount of breeze into the room. But why were the shades pulled down?

Samuel answered the door, stepped closer to the screen, and peered past her. Satisfied she was alone, he opened the door, motioning for her to enter quickly.

"What's going on, Samuel? Why are all these people here?"

Instead of answering, he nodded toward the sitting room. "Go on in. She wants to see you."

What Chloe saw next would be forever imprinted on her mind.

Erin and *Mammi* sat on the couch, hands folded, expressions unreadable. Jacob stood near the wall, fidgeting with his hat and frowning. Dr. Hartman and the nurse stood to the side, deep in conversation. Bishop Levi sat in the chair across from the ladies. And standing by the window, her arms crossed and her foot tapping impatiently against the floor, was Anna.

Chloe felt her world shift, literally tilt, and she shook her head to clear it. She couldn't be seeing what she was seeing. It wasn't possible.

Then Anna looked at her and smiled, and she knew it was true.

She hurried to her friend's side, grabbed her hands, and pulled her into a hug.

Somehow what couldn't happen, had happened. Anna was healed.

CHAPTER 44

Twenty minutes later, they were in the kitchen at the table, just the two of them.

Chloe had a glass of water, Anna had a glass of milk, and a plate of cookies sat between them.

At Anna's insistence, Chloe had taken notes.

"Someone is going to put it in the papers. It might as well be you."

Now Chloe looked back over what she had written. But they were only words on a page—words she expected no one would believe. She glanced up at Anna, who stood, picked up the cookie plate, and said, "I might as well take this to the sitting room. Someone will eat them if we don't."

Chloe watched her walk out of the room. She had a thousand questions. She felt shaky and ecstatic at the same time. Her reporter's brain was fighting with her heart.

How could this have happened?

It was true. There was no doubt about what she was seeing. But how? She'd begun attending church again last winter, at the height of her depression over Anna's condition. She couldn't have explained to anyone why Anna's injury had affected her so severely, but it had. She'd needed to look for answers to her questions about why such terrible things happen to good people. She'd wanted to know what kind of God could allow such a thing. She had hoped to understand all that had happened to her friend.

But church didn't provide her with those types of answers. It did start her reading the Bible again, though somewhat sporadically. It brought her closer to her mother. It reminded her of the faith of her childhood. But she wasn't a child any longer, and now she had more questions than ever.

If she didn't file this story, Eric would probably fire her, and then he'd send someone else to do it. Someone who more than likely would know nothing about the Amish or their customs and beliefs.

The enormity of what she was about to do sank into her heart like a stone. She was about to file a report on a miracle. How could she do that? How could she possibly find the words to report what she was seeing? And be objective? Well, that was impossible.

Anna walked back into the room. "The sheriff says there are even more people out there. He suggested we go away for a while."

"Will you?"

"*Nein. Onkel* has work to do in the fields. Jacob is helping him. *Aenti* and *Mammi*? Why would they leave? And *Onkel* called my mother. She's on her way here. She promised to take the bus today." Anna shook her head. "We can't leave."

"You could go alone. Go back to your home in Goshen."

Anna stood with her back against the counter and her hands in the pockets of her apron. Perhaps she didn't understand the seriousness of what lay ahead, because she smiled and said, "Why would I leave? This is my home."

"Yes, but…maybe the sheriff has a good point. Maybe it would be the wise thing to do until another big story comes along and folks become distracted and leave."

Anna frowned and pulled one of her *kapp* strings forward. "I'm ready to start quilting again, and gardening, and keeping the produce stand—"

"You might be able to do the first two, but there's no way you're going to be able to sell produce out of the stand. Do you realize how many people are out there? Not to mention the newspaper and television crews."

"Media! Oh, my!" Anna nearly laughed as she said it. "You're all the same, aren't you."

Chloe cleared her throat and put on her most serious expression. "I know you're teasing, but many reporters are ruthless. I don't think you understand, Anna. Some people will do anything for a story, and this story? It's big."

Anna waved her concerns away, but then she sat down next to Chloe and grabbed her hands.

"Don't you see? It's as if I've been given a second chance. Am I supposed to be afraid of the people waiting in our lane? I don't feel afraid of anything. I feel marvelously alive."

Tears pricked Chloe's eyes.

"I don't know why, Chloe. You asked me that question. Look back at your notes. I don't know why me or why now. I don't understand any of it." She tapped her feet against the floor. "I only know that I couldn't stand or walk. My life was changed the day the tornado came across my *onkel's* field. And now it has changed again."

Before Chloe could think of how to respond, Erin walked into the room. "If you two are finished, the doctor would like to talk to all of us."

"*Ya*, sure." Anna squeezed Chloe's hand, and together they walked into the sitting room.

Dr. Hartman had stepped out onto the front porch to use his phone. The bishop moved from the chair, though now he was vigorously chewing a piece of gum and occasionally blowing bubbles with it. The image settled Chloe's nerves. Samuel was seated on the couch with *Mammi* and Erin. Jacob walked over and stood beside her and Anna. Sandy stood at the window, dividing her attention between watching the doctor and staring at Anna. The sheriff had left.

A few moments later Dr. Hartman walked back into the room. He glanced around at each of them, but finally turned his attention to Anna. "I'd like you to come back to Tulsa. I want to run a few tests."

CHAPTER 45

"I don't want to go back to the hospital. I don't *need* to go back to the hospital." Anna resisted the childish urge to stomp her foot. She wasn't a child. She was a woman, and they couldn't make her go.

"I understand a little of how you feel." Dr. Hartman stared at the floor for a moment. When he glanced back up, looking directly at her, Anna realized for the first time that he was merely a man. She'd always been a little in awe of doctors and nurses. Of their skill and their knowledge. It was plain from the look on his face that Dr. Hartman didn't understand what had happened any better than they did. His knowledge and his skill only went so far.

"You're well now. You've been given your life back, and you want to be left alone to enjoy it."

Anna nodded slowly. That was exactly what she'd been thinking.

"But you couldn't walk and now you can. I've been your doctor since that fateful day you were brought into Oklahoma Surgical, Anna." He shook his head and the next thing he said was more to himself than to her. "I didn't read those X-rays wrong. You shouldn't be able to walk."

"What is the point of the tests?" Bishop Levi tapped his cane against the floor. "We are thankful for your help with Anna, but she was healed by *Gotte*. A miracle is not something that can be explained. It's not something that will show up on your tests."

"But it will. The MRI will show if her spine is actually healed. And possibly...maybe there is something we would see that would help someone else. I don't know what. I can't even imagine, but I also didn't believe Anna could walk when Sandy called me."

"It might help others?" Anna crossed her arms. She didn't want to ever walk inside a hospital again, but if it could help someone who was enduring a lifetime in a wheelchair, perhaps she should.

"How would you even get her there?" Samuel asked. "You heard the sheriff. A lot of people are waiting to catch a glimpse of her. How would you get her off the farm without at least some of those people following?"

"We'll transport her in an ambulance. The sheriff department would probably provide us with an escort if we need it."

Samuel shook his head. "We live our life separate—and quietly. I don't want Anna to be followed around like some movie star."

"Your *Englisch* vehicle, it has dark windows, yes?" *Mammi* had been fairly quiet all morning. Now she pushed up on her glasses, stood, and walked over to Anna, stopping in front of her.

When she reached up and touched her face, Anna closed her eyes. Her grandmother's love was both deep and wide. It was a miracle in itself.

"Go and help the children, Anna. Perhaps *Gotte* will use you today. You can wear Chloe's ball cap over your *kapp*. If anyone gets close enough to look through the windows, they will only see the ball cap. Perhaps they will think they're seeing Chloe."

"Wearing *Englisch* clothes, disguising herself—I'm not sure that's something we want to do." Samuel also stood, now obviously agitated, but Levi reached out and touched his shoulder.

"It's *gut* that you are thinking these things through, Samuel. It's *gut* that you care about your family as well as your commitment to the *Ordnung*." Levi stood, leaned against the cane with his left hand, and ran the fingers of his right through his beard. "But these are extraordinary circumstances, and perhaps we should deal with them as such. I think Ruth's idea is a *gut* one."

Anna smiled at the use of *Mammi*'s name. Nearly everyone simply called her *Mammi*, but Levi had known her for a long time.

"Will you do it, Anna?" Dr. Hartman looked hopeful. "Will you come with me?"

"I'd rather not go alone."

"I'll go." Sandy stepped forward. "I'll be happy to ride in the back-seat with you."

"It would probably be best if you followed in your car, Sandy. No doubt some in the crowd already know who we are and what we drive. They will only see the doctor and nurse leaving. There will be no need to follow us."

"I could follow in my car if you'd like me to be there with you," Chloe said. "And I can bring you back."

Anna squeezed her hand. It seemed they had found a way to fulfill Dr. Hartman's request.

"That's a good idea," the doctor said. "But perhaps you should wait a few moments—so they don't see a whole convoy of cars leaving at once."

"I'll ride in the back with Anna. No one will be able to tell whether I'm Amish or not." Jacob touched the top of his head. "I'll keep my hat off."

Samuel nodded in agreement, and Anna felt butterflies spin in her stomach. She'd been healed for only a few hours, and she was headed back to the hospital.

She glanced over at her quilting, which sat where she'd left it before she'd first fallen ill with the summer cold. The fabric with frogs was pieced together but not quilted. It was folded and waiting for her to return to the task. The quilt was for a child. And this trip? It was for a child too. Anna didn't know who, and she didn't know how it would help, but she was learning that she could trust God with the details.

Everyone began moving at once.

Erin went to Anna's room to fetch her purse. Jacob had been work-ing on the tractor with Samuel before the morning had taken a dra-matic turn. He hadn't noticed before now, but his shirt was covered with tractor grease. He disappeared for a moment and returned in a clean shirt, one he had apparently borrowed from Samuel.

Erin and the bishop stepped out onto the front porch, where Dr. Hartman was once again on his phone.

Sandy retrieved the nursing bag she carried with her everywhere.

Chloe pulled the ball cap off her head. It was black with a blue letter on the front. "I'm glad I'm going with you—and I don't mean so that I can report on it. I want to be there, Anna. You mean a lot to me." She handed the cap to her friend.

"What's this for?" Anna pointed to the T.

"Tulsa Drillers, minor league baseball team." Chloe placed it on Anna's head. "It's my good luck cap too, so don't lose it."

Anna smiled and started to turn toward the front door, but Chloe pulled her back. "Don't let the crowd frighten you. Okay? They're only people—some curious, some desperate—but only people."

"Got it. They are only people." Anna hurried out into the sunshine to Dr. Hartman's car. She and Jacob slid onto the backseat. It struck her as funny to see Dr. Hartman sitting up front all alone. Anna thought of Clarence, the driver of the handicap van. He always sat up front by himself, though she couldn't imagine much else that the two men shared in common. She suddenly realized that she'd like to see Clarence again. Many of the people who had become important in her life were people she no longer needed. That thought bothered her, and she pushed it away.

They began moving down the lane.

Anna thought she was prepared for what was ahead. She'd certainly seen large crowds of people at the auctions they had held to help the tornado victims and even back home in Goshen, but nothing could have prepared her for the chaos at the end of their lane.

Two officers had positioned their vehicles to allow for a gap barely large enough for their car to pass through. Dr. Hartman must have called ahead, because the officers had been guarding that open space, but at the sight of the black automobile, they moved out of the way.

Instantly the crowd surged forward.

A small scream escaped from Anna. She was sure they would run over someone, but Dr. Hartman simply continued to move forward at a slow but steady speed. When he didn't stop or even pause, the people parted much like Anna had always envisioned the Red Sea parting for Moses.

There were all manner of people waiting in the hot summer sun. Some held signs.

Help me, Anna.
God is alive.
Repent and believe.
Another hoax!

The signs didn't disturb her nearly as much as the faces did. The person holding the hoax sign hollered at the person holding the God sign. They converged on each other and for a moment the majority of people were distracted. Dr. Hartman was able to speed up a little and pull away from the main crowd.

That was when Anna saw that the line of cars stretched well past their farm. That was when she saw the people in wheelchairs, being pushed down the road toward her home.

"Why are they doing this?" she whispered.

No one in the car had an answer.

CHAPTER 46

*J*acob hadn't been in the Tulsa hospital before. He had wanted to visit when Anna was there, but it had seemed that he would be a better help to her by staying at the farm. And at the time he'd barely known her.

That seemed odd to him now.

He couldn't imagine his life without Anna. Glancing at her as they sped along the Oklahoma freeway, he wondered if she realized that. Did she know how much he cared? He'd confessed his feelings to her on at least two separate occasions, but how could words describe the emotions pressing on his heart? Now wasn't the right time to try again, especially with Dr. Hartman in the front seat and possible stalkers behind them.

The physician didn't speak much as they traveled toward Tulsa, though he talked occasionally on his phone through the car's Bluetooth system. A motorist who had given Jacob a ride back in Indiana had explained it to him. It seemed *Englischers* spent a lot of effort and money finding ways to do two things at once, but who was he to judge? His life wasn't exactly a straight arrow.

Jacob noticed that Dr. Hartman glanced in the rearview mirror often, as if to be sure that Anna was still there.

She had been visibly upset when she saw the folks outside her *onkel's* farm. Jacob couldn't say he was surprised at the size of the mob, but then he'd traveled more than she had. He'd seen some strange things. A memory hit him of the time he'd been hitchhiking from one small town in Ohio to another. He'd seen a crowd of folks pulling off from the road. They parked on the grass because the parking area around a small store was full. Curious, he had walked over to see what the fuss was about. A man had been standing under a large tree selling small bottles of water. He claimed the water came from a river in South Africa, and that it had special powers—healing powers.

Jacob had shaken his head and continued walking. He didn't see how water from South Africa could be any different than water from Sugar Creek, Ohio. But the people who had been standing around were reaching for their wallets.

"Have you ever been to Tulsa before?" Anna nervously cracked her knuckles as she stared out the window at the tall buildings.

"*Ya.* My bus came right through the city. I didn't want to go farther south, so I got off." Jacob laughed at the memory. "But I didn't see any Amish."

"What did you do?"

"There's a mission downtown, a place that allows you to sleep for free and gives you two meals a day—breakfast and dinner. I stayed there for three days, and then a counselor met with me. He told me there were only two Amish communities in Oklahoma—one in Clarita."

"I've never been there."

"It's small, with only a few families, or so this man said. The other was Cody's Creek."

"That's why you came to our town."

"Yes."

"I wouldn't have met you if it wasn't for him."

Jacob started to argue. He was certain they had been destined to meet. He had no doubt that God would have found a way to put him in Cody's Creek, but before he could say that, Dr. Hartman began to explain to them what was going to happen when they reached the hospital.

"We'll go in through the doctor's entrance. That should keep you away from the news media."

"They're here?" Anna asked.

"I wouldn't be surprised. With Google it's easy to figure out what hospital you were originally brought to. If I remember right, all the newspapers covered it."

"But they have no reason to believe Anna is here now." Jacob reached over and enfolded her hand in his.

"Standard procedure. They'll position a few reporters and camera crews out front." Dr. Hartman pulled into a parking garage. "I could be wrong, but it's best to be prepared for the worst-case scenario."

A woman Anna seemed to know met them as soon as they exited the elevator. She wore nurse's scrubs and had a pleasant manner, though she glanced at Anna and away constantly—never quite making eye contact. It occurred to Jacob that she seemed almost afraid of her. He could have been imagining that, though. It already felt like a long day, and it was only noon.

Sandy had pulled in behind them. She hurried off to make sure the paperwork was ready for Anna's tests. Apparently, they didn't want her to have to spend any time in the waiting room.

Anna, Jacob, and Dr. Hartman walked down a long hall and through a set of double doors. Beyond that was another set of doors with the word "Radiology" above them. Also on the door was a yellow triangle, bordered in black and sporting what looked to Jacob like a black fan in the middle. When he asked Hartman about it, he explained that it was required to post the sign so that people would be aware they were walking into a restricted area.

"Everyone from nurses to patients to maintenance workers needs to be aware that they are working around contaminated materials."

Anna didn't seem surprised by any of this, but everything the doctor was saying concerned Jacob.

"It's nothing for you to worry about. You'll wait over there, in the waiting area. Anna will go back into one of the rooms with an MRI machine."

"And it's safe for her?"

"Yes. Quite safe."

Anna put a hand on his arm. "I've done this several times, Jacob. It doesn't hurt and allows them to take a picture of my spine."

A nurse stepped through the doors and strode toward them. "They're waiting for you, Anna. I'll walk you back there."

Anna nodded and then turned toward Jacob. "This shouldn't take long."

He reluctantly went down the hall to the tiny room with a television in the corner and a stack of magazines on a table. There was only one other person there—a stooped, older woman.

"Doctors and their tests," she muttered to herself, though he thought it might be for his benefit. "They simply want to drain all the money they can out of us. And for what? I can tell my spine is curved."

She shuffled away when a technician came for her. Jacob was relieved to have the room to himself.

Chloe hurried in. "She's already having the tests? Where's Sandy?"

"Anna went back a few minutes ago. Sandy went to check on the paperwork so Anna could go straight in. I haven't seen her since we arrived. How was your drive?"

"A little strange. I had two cars follow me from Samuel's."

"They followed you here?"

"No." Chloe walked over to a vending machine, put a dollar in, and received a bottle of water in return. "Do you want anything, Jacob?"

He shook his head. What he wanted was to take Anna home. "What happened with the cars? The ones that were following you?"

"I took the exit for the Hard Rock Casino on the east side of town."

"You went to a casino?"

"I didn't go in. I drove through the parking garage, came out the other side, made sure I'd lost them, and got back on the freeway. That's why I'm a little late."

Jacob sat forward, his elbows propped on his knees. "I've seen people act in strange ways before, but this...why would they follow you?"

Chloe shrugged. "It's a big story. A lot of people are looking for miracles. A lot of them pray for one every day but never receive it. And then there are the skeptics."

Jacob thought of the signs folks were holding as they waited outside of Samuel's property. How long would they wait there? What did they expect to happen?

"How did it go here? With the staff?"

"What do you mean?"

"How did they treat Anna? Were they friendly?"

"*Nein*, not friendly. Not exactly."

"What do you mean? I would think Anna would already know the nurses and technicians on this floor. She's been here often enough."

"I think Anna did know the nurse. She greeted her by name. But the woman acted a little distant, almost as if she was afraid to touch her." Jacob shook his head. "I could be seeing emotions that aren't there."

Chloe sighed and took a long drink from her bottle of water. "The next few days are going to be hard, Jacob. Maybe as hard as when she was first injured. Anna's going to need her family and her friends to be there for her."

"I'm not going anywhere. I'll do whatever she needs me to."

"I can see why she likes you so much. You're one of the good guys."

Jacob didn't know how to answer that. Anna had said she liked him? And why was he one of the good guys? What had he ever done that was so out of the ordinary? He was only doing what anyone would do, at least anyone from their community.

But that wasn't exactly true, and he realized it even as the thought crossed his mind. What he felt for Anna—it was special. Other people had been kind to her, but he'd been willing to do anything to brighten her day. He'd stayed in Oklahoma because of her, and he wasn't about to leave now.

The wait seemed to stretch on interminably, but according to the clock they'd been there less than an hour when Anna joined them.

"Any problem?" Chloe asked.

"*Nein*. The test is simple enough."

"What did the technician say?"

"He didn't say anything." She glanced at Jacob and back at Chloe. "But he seemed a little nervous."

Jacob barely had time to think about that because Dr. Hartman walked in.

"I'd like us to go to my office if that's okay."

They went down another long hall that led to an elevator, which carried them to a different floor. When they reached his office, an elderly woman who looked at them kindly sat at a desk outside the main office.

"Cushing?" Hartman asked.

"Already waiting for you."

"Hold my calls please, Judith. I don't want to be disturbed."

"Yes, Dr. Hartman."

They walked into a well-furnished office. Jacob had guessed that Dr. Hartman was an important doctor at the hospital. The bank of windows, expensive cherry wood furniture, and leather chairs confirmed that. On the wall were several diplomas and pictures of Dr. Hartman with various patients. Other photos showed him shaking the hands of city officials. Jacob knew this because each picture was framed with a mat and a label explaining the photo. Another man stood beside Dr. Hartman's desk.

"This is Brent Cushing. He's the president of the hospital."

Dr. Hartman introduced everyone, and then they sat down.

"It's good to meet all of you." Dr. Cushing was middle-aged with short black hair.

"As president of the hospital, Dr. Cushing has access to all records," Dr. Hartman said. "He's reviewed your chart, Anna, and he's also looked over the results from today's test—we both have."

"I'm going to be honest with you. I've never seen anything like this." Dr. Cushing cleared his throat. "I've worked with Dr. Hartman for a number of years, and I don't doubt his records or his assessment. I also don't doubt what I've seen with my own eyes."

He had been talking to all of them, but now he turned and looked directly at Anna.

"Can you explain what happened, Anna? Do you have any idea why you can walk?"

She didn't answer. She shrugged, as if she hadn't a clue. None of them had any idea what had happened. Jacob had been too busy, too excited, to give it much thought. Or perhaps he had blocked the questions, ones that couldn't be answered, from his mind.

"What did the test show?" she asked.

Dr. Hartman opened a file and pulled out two sheets of film. He walked over to a box on the wall and pushed a switch that turned on a light behind it. "We keep most records on the computer now, but I wanted you to be able to see the actual film. This is your spine after your accident, Anna. Clearly, a break is here." He pointed to a spot three-quarters of the way down Anna's spine.

Jacob had an urge to walk across the room and touch the film, to touch the spot where her spine had been severed. Better yet, he wanted to reach out to Anna and clasp her hand as he had in the car. But he stayed where he was, watching, listening, and wondering.

"This is your spine today." Hartman slipped the second picture onto the light box next to the first one.

It was obvious, even to Jacob, that there was nothing wrong with the second picture. There was no break.

"Your spine is healed, Anna. Not only is it healed, but there's no evidence that it was ever broken—no scar tissue, no nerve damage, nothing to suggest you'd had an accident. After nearly a year in a wheelchair your muscle tone had deteriorated markedly, and yet you're able to walk with no trouble."

"That's *gut*, right?" Anna glanced around the room. "I don't understand it any better than anyone else, but it's a *wunderbaar* thing."

"Yes, of course it is." Dr. Cushing steepled his fingers. "However, I'd like to propose that we look at this in the broader context. How did it happen? Why did it happen? Perhaps there's something you did...some herb..."

He stopped midsentence, and for the first time it seemed that his confidence was shaken. He stood and walked to the window, his hands in his pockets. When he turned back to look at them, he shook his head. "That's absurd. I realized it even as the words came out of my mouth. I think we all know an herb can't heal a spinal cord injury. Nothing can. Dr. Hartman is one of the best surgeons in the country. He couldn't have operated on you with these results. There was no need to operate because your injury was irreparable. What we're seeing is...well, it's impossible."

"It's not impossible," Chloe said. "Anna is proof of that."

"Which is why we'd like to run some more tests. If you would be willing to stay a few days—"

Anna stood and drew the strap of her purse over her shoulder. When she did, Chloe and Jacob stood as well.

"*Nein.* I won't stay a few more days, and there won't be any more tests."

Neither physician looked surprised.

"I want to thank you for taking care of me while I was sick, but I'm well now. If the test you did today can help you understand what happened and perhaps help others with my condition, feel free to use it. But after today, I hope never to see you again. No offense."

Jacob wanted to cheer. He wanted to put his arms around Anna and swing her in a circle. He wanted to take her home.

At that moment, there was a knock on the door, and Dr. Hartman's receptionist stepped inside.

"I'm afraid we have a problem."

CHAPTER 47

*C*hloe wasn't surprised that the press had found them. She was a member of that particular tribe. She understood all too well how desperate reporters were to catch a big story, and this story could be huge. She was still struggling to believe it herself.

After the receptionist had explained the size of the crowd outside the hospital, including three major television stations and several national affiliates, Dr. Cushing took charge.

"Dr. Hartman will drive you home now. You can leave the way you came."

"Actually, I was going to drive them home." Chloe looked to Anna and Jacob for confirmation.

They both nodded, though they looked a bit stunned at the latest turn of events.

"We could get a police escort," Dr. Hartman suggested.

"*Nein*. I don't want that. I just want to go home."

"Very well," he said. "Where did you park, Chloe?"

"In the outpatient lot."

"Which is on the other side of the building from our main entrance. Good. Why don't you bring your car around to the employees' entrance. I'll have Judith call ahead and tell the attendant to allow you through."

"I'll release a statement to the press." Dr. Cushing stood and straightened his suit jacket. "That should keep them occupied for a little while."

They had gathered their things and were hurrying out of the office when Anna stopped. She turned to Dr. Cushing. "What will you say?"

"Basically? *No comment*, but I'll say it in such a way as to keep them occupied long enough for you all to get away." He paused before he said, "Anna, I understand why you don't want to be poked or prodded anymore, but if you change your mind—"

"I won't."

Sandy was waiting in the outer office. Dr. Cushing walked out, talking on his cell phone as he left. Dr. Hartman said to Sandy, "We're taking them out the back way—by the chapel and employee cafeteria."

"Is there any way I can help?"

"Come with us in case we need reinforcements."

Chloe finally understood how serious the situation was. Reinforcements? Just so they could leave the building? Reporters were ambitious, but they weren't crazy. There must be more going on outside than what they had been told.

The group of five hustled down the hall and into an elevator. Dr. Hartman put a key into the panel before pushing several buttons. "So we'll go straight down," he explained.

A moment later they stepped out of the elevator into a nearly empty hallway.

They had gone halfway down the length of the hall when two security guards appeared. "Sir, we have a situation."

Everyone stopped. What else could have happened?

"The reporters?"

"No, sir. Dr. Cushing has their attention for the moment."

The taller of the guards glanced at their little group, his eyes lingering on Anna for a moment. The shorter guy spoke briefly into his radio before turning his attention back to Dr. Hartman. His name tag had "Taylor" on it.

"They know she's here. Someone leaked a picture of Miss Schwartz to the media as she was leaving the exam room."

"What?" Dr. Hartman's face flushed in anger.

"There's more. The major networks have released pictures of her tests—both before and after."

"That is a direct breach of our patient privacy laws! I want you to find out who leaked those tests, and they will be held responsible."

"Yes, sir."

The doctor scrubbed a hand across his face. "What is the outpatient parking lot like?"

"Jammed."

"That's where I'm parked." Chloe stepped closer to Anna. "We need to get her out of here."

"Take my car." Sandy fished in her purse for a set of car keys. She scribbled her cell phone number on a sheet of paper. "We can meet up later and swap back. You've seen my car before, a white sedan. It's on the third floor of the employee parking garage. My slot is three-one-four."

Chloe had already pulled out her own keys. "Blue Chevy Cavalier. I'm all the way at the back of the outpatient parking area, probably surrounded by sharks." She gave Sandy the license plate number for her car.

"All right." Dr. Hartman glanced around. "Radio your men, Taylor. Instruct them to split your security force. Keep half out front and send the rest to the outpatient parking area. You two stay with Miss Schwartz until she is able to safely leave this property."

Hartman turned to Anna. "Give us fifteen minutes. That should be enough time for the media to swarm the outpatient lot. You should have a clear path out of the employee lot." He stopped and reached forward to touch her arm. "You're a very special woman, Anna, and I'm sorry that what may be the most amazing day of your life has been marred by all of this."

Turning from her, he said to Sandy, "Come with me," and the two strode off in the direction they had come.

Taylor delivered orders to someone on the other end of his radio. After a moment, he faced them and said, "We can continue down this hall. Once we reach the end, we'll wait for a few minutes until I receive word it's safe for you to proceed."

It all seemed completely surreal to Chloe. She'd covered a lot of stories in her life, but she'd never been through anything remotely like what was taking place.

Apparently, the hall had been cleared, as they passed no one. They didn't see a single other person until they neared the chapel, when someone Chloe recognized stepped out.

One of the security guards held a hand up to stop her from walking any closer. "Chaplain, this hall is supposed to be cleared."

"I know you wouldn't tell me that I'm not allowed in the chapel, Mr.—" She looked more closely at his name tag. "Taylor. Besides, I know these people. At least, I know Anna and Chloe."

She glanced pointedly at Jacob.

"*Ya.* We know each other. Jacob, this is Dora Smith. Dora, this is my friend, Jacob. Jacob Graber."

"Nice to meet you, Jacob."

"It's so *gut* to see you." Anna stepped forward and enfolded the woman in a hug.

Dora held her for a moment. When she stepped back, her hands remained on Anna's arms. "So it's true. You are healed."

No one spoke, but Anna nodded.

"I would like to hear about your experience, Anna. God has blessed you—"

Before she could finish the thought, Taylor's radio crackled again.

"Two reporters have found a way into the building. They're headed your way, sir."

The larger man, whose name tag said "Smith," seemed to have gotten over the surprise of escorting Anna. He frowned at the voice coming over Taylor's radio, and then he said, "Want me to take care of that?"

"If we confront them, it will only confirm that they're in the right part of the hospital. But we also can't let them see her."

"The chapel—we can wait in there." Dora hurried into the small room, and Chloe, Anna, Jacob, and the two security guards followed.

Chloe heard the door shut behind them. Probably no one would realize the room was even occupied. The lights were dimmed. About ten chairs were positioned on each side of the room, and a prayer rail ran the width of the room at the front. No music played. When the door was shut, it blocked out the everyday noise of the hospital. Chloe realized they had entered a haven of sorts, a place where those who were feeling overwhelmed could stop and rest and pray.

The thought had barely crossed her mind when Anna stepped toward the front of the room.

CHAPTER 48

*A*nna hadn't been in the chapel before.

She thought her *aenti* had. It seemed she remembered Erin saying she was going to pray for a few moments back when her mother had been visiting and able to sit with her. She remembered Dora. The chaplain had been a center of calm in the storm. She'd visited Anna nearly every day, and she'd always brought an encouraging word and kind smile. She hadn't sugarcoated what Anna was facing. Instead, she'd offered an unruffled, reassuring presence.

That might explain why Anna now relaxed at the sight of her. Dora Smith was someone she trusted. When Anna stepped into the chapel, all of the tension and worries she'd been carrying melted away. The room had been carpeted in warm brown shag, and the chairs were cushioned in a similar color. Dimly lit, the chapel provided a restful refuge. But those things weren't what caught Anna's attention. Rather, she was transfixed by the sight of the cross, made of stained glass, with some sort of light behind it. She walked toward it, her heart banging a rhythm against her ribs.

And then she had to kneel, to fall to her knees and thank God for what He had done.

She was suddenly overwhelmed by a feeling of complete and total love. Her heart ached as she sank to her knees in front of the prayer rail and raised her face to the stained glass. Anna closed her eyes, but she still felt warmth against her skin—as if she were sitting in a sun-beam of light.

All of the things that had seemed so important became background to the love and joy and acceptance that surrounded her. It no longer mattered that people were chasing her to get her story, that the peace and tranquility of their farm had been shattered, or that her life had been turned upside down for nearly a year and then suddenly righted again. In that moment, the past ceased to exist and the future was something she could once again trust. In that moment, she found her-self surrounded by total love, complete security, and quiet assurance. She felt herself caught up in her Father's arms.

She didn't realize she was weeping until Chloe, Jacob, and Dora sur-rounded her—all going to their knees, all placing their hands on her.

"What is it, child?" Dora's face scrunched in concern, reminding her of *Mammi*.

"Are you okay?" Chloe asked.

"Maybe you should sit in one of the chairs." Jacob's expression was a study of concern.

Anna wondered that they could be worried about anything. To her, everything was crystal clear, but she didn't know how to explain that to them. She closed her eyes again, wanting to hold on to the moment. Already the emotions she'd felt were fading, but the certainty? The serenity? They remained.

She brushed tears from her cheeks, reached toward the prayer rail, and used it as a support to help her stand.

"I'm fine," she assured them. "Better than that. Better than I've ever been."

"I think I need to sit down." Dora went over to the front row of chairs and rearranged them so that they could sit in a circle. "We all should."

"Anna, what happened?" Jacob asked. "Why did you...why did you hurry forward and kneel at the railing?"

"It seemed like...like something I wanted to do. Something I needed to do."

Dora wiped sweat from her forehead. "The need to thank our Father when we've been in His presence, when we've felt His touch—it's not something that a person can resist. In the Gospel of Luke, Christ tells the Pharisees that if the people don't praise Him, the stones will cry out."

"Is that what happened?" Chloe asked. "Anna, you've been so calm through all this. I don't know how you've held yourself together. When you fell to your knees, I was afraid that...I'm embarrassed to admit this, but I was afraid you were paralyzed again."

"*Nein.*" Jacob shook his head. "There is not much about this that I understand, but I do believe your healing is permanent."

Anna nodded in agreement as she reached for his hand.

"Any place set aside for worship is holy ground," Dora said. "We designed the chapel to be a quiet, soothing place. Perhaps it's the first time today that you've had a moment to truly appreciate what God has done for you."

"With so many in this world, in this hospital, hurting...I don't understand why I was healed." Anna pulled her *kapp* strings forward. "But I am certain that *Gotte* will use it to somehow glorify Himself."

"We don't always understand the why of a thing," Dora agreed.

"I'm grateful that we had to hide here for a few moments. That we had this time together." Anna reached for Chloe with her left hand, her right still holding fast to Jacob. She smiled at Dora, who reached forward and squeezed their hands. It seemed at that moment that they were bound together, the four of them. Caught up in some mighty work of God that they couldn't begin to fathom.

Dora glanced over at the security officers, who had remained at the back of the room. Standing, she hurried back to them and then returned.

"We're still not clear to go yet, but they expect to receive word at any moment that we are."

"I don't mind resting here." Chloe drummed the fingers of her left hand against her leg. "So much has happened so quickly."

Anna realized as she ran her fingers from the top of her prayer *kapp* strings to the bottom that she wasn't nervous anymore. Though the intense emotions she had felt while at the prayer rail were gone, the peace remained. "Out in the hall, I was worried and a little afraid. The entire morning has had an unreal quality to it."

She leaned forward, so that she was staring down at the brown carpet. Silence permeated the room, allowing her to find the words to express what she needed to say.

"We don't have to be afraid of the news reporters or anyone else. It's okay. It's all going to be fine. *Gotte* has a plan, and..." She frowned before continuing. "I don't understand it all, but I am sure there's a purpose to all that has happened. It's like the verse *Mammi* is always reading to me. The one from Jeremiah. God knows the plans He has for us—"

"Plans for a hope and a future," Dora added, finishing the Scripture.

Anna looked up at them, a smile tugging at her lips. "*Ya*, but they're not just words. They're the truth. I'm more certain of them than I'm certain my name is Anna Schwartz."

"You've been touched by God, Anna." Dora reached for her hands and clasped them.

"I think you're right. But the thing is, we all have been. Not only me because I'm healed, or us four because we are in this room, or even those men standing at the back ready to protect us. *Nein*, it's not only us who have witnessed something extraordinary. We've all experienced God's touch, and it is an amazing thing."

One of the security officers approached them. "We're clear to leave."

The little group straightened the chairs and formed a line behind the guards. Anna paused to embrace Dora and whisper, "*Danki*."

Dora promised to pray for their safety.

Anna held on to the memory of God's touch, and the miracle of the blessing she had received. She felt no anxiety as they made their way down the hall, out of the hospital, and through the parking area.

They managed to leave the hospital area unnoticed, but Chloe had barely pulled on to the freeway when she informed them that they were being followed again.

"Why can't they leave her alone?" Jacob muttered.

Then Chloe's phone rang. She asked Jacob if he wouldn't mind answering it because she was driving. Anna could tell from the conversation that it was Bishop Levi. He was either calling them from the phone shack or using one of the officer's phones at her *onkel*'s house. Jacob said goodbye and pushed the "End" button on the phone.

"He suggests we not return to Cody's Creek...not right away."

"Why?" Chloe asked.

Anna leaned forward from the backseat. "Are Samuel and Erin all right?"

"Everyone is fine, but the crowds have grown. He thought perhaps we should find a hotel or else return to the hospital, where the security guards can watch over you."

"But I don't need security guards."

"I think I have a better idea," Chloe said. She pulled off the freeway, through a parking garage, and back out the other side, then back onto the freeway heading in the direction they had come. "No one is following us now. We've lost those vultures, and I have the perfect place for us to lie low."

"Vultures, huh?" Jacob glanced back at Anna and then he smiled at Chloe. "Reporters after a big scoop can be ruthless."

"Are you teasing me, Jacob Graber? Because your girlfriend is in the backseat, and I'm pretty sure she's on my side."

"*Ya*, Chloe isn't that kind of reporter," Anna agreed.

The bantering felt like a soft gentle rain to her soul. Anna should have been worried. She had no idea where they were going, she couldn't return home, and the day was once again spinning out of control. Only it wasn't out of control. God had a plan, even in this. She reveled in the feeling of peace that continued to permeate her soul. She didn't have any more answers than when they had driven with Dr. Hartman to the hospital, but she finally understood that those questions and their answers didn't matter.

What mattered were the people with her in the car, the people waiting back home, and the people she was about to meet.

CHAPTER 49

*C*hloe went to her mom's.

Where else could she go? The day had held entirely too many surprises. She longed for the quietness and security of her mother's house.

Teri met them at the door with her usual good mood and grace. She and Anna greeted one another like the friends they were. Other than shedding a few tears when Anna first walked up the front walk, Teri seemed to handle Anna's miraculous healing better than most.

"I'm sure you all are hungry after your long day."

"It's too late for lunch and too early for dinner," Chloe said, glancing at her watch. The digital display told her it was two in the afternoon, but it felt much later. It felt as if she'd received the call about Anna's healing days or even weeks ago.

Teri led them all into the kitchen. "I've set out some sandwich makings."

"We appreciate your taking us in."

"I'm happy to have you here, Anna. Chloe had left me a message earlier in the day, and then of course I've been watching the news."

Jacob shook his head. "Why can't they leave her alone?"

"That's a good question. Unfortunately, I think the answer is probably quite complicated." Instead of explaining further, she waved toward the food. "Help yourselves. Everything is on the table."

As they set about making sandwiches—turkey, ham, cheese, and all of the requisite fixings—Chloe realized that her mom was a real port in the storm. That shouldn't have surprised her.

"Will you go back to your apartment?" Teri asked.

"I think I'll stay here if that's okay. I think we all should."

"That's a great idea. You know I love it when you stay over. You and Anna can share the guest room, and I'll make up the couch in the living room for Jacob."

Chloe's room had long ago been changed into a guest room, something they had laughed about on several occasions. Many of her friends claimed that their room at their parent's house had been enshrined, practically frozen in time. Teri's mom was more practical. She'd quickly set about making the room more inviting for guests, adding new twin beds that could be pushed together for a couple or left separate when that was called for.

"We don't want to be too much trouble," Anna said, as she took a giant bite of her turkey sandwich.

"You're no trouble at all. Jacob, fix yourself another sandwich. A big boy like you is bound to have a large appetite."

"I won't deny that. Maybe one more. I want to leave room for those cookies you made."

Teri laughed and pushed the platter of lettuce, tomato, meat, and cheese closer to him. "I'm sure you have plenty of room for a second sandwich and dessert."

As they ate they were able to relax a little, and then each person began relating bits and pieces of the day's events.

"Sometimes being in the limelight isn't what it's cracked up to be," Teri said.

"No Amish person wants to be in a light of any kind—not if it means a lot of attention." Jacob finished his second sandwich and refilled his glass from the pitcher of water. "We like things quiet."

"*Ya*," Anna said. "I can't imagine how my *aenti* and *onkel* are dealing with all of this, though I'm sure...I trust that they are fine."

"They are fine," Teri assured her. "Your bishop called and told me no one had crossed the police barrier, and he hoped the size of the crowd would diminish by tomorrow."

"Either way, we're going home in the morning. It's where I'm supposed to be right now."

They all considered Anna's words for a moment, and then Chloe turned to her mother. "When we first arrived, you said that the answer to why folks are flocking to Anna was complicated. What did you mean by that?"

Instead of responding, Teri stood, walked across the room and popped a decaffeinated tea pod into the Keurig machine. After asking if anyone else would like a hot drink, she rejoined them at the table.

"Many people are looking for a miracle. We don't know exactly what happened to Anna, but we do know that it was beyond the simple explanation of an injury in her back recovering over time. I'm not giving my opinion there. The fact that you can walk supports that a miraculous healing took place. I don't think there's any doubt that this is the hand of God working in your life."

Anna nodded, Jacob broke his cookie into little pieces, and Chloe studied her mother.

Finally Chloe said, "I agree with you, but not everyone out there does. Not everyone is a Christian or even religious."

"True, but almost everyone is searching at some point in their life for answers to specific needs. And when they're hurting? Or when someone they love is hurting? They often look to God, whatever they know about Him, for help. It's natural that once they hear about Anna, they would be consumed with hope that the same thing could happen to them."

"Consumed is a good word." Jacob frowned at the table. "The people surrounding the hospital were completely irrational."

"Some people have been living without hope for so long that when they finally have a glimpse of it they lose all sense of reason."

No one spoke as Teri seemed to gather her thoughts. Then she glanced up at them as she clasped her hands around her cup of hot tea.

"I suppose I know a little of what they're going through. Chloe's father had what is called a 'dread disease'—multiple sclerosis." She glanced at Anna and Jacob, who each nodded their head acknowledging they had heard of it.

"The majority of people with MS have a dormant type, which is not too debilitating as long as they stay on their medication. However, Gus..." She spread her hands out in a who-knows-why gesture. "My husband had the more active form. He didn't present with MS until he was in his fifties, and then it progressed rather rapidly. Within five years, he couldn't walk."

"I was in college when you first found out." Chloe hadn't thought about that phone call in many years. It had tilted her world. Her father had always been the rock solid center of her life.

"Those years were difficult." Now Teri sipped her tea and smiled over the rim of the cup. "I prayed for a miracle many times, but we didn't receive one. I don't know why. I still believe that God does at certain times work in miraculous ways, but that wasn't His will for Gus."

Chloe reached over and hugged her mom. Anna and Jacob looked on sympathetically.

"I bring it up now because I certainly can understand how people feel when they hear about you, Anna. Some will be hopeful. And others? They will probably remain bitter."

"Why?" Jacob asked.

"It seems to me that when you're going through a terrible illness or accident or disease, you sometimes feel isolated. You feel as if no one understands what you're dealing with, and sometimes you become certain that no one cares."

"I'm sorry, Mom. I should have been there for you. I should have visited more—"

Teri reached out and stopped her daughter's protests with a touch of her hand. "Many people were there for me, and you did the best you could. I can see that now. But at the time? I often felt alone, and yes—a little bitter. I'm not proud of that."

"I think I understand how hard it might have been, but why were you bitter?" Jacob popped a cookie crumb into his mouth.

"Maybe because everyone else goes on with a normal life." Anna cocked her head to the side as she gazed across the table at Teri. "In my case, when I first became a paraplegic, I was stunned and angry that my life had been irrevocably changed. And I mourned because my dreams had died in front of my eyes. I think I understand bitterness."

"All of those were also true in my case. And when I'd hear of or meet someone else with MS, someone who was doing well, I would be filled with so many questions. Why was Gus wheelchair bound? Why did he have the worst form of such a terrible disease? What had we done wrong to deserve such a thing?" Teri shook her head. "I understand now that I was asking all the wrong questions."

"What do you mean?" Chloe asked.

"I should have been asking what God intended for us to do. What did He want us to learn? How had He planned to bless us through our circumstances? How could I reach out to others?" She nodded toward the other side of the house, where her sewing room was located. "I began quilting in earnest the last year your father was alive. I'd played with it before, but suddenly it was an escape for me. It was a way to broaden my world again—a world that had become very small."

"I felt the same way the first time I came here." Anna smiled at the memory. "Looking at what you were doing helped me to envision something besides my own problems."

"The year I began sewing for Project Linus, I'd taken early retirement from teaching. Although there was plenty to do caring for Chloe's father, I needed something else to focus my mind on—so I quilted more than ever before, and I looked for organizations I could donate to. Gus was proud of my work, and I'd often go in and sew while he rested. Those were special times we shared. Now I'm grateful for the years, and the time, we had together."

"The quilting brought a little sunshine into my world, and the fact that I could help someone else who was hurting...well, it gave my days a purpose again." Anna rested her elbows on top of the table and propped her head in her hands. "But now that my life has changed again, I'm not sure how I can help those who are hurting. I plan to continue quilting, but I also want to reach out to the people who are waiting outside my *onkel*'s and *aenti*'s. I am certain that *Gotte*'s hand is in this."

Those words echoed through Chloe's mind as they helped to clean the kitchen. They spent the afternoon reading, taking a walk in Teri's garden, and then playing Monopoly while they ate pizza that Teri ordered. By nine o'clock, everyone was yawning and the girls conceded the Monopoly win to Jacob.

Teri tucked sheets and blankets on the couch for Jacob and showed Anna to the guest room. Everyone prepared for bed, finding toothbrushes and taking showers, though Anna and Jacob didn't have an additional set of clothes. Chloe offered Anna a dress for the next day, but she shook her head and smiled. She did accept a pair of pajamas from Teri to sleep in.

When everyone had settled down for the night, Chloe crept out to the kitchen table, opened her laptop, and began to write the story that was due to Eric before midnight.

CHAPTER 50

The house was quiet. Peaceful, even.

But the questions spinning through Chloe's mind made a racket louder than a train passing through a silent night.

She glanced over her notes, the ones she had taken at Anna's house. She added her own reactions to seeing Anna, for the first time, standing by the window in the living room. It might not go into her report, in which she thought she should maintain an objective tone, but she wanted a record of those first reactions. It helped to crystallize her thoughts about the morning.

She added all that had happened that day—making their way through the crowd, being followed not once but twice, and the experience in Dr. Hartman's office. Again, she wasn't sure how much of that she would include, but she was sure she needed to document the entire experience while the memories were fresh in her mind.

Chloe's fingers paused over the keyboard, and the gravity of her task caused her to freeze. She was going to report on a miracle? She was going to describe to the world this impossible thing that had happened? How? What words would she use? How could she possibly explain what she'd witnessed?

She didn't know, but she did know that she wanted to give a different perspective than what was being offered on the major news networks.

She opened an Internet window and typed in *Anna Schwartz* and *miracle.* Only three words, but she suddenly found herself staring at thousands of hits. There were news reports, blogs, a live Facebook chat, images, and YouTube videos. There were also thousands of Tweets with the hashtag "Anna-Schwartz-healing."

She began clicking through the results quickly. In most cases the headings were enough to tell her the general gist of the piece. Basically, the reports seemed to fall into four categories. The first was the worst, most sensational, which adamantly denied any such thing as a miracle could take place and assigned ulterior motives to Anna and her family.

Miracle or Child Abuse?

Amish Girl Paraded Before Press

Miracle—Another Day, Another Scam

Miracle Myth

Miracles—the New Amish Industry

Miracle Exposed

Secret Story—Amish Miracle Explained

These headlines sickened Chloe. Not only were they way off base, but they were mean. The writers weren't reporting at all. Instead, they took the approach of dismissing what they considered a ludicrous idea before any actual investigating had been done. She remembered her mother talking about bitterness and wondered if these were the people she was referring to. When would their attention turn away from Anna?

The second type of headline was more what she would have expected. Reporters sent to cover something they had no way to gain actual information on, so instead they reiterated the questions people were asking.

Miracle Healing?

Miracle or Not? You Decide

Proof of God?

An Amish Miracle?

Miracle in Cody's Creek?

Chloe related well to these reporters. If someone had told her when she'd awakened that morning that before the clock turned to a new day she'd be reporting on a miracle, she wouldn't have believed them.

She would have probably laughed. Twenty-four hours ago, she didn't believe in miracles. She was willing to admit that to herself. What did that say of her faith? There were miracles in the Bible, but she simply hadn't thought they were still possible. She hadn't thought God was that big. No, that wasn't right. She hadn't thought He was that involved in His creation.

The third type of headline was almost worse than the first. These were people trying to capitalize on what was happening.

Miracle Berries Found in Oklahoma
DIY Miracle—Follow Anna's Simple Steps
Miracle Healing Power Revealed
Holy Water from Cody's Creek

The list of articles went on for pages. She sat back, stunned. How could people claim such things? She'd been reporting a long time, and she understood that often there was someone trying to make a buck off a big story. This seemed to go beyond that. She had a feeling that these people had a well-oiled operation. Clicking on one that looked promising, she found that she could order a packet of "Miracle Berries" that had been harvested there in Cody's Creek. Very few berries grew in their area, and she was certain none were ready for harvest. Whatever these folks were selling, they basically slapped a new label on it to match the headline. She could even use her Paypal account to purchase the items.

How could she counter such sensational reporting? How could she present the truth of what had happened to her friend? Especially in light of the fact that she didn't understand it? Going back to her search results, she began narrowing her search terms and—on a hunch—she took out the words *Anna Schwartz*. She found herself looking at a much smaller list, this time of past miracles.

One was of a boy in Colorado, healed of a debilitating virus after being prayed over by two nuns.

Another spoke of the Pope, and how through him, God had healed an unborn child. In fact, a good number of the purported miracles were investigated in some way by the Catholic church. "The healing is not considered a certified miracle until it is approved by a team of theologians and the current Pope. But the most difficult step in this process is usually the recognition from the medical commission."

At least Anna's community of believers would require no such thing. She had a feeling the Amish community would continue on much as it had before, unfazed by the events or the attention. But perhaps she was wrong there. A miracle was a rare occurrence, regardless of your denominational beliefs.

Another headline claimed that a priest had shown up at a horrific auto accident before mysteriously vanishing. A miracle? An angel? Chloe investigated that one a bit further and found that a parish priest had stepped forward and explained that he'd been in the area, prayed over the people in the accident, and then he had quietly slipped away. Not a miracle.

But the story held her attention. People wanted to believe in miracles, and there were some out there who attempted to report on it fairly and objectively.

She shut down the Internet browser, pulled her notes closer, and opened a new document.

Slowly she began to type.

The Healing of Anna Schwartz

Anna Schwartz woke this morning to a completely different life. After more than nine months in a wheelchair, Anna found that she could walk. She was injured in the tornadoes which struck the community of Cody's Creek in September of last year. Thrown from the wagon that two of her uncle's horses were pulling, she experienced a complete spinal break.

Doctors from Oklahoma Surgical Hospital confirmed that diagnosis with MRIs as well as physical assessments. Anna was kept at the hospital for observation a few days, and eventually she was moved to a Tulsa-based rehabilitation center. Since that time, she has been wheelchair bound, spending her time quilting for Project Linus, working in her uncle's produce stand, and living the quiet life typical of Amish families in this northeastern Oklahoma community.

Chloe considered deleting the last sentence but decided to leave it in. She wanted her readers to connect with Anna, to know that she was a person, not just a story.

On the morning of July 14, Anna's life changed once again. She woke and found that she could walk. Her family immediately consulted Anna's physician from OSH, who insisted on a follow-up MRI. That test showed that Anna's spinal break—which had been deemed irreparable—was healed. The doctor could find no evidence of the previous injury.

When asked about the day's events, Anna said, "I don't understand it any better than the doctors do, but I'm grateful. I'd like to thank everyone for their prayers and support over the last year."

Crowds have grown outside Anna's home, requiring the presence of the local police department, who is tasked with ensuring the Schwartzes' safety. Officer Glen Starnes has been placed in charge of the security details. "I understand everyone's curiosity, but I would ask them to respect the family's privacy."

Anna seemed less perturbed about the crowds. "I appreciate their interest in my well-being. For the moment, I'm looking forward to resuming a normal life."

Chloe checked her notes to be sure she had her quotes exactly as they'd been given to her. She read through the piece one more time, prayed that what she was writing might serve to calm the situation, and hit "Send."

She thought she might toss and turn, worrying over her piece or what was to happen the next day, but as soon as her head hit the pillow, she was out and slept deeply through the night.

CHAPTER 51

Jacob was eager to get back to Samuel's place the next morning. He understood all too well how much work there was to do on the farm, and he didn't think his being gone was helping one bit. He was glad he'd accompanied Anna to the hospital. He'd felt close to her from the first day, but now they seemed to understand one another with a simple look, casual touch, or half-finished sentence. He had never felt so intimately connected to another person. If he had stayed at the farm, he would have regretted it.

They left Teri's house early the next morning, stopping at a fast-food restaurant to meet Sandy and swap cars.

Chloe spoke on the phone with Officer Starnes. What he told her must not have been good because even from the backseat Jacob could look in the rearview mirror and see the worry lines across her forehead.

"What has happened? Has the crowd grown even larger?" he asked.

Instead of answering him, Chloe turned to Anna and said, "I have one piece of good news. Your mother arrived this morning."

"She's here? Already?" Anna turned and smiled at Jacob. "I can't wait for you to get to know her."

He hadn't had a chance to meet her when she'd come to visit the year before. Anna's mom had spent nearly all of her time at the hospital, and she'd left when Anna had been moved to rehab. The few times she'd spent an evening at Samuel's house, Jacob had already been gone for the day. By the time he'd arrived for work the next morning, she had already returned to the hospital.

"I knew you'd be happy to hear that," Chloe said.

"I'm not sure how she managed to arrive so quickly," Jacob muttered. "It took me several days to get from one state to another, but then I stopped to work along the way. Is she in Tulsa? Should we turn around and pick her up?"

"Not necessary." Chloe took the Cody's Creek Exit off Highway 412. "She was able to change buses in Joplin, where she spent the night. She arrived in Cody's Creek first thing this morning. Samuel has already been to town to pick her up."

"Oh, my. He took the tractor to town? Through the crowd?" Anna practically cringed.

"Actually, Officer Starnes took him." Chloe started to say something but stopped herself. Jacob wondered what else had happened, what Chloe wasn't telling them. He decided she had her reasons for not sharing. They would know everything soon enough.

The line of cars now reached past the bishop's property. Though it was only seven thirty in the morning, folks were already arriving, exiting their vehicles, and moving toward Samuel's place. The road was crowded with people walking, others being pushed in wheelchairs, and news crews. Chloe had to inch along in order to avoid hitting anyone. By the time they reached the lane leading into Samuel's place, Jacob was ready to get out of the car to shoo people away. What were they thinking? And how long were they planning to stay?

He groaned when he saw a food vendor truck selling coffee, donuts, and even advertising hot dogs for lunch. "I can't believe these people. If they can buy food, they are going to stay even longer."

"It's definitely worse," Chloe agreed.

But Anna only stared out the windows. She silently considered the mass of people.

Chloe had called the local police department and was transferred over to the officer heading up the road block details. She'd given a description of her car, so now the officers allowed them through without her having to stop or lower her windows.

The family must have heard the car approaching, or perhaps Officer Starnes had radioed ahead to the officer who was stationed at the corner of the house. Samuel, Erin, *Mammi*, and a woman Jacob decided must be Anna's mom stood waiting on the porch by the time Chloe parked.

Suddenly there was no doubt as to the woman's identity. Anna opened the car's door and ran into her mother's arms, not bothering to shut the door or pick up her bag.

And in that moment Jacob realized there was a big difference between himself and Anna. He had always loved his parents. He definitely respected them. But he would never have run into their arms. Anna's family had been through a terrible and wonderful thing together. Perhaps it had brought them closer together as a family.

Jacob picked up Anna's purse, shut the door, and walked with Chloe to the porch.

"Morning, Jacob." Samuel looked better than he had since Jacob had arrived to help with harvest in September of the previous year. He looked, somehow, younger as he smiled at Jacob and glanced back at Anna. "Anna looks like she's still feeling well."

Jacob grinned. "*Ya*. I believe she is. We all had a good night's rest."

"You don't have to speak of me as if I'm not here." Anna swiped at the tears on her cheeks, and then she pulled on her mother's hand, tugged her in their direction. "*Mamm*, I want you to meet two of my friends. This is Chloe—"

"Chloe and I met at the hospital. It's good to see you again, dear."

"And this is Jacob."

"It's so nice to meet you. I'm Martha, and I've heard a lot about you from Anna as well as the rest of the family." There was a strong family resemblance between Anna and her mother, including the habit of cocking her head slightly to the side when she was waiting for a response. "Thank you for taking care of Anna yesterday while she was in Tulsa."

"I was glad to go with her." He glanced past Martha. *Mammi* was holding on to her cane and staring out over the front yard, an unreadable look on her face. Erin looked upset, not making eye contact with any of them.

It was *Mammi* who broke the silence that had settled over them. "Coffee is what we need, and some of the hot biscuits Samuel didn't eat this morning."

So they all went inside. Erin poured coffee for everyone, Martha jumping in to help. There was indeed an abundance of fresh biscuits. Erin placed a jar of honey on the table, along with some bacon that had been cooked up but not eaten. Perhaps she had expected them to arrive earlier. Or maybe cooking was how Erin handled stress, and it was obvious to Jacob that she was feeling rattled. Because of Anna? Or because of the crowd at the end of the lane? Perhaps it was simply the police presence, which now extended to the front porch. He wanted to ask about that, but before he had a chance, Chloe and Anna began reciting the events of the day before.

Jacob half listened to the various conversations. By the time they had finished eating, Anna and her mother stood and declared they were going for a walk through the garden. They invited *Mammi* and Erin to join them, but both begged off. *Mammi* claimed her rocker was calling her name, and Erin said she wanted to put on some soup for lunch. Samuel caught Jacob's eyes and nodded toward the barn.

They walked there in silence, past the watchful eye of the Cody's Creek police officer. When they'd entered the barn, Samuel turned toward him. The smile he'd worn earlier had been replaced by a more thoughtful look, nearly one of awe if Jacob had been pressed to describe it.

"Anna's healing...I still don't understand it, but I believe it. *Ya*, I definitely do. I carried her to the bathroom countless times over the last year. I watched that little girl's heart break and eventually begin to mend. And I prayed. We all did."

He looked to Jacob for confirmation. They had both taken a seat on overturned crates. Jacob nodded. Yes, they had both prayed for Anna after the accident.

"I believe without a single doubt that *Gotte* can do mighty things, and He has done something big here—something we may never understand." Samuel ran his fingers through his beard and leaned forward, his elbows braced against his knees. "But that's not why I called you out here, son. We have a problem."

CHAPTER 52

*A*nna and her mother walked with Chloe out to the front porch. Chloe explained that she needed to go to her office, but she also seemed hesitant to leave Anna without her protection.

"Which is silly, I know, because you have—" Chloe spread her hands to encompass the officer at the corner of the porch and other policemen farther down the lane. "Your own security force."

Anna frowned and shook her head. "I think they should leave. It's very disruptive."

"I don't think those men and women who are gathered at the lane are bothering the farm, though they do make coming and going difficult." Martha reached over and looped her arm through Anna's. "Perhaps in another day or so we won't need anyone to stand guard on the property. It's certainly not our way. Thank you for helping Anna get through yesterday, Chloe."

"It's a day I'll never forget." Chloe reached forward and briefly hugged Anna. She touched her friend's face once before walking to her car and driving down the lane.

"She's been there for you since the accident," Martha said to her daughter. "I remember her coming to the hospital."

"*Ya*, she was always there, even through my darkest days."

"I could tell from your letters that you've had your ups and downs, and your *aenti* has kept me posted. But tell me about your healing. How did it happen, Anna?"

They walked through the garden, and Anna told her everything—about her dark days, about finding a new purpose in the quilting, and about what had started as a summer cold and nearly ended her life. She also recounted the dreams that had plagued her since the accident. She described her despair as her health grew worse and her depression deepened.

"I almost came when it was obvious the cold was lingering. Your *aenti* would send someone to the phone shack each evening. They would call and tell me to wait one more day, and that the doctor was doing all he could. They would tell me not to worry. Four days ago, I went to the bus station and purchased a ticket." Her mother stopped, reached out, and ran her fingertips over a white rose. "I was waiting for the bus when Menno showed up begging me to come and help with the birth."

"How is my *bruder?*"

"Good now, but if you could have seen him then—" Martha shook her head and they resumed walking.

"The baby is fine?"

"*Ya.* A few weeks early, but she is doing well. They named her Ruth."

"*Mammi* will be happy about that."

"She seemed to be. She was going to write the *boppli* her first letter this morning." Martha motioned toward a bench Jacob and Samuel had placed in a corner of the garden. "You and *Mammi*—you've grown very close, haven't you."

"Sometimes I think it was worth moving here, worth everything I've been through, to spend the time I've had with *Mammi*. She's...well, she's very special."

Her mother smiled in understanding. "Tell me about the last few days."

Anna took a deep breath. "The dreams changed two nights ago. They were intense and disturbing in one way, but they were also comforting and wonderful." This time when she described walking through the wildflowers she went into more detail. She told about the colors, how the petals felt when her hand passed over them, and the rainbows in the sky.

Her mother stopped her. "More than one?"

"*Ya.* It seemed the sky was full of them."

Martha turned on the bench so that she was facing Anna. "Did you tell Erin about this?"

Anna thought back. "No. I started to, but...*Mammi* and I have talked about the dreams before, and she asked me about the rainbow too. What does it mean?"

"It's not for me to say, Anna. But we'll share this with your *aenti* later. I think she'd like to know. You were saying the sky was clear and then you looked up."

"Jacob, he pointed to the sky."

"And you saw the rainbows—more than one."

Anna again recounted the dream, down to the last detail she could remember. Describing everything sent goose bumps down her arm.

"And when you woke you could walk?"

"*Ya.* I didn't realize it right away. I opened my eyes, looked out the window, and heard *Mammi* reading the Bible."

"She did that every morning?"

"Every morning, every afternoon, and before I slept." Anna cocked her head to the side. "It was like being bathed in Scripture and prayer three times a day whether I needed it or not."

They sat there for another few moments wrestling with the miraculous nature of what had occurred. "At first it frightened me a little, but now I'm sure—absolutely certain—that *Gotte* will guide me." She shook her head. "But I still don't understand why this happened. Why me, and why not others?"

"It's not for us to say or even to understand, but I might have an idea as to why."

Anna glanced at her mother in surprise. It was so good to be with her, to have her near and to hear her opinion on all that had happened. She'd understood why her mother couldn't stay after her accident, and though she would have liked to have gone home with her, she'd also felt a need to stay in Oklahoma. Now it seemed as if her two worlds had joined together again, if for only a few days, and she felt a peace that was precious.

"If you understand why I was chosen, among all the people who are hurting, to receive God's healing touch, please tell me. I'm all ears. Because that baffles me."

"Maybe I should start with *Mammi*. She's always been a very special person from the time I first met her, when I started dating your *dat*. My own mother was a fine woman, but a bit distant if you remember."

"I do."

"She wasn't an openly affectionate person, though she cared for us all in her own way. You never would grow hungry or cold with *Mamm*. She provided for our needs." Martha reached out and touched Anna's arm. "Remember that, dear. People show their love in different ways. Sometimes what we take as indifference is merely a person's particular manner."

Anna nodded, wondering what she was getting at.

"*Mammi* was different, though. She always had an almost childlike faith. At times it was frustrating because she didn't seem to have the same questions the rest of us did. When some tragedy would strike—whether it was death, drought, floods, or illness—your grandmother would smile and carry on." She laughed in spite of herself. "That's precious in someone as old as your grandmother, but in a younger woman it's sometimes hard to understand. How could she stand over the body of a loved one and not shed a tear? Your grandmother—she would be quoting the Psalms and rejoicing."

Anna could picture that well enough.

"As I've grown older I've learned to respect your grandmother's faith and to try to learn from her. Maybe somewhere deep inside I always knew that her faith would make a difference in our lives, but I didn't know how. I certainly never envisioned...this."

"This? You mean—"

"Does it surprise you so much? Yes, I think your grandmother is responsible for this miracle. We all prayed for you, Anna. I shed many tears, as I know your father and *aenti* and *onkel* did. The rest of the family back in Goshen didn't forget about you for even one day. You were always in our hearts and our prayers. But we probably didn't believe that our prayers were making a difference." Martha smiled. "Don't look so shocked. We're not saints. We believe in God's holy Word, and we hope, but we have doubts like everyone."

"Not *Mammi*."

"No. Your grandmother's faith is complete. She's a special one."

"And you think her prayers healed me?"

"Only God can heal, but I believe He smiled on your grandmother the day He healed you."

Anna allowed her mother's words to sink in. Finally she said, "*Mammi* asked me once if I believed in miracles. I didn't know what to tell her. I didn't think they were even a possibility."

"But for *Mammi*, there is no limit to what God can do."

"I've barely had a chance to talk to her since yesterday morning. I think I'd like to go back now and see her. I think you may be right. It feels right, and the way that she studies me from behind those big glasses...well, I think she understands more about this than she's admitting."

Together they walked back to the house. Martha joined Erin in the kitchen, but Anna walked over to where *Mammi* was sitting by the front window, her Bible beside her and her knitting in her hands. As Anna walked across the room, she had every intention to pull up a chair and sit and have a good chat with her grandmother. But then *Mammi* glanced up, a smile tugging on her lips and the joy of her secret in her eyes.

Anna went to her knees beside her grandmother's chair. "I didn't know, *Mammi*. I didn't understand. You were always there for me. Through every dark night and every bitter morning."

Her tears began to run in rivulets down her cheeks, but Anna didn't bother to wipe them away. "You never doubted, and your prayers...God heard them, didn't He?"

Mammi set aside her knitting and put her hands gently on Anna's head. The warm, soft, gentle touch of her grandmother's hands calmed Anna's spirit.

"God always hears His children."

"But you were faithful to ask, weren't you? To ask that I be healed?"

"I only asked for God's will. I asked for Him to use you and me, Anna. And it would seem that He has."

CHAPTER 53

During lunch, Samuel explained the situation with the officers stationed outside. Anna could tell her *onkel* had already shared the information with Jacob because he chimed in from time to time clarifying a point.

"The local police simply cannot handle a situation of this magnitude," Jacob said. "They do not have enough officers."

"And though we would rather not have any outside presence, it seems we have no say in that." Samuel ran his fingers through his beard. "The two-lane road is public property, and the crowd there is growing. Instead of folks losing interest in Anna's story, it seems that more people show up every hour. Yesterday there was a news crew from Washington, DC, and a movie van from California."

"So you've already agreed? The governor's special task force is coming here?" Erin frowned at her food, which she was again scooting around on her plate rather than eating.

"For now, yes."

Anna glanced around the table. No one seemed shocked by the news, but her mother and aunt were frowning.

"Why do we even need them?" Martha asked. "Perhaps if the police leave, the people will leave."

"We hope, given time, that they will," Samuel said. "But until that happens, it doesn't seem wise to turn away the help. Even Levi is afraid the people would crash through the barricade the police have set up. They would be here at the house before we had a chance to stop them."

"I think I should talk to them." Anna had taken a big bite of corn bread, so the words came out somewhat distorted and she had to repeat herself.

"Why would you think that?" Samuel said. "Those people are trying to profit off you or get a big story. I don't know when they'll go away, but certainly something else will grab their attention soon. That's what Officer Starnes thinks, and I agree with him. Wait this out, and eventually things will return to normal."

Anna wasn't sure if things would ever be normal for her again. Would standing up and walking across a room ever seem ordinary? Would there come a day when she didn't revel over the feel of her toes against the wooden floor? She doubted it, but she kept those thoughts to herself.

"We're fortunate the governor has offered to provide men from a special task force to help with our protection."

"I've never heard of such a thing," Anna said.

"The way it was explained to me, these folks are normally used to help with security for visiting dignitaries, especially in small towns where resources are limited."

"I'm not visiting, and I'm hardly a dignitary."

"True, but what has happened to you is special, Anna. Normally..." Samuel glanced around the table, taking in each person seated there. "Normally I would remind you of your commitment to Scripture and to our *Ordnung*, both of which call us to be a separate people. But there are times when our lives and the lives of the *Englisch* cross paths. This is one of those times. I think the governor and the bishop are right. We need help."

So it was decided. The officers from Cody's Creek would hand off the protection of the Schwartz family to the governor's task force. Jacob touched Anna's shoulder as he walked out of the kitchen, "See you tonight?"

"*Ya*, sure."

He trailed his fingers down her arm, and Anna couldn't stop the smile spreading across her face. She hadn't had time to consider what her healing meant to her and Jacob's relationship. Did they even have a relationship? Could the dreams she'd harbored possibly come true?

Everyone began moving in different directions.

Anna's mother ducked her head close to *Mammi*, and they spoke in a whisper. What was that about? *Mammi* nodded and Martha glanced up at Anna, as if she wanted to say something. Anna started to ask her about it, but Martha quickly shook her head. Erin had begun clearing the dishes.

Anna glanced around, and then she moved forward and stopped her *onkel*, who was headed back outside. "How did the governor even know about us?"

"He read a newspaper story—one written by Chloe. He said it touched his heart, and then he called the police department here to see how he could help."

Samuel clumsily patted her arm, and Anna remembered him picking her up. She remembered the way he cared for her each day when she couldn't walk.

"Everything will be fine, Anna. You concentrate on staying well."

She didn't think that would be necessary. She knew, deep in her bones, that she didn't need to fear returning to her wheelchair. As to everything being fine, she wasn't so sure. Her *aenti* and *onkel* had become much more sociable since her illness, but they were still very private people. She didn't like the idea of their quiet lives being paraded before the public, and she wondered how long it would take for the pressure to begin to take its toll. She remembered her time in the chapel and the sense that God had everything under control. She looked down at her legs, and she had no trouble believing He could handle a crowd of gawkers.

She was standing in the mudroom, watching Samuel and Jacob walk across the yard to the barn, when her mother walked up behind her. Martha put her hands on Anna's shoulders, turned her around, and kissed her forehead.

"Could you come into the kitchen? *Mammi* and I would like you to speak to Erin."

"Now?"

"Yes."

"About what?"

"You'll see. It's important, Anna, and I think that now—well, I think now is the time that we share everything with her."

CHAPTER 54

*E*rin was seated at the table when Anna walked back into the room. She was staring down at her hands, which were folded on top of the table. A dishcloth sat discarded beside her. *Mammi* had taken the place to the right of her, and Martha sat on the left. Anna's *mamm* nodded toward the seat across from Erin, and Anna took it quickly. Whatever this was about, she could tell it was serious.

What now? Was someone else sick? Had something happened while she was gone the night before?

But no one had mentioned anything at lunch. Whatever was going on, it didn't seem to include Samuel or Jacob.

"Anna, your *mammi* and I would like you to tell Erin your dreams."

"My dreams?"

"Yes, especially the one where you walk through the wildflowers. But perhaps you should start at the beginning."

Erin glanced up, and Anna realized her *aenti* had no more idea as to what was going on than she did.

Her mother and *Mammi* shared another glance, and then *Mammi* removed her glasses and polished them on the hem of her apron. "Do you remember in Joel and again in Acts when God's Word talks about dreams?"

Anna shook her head. She knew dreams were described a few times in the Bible, but she couldn't recall the specific section of Scripture *Mammi* was talking about.

"'Your sons and daughters will prophesy, your old men will dream dreams, your young men will see visions.'"

"What does that have to do with me?"

Her mother smiled even as she folded her arms, rubbing her left arm with her right hand, as if to warm herself. "We think that your dreams may have a purpose beyond what we can understand."

"That isn't too hard to imagine. I can't understand them at all!"

The three women—the women who meant the most to her and had stood by her through the trials of the last year—stared at her. *Mammi*'s face was a study of curiosity. Her mother looked more solemn, and Erin—well, Erin glanced from one to the other but still said nothing.

Anna cleared her throat and combed back over her memories of the dreams—searching for a place to begin.

"The first dreams were in the hospital. There was the quilting dream, where I couldn't quite get the pattern right. My thread was always too short, my needle sometimes huge." She shook her head. "I don't know why I would have dreamed about quilting since I didn't do much of it."

"Until you began quilting for the children." *Mammi* tapped the table. "You found the work *Gotte* would have you do."

"Maybe so. While I was in the hospital, I couldn't have imagined that, but maybe so. The dream which bothered me the most was the one where Jacob was holding my hand." Anna found herself falling back into those days of loss and confusion. "I couldn't remember who he was, but I could see the look of worry in his eyes. It seemed to me—in the dream—as if his heart was breaking for me. It seemed as if we knew each other very well. And then I asked him to hold my hand. I was embarrassed that I had been so bold, but I was also terribly afraid of being left alone."

"Jacob did hold your hand. By the time we reached you, he was hovering over your body, protecting you." Erin's voice was a whisper.

Anna nodded. She knew that what her *aenti* remembered was how it had actually happened. She had talked with Jacob about this more than once. "I also had a dream of walking through the wildflowers. I didn't tell you this before?"

Erin shook her head.

"It is afternoon and I am walking through a field of wildflowers—they are red, orange, pink, and blue. It seems that every color I can imagine is there. In my arms, I'm holding a quilt. The fabric has a blue background and contains a pattern of rainbows. I hug the quilt and continue through the flowers, but then suddenly I'm in a field of corn that is ready to harvest. When I first dreamed this, I feared becoming lost in the rows of corn."

"But not the last time," her mother said softly.

"*Nein*. I'm not afraid at all. I walk through the corn, wondering where it will lead, when suddenly I see picnic tables in the middle of the crops. You all are there and sitting around the tables. All of my family is present, the people here and those in Indiana. Chloe and Jacob, they are there as well. I'm overwhelmed by the amount of love from the people around those tables. Each person there cares and prays for me."

"As we do, child." *Mammi* reached forward and squeezed her hand.

"My heart begins to beat faster and faster, until I can feel it thrumming through my veins. Everyone is excited. I look at Jacob, and he points to the sky. When I look up, I see colors of the sunset splashed across the sky and stars beginning to appear. But that's not what we're all looking at. There are rainbows as far as the eye can see and in every direction."

Erin clutched the edge of the table, her hand shaking and her eyes widening. "You dreamed this? The rainbows—"

"*Ya,* and more than once. It was as if my mind was in a loop it couldn't shed. The quilting I suppose makes sense—I never was good at it. Perhaps I felt guilty. I don't know. Chloe and I had visited a few of the quilters from our district a few days before. Maybe a part of me was remembering that trip. As far as the dream about Jacob—well, my mind must have been trying to reconcile what had happened. But the flowers...I couldn't figure them out. We have a few here, and there are some in Indiana." Anna turned to her mother. "Have you ever seen so many, with so many different kinds and colors?"

"Only once."

"I've seen them too—" Erin raised her fingers to cover her mouth, even as tears slipped from her eyes. "The year that Susan died."

"Susan?"

No one spoke for a moment. Finally her mother said, "Your *aenti* had a child who lived for three years."

"She loved the flowers. She would laugh and twirl as we walked through them." Erin's voice shook as she spoke. "The year she died, we had good rains. The flowers...they were more abundant than I'd ever seen.

Now Erin was weeping openly. "When she died, I walked out into the flowers, my heart aching, my soul longing for my child. I remember sinking to the ground and asking God why such things happen and how I was to bear the pain."

"I'm so sorry, *Aenti*," Anna said. "I had no idea."

But Erin wasn't listening. She was confessing, and as the weight of her sins lifted, Anna saw the woman her *aenti* had once been. "I looked up, Anna, and I saw not one, not even two, but three rainbows. I've never seen such a thing since, and I knew in that moment that *Gotte's* promises were *gut*. I knew I could trust Him."

"*Gotte* blessed you even as you walked through the valley," *Mammi* said.

"I swore I'd never forget, but I did. I pushed that memory away. I allowed my grief to consume me. Every time another *boppli* would be born to a woman in our district, the pain in my heart increased. Why were they so blessed when my Susan had been taken? And how did I know, how could I be certain, that I would be reunited with her in heaven?"

Anna's mother placed an arm around her sister-in-law. "No one blames you for your grief, Erin."

"But I've indulged it too long. My faith—it wasn't strong enough to see me past those dark days. Then you came to stay with us." She looked at Anna as she brushed the tears from her cheeks. "You came, and it was like I had a daughter again. I was afraid to let you close at first. I must have seemed terribly cold. I was afraid you would leave us or reject us or—"

Anna remembered those first few months and her *aenti's* distance.

"After you were hurt, I prayed to *Gotte*, Anna. I prayed that if He would save you, I would set my grief aside."

"And you did. You took *gut* care of me."

"Until you were healed, and the old questions returned. Why wasn't Susan healed? If *Gotte* was willing to allow a miracle in one situation, why not the other?"

Anna remembered what Chloe's mom had said, about the people waiting at the end of the lane, about people searching for a miracle.

Erin stood, walked around the table, and pulled Anna into a hug. The woman's arms were shaking, but she held on tightly. "*Gotte* sent you a vision of my time of grief, and His deliverance and love."

She stepped back and touched Anna's face. "I will see her again. Won't I?"

Anna nodded. She hadn't understood it at the time, but of course the scene at the table, in the center of the harvest, was a promise of another reunion—one that would last for all eternity. A holy gathering of those she loved—both those present and those who had gone ahead.

What was the verse *Mammi* had read to her when she was sick? Something about God wiping away every tear. A promise of no more death or mourning, crying or pain. One day they would be together again, and when they were Erin would be reunited with her only child.

There was a knock at the front door.

"I'll get it," Martha said.

Mammi stood and walked over to Anna and Erin. Placing one hand on each of them, she said, "He cares about both of you. He always has, and He'll see you through the troubles that lie ahead." Then she turned, clutching her cane, and hobbled into the other room.

CHAPTER 55

*J*acob sat through the Sunday service, tense and barely able to control his anger. He realized how hypocritical he was being—pretending to worship but in fact seething. However, he was honest enough to admit his emotions to himself, even to lift them up in a silent prayer and pray that God would forgive him.

The problem was that he had been watching Anna all morning, ever since she'd first walked through the bishop's front door for their worship service. On the surface, people were friendly enough. He'd see them smile and a few even enclosed her in a hug. It was plain that many of their congregation were truly happy for her and grateful for the miracle that had occurred.

It was the mumblings when they stepped away that caused Jacob's temper to rise.

"She's the reason we have *Englischers* posted at the lane."

"Why couldn't she stay home? Surely it's a sin to have our service disrupted like this."

"It might be better if she'd never been healed. For all we know, the accident was *Gotte's* judgment on her. And this? How do we know it's of *Gotte*?" This was said by Sally Hershberger, who had always struck him as a bitter person. No doubt she had her reasons for her dark attitude toward life, but he couldn't abide her speaking ill of Anna.

He had stepped forward to confront her when Samuel tugged him away. "Let it be, son."

Samuel had taken to calling him *son* months ago. Jacob didn't see it as a slight on his parents, who he now wrote and called on a regular basis. They weren't the perfect family, but they were communicating, and he saw that as a good thing. At least he wasn't running away anymore. He'd found a place where he belonged, and somehow communicating that to his family had erased the tension that had always hung beneath the surface of their relationship.

Jacob knew that Samuel had come to see him as a son, and in truth he enjoyed working for the older man.

"But she said—"

"I heard her myself, and nothing you can say would change her mind. Leave that to *Gotte*. Perhaps He will speak to her through our sermons today."

Jacob had allowed himself to be pulled away. He'd joined the men on the far side of the room, but he'd kept his eyes on Sally as well as some of the other women. It was plain enough to tell when they were speaking of Anna, as they would cover their mouths or duck their heads, but always their gaze would return to the girl he loved.

He did love her, and he wouldn't allow this to continue.

Gossiping was a sin, as surely as adultery or swearing or pride—though Jacob thought it was more damaging than most transgressions. What was it he had read in one of the books that he picked up from a swap shelf? *Great minds discuss ideas. Average minds discuss events. Small minds discuss people.* Apparently, the wife of a president had said that, though a footnote in the book had explained that it originated with a Greek philosopher. Regardless, Jacob felt it applied perfectly to what he was seeing—and hearing.

After the service he would make a point to speak with Bishop Levi. He was still living with the bishop and his family, and Jacob knew the man well enough to have faith that he would stop any gossiping before it spread into something they couldn't curb.

The sermons that day, not surprisingly, were on miracles recorded in the New Testament. Jacob listened with one ear. Mostly his attention was focused on how he would confront Sally.

They stood for the final hymn, jostling against one another as the room barely held everyone.

Their Sunday gatherings were always crowded because they met in someone's home. But this morning more were in attendance than normal. It was rare to have *Englischers* at their service, but today there were a few. They were people Jacob had seen in town, so they had probably attended various weddings or funerals within the Amish community. This wasn't as rare as some outsiders thought. Though the Amish were encouraged to remain separate, their lives often crossed paths with others in their community. When an Amish person married, or when one passed on, it wasn't unusual to see folks from the Mennonite and Christian churches attend. Today he guessed the *Englisch* visitors were there to catch a glimpse of Anna.

There were also more Amish family members than normal—older brothers and sisters who happened to be visiting in the area. Jacob had heard the Stutzmans talking as he walked in. An older man standing with them had asked, "Is that her? The short, plump girl?"

He doubted their being in attendance at the first worship service after Anna's healing was a coincidence. It seemed morbid curiosity didn't stop at the police barricade or with the group of *Englischers*.

Grabbing a seat next to Anna during lunch was impossible. He did catch her glancing his way several times, which gave him the confidence to walk over to her table once she was done eating.

"Care to go for a walk?"

Anna's family glanced at one another, smiling.

The Bylers were also sitting at Anna's table. Rebecca said, "*Ya*, Anna. Go for a walk. I'm sure you've heard enough chatter from us old folks."

Jacob carried her plate to the washtubs, and when he returned to her table Anna was ready to go. Volleyball games and baseball games had already started, but she turned in the other direction, toward the barn.

Good. They would have a few minutes alone.

They had barely stepped into the shadow of the barn when Anna turned toward him, resting her hand on his arm and gazing up into his eyes. "I'm glad you're here, Jacob. I don't know what I'd do without you and your friendship."

Is that what they shared? Friendship?

She turned and moved slowly down the side of the barn, stopping to call over the bishop's mare. Pulling a carrot from her pocket, she offered it to the dappled gray.

"You'll spoil her doing that."

"Will I?"

"*Ya*. I tell the bishop the same thing. He gives her everything from apples to carrots to sugar cubes."

"Bishop Levi has been such a *gut* friend to me, from my arriving here, through my accident and now..." She waved toward her legs. "Now this."

"He's a *gut* man."

"Many in our congregation are not happy about the guards at the lane."

Jacob didn't answer. He was thinking about Sally Hershberger. Should he share with Anna the things he had heard?

She turned to him again, though this time she kept some space between them. "The leadership of our church asked to speak with me and my family later this afternoon."

He attempted to keep his expression neutral, but he apparently failed because she said, "Don't worry, Jacob. This is a difficult thing for all of us to understand. I only bring it up because I'm not sure what *Gotte* would have me say. How do I explain something I don't understand? Can it even be explained?"

Jacob reached for her and pulled her into the circle of his arms. "You've been through a lot this last year, and no doubt your mind and emotions...no doubt they're tumbling as fast as an *Englisch* carnival ride."

When she looked up at him in surprise, he said, "Surely you've ridden one. It seems they stopped at every small town I've worked in."

She shook her head, and he peered up toward the sky, trying to remember the names of the rides the children and teens frequented at the carnival.

"The Helter Skelter?"

"*Nein.*"

"Tilt-A-Whirl, Tumble Bug, Pirate Ship—"

"You're making those up."

"I'm not." He slipped his hand over hers as they began to walk back toward the grouping of tables under the large maple trees. "If you didn't ride carnival rides, what did you do on your *rumspringa?*"

"I came to Oklahoma!"

As he laughed and Anna began to giggle, Jacob found that the tightness he'd been experiencing in his chest loosened. He could trust her to say what needed to be said. He knew that Bishop Levi would lead the discussion fairly. But at the very center of things was neither of these individuals. At the center was God. Yes, he had heard the sermon that morning. He didn't need to worry about Sally Hershberger or any of the other naysayers.

He planned to stick around until after the meeting took place in case Anna needed moral support. Where did he have to go? This was where he lived, and Anna was his girl. It occurred to him that he'd like to make that permanent. He wanted to ask her to marry him.

It might be best to wait, though, until the time was right.

For now, they had quite enough going on. He was satisfied to simply walk beside her, their fingers laced together, her laughter still ringing in his ears.

CHAPTER 56

As usual the luncheon and games lasted all afternoon. Anna had thought that perhaps Jacob would ask her to the singing, but in the end she'd needed to wait for the meeting with their church elders. Jacob had waited with her. Soon the benches they had used in the service and around the makeshift picnic tables were loaded into the bench wagon. Anna loved the sound of the horses clip-clopping down the lane and into the twilight.

Unfortunately, a line of buggies developed at the intersection of Levi's property and the road. Lacretia Gates was a young black woman in charge of the governor's task force. She offered a calm, assuring presence and had been faithful to keep the Schwartz family updated each day. For the Sunday service, she had divided her group, putting half at the lane leading to the Schwartz place and half at the end of Bishop Levi's lane. Though it signaled to the onlookers where the family would be for the day, she explained the people would have followed the buggies anyway.

Now those very same buggies backed up down the lane, waiting for the barricade to be moved and the security personnel to allow them to pass. The sight seemed incongruent with the simplicity of the buggies and the peacefulness of the July evening.

Their lives had become a bit of a circus all because of her.

Gradually, one family after another managed to find their way out onto the two-lane blacktop until all that was left was Anna, her family, Jacob, and the leaders of their church.

There was Bishop Levi, who smiled at her now as they all sat down around the remaining picnic table. There were also the two ministers—Luke Hershberger and Daniel Stutzman. The last man to take a place on the far side of the table was Joseph Byler, who was their deacon. He'd arranged several of the fund-raisers that had taken place over the last year.

Levi was the oldest, confirmed by the whiteness of his beard. The other three were probably the age of her *onkel*, though perhaps Luke Hershberger was younger by a few years. Her mind flashed back on all the boys at the Hershberger place. Were there eight? No nine. Nine boys and the only girl, who had died. She'd caught Sally staring at her a few times during the service. Perhaps, as Chloe's mom had suggested, she was resentful that her prayers for a miracle had gone unanswered. What was it she had said exactly? "Some will be hopeful. And others? They will probably remain bitter."

On Anna's side of the table were Samuel and Erin, her mother, *Mammi*, and Jacob. No one disputed Jacob's right to be there. They didn't actually fit around the table. Extra chairs were brought over to encircle the ends.

Levi began the meeting with a time of silent prayer, and then he said, "We appreciate your all staying late so that we can discuss this matter."

"What is the matter we're discussing?" Samuel asked. "Anna's healing? Or the guards at the end of our lane?"

"Both. I believe we should discuss both. Actually, one is a product of the other, is it not?"

"One is a gift from God. The other—" Samuel's hand flattened against the table. "Not so much."

"How do you know it is a gift from God?" Luke frowned as he studied Anna. "This thing that has supposedly happened. How do we know the truth of it? Perhaps she was never really injured."

Anna couldn't pretend to be surprised by the accusation, but she also didn't know what to say. *Mammi* had cautioned her about this very thing before they had left for the church service. "Some people long to believe, Anna. And some people will refuse."

Instead of arguing, she watched Levi, who sighed and chewed vigorously on his ever-present bubblegum.

"I have visited with Anna once a week since the accident, Luke. In fact, I was there when the paramedics first arrived. She was grievously injured, of that you can be sure."

"Then how do you explain this?" Luke shook his head, as if to ward off any possible logic the bishop might use.

"God's miracles have never been explainable," Joseph said.

"So you believe?" Luke turned on the man sitting next to him. "You're willing to stake the integrity of this church on something a young girl claims, a young girl who only moved here a little over a year ago?"

"I'm willing to do so." Martha's voice was calm.

Anna was surprised she spoke up. Women as a rule remained silent in church as well as in such meetings. Not that she'd ever attended one before, but she'd heard about them.

"Anna's father couldn't be here. As you know, we have a farm in Goshen that required his attention. But he has called and spoken with her."

Anna smiled at that. She had been able to feel the love of her father radiating through the phone as they talked, and she'd promised to return home—to visit or to stay—soon.

"Since he can't be here, I will speak to Anna's character. She's a *gut* girl. She never attended the parties our youth are now famous for. Never owned one of the smartphones many of our sons and daughters keep hidden even after they are married."

"How would you know?" Daniel asked. His tone was less argumentative than Luke's. He seemed genuinely interested as he waited for an answer. "We can try to enforce the rules of our *Ordnung*, but we can't know for certain what our children prefer to keep hidden."

"*Ya*. At times it is hard to be certain," her mother agreed. "But a parent? A parent knows. We may occasionally look the other way, or pray that a particular sin in our children's lives will pass, but we know. I can tell you that Anna was never one to rebel. She…she had trouble find-ing her place in our community and so asked to spend a year with Sam-uel and Erin."

"And we have been blessed to have her," Samuel said. "In spite of all we've been through the last year, I wouldn't change the fact of Anna's coming into our lives, our community, and our family of faith."

"So she hasn't rebelled before." Luke sat back and crossed his arms. "That still isn't proof that what has happened is real. Perhaps she longs for attention. There's certainly enough of it now at both your lane and Levi's."

"I believe we're a little off track." Levi popped his gum and smiled at Anna. "We'd like to hear your version of what has happened, Anna. Some of it you shared with me the first day, but these men who are the leaders of our church would like to hear it from you."

Anna drew in a deep breath, closed her eyes for a few seconds to gather her thoughts, and then she told her story—simply, directly, and without embellishment. She didn't tell about the dreams because they hadn't asked specifically about those. She described the initial accident and diagnosis, her rehab, the illness she had endured the last few weeks, as well as waking in the night and weeping. She described *Mammi*'s prayers.

"I am not surprised about Ruth's praying." Levi nodded toward Anna's grandmother. "She has been a faithful member of our congre-gation for many years. Often she has prayed for me and my family—for each person here, no doubt. The prayers of a righteous man, or woman, availeth much."

"You quoted that Scripture from James this morning, but I'm not sure I see how it applies here." Daniel frowned at his hands. "Haven't we all prayed for loved ones?"

He paused and ran his thumb under one of his suspenders before continuing. "I myself have prayed for my son many times since his leg was broken. For whatever reason, *Gotte* hasn't seen fit to heal him com-pletely from that accident. The doctors say he will walk with a limp the rest of his life—a limp that will limit what type of work he can do. No disrespect intended, Levi."

"None taken, but I would remind you that *Gotte's* ways are not our ways. I, too, know a bit about answered and unanswered prayers, but what we must remember is that every prayer is answered—though not always in the way we would wish and not always as soon as we would like." He paused, glancing slowly around the table before he continued. "I have no doubt that all of Anna's family prayed for her from the moment the accident happened—and it did happen. There's no dispute there. So why was she healed now, nearly a year later? Why was she made to endure the months of rehabilitation and life as a paraplegic?"

Daniel leaned forward as if to offer an answer, but Levi stopped him with a raised hand. "I don't want answers from you right now. What I'd like is for us all to take this up as a matter of prayer, that we might understand and know *Gotte's* will for us, for Anna, and for her family."

Anna thought the meeting might break up, but Luke wasn't done. He waited a moment for Levi's instructions to fade into the night. Then he said, "We need to talk about the money."

"The love of money is the root of much evil," *Mammi* murmured.

"I'm talking about our money, and the money of the families who donated to Anna's cause."

"What about it?" Joseph asked. As a deacon, he helped to distribute funds given in hardship cases. Anna remembered that Samuel had insisted he be a cosigner on the account set up for her so that he could ensure all funds were handled properly.

"A balance remains?" Luke asked.

"*Ya*. We received donations from across the country that totaled a little more than half a million dollars. We had anticipated that Anna's needs would stretch far into the future. People have been faithful—both within our congregation and the community of Cody's Creek."

"Even farther than that," Levi murmured. "We received donations from all over the United States, and from many different groups and individuals."

"But she's no longer handicapped," Daniel said.

"Not handicapped, and so not entitled to the monies." Luke studied her as if he was waiting for a response.

Suddenly Anna realized that Daniel and Luke had spoken of this before they sat down to talk. They glanced occasionally at one another, and their comments sounded rehearsed.

Her uncle leaned forward, his forearms resting on the table. He'd rolled up his sleeves and his arms looked like rope to her—aged but muscular from years of working in the fields. He was a simple man. A good man, and it hurt her to see him having to endure this type of interrogation.

"We will gladly return any remaining funds to the general benevolence account."

"Yes, but what of the money you've already spent? It's paid for your help." Luke cast a pointed look at Jacob, who had remained silent throughout the meeting. "I would have been happy to have an extra hand—a free hand—on my place."

"The monies spent to date were done so in good faith and in a time of need." Levi's tone brokered no argument. "They will not be returned. I agree with Samuel's suggestion to return the balance of the funds to our general benevolence account."

After that they spoke for a few moments about the governor's task force, but Anna's attention wandered. She couldn't believe that what had happened to her—a lovely, beautiful, miraculous thing—had been turned into a discussion about money. She didn't want to believe that the two men sitting across from her would imply that her uncle may have behaved dishonestly in regard to the donated funds.

She tuned back into the discussion when Levi suggested they close with a silent prayer. When she raised her head, she found Jacob watching her. She could tell by the set of his mouth and the lines between his eyes that the entire meeting had been as painful for him as it had been for her.

"I will get the buggy," Samuel said as they stood and began gathering their things.

Anna said, "I think I'd rather walk home." She shook her head when Jacob offered to go with her. "I'd like some time alone, but *danki*."

Her mother patted her hand. "All right, dear. Don't be long. It's late already."

She could have cut straight across the field. The roofline to her uncle's barn was clearly visible even in the waning light. But suddenly she longed to be away from it all—the stares, the comments barely heard, even the guards at the lane. She wanted to walk around the pond and enjoy the fact that she was able to do that very thing, something they had barely talked about.

Anna made her way toward the back of the property, walking through knee-high grass and pausing to study the occasional wild-flower. She brushed her dress down with her hands and tried to still her mind, listening intently to the rustle of the summer breeze in the trees. She'd made it to the pond and was sitting on the bank when she heard footsteps. Thinking it was Jacob, she turned.

Before she could scream, before she could even think to call out, a rough hand was clamped over her mouth and she was being pulled back, away from the pond, and into the surrounding woods.

CHAPTER 57

*C*hloe answered the phone as soon as she recognized the number. After Anna's accident she had added the phone shack in Cody's Creek to her list of favorites. She hoped it was Anna calling. She'd missed talking to her the last few days, but the response to her article had been overwhelming. She'd been fielding phone calls and returning emails since the paper had run the piece featuring "Anna's Healing"— which was what everyone was calling it now. Eric was beside himself with glee, which for some reason only served to irritate her.

She was surprised to receive a call so late in the evening. Until now, her Amish friends had walked to the phone shack during daylight hours.

"Chloe? This is Jacob."

She instantly understood that all was not well. "What's wrong?"

"It's Anna. She's missing."

"What?" Chloe had been lying on her couch, reading through the email on her tablet. Now she sat up, knocking the device to the floor. "What do you mean *missing*?"

"She's gone! She stayed late at the bishop's, her entire family did, and then she said she wanted to walk home alone. I think the meeting...I think it upset her."

Chloe checked her clock again. Nine twenty-eight. Not so late.

"Maybe she needed a few hours to herself. I wouldn't panic."

"The meeting ended three hours ago. The bishop lives next door to Samuel's. There is no way she would stay out that long. She would know…she would understand that everyone would worry."

"Have you looked—"

"*Ya.* We've all looked. Even the governor's people. They have scoured the place. There's no sign of where she's gone."

Chloe was tugging on her shoes as he spoke. She snatched up her keys and purse and hurried out her apartment door. "I'm leaving now, Jacob. I'll be there as soon as I can."

Chloe had spent the last year becoming reacquainted with the faith of her childhood. She understood, now that she was an adult, that somehow those beliefs and those people had rooted her and helped her grow into the woman she was. She understood that the God they worshipped cared about them on a personal level. Perhaps she had doubted that when her father was ill, but she didn't any longer.

As she drove toward Cody's Creek, she petitioned her heavenly Father. She prayed for Anna's safety. She prayed for the people who were searching for her friend. And she prayed that somehow she would be able to help.

Turning down the two-lane road that led to Samuel's farm, she was surprised to see so many people camped outside of his property. She'd assumed they went home each evening and returned in the morning. Perhaps some did. But others pitched tents or simply slept in their cars.

Why? What were they expecting to happen? And how long would it take until their attention turned elsewhere?

The cars parked on both sides of the road barely left enough room for passing, and the scarcity of streetlights didn't help. The last thing she needed was to have a fender bender. She slowed her car to a crawl. When someone tapped on her window, a small scream escaped her. Stomping on the brake, she peered out of her window and could barely make out the camera crew from one of the Tulsa television stations. The population of Tulsa had grown over the last decade, but still most of the reporters knew one another.

"Justin, what are you doing here?"

He looked like a typical cowboy—wranglers, pearl-snap shirt, and either a cowboy hat or baseball cap. Today he wore a cap with his television station's logo.

"Hey, Chloe. There's a rumor that Anna is missing. Can you confirm that?"

Chloe stared toward the farmhouse. A glow of light rose above the trees. It looked odd to her, like a beacon in the middle of a group of Amish homes. It reminded her how unnatural all of this was. "I can't confirm anything. I just got here."

"Why are you here, though? Why are you visiting so late in the evening?"

Chloe glanced left and right. No one else was close enough to hear their conversation. She'd known Justin for years, and she thought she could trust him. "Look, this is between us. Okay? You cannot report this until someone releases an official statement."

"Sure. You have my word."

"I did receive a call that Anna's missing. No one knows what happened, and I'm worried. She's my friend. You know? She's more than a story."

"I get that."

"Keep your ear to the ground, and if you hear anything—anything at all—call me." She reached into her purse to grab a business card with her cell phone number. Finding one, she handed it to him.

Justin accepted the card and tucked it into a pocket. "I'll work the crowd out here. See if anyone is saying anything new about it. There was some activity at the gate a few hours ago with the governor's people, so we thought something was up. I'm sorry about your friend. I hope they find her and that she's okay."

"Me too, Justin." Chloe rolled up her window and pulled forward to the makeshift barricade.

The guard there checked her ID and consulted a list on his clipboard. Then he called out, "She's good. Let her pass."

Chloe drove toward the house. The area around the home and barn was ablaze with light—much more than the gas lanterns Samuel and Erin used. As she approached the place where she usually parked, she saw that the task force had set up emergency lights. She could make out the front porch, where several people were standing in a huddle—including the head of the governor's task force. Lacretia was speaking with a Cody's Creek police officer and Anna's uncle.

Chloe took a moment to text her mom. She briefly explained what had happened and asked her mom to alert the prayer group at their church. She knew she could count on them to be discreet, and she believed that their prayers could make a difference. Something told her they were going to need all of the help they could get.

CHAPTER 58

$\mathcal{A}$nna figured she must be in shock. That was the only thing that could explain the calmness she felt. After all, she'd been abducted. She should have been afraid for her life.

Studying the man beside her, the man driving the old Dodge truck, she didn't think he looked so dangerous. He seemed more desperate to her, though she supposed that sometimes desperate people could become dangerous.

He caught her staring and glanced over at her. "Won't be long now."

He gripped the wheel harder, causing his knuckles to turn white in the glow of the dashboard lights. She guessed him to be about Samuel's age, possibly in his sixties. He was thin but had a bowling ball belly, and his hair was thin on top. His face and hands were marked with sun spots. Anna thought she could give a good description to the police if she ever had a chance.

The truck smelled of cigarette smoke, but he hadn't lit up since he'd pulled her away from the pond, through the woods, and forced her into the battered truck. She didn't know how long they had been driving, but it felt like several hours. Her family must be worried sick.

No doubt they would have contacted Jacob by now and maybe the police as well.

There wasn't much she could do other than jumping out of the moving vehicle. Because it was going sixty miles an hour, she didn't think that was a good idea. Better to wait for a more opportune chance to escape. So instead she spent her time praying. She prayed for her parents. She'd caused them so much worry in the last year! She prayed for Samuel and Erin. She even prayed for the men who had met with her and her family after church. Her mind kept going back to that meeting, like a tongue seeking out a sore tooth.

They weren't bad men—though Luke Hershberger and Daniel Stutzman did seem bitter. Both had suffered hardships. Both of their families had endured what must have seemed unendurable. Luke and Sally had lost their baby girl, and Daniel and Margaret Stutzman were dealing with their son's injury. Did they all wonder why she'd been healed but not their loved ones? If so, she didn't blame them. She didn't understand it either. Why had she been chosen? Why had she been healed?

She prayed that God would soften their hearts. And then she found herself praying for the man beside her. Why had he taken her? And where were they going?

As if in answer, he took the next exit off the interstate. She tried to catch the words on the road sign, but they were past it before she could make out more than one or two letters.

She remembered crossing the state line into Texas nearly twenty minutes ago. She'd thought about visiting the state to their south, especially when Jacob talked about his travels. But there weren't any Plain communities to speak of in Texas—only Mennonite groups and a very small Amish group in the southern part of the state. She didn't think this man was taking her to either of those places.

Why would he take her to Texas? Why would he take her anywhere?

As they pulled up to a four-way stop, the sign said *Paris* and pointed to the right. They went left. Soon she saw a sign that said, *Welcome to Blossom, population 1,439*. She didn't see much evidence of a real town. Perhaps he was staying off the main roads.

He turned right, then left again, and finally slowed and pulled into a trailer park. It didn't look like the mobile homes they had in Cody's Creek. This looked more like a place for motor homes that *Englischers* took on vacation. But these motor homes looked as if people were living in them permanently. There were porches built around front doors, a few attempts at planting scraggly rows of flowers, even an occasional handicap ramp. There were streetlights spaced every third trailer, and all of them had picnic tables and hoses stretching from the trailer to a water spout.

Her kidnapper pulled into a small yard surrounded by a waist-high fence. It, too, had a handicap ramp to the left of the porch steps. Parked next to the trailer was a longish white car. It looked as if it had seen better days. The paint was faded in places, and it sat low to the ground, as if it needed maintenance work.

The man turned off the truck and just sat there, rubbing his hands over his face. Finally he turned to look at her. "Don't do anything stupid. We've come too far for that."

Anna nodded, but she wasn't sure she agreed with him on what would be considered stupid. If she had a chance to run for it, she would.

He didn't give her that chance. Instead, he scooted across the bench seat, grasping her by the arm and pushing her out her door. He didn't let go of her arm until they had walked up the three steps of the porch and into the home.

The first thing Anna noticed was the stale smell of cigarettes. Under that odor she noticed several things that brought back the early days after her accident—the scent of antiseptic and the soft beeping of a machine in the background. The home was permeated with the sour smell of death, at least that was the odor in Anna's mind. Someone had made a feeble attempt to cover it up with a citrus air freshener.

She'd barely stepped inside, the man close behind her, when a small dog hurled itself across the living room, barking madly. "Shush, Peanut. Shush now. You'll wake up Momma."

Peanut now threw herself against the man's legs. He reached down, picked her up, and tucked her under his arm. With his other hand, he guided Anna to a small kitchen at the end of the trailer and motioned for her to take a seat at the table.

A large woman walked into the room, rubbing her eyes and wearing a housedress similar to one Anna had seen advertised at their local thrift store as a muumuu. The fabric displayed large flowers in a variety of colors. She blinked several times at Anna, as if she couldn't believe what she was seeing.

"Who is this?"

"You know who it is."

"Spencer, what have you—" She sat down across from Anna. "Why would you—"

"Stop asking me things you know the answer to, Peggy. I don't need you questioning my decisions."

"Decisions? You call this a decision? It's crazy. You're crazy." Her hands came up and she waved them back and forth. "Kidnapping? You think you had problems before? Add a kidnapping charge, and...you crossed the state line with her?"

Peggy sank back against the chair, causing it to groan beneath her weight. "That makes it a federal offense. What were you *thinking*?"

"Don't worry about that." Spencer poured a cup of coffee from the coffeemaker, downed it, and then grimaced.

Anna could smell the coffee from where she sat. It must have been stewing in the pot for several hours.

"Watch her for me."

He made it to the doorway before he turned back toward them, avoiding Anna's eyes and instead staring at Peggy. He was still holding the dog, who had quieted down and now looked up at him with complete adoration. "How is she?"

"Same."

"Is she sleeping?"

Peggy waved away the question and then clarified. "With the pain meds they have her on, she doesn't actually sleep. Mostly she fades in and out."

Spencer looked at Anna for a moment, directly at her, and she finally understood what was happening. She understood why he'd brought her to his home and how desperate he was.

The question was, how would Spencer react when she couldn't do what he wanted? She didn't have an answer for that, but the despair in his eyes told her that this evening probably wouldn't have a happy ending.

CHAPTER 59

Jacob sat on the back porch steps next to Chloe. They had been there for a good ten or fifteen minutes. He appreciated that she didn't talk. She didn't try to assure him that everything would be fine. Instead, she sat by him and allowed the quietness of the night to envelop them.

He heard the crickets, frogs, and even the occasional low of a cow. He heard those things, but his mind was not on them. His mind and heart were on Anna.

"I thought the day she was hurt, the day of the tornado, was the worst day of my life. I thought it couldn't get any worse." He shook his head at his naïveté. "I never even imagined something like this could happen."

"The police are working hard to find her, Jacob. I think deciding to release a statement was the right thing to do. Maybe someone out on the road saw something."

He didn't answer. His mind had drifted to Sunday afternoon, when he'd walked with Anna to see Levi's horse. He thought back over the conversation. He'd teased her about spoiling the horse. She'd worried over the afternoon meeting, and he'd talked to her about carnival rides. Carnival rides! What was he thinking?

"You're awfully quiet over there, Jacob, even for an Amish man."

Instead of answering her, he closed his eyes and covered his face with his hands.

"Hey! Don't give up on Anna. She's tough, you know. Not to mention that I don't think God healed her only to have her—" She stopped, apparently unwilling to voice their worst fears. "She's going to be fine."

"It's not that."

Chloe waited, and he finally sat up straighter, still shaking his head.

"I had the perfect chance yesterday. I could have asked her to marry me then. If I had, we would have walked home together—"

"If she'd said yes. If she'd said no, she probably would have still walked home alone. You're not to blame for what happened, and you can't know what would or wouldn't have changed it."

"You think she would have said no?" New fears flooded his mind and heart.

"Relax." Chloe stretched, patted him on the back, and stood. "I don't know how she would have responded. I don't know that she's ready for another big change in her life. I'm not sure. Maybe. You probably know her better than I do."

"What if I don't get another chance? What if we missed our one opportunity to be together?"

"Jacob." Chloe was standing below the steps now and he remained seated, so they were roughly the same height. She reached forward and put her hands on his shoulders, shaking him slightly. "She's missing. That's all. Give her a little credit. Because she's Amish doesn't mean she won't find a way to escape. If someone did nab her, and I'm not saying that happened, it's possible they may have grabbed more than they bargained for. The Anna I know won't sit back. She'll have a plan. She'll find a way back to us."

An image popped into Jacob's mind—of Anna attacking the garden plants with a vengeance when she'd had a bad day. "The girl has a temper, that's for sure and for certain."

"A temper can be a good thing," Chloe said brightly. "It might serve her well tonight."

The weight on Jacob's heart, the weight of his love for Anna, lifted. He had been thinking of her in the past tense, which was ridiculous. His fear had been driving that train of thought. He nodded and even managed a small smile.

"So you've seen her temper, have you?"

Jacob stood and they walked toward the back door. When he turned to answer her, he saw the stars blazing in the evening sky. He saw them and he remembered the verses *Mammi* had read to them the week before, when Anna was still sick. Verses about considering the heavens, the work of God's hands, the moon and stars. He couldn't recall the exact phrases from the Psalms, but the thought was something about God being mindful of man and the wonder that He cared for them.

"Hello? Jacob? Did I lose you for a minute?"

He smiled at Chloe and nodded.

"I was asking you about Anna's temper."

He glanced at the stars again, and though he was still worried, he allowed the assurance of God's care to permeate his heart and mind.

"*Ya*, quite the temper."

"Give me an example." Chloe cocked her head. Maybe she was genuinely interested, or maybe she was trying to distract him.

"You know, one of the reasons I love her is because of that temper. Many Amish women—or women in general—seem to hide their hurts and fears." He straightened a suspender that had become twisted. "My *mamm* always did. She'd become silent and no one would know what they had done wrong."

"That can be tough."

"*Ya*. But Anna isn't like that. If she's mad, she doesn't mind telling you why. While she was recovering, when she still couldn't walk, she'd have bad days—times when she struggled against what her life had become."

"I know she did."

Jacob's smile grew. "But she didn't mind hollering at the plants in her garden, or attacking the weeds with a spade as if she could right the world's wrongs. She was always honest. You know? About how she felt or what was going on. You don't have to guess around her."

Chloe nodded. "I know what you mean. One time we—" Her phone chirped, and she pawed through her purse until she found it. "Hello?"

Jacob watched her expression closely, which went from polite to curious to excited. "Hang on, Justin. Let me get Lacretia. You need to tell her exactly what you told me."

They both hurried into the house and found Lacretia on the front porch.

"It's a reporter from a Tulsa television station. His name is Justin," Chloe said to her, holding out the phone.

"I don't have time—"

"Someone saw a truck driving down the adjacent road where it connects to the back of Samuel's property. It pulled to a stop off the pavement, kind of in the trees. They didn't think much of it at the time, but they noticed it had a Texas license plate."

CHAPTER 60

$\mathcal{A}$nna stared at the woman across from her. Her first impression had been correct. She was quite large. But now that they sat across from each other, Anna noticed that she had a beautiful face framed by black curls streaked with gray. Her eyes, though, spoke of a sadness Anna could understand.

"I'm Peggy, Spencer's sister." She studied Anna a moment and finally admitted, "I probably wasn't supposed to tell you that. But I don't see how this can get any worse. You don't have a cell phone on you, do you? Because I don't think you should call anyone yet. Do you have a cell phone?"

Anna shook her head.

"I didn't think so. I read about you people. I know that most of you don't abide cell phones. Can't afford one myself, but I use Spencer's sometimes." Peggy nodded toward what looked like a closet on the far side of the kitchen door. "Did he even stop so you could use the bathroom?"

"*Nein.*"

"There's one through that door. Go on and use it."

Anna didn't have to be told twice. She was surprised to find that the bathroom was rather modern. In fact, the entire motor home seemed rather new, though awfully small. She finished in the bathroom, pausing only to splash water on her face, wash her hands, and say yet another prayer for deliverance. The only window was the size of a shoe-box. There was no way she'd fit through that, so for the moment escape seemed impossible. She could possibly run past Peggy, but Spencer would hear a ruckus and catch her. He knew the area. It was better if she waited for a clear chance.

She walked slowly back to the kitchen, which was only a dozen steps away.

Peggy had placed a bottle of water and assorted cereals on the table along with a half gallon of milk. "Did you eat?"

"I didn't, not since our luncheon."

"Better do so now then. You've a long ride back ahead of you. I still can't believe he would be stupid enough to—"

"I'm going back?"

"Well, honey, we can't keep you here. Have you seen how small this place is? I have to step outside to change my mind." She pushed a bowl and spoon toward Anna. "Sorry, but we don't keep a lot of food on hand. This will at least give you something in your stomach, though Spencer doesn't choose the healthiest kind of cereal. He's still a little kid as far as that is concerned."

Anna stared at the boxes—something with a rabbit on the front, another with a leprechaun, and one with cinnamon toasted oats. She chose the last and filled her bowl, adding milk, and diving into the food. She hadn't realized how hungry she was.

Peggy poured herself a cup of the coffee and held up another cup to Anna, but she said, "No, thank you." The last thing she needed on her stomach was day-old coffee.

Peggy glanced down the hall, and then she sat down across from her again. "What did he tell you?"

"Nothing."

"You don't even know why he brought you here?"

Anna scooped up another spoonful of cereal, but paused with it halfway to her mouth. "Someone's sick?"

"His wife, Karen. She's been a good friend to me these many years." Peggy stared out the small window beside the table, as if she were seeking answers from the darkness. "She has cancer. Not much time left now. Maybe a week."

Anna set down her spoon and placed her hands in her lap. "I'm sorry."

Peggy nodded. "Thank you. And keep eating. The living need to eat."

"He thinks I can heal her?"

"He isn't thinking. That's the problem. But he probably hopes you can. That man's mind shut off when he found out she had cancer and couldn't beat it."

"I doubt I can help her. I don't even understand what happened to me, not completely."

"It's true, though? You were handicapped?"

"*Ya.* I was driving a wagon, pulling our harvester when the tornado hit."

"And you couldn't walk?"

"Spinal break. I couldn't use my legs at all."

"But you woke up nearly a year later, and you could walk?"

Anna nodded.

"I heard your story. It's all over the local news. Some are saying it's a miracle, and others are claiming it was all a hoax. Spencer is banking on it being the real deal."

Anna didn't know what to say to that, so she resumed eating.

"It's been too much, is all. Too much for him to handle." She ran her fingers through her curls. They straightened before bouncing back into place. "They've been replaying the story of when that tornado hit on the news because of your miracle. That same week of your tornado, Spencer bought this motor home. He'd finally retired from his job."

"What did he do for a living?"

"Maintenance man for the school district in Paris. He was good at it too. Nothing to be ashamed of doing maintenance work. He always showed up, always on time and willing to do what needed to be done. I went to his retirement party, and even the superintendent was bragging on old Spence, saying what a dependable person he was."

Anna realized she didn't want to eat any more. She pushed the bowl away and focused her attention on the middle-aged woman across from her.

Peggy, for her part, seemed to be talking to herself as much as she was to Anna. "I wish you could have seen him then. He had all these brochures—different kinds of motor homes, different states they were going to visit. Karen, she was tickled pink. That's the way it's always been with her. Spencer's dreams became her dreams, and who could blame him for wanting to get out of Texas after forty years of cleaning up other folk's messes?"

"So they bought this trailer?"

"Sold their home, went down to the factory, and paid cash for it. They made it all the way to Mount Rushmore in South Dakota. You know, the place where the presidents' heads are carved into the mountainside? I've heard it's quite a sight."

"I saw a picture of it once in a magazine."

"That's about as close as I've been too. Anyway, that was when Karen first got sick. It was last September, about the time you were wrestling with the tornado. By January, he'd called me to come and help. Taking care of her full-time was too much of a strain. I arrived to find he'd settled down here, even built a handicap ramp for her chair, though she's been bedridden for weeks now."

Peggy stood and put the boxes of cereal back into a cabinet. She returned to the table, sat down, and stared at her hands. "I don't blame you for judging him. What Spence did—grabbing you and bringing you here—that was totally out of line."

She glanced up at Anna. "But he loves her, and love sometimes causes you to do things you'd never imagine. He even gave up smoking for her. Twenty-five-year habit, and he stopped cold turkey the day they delivered Karen's oxygen machine. I thought he'd accepted the inevitable, but he's still clinging to the hope there's a way to rid her body of the cancer. Last week it was an herb he'd ordered from South America. This week...well, this week it's you."

"What kind of cancer does she have?"

Peggy waved away the question. "It's spread. The stuff has eaten her up."

"She's dying?"

"Yes. She is. And after forty years of marriage, I'm pretty sure that Spencer is dying with her."

CHAPTER 61

*F*ive minutes later, Spencer walked down the short hall and stopped at the doorway. He nodded toward Anna, motioning for her to join him. Because she had no idea what else to do, and hoping that in Karen's room there might be a way out of the motor home, she followed him down the hall.

"I told her who you are, but she's on a pretty heavy dose of painkillers. Not sure she'll remember."

"What exactly—"

"I wanted to go in with you, but Karen wants to see you alone. She can be...stubborn, to say the least. A mite of a girl like you, I don't think you can hurt her. I don't believe you would hurt her." Spencer shook his head. "Go in. Do what you can."

He began to turn away but stopped with his back to her. "She's everything to me."

Without another word, he walked toward the kitchen.

Karen's room was nothing like what Anna had expected, though it wasn't as if she'd ever been in a motor home before. From the looks of things, this was a top-of-the-line model. She'd known a few men back in Indiana who had gone to work in the RV factory outside of Shipshewana. They had mostly done cabinetry work. The jobs paid well, but once a man married, he'd rather be working near his home and not in a factory all day.

Karen's room was much tidier than the other rooms in the trailer.

Small windows on both sides of the bed were positioned near the top of the ceiling. At less than six inches, Anna couldn't have fit through them even if she managed to hoist herself up that high. Toward the back of the room was a skylight. One wall of the room was an oak cabinet—complete with shelves and built-in drawers. She stepped closer and ran her hand over the cabinet face. It looked like Amish work to her, so maybe this motor home had been built in Shipshe.

The large-sized mattress was tucked into the shelving unit so that it made a sort of headboard across the top of the bed.

An oxygen machine and IV drip were crammed next to Karen's side of the bed, and beside that was a small, straight-back chair. There wasn't room for anything bigger.

But Anna saw Karen's touch in the bedroom. Apparently, she'd decorated it before falling ill. The spread on the bed was a paisley print with red, gold, and purple designs. Short curtains that coordinated with the spread adorned the windows. And on the shelf nearest her was a worn Bible and a hand-stitched embroidery piece, which was placed inside a white wooden frame. It read, "God is our refuge and strength."

Anna picked up the frame and studied the verse, one from the Psalms that she recognized all too well. *Mammi* had reminded her of it often enough in the last year.

"You're a believer?" The voice was a mere whisper, but the eyes that studied her seemed alert enough. Karen was probably Spencer's age, certainly in her sixties. She'd lost her hair, and her shiny head reminded Anna of the new niece she had back in Indiana. Would she ever meet her? What would Spencer do when she couldn't heal his wife?

"*Ya.* I was baptized a few years ago, back at my church in Indiana."

Karen nodded. "That's good, child."

Anna couldn't tell much about the woman. The bedspread was pulled up nearly to her chin. However her eyes were the light blue of an early morning sky. Her face sported plenty of wrinkles, even laugh lines around her mouth and eyes. Anna suspected she would have liked this woman if she had met her under other circumstances. The clatter of the oxygen machine and the occasional beep of the IV unit faded into the background as Anna sank onto the chair.

"It's true, then?"

Anna didn't have to ask what she was referring to. Evidently Spencer had told Karen why he'd brought her to their home. "*Ya.*"

"That's wonderful. I'm glad for you, Anna—that you'll be able to live a normal life. A young girl like you—" She paused to cough up phlegm caught in her throat.

Anna jumped up to pull a tissue from the box on the shelf. She handed it to her and asked if she would like a sip from the pitcher of water.

Karen ignored her question. "Spencer thinks you can save me."

"I know he does, and I would if I knew how. I can see how much he loves you, and his sister does too. It's...it's very obvious that you all mean the world to one another."

"Sometimes that much love can smother a person."

Anna understood that. She'd felt that way when she was confined to her wheelchair, when everyone wanted to help so badly. But sometimes what she needed most was to be alone. Was that what Karen wanted?

She seemed to drift into a light sleep.

Anna was debating whether to stay or walk back down the hall when Karen said, "Tell me about it. Tell me what it was like."

So she did. She told her about the accident—how frightened and angry she had been. She explained how her family had cared for her, prayed for her, never left her side.

"Like Spencer."

Anna wasn't sure whether Spencer and her family were very much alike. One thing was certain, though. They both loved and cared for their family. In Spencer's case, he'd become lost in that love, or perhaps in the grief that accompanied it.

Karen was staring at Anna, the look in her eyes calm but curious.

"And you never expected to walk again?"

"*Nein.* I met people in the hospital and in rehab—some who had been injured for many years. They would come back to learn to operate a new prosthetic or maybe because they had experienced a setback. Their condition never improved. Why should mine? But...there were the dreams."

"Dreams?"

"Yes. Some I didn't understand, but most of them included family members." She hesitated and finally added, "Though they frightened me at first, more recently they comforted the ache in my heart."

"I've had similar dreams," Karen said softly.

Anna didn't know how to respond to that, so she continued telling about her dreams, how they had changed when she was so sick, and she described waking and finding herself able to walk.

"God has blessed you." Karen raised a wrinkled, weak hand and grasped Anna's. "He's blessed me too. Spence doesn't see that, but I've had a good life. We know there's more than this. Don't we, dear?"

Anna nodded, the lump in her throat preventing her from speaking.

"And now it's my time."

Tears slipped down Anna's cheeks. She wasn't sure why she was crying for Karen—a person she had just met, but she did understand there was no danger from the elderly woman. Perhaps it was the exhaustion in her eyes. Anna could relate all too well to that. Or maybe...maybe it was the peace she saw behind the fatigue. She thought of the embroidered verse and the Bible. Karen's faith had somehow remained strong. It was Spencer who was struggling. Spencer who had lost his anchor and was awash in a sea of pain.

"My *mammi*, she likes the Psalms. Could I read some aloud to you?"

"That would be good."

Anna started with the first chapter and made it to the end of the fourth. "'In peace I will lie down and sleep, for you alone, Lord, make me dwell in safety.'"

She stopped reading when Spencer walked into the room.

If anything, he looked worse than he had before. Perhaps he'd been arguing with Peggy. Anna hadn't heard anything from their end of the motor home, but she had been completely focused on Karen.

Spencer gazed at his wife, and in that moment Anna saw on his face the depth of his love for Karen. It caused her heart to ache. Her mind was filled with images of her own mother and father, *Mammi* and *Daddi*, even Erin and Samuel. Each couple experienced love in their own way, but they were all completely devoted to one another.

She thought of Jacob, and she realized how much she wanted to experience that kind of love. The kind that sees you through a lifetime, even if in the end it breaks your heart.

Spencer stared at the sleeping form of his wife for another moment, and then he motioned Anna out of the room.

CHAPTER 62

*C*hloe hit the "Send" key on her tablet.

The report she'd filed had been brief, barely more than a hundred words, but it pretty much summed up the current situation.

> The Cody's Creek Police Department is seeking information regarding the possible abduction of Anna Schwartz. Miss Schwartz has been the subject of much media attention since her healing from a complete spinal break.
>
> Police have reported that Miss Schwartz was last seen at a neighbor's farm. Though she left at 6:20 last evening to walk the quarter mile home, she never arrived at her uncle's house.
>
> A late model Dodge truck with Texas plates was seen in the area. Police would like to question the driver, an older white male. If you have any information regarding Anna or the Dodge truck, contact the Tips hotline immediately.

It wasn't her best writing—not that she cared. At the moment all Chloe cared about was finding her friend. It was a few minutes past midnight, but Chloe felt as if she'd devoured an entire pot of coffee and a dozen donuts. Her blood was practically thrumming through her veins, or perhaps that was hope energizing her. She walked out onto the front porch and stared up at the dark sky. Though gas lanterns still shone from the living room, at least the officers had cut the floodlights around the house. There were no clues there and no reason to continue searching. Anna was in the Dodge truck, or she had been. They'd had at least three separate confirmations of an Amish girl leaving with an older *Englisch* man.

She'd texted her mom the latest news, and Teri had responded that she'd sent a request through the prayer chain for Anna's safe return. She reminded her daughter to *keep the faith* and *not lose hope*. Those two phrases would have sounded cliché to Chloe a year ago, but now she clung to them like a life raft in a turbulent sea.

After reading her mom's text, she'd emailed Eric. He'd promised to put her post directly on the website within the hour. He actually congratulated her on getting the scoop. Yup. Her boss was still counting website hits, and he didn't seem worried at all that a woman was missing.

She wasn't the only one who would report the story. At that very moment Lacretia Gates was briefing the press people assembled out on the lane. The Cody's Creek Police Department had been hesitant to issue an alert because, technically, Anna needed to be missing forty-eight hours before they could open an investigation. Lacretia offered to call the governor and confirm that this was a special case. Officer Starnes had quickly backpedaled and agreed to make an exception.

Suddenly the screen door behind her slammed shut. Jacob didn't pause to look at or speak to her as he hurried down the steps.

"Where are you going?"

He didn't answer, so she jumped up and ran to catch up with him.

"Jacob, where are you going?"

She reached for his arm, but he brushed her off.

"I have a car, Jacob."

That stopped him. He turned, studied her a moment, and then said, "Good. Let's go."

"Not until you tell me where we're going."

"To Texas. I'm going to get Anna."

"You're what...going to speed down there and find her? Do you realize how big Texas is? Where will you look?"

"I don't know. I do know that I have to find her!"

"Jacob, listen to me."

He turned and continued down the lane.

"You need to be here."

Again, he stopped, but this time he didn't turn toward her.

"You need to be here when they call. Let the police do their job. They will find her, and when they do, you need to be here to talk to her, not out traveling the interstate."

At that moment Anna's mother stepped up beside them. Chloe hadn't even heard the clatter of the front screen door. She'd been too focused on Jacob, on trying to think of a way to stop him.

Martha paused a moment beside Chloe, squeezed her hand, and then she moved on toward Jacob.

"So much has happened since I arrived. I haven't had a chance to thank you properly."

When he looked at her in surprise, she continued. "Anna wrote me weekly, and we talked sometimes on the phone when she could get to the phone shack. She told me, Jacob. She told me all that you have done, and what good friends you two have become."

"That's what she called us? Friends?"

To Chloe, it looked as if his face had become a caricature for misery.

Martha linked her arm through his and guided him back to the front porch. "She may have hinted at something more, though I wouldn't want to share anything from her letters that she hasn't shared with you already."

Jacob shook his head, "We haven't had time to talk about it. I didn't take the time when I had the chance."

As Chloe was wondering whether she should give Martha and Jacob a few moments alone, Martha sat on the step and patted the spot to her right and left. Jacob and Chloe sat with her.

"You think she didn't know? That you care for her?"

"If you ask me, she knew," Chloe said. "She would break into a smile at anything you said, her face would blush, and she'd forget whatever she was doing at the moment." When Jacob and Martha looked at her, she added, "I'm a reporter. They pay me to notice things."

Jacob's arms were propped on his knees, and he dropped his head into his hands. "I don't know. I hope she did, but—"

"My Anna. She's a bright girl." Martha paused, and then she added, "I wouldn't be breaking her confidence to say that she cares for you, Jacob."

Chloe watched the expression on Jacob's face as misery gave way to hope. It was like watching the sun come up over the Oklahoma fields.

He wiped at his eyes. "I should go and look for her—"

"No, I think Chloe's right. Let the officers do their job. Not only does Anna need you here, but Samuel will need help with the livestock."

"I hadn't thought of that."

"Well, I suspect you've been a bit distracted." Martha stood and straightened her apron. "Now, I think we should all go inside and try to get some sleep. Erin made up the couch for you, Jacob. And Chloe, you can sleep in Anna's bed."

"I couldn't sleep," he said.

"Better try. Tomorrow's bound to be busier than today. *Mammi* keeps reminding me that *Gotte* has a plan for Anna, for each of us. This time, I think I'm going to trust her. I don't know why, but it seems the Lord has His hand on my girl."

Jacob stood, and he and Martha walked back toward the front door. Chloe assured them she would follow soon. She wanted a few moments to let the quiet and peace of the evening slip into her soul. She wanted to think about that look on Jacob's face, and her own ideas about love and relationships. But more than anything, she wanted a few moments to pray.

CHAPTER 63

$\mathcal{A}$nna followed Spencer back into the kitchen.

She hadn't noticed the small television on the counter, but now it was turned to the news, though the volume was muted. It was plain enough to tell what the story was about. She recognized Lacretia and the scene outside her uncle's farm. Before she could fully comprehend what was being reported, Peggy and Spencer began shouting at each other.

"You have to take her back, Spence. Now!"

"I do not!"

"Yes, you do. What you've done is *illegal*, and the only hope you have is to return her."

"They'll never find us, and besides—"

"Never find you? Are you watching the news? They know you're in Texas—"

"It's a big state, Peggy."

"They know that you're driving a Dodge truck—"

"Plenty of those around."

"And they know you're an older white male." She held up her fingers to put imaginary quotation marks around the last three words.

A small groan escaped Anna's lips as she stared at the television. She'd caught sight of her uncle, and he didn't look good. This was too much stress for him. She had once again turned his world upside down.

Peggy and Spencer had stopped shouting at one another and were now watching her closely.

"I think I need to sit down." Anna walked to the table and plopped down in one of the seats. Until she'd seen her uncle's farm on the television, this entire episode had seemed like a dream. Seeing Lacretia standing in front of the large group of spectators reminded her that this was very real—and also that she had more problems than Spencer, Peggy, and Karen. Seeing her uncle standing beside Lacretia reminded her of how worried her family must be.

"I can't walk in there and drop her off." Spencer stabbed a finger in the direction of the television. "Do you think I'm daft?"

"Yes!"

"What good am I to Karen if I end up in jail?"

"Then why did you kidnap her? It's always about *feelings* with you two. You don't stop to consider consequences!"

"I'm well aware of the consequences! Maybe *you* aren't aware how sick Karen is."

"Spencer, she's not just sick." Peggy had been standing and wagging a finger at her brother as she argued. Now she collapsed into the seat across from Anna, the trailer rocking slightly when she did so. "She's also dying."

"Don't say that." Spencer walked to the sink, placed both of his hands on the counter on either side of it, and stared down into the depths of the drain. "Don't say that word in my house."

"Dying? You want to ban the word *dying*? Whether you say it or not—"

"I will not give up on her!" He turned toward them, and Anna was able to see the tears streaming down his face. "Maybe Anna needs more time. Maybe she needs a few hours with her. If there's any chance she can help her—"

"I can't."

Both Peggy and Spencer turned to stare at her.

"I'm not sure why I was healed. I don't know what plan *Gotte* has for me, but it's not healing others. I don't have the ability to do that."

Spencer seemed to crumple before her eyes, as if until that point the power of his hope—no matter how slim that hope was—had bolstered him up. He slipped to the floor, his back against the cabinets and his legs splayed out in front of him. Peggy and Anna hurried to his side.

"Spence. Talk to me. Tell me you're okay."

"Perhaps he needs a drink." Anna opened the refrigerator, retrieved a bottle of water, popped the top open, and handed it to him.

Peggy helped to steady his hand. After he'd sipped from it twice, he pushed it away.

"I'm a fool. I know that, but if there had been any chance—"

"I love her too, Spence. She's like the sister I never had. She's like my only sister. Do you think that I want to see her go? But facts are facts, and the truth is that Karen doesn't have long left. The nurse has said so the last three visits."

Spencer wiped at his eyes with the heels of his hands. To Anna, the gesture reminded her of the young children in their congregation after they had fallen and scraped a knee or elbow. It softened her opinion of him, seeing him so vulnerable.

Peggy had sat beside him on the linoleum floor, and now Anna sat as well.

"I wish I could," she said softly.

"I don't understand God. I don't understand how He works. Is it because of me? Did I do something terrible, so that...so that He has looked away from us?"

"*Nein.* I can't say I understand a lot either, but I am certain of God's love for all of His children. My grandmother finally pounded that into my thick skull."

"I have so many regrets." He glanced around the kitchen, and then he shook his head. "So many things I wanted to give her, experiences I wanted to share with her..."

"While I was sitting with your *fraa*—that is, your wife—she said she'd had a good life."

"She said that?"

"*Ya*, and she also said she knew there's more than this."

"This?"

"This life. There's something after it. There's heaven."

"Karen told you that?"

"She did." Anna pulled her knees up under her dress and encircled them with her arms.

"We've never actually prayed together. You know? Except when we went to church—mostly on holidays like Easter and Christmas. Seemed life always kept us too busy. But Karen...she's always been one to read the Bible."

"You should talk to her, Spence. While you can. Make your peace with her passing. Tell her how much you love her, and that you're ready to let her go. I read somewhere that folks need to hear that." Peggy brushed at her own tears, and then she heaved herself to a standing position.

"Where are you going?"

"To take this girl home."

Spencer shook his head and stood as well. "I brought her here. I'll take care of it."

Anna hopped to her feet. Could she believe what they were saying? Were they actually going to take her home?

Peggy opened a coat closet and removed her purse from the top shelf. "I have a feeling you wouldn't get far with as much surveillance as they have now. Cameras are on every road. An older white male and an Amish girl are going to get pulled over immediately. You'd be in jail faster than I can snap my fingers. I expect they know the direction you went and have sent out an alert to all agencies."

"But—"

"I'll do this, Spence. Let me do it—for you and for Karen."

Spencer studied the floor, which Anna supposed was his way of agreeing.

"Come on, honey." Peggy motioned Anna toward the front door.

As they were hurrying to the white car, Spencer's head popped out of the motor home. "Do you even know where you're going?"

"I have your cell phone, and I've already looked up the route. The phone is fully charged, and my gas tank is full."

Anna had reached the passenger side and opened the door. Peggy touched the handle on the driver's door, but she didn't open it. Instead she turned to give Spencer one last piece of advice. "Go and sit with Karen. Stop trying to fix this and tell her how you feel. She already knows, but it will make her happy to hear it."

She ducked into the car, put the key in the ignition, and turned it. The engine roared to life.

"Ready, honey?"

"*Ya*. I am."

"Good. Let's get you home."

CHAPTER 64

The ride back to Oklahoma was a completely different experience than the ride down to Texas. Anna realized she must have been in shock before. She'd noticed very little. This time she read the many signs they passed.

Leaving Texas—Drive Friendly, The Texas Way

Red River

Welcome to Oklahoma, Discover the Excellence

McAlester, Exit Here

Eufaula Lake, Next Exit

Muskogee

She must have seen the same signs in reverse on the way down, but they hadn't registered in her mind. Now she craned her neck to see dark hills barely illuminated by the car's headlights. She was surprised to see so much traffic in the middle of the night, much of it truckers but some families too. They stopped at an all-night gas station.

"Let me get the key to the restroom. If you go inside, I have a feeling we'll be detained here for the evening."

Anna nodded in agreement. For some reason she trusted Peggy. Perhaps it was the firm, honest way she'd spoken to her brother, or it could have been the fact that she'd offered to make the drive to Cody's Creek. They all knew that she was putting herself directly in the police's path. She had sacrificed herself for Spencer so that he could spend a few precious final moments with Karen.

Anna was moved by that love and sacrifice.

It had never occurred to her what other families were going through, how much they cared for, hurt for, and prayed for one another. She'd been pretty consumed by the drama of her own life—for the past year because of the accident, but even before that. When she'd first moved to Oklahoma, her biggest problems had been boredom and a general sense of aimlessness. They had seemed huge issues to the girl she used to be. But she saw now that life was precious, and each day was a gift.

She wanted to go home.

She wanted to live the life she'd been given, and it didn't matter anymore whether it was in a wheelchair or not. What mattered was who she spent her time with.

Peggy kept the radio turned low to a station that played country music. Anna recognized some of the tunes from shopping in town. Often stores had such music playing over the speakers. She even recognized one singer—George something. His voice was low and smooth and helped to calm her jitters. The lyrics filled the car—something about how he saw God today.

That idea bounced around in Anna's mind. What the singer said made sense. God was all around them. You could see Him in the colors as the sun sought the horizon over the hilltops. You could hear Him in the lyrics of a song. You could experience Him in the love that others shared. Love like that of Peggy for Spencer, Peggy and Spencer for Karen, and Karen for the two of them.

"Pull over," Anna said.

"I thought you said I need to turn left at the next stop sign."

"Pull over." Anna had been giving Peggy turn-by-turn instructions as they had entered the outskirts of Cody's Creek. Now she directed her to a graveled spot on the side of the road, under a tall oak tree.

"Is something wrong? Do you need out of the car?"

"I do need out of the car, but nothing's wrong." She turned and studied Peggy. It felt as if she'd known the woman much longer than she had. In Peggy's eyes, she saw the dawn of understanding.

"I don't mind taking you in, right up to the police barricade. It's what I planned to do. Spence is going to have to turn himself in eventually unless I can convince them I'm the one who did it, and then—"

"I think there's another way."

As Anna explained her plan, Peggy shook her head, causing her curls to bounce back and forth. When Anna had finished, she reached out a hand and squeezed her arm. "You don't have to do this."

"It's not a hardship for me. My uncle's place is a little over a mile from here. It's an easy walk."

"Coming from a girl who was in a wheelchair last week."

"All the more reason to enjoy walking down a country road as the sun comes up."

Peggy looked out the front window and tapped her fingers against the wheel. "Why would you do this after we've disrupted your life? After we scared you half to death, and don't deny you were scared. I saw your expression the minute you walked into the motor home. Your eyes darting here and there looking for an escape hatch."

Anna laughed. Now that she'd made up her mind, she knew her plan was the right thing to do. "I was scared, but that was before I knew you or Karen. And even Spencer is not all that dangerous. His love for his wife made him do things he wouldn't normally do."

"He's never listened to reason where Karen was concerned."

"But he listened to you." Anna opened the door and got out of the car.

To her surprise, Peggy wrestled herself out from behind the steering wheel and walked over to her. The big woman enfolded her in a hug. Anna inhaled the scent of the shampoo she used. Peggy had already sacrificed a lot for Spencer's wife, and she'd been willing to sacrifice a lot more. The depth of folks' love sometimes amazed Anna. She stepped back and waved her toward the car.

"Better get going. I'll give you fifteen minutes before I start walking. That should give you plenty of time to reach the interstate."

"Thank you."

"Please tell Spencer I'll be praying for him and Karen."

Peggy nodded, wiped at her eyes, and then climbed into the car.

It took her three tries to turn the vehicle around on the small country road. Anna stood staring at red taillights. She sat on a tree stump and gradually became aware of the freshness of the morning air, the sound of the breeze through the cornstalks behind her, and the call of one bird to another.

When she was sure fifteen minutes had passed, she stood and began to walk home.

CHAPTER 65

*J*acob had already taken care of the animals in the barn. He was checking on the horses in the far pasture when he looked up and saw a small form walking down the road. As he watched, his pulse beat faster and his hands began to sweat. He forgot about the apple he was feeding to the horse. He dropped it on the ground and walked toward the fence.

Now he could see that it was a woman. He could make out the dress and apron and *kapp* as she drew closer. The woman was definitely dressed in Sunday clothes, not workday clothes. The same clothes Anna had been wearing the last time he'd seen her. He began to run toward her, hoping and praying but afraid to believe, and then she raised her hand in a wave.

His Anna, waving at him as if it were any summer morning.

As if his life hadn't just changed, again.

He ran faster. The fence didn't stop him. When he reached it, he scrambled over the top. To the left, over the hill and out of sight, were the long line of cars and spectators. To the right was Anna.

He scooped her up in his arms, twirling her around, and holding on to her as tightly as he dared. She was laughing, and that sound was sweet indeed. She was okay, and she was home.

"Let me down, Jacob. You're going to hurt your back."

"With you? I could carry you home or anywhere else you want to go." He set her on the ground, and gently framed her face with his hands. "Oh, Anna. I was afraid I'd never see you again. I was afraid I hadn't told you often enough—"

"Told me what?" The familiar teasing look was in her eyes, but that didn't stop him.

"That I love you. I love you and I adore you and I want you here with me."

Anna reached up and covered his hands with hers. "Jacob, I am here."

"And you're safe?"

"I am. Can't you see? I'm fine." She cocked her head to the side. "Did you just tell me that you *loved* me?"

"*Ya*. I suppose I did."

She pulled his hands away from her face, but she didn't let go. "On a country road, before the sun has properly come up?"

"Best time for admitting such a thing."

She stepped closer and lowered her voice. "I happen to feel the same way, and you're right—I can't think of a better way to begin our day."

Finally Jacob did what he'd dreamt of doing. He pulled her closer and kissed her on the lips. He had loved Anna for so long, and imagined this moment so many times, that he was surprised to find the reality of it was even better than the anticipation.

As the sun pierced the horizon, bathing them in its glow, he remembered—suddenly—the horror of the last twelve hours. Pulling her toward some large rocks along the side of the road, he sat down and she sat beside him, their mood suddenly quite serious.

"Chloe and I were so frightened. Your *mamm*, she said not to worry. She said *Mammi* was right and that God had a plan for you. But I was so scared, Anna."

"I was scared too, at first."

"What happened?"

"It's a long story."

Jacob glanced around. "I'm in no hurry."

But now Anna was worrying her thumbnail. "And I want to tell you all of it, but first there's something I need to do."

"What is it? Anything you need. I'll help you."

"Walk with me?"

He nodded. They stood and made their way down the road, approaching the line of spectators. He could have helped Anna over the fence back where he'd first seen her. She'd have been able to go up to the house undetected. But somehow, he knew the thing she needed to do involved going through the front barricade.

The crowd was beginning to move about. Some people had slept in their cars. That still made no sense to Jacob. What were they waiting for? Why were they still here? Others had pitched tents and slept in those. Still others were arriving. Apparently they'd found lodging in town or maybe even in Tulsa. He'd heard the officers say that folks were making the daily trek from area hotels. He'd heard them say that perhaps when the money ran out, the crowds would thin and then the spotlight would be off Anna. In their opinion, it was all a waiting game.

But they didn't have to wait any longer. They suddenly realized that Anna was the girl walking past their cars.

"It's her. She's back!"

"Where has she been?"

"Why is she walking?"

"I can't see. Move out of my way."

"Anna, over here! Please, come see my child."

"Help us, Anna."

Anna kept moving resolutely forward, and Jacob clutched her hand, determined to protect her from any other crazy person who might have taken it into their head to whisk her away. He wasn't going to let that happen again. He wasn't sure how he could protect her twenty-four hours a day, seven days a week, but he was determined to find a way.

The crowd pushed in around them.

Finally they were close enough to the entrance of Samuel's lane that the officers took notice. One spoke to another. A third talked into a radio. The first two began to walk toward them, but Anna held up her hand and shook her head. They hesitated but stopped.

A wooden platform stood behind a small stand that had been built the night before, so that Lacretia could speak to the crowds and be seen and heard. There was even a microphone there, plugged into a generator. Somehow Anna seemed to know all this, and it occurred to Jacob that perhaps she'd seen it on a television. The thing he couldn't imagine was what she was planning to do. He reluctantly let go of her hand as she stepped up onto the platform. She smiled at him again, and then she pulled the microphone closer, causing it to send out a squeak through the morning's dawn.

"*Gudermiraye.*" She glanced down at Jacob, and he did his best to encourage her with a smile. "Or maybe I should say *good morning.*"

There were murmurs and questions and a few returned her greeting. Mostly they pressed up to the platform, including the news reporters who were zooming in with their cameras. Anna must have noticed the reporters too, because she turned to her right to address them directly.

"I appreciate what you have done to help me since yesterday evening. Thank you for your news reports..." Now she turned back to the people in the crowd "And your prayers."

The crowd was silencing. They were hanging on to her every word, but Jacob was still worried. What was she doing? And what would he do if someone jumped up and tried to grab her? That was a foolish thought. The officers had formed a semicircle behind her. No one would be snatching Anna this morning.

"I would like to go to my *onkel*'s house now and speak with my family. I know they have been very worried. I would also like to eat a little breakfast. No doubt you are hungry too." She stepped back and said something to one of the officer's behind her.

"It's nearly seven now. I'll be back at eight thirty, which should give everyone plenty of time to eat. I hear there's a *gut* breakfast at the Dutch Pantry in town."

A light laughter rippled through the crowd, like a breeze Jacob had been waiting for. Could it be that these people meant her no harm? Could he trust that this was all going to turn out all right?

Anna had turned away from the microphone, when one of the reporters called out to her. "Where have you been, Anna? Is it true that someone took you? Can you tell us—"

"Eight thirty. I'll answer all the questions I can at that time."

As she stepped down, Anna reached for Jacob's hand, and his heart swelled until he could actually feel it beating in his chest. They turned and started up the lane. Already, Anna's family was running toward them—Martha, Erin, Samuel, and Chloe. She was a part of their family too. Their lives had been irrevocably bound together through the course of events Anna had endured. Jacob looked past them to the house and saw *Mammi* standing on the front porch. Her hands were raised, and he knew, he understood fully, that she was giving praise that Anna had returned home.

The sight humbled Jacob. He had been so caught up in his emotions that he hadn't thought to thank the Lord. His prayers had been answered, but his mind had rushed ahead to the next problem. As Anna's family surrounded her—hugging and laughing and making sure she was fine—Jacob continued to the house. He sat down beside *Mammi*, allowed his head to drop into his hands, and uttered a prayer of gratitude.

CHAPTER 66

*A*nna had known, somewhere in the back of her mind, that her family wouldn't like her plan.

"I don't see that it's necessary," her mother said.

"*Ya*, and you're just now home. Why stir them up again?" Samuel poked at his scrambled eggs with his fork. "We're so glad you're back, and now if life could return to normal—"

"Can't you see? Don't you understand?" Anna felt frustration bubble up inside of her. She forced herself to take a calming breath and pushed on. "We won't be normal as long as I'm hiding away in here. We'll pretty much be waiting for the next desperate person to do something crazy."

"What will you say to them, Anna?" Erin fidgeted with the strings to her prayer *kapp*. "What can you possibly tell them that will make them go away?"

"And why can't you simply issue a press release?" Chloe had been the most adamant voice against her speaking directly to the crowd. "We can type up anything you want to say. There's no need for you to go out there—"

"Anna's changed." *Mammi* poured syrup over her hot biscuit, pausing only after she had it to her liking. "She sees things differently now."

"What can that possibly mean?" Martha asked.

"*Mammi* is right." Anna was grateful for the cup of coffee she held in her hands, and she wanted one of the hot biscuits, but her stomach was flipping and flopping, and she didn't trust herself to eat yet. "I am seeing things differently, and I'm sure this is the right thing to do."

No one had an answer to that, so they finished their breakfast in silence. She glanced up from her coffee cup, saw Jacob watching her, and realized they hadn't shared with anyone their feelings about each other. There would be time, though—plenty of time. For now, it was a sacred and intimate confession between them. She held on to that thought as her family finished their breakfast. It was good to be back with them. It was good to be home.

Lacretia stepped into the kitchen. "It's time if you still insist on doing this."

Anna nodded, and everyone pushed back chairs and carried plates to the sink. It was decided that they would all go down to the area where the lane turned into Samuel's property together. Because *Mammi* also wanted to go, Samuel cranked up the tractor after he and Jacob had attached the truck bed with the benches. They all fit inside—but barely. Lacretia had offered to drive them down in one of their cars, but Samuel had declined. "If we must do this, we'll do it as simply as possible."

As they drove closer, Chloe leaned in and said, "Looks like twice the number of news crews as we had last night. Didn't take long for the word to get out."

There were indeed even more news vans lining the lane.

Instead of being filled with despair at the sight, Anna felt a surge of hope. Perhaps if they could get the word out, this might work.

She squeezed Chloe's hand. "Stop worrying. You look like a mother with a wayward babe."

"I feel like one too!" Chloe shook her head before squaring her shoulders and smoothing frown lines away from her forehead. "Always smile for the camera."

"*Ya*. Sounds like *gut* advice." The cameras made Anna uncomfortable, but she understood that a statement wouldn't be enough. The people who were hurting needed to see and hear her. Not because of who she was, but because of what God had done.

Lacretia had briefed the team at the entry on what was about to happen. They had spread out around and in front of the podium.

Anna's family stood behind her. There wasn't enough room up on the wooden platform for everyone to stand together, but they waited close by. She could hear them and feel their support and love and prayers. She reminded herself of the real reason she was doing this, took a deep breath, and began.

"As many of you know, I was injured in an accident nearly a year ago here on my *onkel's* farm. Jacob..." She turned and smiled at him, and he looked back at her with complete love and steadiness. That look, that love, gave her courage. "Jacob saved me. He's a friend, and he helps out around here."

There was the flash of cameras, and she could hear the whir of film crews. They had spoken of this, and it may have been the main reason her uncle resisted the plan. The Amish preferred not to be photographed. In this case, however, it seemed they were way past that problem. After all, her picture had been leaked all over the news when she went missing. Anna stood straighter and smiled for the cameras. She might need to ask forgiveness from her church later, but it was time to do this.

"I think you all have probably looked over my medical records by now. You probably know a lot about me—even what I had for breakfast this morning."

Laughter spread through the crowd, and the tension eased. The sun was now shining fully. It was going to be another hot day. Anna noticed several families in the crowd, families with little ones who needed to be back at their home, not camping outside an Amish farm.

"I suffered a complete spinal cord break. After some time in the hospital, I was transferred to a rehabilitation facility. Eventually I returned here to my *onkel's* farm. I'm not telling you anything you don't know, but I wanted you to hear the basic facts from me."

"How is it that you can walk now?" This from a newswoman who was scribbling madly on a pad.

Anna waited for her to look up. "I don't know."

"You mean—"

"I mean I don't know. I went to sleep one night a paraplegic and woke the next day able to walk." People in the crowd shifted to better see her, but there was total silence. She could hear the call of a cow to a calf, and the neighing of one of the horses. "What I do know is that my family, my entire family and church and friends, prayed for me while I was ill. I believe that their prayers are what caused God to answer and to heal me."

The reporters had stopped writing on their pads. Every eye was now trained on her, but Anna turned and sought her grandmother. *Mammi* smiled and nodded slightly, one hand lifted halfway to heaven.

"I can't tell you why God did that. I don't understand anymore than you do, but what I do know, what I'm certain of, is that He cares for us. He has a plan for me and one for each of you. Whether I'm in a wheelchair or standing in front of you, He can use me, and one way is as good as another."

"But what of my child?" This from a woman who rolled a stroller back and forth. She looked frail and worn. She looked as if she wanted to lie down and sleep for days. "My child is dying. Are you saying that God can use her death? I'll have nothing to do with such a terrible deity."

Anna thought of Karen and Spencer and Peggy. She had refused to give Lacretia their names, only saying that it had been a misunderstanding, one they had managed to clear up. No one had been hurt, and she didn't want to press charges. But the pain in this woman's eyes, the woman whose babe was dying, it was the same pain she'd seen in Spencer's eyes.

"When I was a child, I would play outside until darkness fell." Anna swallowed and pushed on. "I'd stay there as long as my *mamm* would let me. But she cared for me, and so she would call me inside. She'd call me home. She didn't do that because she was angry or because she disliked me. She did it because home was where I belonged."

The woman who had asked about her child began to weep. Anna wanted to go to her, but she knew she couldn't. She was relieved when a man stepped forward and put his arm around her.

"Are you saying there's nothing you *can* do for us?" A man with one leg stood near the back of the crowd leaning on his crutch, but his voice could be heard clearly. "Or that you *won't*?"

"I was not given the gift of healing, if that's what you're asking me."

"Then why? Why were you healed and so many others are still hurting?"

"I don't know." Tears slipped down Anna's cheeks. She'd asked the very same question so many times in the last week, and still she had no answer. "What I do know is that we all have a finite amount of time. We should spend that time wisely, with the ones we love."

There were many more questions. Anna tried to respond to each one, though after a few minutes she was aware that she was repeating herself. Obviously, she was not giving them the answers they had sought.

She had no miracle cure.

She had no answers.

She was a young woman, and she was still figuring out what had happened. As two reporters in front vied for her attention, she thought again of Spencer and Peggy, and their love for Karen.

She held up a hand to stop the reporters, stepped closer to the microphone, and tried one more time. "Our families are a gift, *ya*? Our love for one another, that is a true miracle. *Gotte*'s love for us? It's difficult to understand, but we can still believe in it in the same way we believe that the sun will set this evening and rise again tomorrow. You want me to tell you how to stop the pain that plagues you."

She looked out, scanning the crowd from left to right, and seeing some from her Amish community on the edges.

"I can't tell you that. But I can tell you, with certainty, that your love for each other is stronger than the suffering. And *Gotte*'s love?

"The length and width and height and depth of our Father's love is greater than anything we can imagine."

CHAPTER 67

Chloe stayed another hour. They all rode back to the house, where Anna insisted that she wanted to spend a little time in her garden. They walked together down the rows, pausing to prune some plants and pull ripened vegetables. The tension from the morning, from the last week, seemed to drain into the soil.

But soon Anna began rubbing her eyes and yawning. Chloe laughed when she dropped onto the wooden bench in the corner of the garden.

"You're exhausted, and yet you fight it."

"*Ya*, I feel like a child who refuses to take a nap."

"Well, you were up all night."

Anna nodded, and then she told Chloe everything that had happened—she described Spencer and her fear and the drive and the motor home. She told her about Peggy and Karen. She tried to put into words how much that family loved one another.

"I suppose all families do."

"*Ya*, but we don't always show it. Life keeps us busy. In Spencer and Karen's case, life had finally slowed down. The job was over. The house was sold. What was left was the relationship between them."

Chloe stood, reached for Anna's hands, and pulled her to her feet. It was obvious her friend was exhausted. She finally convinced her to go inside and rest.

Jacob and Erin walked Chloe to the car.

"Thank you for everything," Erin said, enfolding her in a hug.

"Jacob, call from the phone shack if Anna needs me." She waited until he nodded before starting the car and driving down the lane.

Already the crowd had dwindled to only a few folks.

Anna had been right. Hiding had made it worse. When she answered their questions, when she allowed them to see her, the need to wait and stare and photograph disappeared.

Chloe pulled out onto the blacktop and waved at the two officers who remained. It had been decided that they would stay until evening. Samuel wanted the farm to return to normal. If people insisted on trespassing...well, the Amish in general didn't mind a visitor or two. Perhaps he could sell them something from the produce stand.

As she pulled down the road, she spied a dog walking along the fence line. She couldn't remember ever having seen a dog at Samuel's place before. Maybe it was a stray. The dog was medium build, a mottled blend of Labrador and blue heeler if she guessed right. As she looked in her rearview mirror, the dog slunk down beside the property fence, ducked under it, and trotted toward the house. The stray moved as if he had a destination in mind.

Tonight she would file another report, perhaps the final report on Anna. What would she say? How could she possibly describe the events of the past week?

Suddenly she realized that people's responses weren't dependent on her or her ability to turn the perfect phrase. There were three types of people who would read her piece. The first would be those who were simply curious. She couldn't blame them. Miracles were rare occurrences. These people weren't personally invested in the story, but they would want a conclusion, as if it were a book they needed to finish and feel good about. They were waiting for the happy ending.

The second type of people was more desperate. They longed for a cure to whatever ailed them. When they realized the cure wouldn't come through Anna's hands, they would quickly turn to the next story or prophet or remedy.

Chloe didn't need to write an article for either of those two groups. She realized now that writing was more than a job, it was a calling. She needed to approach it with prayers for wisdom. She needed to consider the influence her words had on people—and at the moment she was concerned about the third group. The group that would recognize the truth when they heard it. The people who needed to be nudged back toward home, toward their faith, and toward the future God already had planned for them.

The words formed in her mind as she drove toward her apartment. She could see the article taking shape, and she stopped worrying about whether or not she could do it. Her mind moved past the job, and she realized she hadn't seen her mother since they had spent the night at her house.

Chloe reached the suburb where she lived in a downtown apartment. As usual, vendors had opened up their shops and had moved displays out onto the sidewalk. She nabbed a parking spot in front of her building, grabbed her purse and computer, and locked the car. Turning, she walked back toward the corner store, which carried fresh coffee and hot pastries. She could use one of each. But that wasn't what had caught her eye as she'd driven by.

Near the door was an old washtub filled with water and holding various bouquets of flowers. She chose one with yellow and white daisies—her mother's favorite. She would go upstairs, file her report, and then she would call her mom. Perhaps they could share a meal. It was time that she stop avoiding her childhood home because her father wasn't there. Admitting that she had done so for so long hurt. She'd thrown herself into her job so that she could avoid the hole wrought by her father's death. But she still had family, and she wanted to embrace that.

Her mother was alive and well, and Chloe wanted to spend time with her. She'd slowly come to realize, over the last year, that she missed her mom, something that was completely unnecessary because she lived only a few miles away.

"It's a beautiful morning to buy flowers." The clerk smiled at her as he rang up her purchases. He was probably Chloe's age, tall, with a crew cut and wearing a green work apron.

"It is," she agreed. "I don't believe I've seen you here before."

"I started a few days ago. My brother—Andre—is expanding to

include a deli. He needed some help, so I volunteered." He shrugged and handed her the change and a drink carrier holding her coffee and a pastry stuffed in the side. "My name's Carlos."

Normally Chloe would have thanked him and turned away, but today was different. In the back of her mind she was still thinking of Anna and her admonition that they all had a limited amount of time. She was thinking of the length and width and height and depth of God's love. So instead of walking away, she juggled her packages and held out her right hand.

"I'm Chloe. Nice to meet you, Carlos."

His polite smile turned into a grin. "Nice to meet you."

She started toward the door. She stopped with her hand on the glass, turned back, and added, "Welcome to the neighborhood."

CHAPTER 68

*A*ugust gave way to September, cooler temperatures, and another approaching harvest. The weeks since Anna had been healed, abducted, and returned had been filled with highs and lows. Some days she was sure what path her life should take. Other days? Not so much.

One surprise was that they had adopted a stray hound dog and named him Jake. He was completely devoted to them, and Anna delighted in sitting on the porch and running her hand through his fur.

Looking out the window over the kitchen sink, Anna realized that winter wasn't far away. She would need to decide soon if she was staying in Oklahoma or returning to Indiana.

They had finished dinner, and Anna was helping with the dishes as Jacob walked to the barn with Samuel.

"Those two, they walk about like father and son." Erin smiled as she dipped dinner plates into the sudsy water.

Anna noticed that her *aenti*'s moments of introspection and gloominess occurred less often of late. It was easy enough to guess the reasons for that, or part of the reason.

It was harder to understand why the last year had occurred as it had.

Why had the storm taken so much from them? Why was she grievously injured? Why was she miraculously healed?

The questions were never far from her mind, but as usual, life often interrupted her thought process about the time she started chasing those questions round and round.

"I've forgotten my glasses again." *Mammi* had settled in her rocker with the Bible on her lap. When she pushed her hands against the arms of the chair, Anna stopped her.

"I'll get them."

"*Danki*, Anna. Probably they're in the sitting room next to my sewing."

Hurrying from the room, she caught the smile exchanged between the two women. Yes, she could walk from one room to another without help now. That had lifted her *aenti*'s burden of guilt, she was sure, but there was something else too.

Perhaps it had to do with the dream of the rainbows. Had God given her that vision? Had He used her as a vessel to bless others?

Was that why she had been injured? To provide her *aenti* with assurance that she would see her daughter again once she passed from this life to the next? And if that was the reason, why was she healed? She would have shared the dream with her *aenti* whether she'd walked again or not.

She shook her head and retrieved the glasses.

There was no way to know. All of the talks with Bishop Levi, letters exchanged with her parents, and evenings spent listening to *Mammi*'s prayers hadn't answered her questions. Perhaps she would never have those answers. It was enough to know that her *aenti*'s heart had been lifted from a pit of misery and despair.

She returned with *Mammi*'s glasses. When she handed them to her, *Mammi* reached up, placed a palm against Anna's right cheek, and planted a kiss on the other. Pushing the glasses onto the bridge of her nose, she smiled at her granddaughter and shooed her away.

For some reason *Mammi*'s gentleness brought tears to Anna's eyes. She never used to cry. Now it seemed to be a daily occurrence. Her tears weren't from sadness, but more from the fact that her emotions, her heart, felt raw.

She felt as vulnerable and sensitive as a newborn child. Perhaps she had been reborn, in more than one way.

Erin and Anna finished the dishes quickly, with only a few words exchanged. But now the silence that pervaded the kitchen soothed

Anna's soul rather than irritating it the way it had done when she'd first come. More and more she sought such moments of peace.

All three women moved to the sitting room. Anna sat on the couch and picked up the lap quilt she was currently working on. Her mind flashed back to the other dream, the one where she had sewn the quilt pieces together incorrectly not once but many times. The nine patch in her lap showed the improvement in her quilting. Had it taken being confined to a chair for her to learn to appreciate being still, the feel of pushing a needle through fabric, the simple beauty of a pattern put together in a pleasing design?

"Those colors are coming together quite well, Anna." *Mammi* pushed up her glasses and clucked as she took up her own sewing—a small blue dress for one of her grandchildren in Goshen.

"*Danki.*" The solid squares of brown, blue, and dark green against the specialty print of puppies in rain boots made for an interesting contrast. Anna thought of Chloe's mom and the modern quilts she made. She glanced over at her *aenti*, who was working on a traditional log cabin pattern. Turning her attention back to her own work, she realized it represented a bridge between the two styles—between the traditional Amish and the modern *Englisch*.

She continued to quilt until a knock at the front door interrupted the silence.

"I'll get that." Erin was out of her chair before Anna could argue. Anna understood that not only was her *aenti*'s heart lighter, but she moved and reacted like a younger woman now. Could guilt affect you physically? Could it slow your body as well as your spirit? If so, Erin was proof that the opposite was true as well. Forgiveness spoke to both the earthly body and the eternal spirit.

"Jacob. We thought you were in the barn with Samuel."

"*Ya*, I was for a moment, but then I went back to the bishop's."

"Well, come in. There's no need for you to use the front door, you know."

Jacob stepped into the room. Anna's pulse had quickened at the sound of his voice. When she looked up and saw his clean clothes and still wet hair, her heart plunged. He had gone home to wash up, and now he'd come to them with news. She knew it by the set of his mouth and the look in his eyes.

Was he going home? Returning finally to New York?

Had he found other work on another farm or in a different district? Her *onkel* paid him as best he could, but Jacob was a good worker. There was little doubt he could do better elsewhere.

They hadn't spoken of that morning on the lane when they had both confessed their love. They hadn't mentioned it even once in the days since.

"Would you like a piece of pie?" Erin asked. "We have a Dutch apple cooling on the stove."

"Maybe later." Jacob had removed his wide-brimmed straw hat when entering the house. Now he twirled it in his hands as he looked directly at Anna. "I was hoping you would like to take a walk with me."

Heat crept up her neck, but she folded the quilt and placed it on top of her basket of notions.

Mammi was suddenly terribly interested in her sewing, though a smile wreathed her face. *Aenti* had resumed her needlework without another word.

There was no need for a shawl or sweater. Though fall should be arriving, the evening was still quite warm. The sun hung in the western sky, refusing to give up the day.

They walked shoulder to shoulder toward the corn maze, which her *onkel* had carefully reconstructed. Anna now understood that was a work of love for *Mammi*. As long as her grandmother was alive, the fall festival would continue. The corn had once again grown taller than Anna. In a week they would begin to prepare the farm for visitors.

She tried to mentally prepare herself for whatever Jacob wanted to tell her. It seemed that her life was about to take another turn.

CHAPTER 69

*J*acob watched as a car on the main road slowed, its driver staring in their direction.

"At least there's only one of them this evening," he muttered.

They stepped into the maze, and the worries of gawkers and newspeople fell away.

"I suppose I should feel afraid here in the maze, here where the storm found me. I don't, though. It seems more like a sanctuary, like a holy place almost."

"*Gotte* touched you here, Anna."

"Do you think so?" She turned and studied him, causing him to wonder if his hair was sticking out below the rim of his hat.

He no longer felt like the boy who had arrived a year ago looking for work. He'd grown stronger since working with Samuel. He'd always worked in the fields, but the daily responsibility of caring for crops and animals had changed him. He found he enjoyed the rhythm of working on a farm much more than spending days riding buses or trains.

It was time to speak frankly with Anna, though, and depending on her response he would know whether he should stay or go.

"I do believe *Gotte* touched you." He hesitated and added as an afterthought, "Remember, I was here."

"*Ya*. I remember. You saved me, Jacob."

"*Nein. Gotte* saved you, and then He healed you."

"But why?" Her eyes filled with tears, causing her to blink and look away.

"I can't say, but I suppose one day we'll know."

She looked at him sharply at the use of *we*.

Jacob reached for her hand.

"I believe you know how I feel, Anna. We haven't spoken of this since the morning you returned. I wanted to give you time to heal and settle into a normal life." He rubbed his thumb over the back of her hand. "But perhaps it is better that I say it. I love you. My heart's desire is for you to be my wife. I can't imagine my life without you, and I think *Gotte* put us together for a reason."

"Are you asking me to marry you?"

"I am."

"Then my answer is yes," she whispered.

Instead of pulling her into his arms, he fiddled with his suspenders. "So much has happened since that day, and I wasn't sure, that is, I was afraid to hope—"

She moved closer, stood on her tiptoes, and placed both palms on his face. "My answer is yes, and I meant it. I'm sure. I've been waiting for you to ask."

"*Ya?*" A smile slowly spread across his face.

"*Ya.* Do you need me to write it down so you can carry my answer in your pocket and check it now and again?"

"No need for that. Your word is good enough for me." He pulled her into his arms and kissed her softly on the lips as the breeze brushed through the cornstalks and across them. Then he held her at arm's length, smiling at her as if he'd discovered some marvelous surprise, and perhaps he had.

Anna relaxed in his arms for a moment, but then she pulled away. Was she having second thoughts? Did she doubt whether he could provide for her?

They resumed walking through the maze.

Jacob waited, content to walk beside her and allow her to consider his words.

"There's so much I still don't understand. I love it here, and as you say, this does seem like a place where I came into the presence of God. And yet, I'm not sure..." She glanced in the direction of the road but couldn't see it through the tall stalks for corn.

"I'm not sure I should stay. The attention brought on my *aenti* and *onkel* isn't good. It makes them uncomfortable, and I know they worry about the constant offers from news and book and television people."

"Have they told you this?"

Anna shrugged. "A girl can tell. And then there are the people who traipse onto our property to steal things. Last week it was one of my *kapps*. Yesterday, if it hadn't been for Jake, a woman would have made off with a quilt I was airing across the front porch banister."

"It's *gut* that he showed up when he did. He's like an *Englisch* burglar alarm."

"*Ya*. He started barking, which brought me to the door. I tried to talk to her, but she turned and fled."

"Chloe says that people will try to sell your things, claiming they have special healing powers." He nudged her shoulder. "Perhaps you could heal my thumb. I'll lose the nail, it's so black."

She stopped, pulling his hand closer to look at it. "Another tractor accident?"

"*Ya*. Tractors are worse than horses in many ways."

She kissed the thumb and they continued to walk through the maze, finally exiting on the far side. The sun had dropped to the horizon and was splashing a painter's palette of colors across the sky. Anna stood there, her back to Jacob, apparently mesmerized by the sight.

"Do you love me, Anna?"

He had moved closer, and now he circled his arms around her as they both stared at the beauty—the miracle—of another day ending over an Oklahoma field.

"*Ya*, Jacob. I've loved you for a long time."

The words made him want to shout. He wanted to tell somebody—tell everybody. But Anna was shaking her head now.

"I haven't allowed myself to hope that we could live a normal life like a normal couple. Our lives will always be difficult, with people intruding and gawking."

"I'd rather live an unusual life with you than a completely normal one with anyone else."

"Where will we live?" She turned in his arms and stared up into his eyes. "Where—"

Instead of answering he again dipped his head to kiss her, hoping to melt away the questions in her soul.

Jacob stepped back, his heart lighter with the hope in Anna's smile. They turned and walked back toward the house, around the maze this time.

"We will move if you'd like."

"Move?"

"Yes, we can marry and move away. We can start over again."

CHAPTER 70

$\mathcal{A}$nna stared at Jacob, her thoughts and feelings twirling like an Oklahoma twister. "I don't know what to say."

"Say that you will." When she didn't answer, he continued. "I know how difficult it has been, Anna. Your speech to the crowd did help, but still they come. As you say, they take your *kapps* and even your quilts. Erin said someone stole a pie from the back porch the other day."

"That could have been Jake."

"That mutt looks as if he could eat anything, but he would have left paw prints and a tin pan." Jacob laughed at the image but quickly grew somber. "We can stay here and hope the gawkers will find their attention consumed by something or someone else or we can move."

"Where?"

"My family would be happy to have us in New York. I've talked to my *mamm* and *dat*. We're welcome there."

"You spoke to your parents about us?"

"I have." Jacob laced his fingers with hers, and they slowly walked toward the house. "I've also taken the liberty of writing to your family in Goshen."

"My family?"

"They would be happy to see you move back."

Anna glanced out at the evening sky, which was quickly deepening to a dark blue velvet. The constellations appeared, filling the heavens and causing her heart to lighten. It would be a moonless night—a perfect night to watch for falling stars. She didn't realize until that moment how much she had grown to care for Oklahoma, with its vast horizons and challenging land.

"I love it here," she murmured.

"There is a third option."

They had reached the house, and the gaslights from the sitting room allowed her to see his expression. If she had to describe the look on his face with one word, it would have been *hopeful*.

"What is our third option, Jacob?"

"To move to a more remote area of Oklahoma." He mentioned the name of an Amish settlement she recognized. "It's a smaller community, and a bit off the main road. I've asked around. They are looking for new Amish families to join them."

"We'd move."

"*Ya*, if that's what you want, Anna."

She pulled her *kapp* strings forward, ran her fingers from top to bottom. Suddenly she froze. *Mammi* had stepped in front of the gaslight and was silhouetted against the sitting room window. With a force stronger than any wind, she remembered the prayers that her grandmother had uttered over her—each morning and each night. She remembered her grandmother's look of pure love as she asked, "Do you believe in miracles, child?" Had she been healed by *Mammi*'s faith? The Gospels described friends bringing a paralyzed man to Jesus, who healed the man. But what else did the Scripture say?

Anna knew the verses from Matthew well. She had pored over them many a night. Suddenly she understood—not everything, but one thing.

"Jesus saw their faith," she whispered.

Jacob didn't interrupt, didn't question the strange turn in their conversation.

"He saw their faith and healed the man who couldn't walk." She placed her hands on Jacob's shoulders and looked up at him. "I think my grandmother's faith made me whole."

It wasn't the first time she'd had this revelation. The evening with Spencer and Peggy and Karen, the ride home through the southern portion of the state, the moments standing in front of the crowd, the conversation with her mother. She'd had clarity on all that had happened before, but each time it slipped away. And when it returned, she felt as if she were discovering it for the first time. She felt as if she were viewing the miracle anew.

Jacob took her hands in his and kissed each one.

"I will marry you, Jacob. But I can't leave *Mammi*. There are things I need to learn from her, and she means so much to me."

"So you wouldn't mind if they moved with us?" Now Jacob had a twinkle in his eyes.

"With us?"

"Sure. Samuel and I thought you might prefer the third option."

"You've spoken with Samuel?"

"We both realized you wouldn't want to leave *Mammi*."

"You spoke to him about us marrying?"

"It would be good to have family with us when we make such a big move." Jacob clasped her hand in his as they walked up the porch steps.

She had no idea what to say. Jacob had known what she needed before she did. How was it that she had come to be so blessed? And what was God's plan for their future?

All questions that would wait for another day.

Instead of going inside, they sat on the porch steps. Jacob put his arm around Anna, and she rested her head on his shoulder. Together they watched the evening sky twinkle with the light of a million stars.

EPILOGUE

Late October

*T*hat is Anna's story.

Was she healed?

I know for a fact that she was a paraplegic. I was there when the doctor explained her injury. I visited her each week as she learned to adjust to the confines of a wheelchair. And I received a phone call the morning she first walked.

All of these things I know, and I reported on them in the *Mayes County Chronicle*. I've included some of those posts here, but you can find the rest if you go and research the newspaper archives.

What you won't find is the *why* of Anna's healing. You can reread Anna's explanation to the crowd outside the entry to her uncle's farm. I have studied the transcript of that morning time and again. And yes, I still have questions.

I'll admit I've spent many a night wondering *how* as well as *why*. Perhaps it's not for man to understand the mysteries of God. Or, as *Mammi* is fond of quoting from the book of Job, "He performs wonders that cannot be fathomed, miracles that cannot be counted."

I recently visited Anna and Jacob. They were settled in their new home with Samuel, Erin, and *Mammi*. As I drove toward their house, passing fields that had mostly been harvested, I could see Anna, shielding her eyes from the noonday sun as she tracked my small blue car making its way down the dirt lane.

I fought the desire to abandon my car in the middle of the lane and run to her. I'd missed my friend more than I would have thought possible. As I parked, she stepped off the porch and slowly crossed the yard.

I shut down the engine and bolted toward her. "Your letters didn't quite describe the changes in you."

Anna enfolded me in a hug, as much as possible given that she had entered the ninth month of her pregnancy. The child kicked and I let out a squeal. "He's a feisty one."

"*Ya. Mammi* says it's a boy for sure and for certain. Any problems getting here?"

"You gave good directions. Otherwise I may never have found you."

"It's a bit remote."

"I'll say."

We sat at the picnic table under the pecan tree. Erin had already laid out sandwiches and tea.

"You like it here?"

"I do. We all do."

Erin and *Mammi* joined us for lunch, as did Jacob and Samuel, who had been working in the fields, completing the last of their harvest. Jake, the old hound dog I'd seen the morning of Anna's speech, lay beneath the table—no doubt hoping for a stray scrap.

If anyone had driven by, which was doubtful, they would have seen an ordinary Amish family sharing lunch with an *Englisch* woman. Not such an odd sight.

But we realized what a special celebration it was. Three years had passed since the accident. Each person sitting under the pecan tree that day had witnessed something incredible. We had been a part of something quite special, and we would never be the same.

Perhaps that is the definition of a holy encounter—you come away forever changed.

AUTHOR'S NOTE

I highly recommend *Samuel: The Amish Boy Who Lived* by Robert J. Hastings. This book was a great resource for me as I wrote Anna's story.

The town of Cody's Creek does not exist in Oklahoma. The place I visited and researched was Chouteau, which was originally called Cody's Creek when it became a stop on the Katy Railroad in 1871. The Amish community in Chouteau does allow the use of tractors, both in the fields and in town. They still use the horse and buggy when traveling to church, a wedding, or a funeral.

Project Linus is an organization that began in 1995 and now has chapters in all fifty states. Please check out their website for more information at www.projectlinus.org.

I would like to offer a special thanks to all the people who wrote me regarding miracles they had witnessed or experienced. Their input helped tremendously in the writing of this story.

DISCUSSION QUESTIONS

1. At the beginning of the story, Anna is full of self-doubt. She doesn't understand why she isn't interested in dating. She isn't sure her aunt and uncle want her staying with them. She has no idea what direction her life is going to take. Have you ever had a deep level of self-doubt? What did you do to remedy it?

2. Anna and Chloe's friendship may seem a bit strange to some, but I have witnessed and even experienced many such friendships between Amish and *Englisch*. What makes friendships stick? And how can we nurture this very important gift God gives to us?

3. The Amish of Cody's Creek (my name for the town of Chouteau, Oklahoma) are quite different. They allow tractors to be used both in the fields and to ride to town. They are a little less put off by contact with the *Englisch*. What do you think of this? Does it make them any less Amish? Are they still following God's path for their families and their communities?

4. After Jacob rescues Miguel, he meets with the church leadership. They remind him about the commandment to turn the other cheek. Jacob replies, "I'm familiar with Christ's words, and if I had been slapped I am certain that I would have been able to turn the other cheek." He's not smarting off. He honestly believes the situation with Miguel required a different response. What does the Bible teach us about dealing with others, especially those who would intend us harm?

5. When Anna first learns of her paralysis, she has trouble accepting the diagnosis. The Bible has many verses that assure us that God will help us through the most difficult

of times. What are three verses you depend on when life
becomes a struggle?

6. *Mammi* loves Anna. She also is an amazing example of
Christian faith. Who in your life has been this sort of
example for you? How have they helped you in your faith
walk?

7. Do you believe miracles are possible? What does the Bible
say about miracles? And why do miracles happen to some
people but not others?

8. When Anna is kidnapped, we want to dislike Spencer, but
the more I wrote about him, the more I felt sympathy
for him. He is a desperate man who is doing desperate
things he will regret, but he's also someone who loves his
wife dearly. Did you feel Anna's response to Spencer was
believable? Why or why not?

9. Dreams figure strongly in Anna's story. What do you think
about dreams? Should we ever pay attention to them? And
what does the Bible say about dreams?

10. In the end, Anna decides to move away. It seems, for her
and her family, that starting over is best. I could have
written a different ending—one where she stays and
ministers to the people in Cody's Creek. How do you
make the decision of whether to stay (in a job, a town, or a
relationship) or whether to begin again?

GLOSSARY

Aenti—aunt

Boppli—baby

Bruder—brother

Daddi—grandfather

Dat—father

Danki—thank you

Dochder—daughter

Englischer—non-Amish person

Fraa—wife

Gotte's wille—God's will

Grandkinner—grandchildren

Grossdaddi—grandfather

Gudemariye—good morning

Gut—good

Kapp—prayer covering

Kinner—children

Lieb—love

Mamm—mom

Mammi—grandmother

Nein—no

Onkel—uncle

Ordnung—the unwritten set of rules and regulations that guide everyday Amish life.

Rumspringa—running around; time before an Amish young person has officially joined the church, provides a bridge between childhood and adulthood.

Schweschder—sister

Wunderbaar—wonderful

Ya—yes

ABOUT THE AUTHOR

Vannetta Chapman writes inspirational fiction full of grace. She has published more than one hundred articles in Christian family magazines, receiving more than two dozen awards from Romance Writers of America chapter groups. She discovered her love for the Amish while research-ing her grandfather's birthplace of Albion, Pennsylvania. Her novel *Falling to Pieces* was a 2012 ACFW Carol Award winner. *A Promise for Miriam* earned a spot on the June 2012 Christian Retailing Top Ten Fiction list. Chapman was a teacher for 15 years and currently writes full time. She lives in the Texas hill country with her husband. For more information, visit her at www.VannettaChapman.com

Fall in Love with the
Amish of Pebble Creek!

A Promise for Miriam, A Home for Lydia, and *A Wedding for Julia* introduce the Amish community of Pebble Creek, Wisconsin, and the kind, caring people there. As they face challenges to their community from the English world, they come together to reach out to their non-Amish neighbors while still preserving their cherished Plain ways.

Enjoy These *Free* Short Story E-Romances
Download Them Today from Your Favorite Digital Retailer!

These two short story e-romances are an exclusive bonus from the Pebble Creek Amish by Vannetta Chapman. Fans of the series will enjoy this chance to briefly revisit Pebble Creek, and new readers will be introduced to an Amish community that is more deeply explored in the three full novels.

To learn more about Harvest House books and
to read sample chapters, visit our website:

www.harvesthousepublishers.com

HARVEST HOUSE PUBLISHERS
EUGENE, OREGON